WHEN HOPE

THE LAST SECRET KEPT

ELAINE STOCK

Black Rose Writing | Texas

ISBN: 978-1-68513-590-4
LIBRARY OF CONGRESS CONTROL NUMBER: 2024948424
PUBLISHED BY BLACK ROSE WRITING
www.blackrosewriting.com

Printed in the United States of America
Suggested Retail Price (SRP) $21.95

The Last Secret Kept is printed in Garamond Premier Pro

*As a planet-friendly publisher, Black Rose Writing does its best to eliminate unnecessary waste to reduce paper usage and energy costs, while never compromising the reading experience. As a result, the final word count vs. page count may not meet common expectations.

PRAISE FOR
THE LAST SECRET KEPT

"Elaine Stock's *The Last Secret Kept* is a captivating and profoundly moving book that explores complex and universal themes such as guilt, forgiveness, and human nature. Through well-developed characters and a gripping narrative, the book offers a profound perspective on historical and personal challenges, inviting readers to reflect on the power of hope and kindness in a world marked by conflict and injustice."
–The Historical Fiction Company

"This historical fiction legal drama leaves you guessing and hoping. While themes of bigotry play out on the global stage at the end of World War II and the beginning of the Cold War, we are glued to an upstate New York town where a man with developmental disabilities faces not only a murder charge, but also society's stigma. With deeply developed characters, Elaine Stock has crafted a beautiful story of humanity, empathy, and found family."
–Lisa Montanaro, author of *Everything We Thought Was True*, Webinar Host for Women's Fiction Writers Association (WFWA)

"*The Last Secret Kept* is a captivating story of the determination and strength of women. Elaine Stock effortlessly weaves together the darkness of a world at war in the 1940s and women's fight for equality in the 1960s. Using the combination of a legal procedural plotline as the Berlin Wall is being built and a historical mystery from World War Two, Stock reveals her characters' strength, vulnerability and ultimately resilience. The journeys of Fanny, Gina, and Helene are handled with great care and deep empathy, eliciting a true emotional connection between them and the reader and bringing to life stories of the past that must never be forgotten."
–Lelita Baldock, author of *The Baker's Secret* and *The Girl Who Crossed Mountains*

"This well-written and well-researched new book by Elaine Stock is about the women in a family during three time periods. It's about family love and what happens to a family when important information is kept secret through the generations. And how it affects everyone when the secrets are finally revealed... I'm not ready to say goodbye to this family!"
–**Susan Roberts, reviewer from** *Girl Who Reads* **blog**

"Alternating between a female lawyer and newlywed waitress in post-WWII America and a frightened grandmother in Nazi Germany, Elaine Stock deftly weaves an intriguing tale of long-buried family secrets and the struggle to save a man accused of murder. At its heart, *The Last Secret Kept* highlights the power of love, friendship, forgiveness, and hope. Grab a blanket and a warm cup of tea and sink into the spell of this satisfying story."
–**Jill Caugherty, author of** *The View from Half Dome* **and** *Waltz in Swing Time*

"The year 1961 is proving a challenge to Fanny, a female lawyer who meets Gina, whose husband is accused of murder as Gina's emotionally detached grandmother, Helene, keeps secrets that can either strengthen or shatter Gina. Also, the Berlin Wall is built, separating East Berlin from the West, and forbidding people the freedom to leave. What strikes me most about the characters in Elaine Stock's novel, is that even though each of them has come from a difficult childhood, they know how to find the good in each other and build a strong, loving connection. If you're looking for an uplifting novel with the addition of wonderfully engrossing lawyer scenes, you're in for a treat."
–**Jacquie Herz, author of** *Circumference of Silence*

"A thoughtful coming-of-age story that is also a compelling legal thriller and a touching love story."
–**S.M. Stevens, author of** *Beautiful and Terrible Things*

"Who doesn't love a family saga chock full of unexpected heroes, evil villains, and worldwide chaos? *The Last Secret Kept* takes us down the proverbial path of family dysfunction with pathos, passion, and a dose of reality called Fanny – my new personal fav fictional legal eagle! Don't miss the latest tale penned by the lovely Ms. Elaine Stock. An entertaining read, and yes, the ending holds surprises."

–**Kay Smith-Blum, author of** *Tangles*

"Elaine Stock's wonderful book explores a variety of themes, particularly those surrounding love and sacrifice. It shows that we must look below the surface when judging people and that nothing is as it seems. I believe that this is the first book in a series, and I am already counting the days before the next one is released."

–**Diane Nagatomo, author of** *Finding Naomi* **and** *The Butterfly Café*

In loving memory of my Aunt Sandra, one of the smartest and most creative people who dared to step to her own beat. It looks like your story of The Spaghetti Man is happily still with me after all these years, something I didn't realize until after completing this story.

To my amazing real-life superhero, Wally. You've filled my life with color and after all our years together, I am still thanking God daily for you.

In writing a dual-timeline story that takes place during the WWII years and 1961, I feel I would have done a disservice to both the story's characters and these eras poised on the cusp of change if I did not use the correct atmosphere to reflect these times. Therefore, I used what has now come to be viewed as politically incorrect words and phrases, and rightly so. The R-word, for instance: *Retarded* was purposely used to capture the then cultural mood and societal way of thinking. These words were never intended to exclude, marginalize, insult, or discriminate against anyone, and they are not a reflection of myself or my publisher.

THE LAST SECRET KEPT

"Love is the highest form of intelligence we can experience."
–John Pierrakos

PROLOGUE

Berlin, December 15, 1943

The fierce wind pushing on her back is a help, not a hindrance as she had feared before she left home. She needs to keep moving. Needs not to flirt with turning back. Not with another's life dependent upon her. Rosa, the poor little dear, may be needy but like any other child, she deserves a chance to live. Her grandchild will flourish, no matter what. If she could do one good feat in life, especially with a war raging full of death and hatred, pelting down destruction indiscriminately, she would do whatever it takes to provide a chance for Rosa. No other option is possible.

Cold slides into the collar of her ragged coat and creeps down the neckline of her threadbare dress. A few snowflakes float down, one landing on the tip of her nose. Accustomed to wintery weather, she will manage what nature has in mind. Worse dangers exist. Out after curfew, she could be stopped and interrogated. Arrested. She resists shuddering and again summons her will. For Rosa, there is no obstacle. Not the weather, nor a confrontation with the police, nor her daughter's wrath. This child will live.

With summoned energy and long strides, she arrives at the convent on the city's outskirts—a nearly ancient institution built in the early 1100s. A place added to through the centuries. A sanctuary she can only hope will continue, with grace, to avoid the devastation by man's hand.

Careful not to slip, she hurries down the hillside and through the stone colonnade. Standing before the brass doorknocker, she hears a rattling from within. The heavy oak door creaks open. A smile fails to greet her. Although, the words she longs to hear do.

"Come in."

CHAPTER ONE

Fanny, Bridgehaven, August 14, 1961

The day began for Fanny Stern with one too many ifs. *If* she had listened to her reliable Zenith Royal radio, she would have noticed the major *if* occurring in the world. *If* she was more prompt in dressing for court. Most of all, *if* the young woman had not walked past her house with a disheartened look on her pale face. About to rush from the window to the front door and call out to see if the stranger needed help, Fanny's cat brushed across her legs. When she glanced up, the woman was gone. Fanny buzzed around the house, grabbing her briefcase and tossing a goodbye to her feline companion, who wore a smug look of accomplishment from slipping between Fanny and the real world.

Forty-five minutes later Fanny stood in the fatigued courthouse centered in the three-block downtown strip of the Monroe County, New York town of Bridgehaven, on the shoreline of Lake Ontario, halfway between Rochester and Sodus Point. The foreman of the jury, composed of ten men and two women, presented the written verdict to the judge. Fanny gave a reassuring smile to her client, Clarence Dibbs, accused by his landlord of burning down his garage despite the lack of witnesses and a sound alibi. A good, kind man, Clarence was young enough to continue making a professional name in advertising for the *Democrat and Chronicle*, yet not old enough to sit in a dusty jail cell for one day more than necessary. Fanny hoped he could read her thoughts: We will win; you will be fine.

"On all five counts, the defendant is found not guilty," the foreman said.

The usual serious-looking Clarence smiled and pumped her hand while saying thank you, over and over again. Clarence's mother approached and tugged her into an embrace of wet kisses. The cloying jasmine and lily-scented White Shoulders itched Fanny's nose. She suppressed a gag and pulled away from the well-meaning, big-haired woman, focusing on the win. Everyone deserves justice, regardless of age, faith, or social background. The quest for equality was exactly why she chose to practice law, specifically becoming a defense attorney. Tourists typically visited Bridgehaven just long enough to take snapshots of the lake and tour the seven-house historic district of still-painted battleship gray Victorian homes before continuing their journey to the Thousand Islands. They presumed the town residents enjoyed an unblemished carefree lifestyle, absent of crime and assorted misconducts. If only they had the same scoop as Fanny did of her hometown. Middle-of-the-night distress shouts of mischievous teenagers, abusive husbands, and busybodies who made it a hobby to point an accusatory finger further drove Fanny to practice law. She set up her practice in a two-room office a block off of Haven Street, the vein of the town, closing her eyes to the naysayers that a woman's place was at home.

There was only one true way to celebrate a court win: beating the lunchtime rush to Bertine's Malt Shoppe and enjoying a chocolate egg cream and a sandwich. With a pat to her white skirt with its trim of a narrow black band and a check to see if the top of the two-piece outfit had its three pearl-white buttons clasped, she was off to the favorite town joint of good food and relaxed, come-as-you-are atmosphere. Typically, she made little eye contact with passersby. In a spirited and daring mood, she rode a high between confidence and pluckiness and enjoyed every second of this feeling. Ah, the satisfaction of victory.

On this fine morning, Bridgehaven's downtown area had no shortage of black-suited men carrying leather briefcases. Clusters of two or three stood on street corners or by store entrances with open copies of the Canandaigua-based *The Daily Messenger*. She approached two men she had seen often, though they avoided introducing themselves to her by name. She tipped her imaginary hat to them. "Good morning, gentlemen." She glanced at the newspapers tucked under their arms. "Anything of interest?"

"For sure," replied the taller of the two. He nudged the other's shoulder. They exchanged nods and stepped away.

Odd. Last week, folks were buzzing with comments about the growing popularity of young men with outrageously long hair, women wearing skirts with nearly show-all short hems, and the loud rock 'n' roll music played at rapid-pulse-inducing volume. Now, she had extracted only two words. Despite one of Fanny's biggest pet peeves of others ignoring her as if she was a pocket of air, she resisted the urge to run after the wisecracker, yank the paper from the crook of his arm, and tell him she would have to read the news for herself. Maybe she would have better success a few steps over at Sylvia's Boutique, Bridgehaven's glitzy dress shop. Perfect timing. Sylvia, the proprietor, stepped outdoors. She was a large woman, both in height and girth and always dressed as if attending a formal dinner party. She held the door open for a customer. The frizzy-haired slimmer woman carried a garment bag with SB in big red lettering.

"It's like the Union versus the Confederacy," Sylvia said, capturing Fanny's attention. As if sounding an alarm, a crow landed in a nearby tree and cawed nearly in the same pitch and length as Sylvia's words.

The customer fanned herself with her hand. "Thank goodness it's not happening in this country. We deserve peace and quiet, don't you think?"

"Good afternoon," Fanny said in the hope of an invitation to chat with them. The shopper mumbled it was time for her to dart off to the post office. Sylvia finger-waved a toodeloo, then ducked into the shop without acknowledging Fanny.

No way would anyone ruin her day of joy. She reached Bertine's and pushed open the stainless steel door. The packed eatery, unusual for the pre-lunch hour, thrust her into an unfamiliar atmosphere as if she had blasted into a distant universe.

A cloud of stale cigarette smoke engulfed her. A clap of noisy chatter further jolted her senses. Threads of conversation erupted from the first booth where three men were seated. Before them on the white and red Formica table were platters of a thick beefy burger and steak fries, a BLT with more bacon than the L or the T and accompanied by a hefty side of slaw, and what looked like a fried egg slipping out of a hard roll.

"Them poor folks. First, there was the inner German border, but this? It was bad enough to be taken over by the Soviets, but sheesh, these people are stuck on the wrong side. They can't leave to save their lives."

"Poor folks? Ted, are you out of your loony mind? You're talking about those worthless Krauts."

"Holy moly, Pete." Ted craned his neck and peered at the crowd. A stamp of worry wrinkled his forehead. "Loosen up about the Germans. No need to insult anyone. The war's over, pal. It's the Reds taking control."

"Then why didn't people leave Germany when the odds of a better chance were higher? Maybe they had it coming to them?"

"Hold on—are you saying even the children born after the war deserve governmental regulation of their lives?"

"Let the Nazis learn what it's like to have their freedoms taken away, for once. I didn't serve my time fighting in the war for nothing."

Fanny did a double take at the waitress weaving a path between patrons lingering near the jammed tables, hopeful for a vacant seat. The young woman was the same one who had passed her house earlier that morning. Her name badge read Gina. Her chestnut shoulder-length hair couldn't conceal her sad eyes and lack of smile radiating she had not one thread of hope tucked in her pocket. Fanny planned to ask Mitch, the proprietor, for the scoop on her. For now, if she could find a seat and order a drink, she stood a chance to shake a brewing headache without the aid of the aspirin she left behind at home.

A whoo-hoo call shifted her attention. She looked left and saw Dawn, her neighbor, waving frantically. Really? Did Dawn want to suddenly get cozy with her as if they were long-lost girlfriends? Something about the day differed from the ordinary. And it had to be a major something. The enthusiastic clamor of four women drew Fanny's attention away from her neighbor. Dressed in a crayon box of pastel blue, cotton candy pink, canary yellow, and tulip purple, the chatty friends carried on as if they just lost a round of bingo at the firehouse.

"Did you hear about the young wife left alone on the west side? You know, the one whose husband had taken the children to visit his mother, and now they're stuck on the east side. Imagine not being able to see each other again?"

"Not seeing my old man would be a fine adventure for me." A round of loud snorts erupted like fireworks at a private backyard barbecue.

The silver-haired woman sobered first. "You're awful, Rosalind. You wouldn't be saying that if Benny had a gun pointed at him and was told if he wanted to keep his kids alive, to turn around and go back to his mother's and stay there forever."

"Ed and I got down on our knees and prayed for all those people last night after hearing about this wall on the news. Forget their recent past— no one deserves forced separation."

"You're right, Bea. It's only been sixteen years since the end of the last world war—you think they'd all know better."

When a touch came to Fanny's shoulder, she jumped. She pivoted and saw Mitch Bertine, one of the few who always greeted her with a smile. A mixture of genuine pity and its opposite, disgust, chiseled his face like she had never seen from the fifty-something-old graying man.

"What's going on?" She peered into Mitch's eyes, remembering he had cousins living in Germany, near Berlin. She tried again, gently, hoping he would hear her despite the lively volume. "Mitch, what has happened? Are you okay?"

"Yesterday, while we were enjoying a fine late summer day doing the Sunday paper crossword puzzle or throwing Frisbees, the Germans paraded their vehicles, guns, and barbed wire through Berlin to stop folks fleeing from the Soviet-influenced—if you get my gist—east side. And up goes a wall to separate the two sides into two countries." He picked up a newspaper that lay haphazardly on the counter. "Look at this, will ya? It's *The New York Times* with this leading article.

As Fanny scanned the article, "East German Troops Seal Border with West Berlin to Block Refugee Escape," the snatches of conversation she had heard since starting the day stormed through her mind. *Blame the Germans. Blame the Soviets. No one deserves forced separation.*

She lowered the newspaper. "Any word about your family in Germany?"

"Not a peep. There's probably no way for them to use the phone with the lines plugged up from the mass hysteria spreading from one end of the globe to the other." In a growly deep voice, which sounded more like the roar of a wild animal, he let his sarcasm rip. "Let families get torn apart. Who cares if folks can no longer travel to work because the employer is suddenly on the wrong side of a worthless wall? For crying out loud, a wall is a manmade barrier, only enforced by the authorities who erected the foolish thing. This garbage is the last thing we need." Mitch grumbled a few expletives as the volume at a nearby table of men grew loud enough to detonate into a full out-and-out brawl. "Excuse me, Fanny. I have my hands full. Oh, yeah. I heard about your court win. Tell whoever waits on you that your meal is on me." He dashed off before she could thank him. While a small part of her wondered how the news of her good day at court preceded her footsteps to Bertine's, she shrugged it off. The town excelled at maintaining its telegraph rate of spreading news, especially with gossip.

No longer desiring a sweet drink or food, Fanny stood still, too stunned to decide whether to stay or leave. From behind her, another shout erupted, a verbal crossfire between a man and a woman.

"What's going to happen next?" the woman said. "Are we going to build a wall separating the North and South here in the good old USA? Or maybe a nice brick barricade between us and Canada and Mexico? Who needs diplomacy?"

"Don't go giving anyone ideas, Dorothy. Understand?"

"I don't understand a thing these days."

The man gulped his water, then wiped his mouth with his hand. "I doubt this bunch understands the craziness going on any better than we do."

The attendant who pumped Fanny's gasoline at the station she frequented for years sat at the lunch counter. Beside him was her veterinarian who had performed a few miracles on her cat. The men stood, tossed a few coins by their empty plates, and then shoved their way through the crowd toward the entrance. Drained of all energy, Fanny barreled toward one of the vacated chairs and slumped down. Although her stomach pinched from all the commotion, maybe she needed a strong cup of coffee.

Clad in a white uniform with a blue and white checkered apron, Gina exited the kitchen's swinging doors as Mitch entered. The two collided. She dropped a tray of four sandwich plates. The rattling of the falling dishes became muffled by the boisterous crowd. A curse sailed from his lips, an apology from hers. He blanched. She flamed red.

"I'm so sorry," the young woman warbled. "Clumsy me. I won't do that again."

Mitch clutched her arms. "Relax. We're all tense." He pointed at Fanny. "Go see what she'd like—and the tab is on me. I'll get the busboy to take care of the mess, then tell your customers their lunch will be out, pronto."

After Mitch walked into the kitchen and bellowed a guy's name, the waitress stood before Fanny. With her eyes averted, Gina rattled the ice bin on her side of the counter, filled a glass with water, and plopped it on the counter. Water sloshed over the rim. She yanked out a couple of napkins from the dispenser and mopped up the spill.

"I can't do one thing right today," Gina said.

"We all have bad days. Today's not exactly a day to fret about the little things in life."

Gina remained silent. She stared at a miscellaneous spot on the counter.

Oh, dear. The gap in conversation would not do. "Let's start from the beginning. Hello. My name is Fanny. Fanny Stern."

"Sorry, miss. I didn't mean to be unfriendly."

"That's okay. No need to apologize." The young woman was frazzled enough. Fanny did not want to contribute more stress by mentioning she had seen her walking past the house earlier. "I noticed you when you first came in. It's Gina, correct?" Gina appeared surprised. "I read it on your name badge."

"It should be Miss Nervous." She lifted her gaze to meet Fanny's. "That's a bad joke."

"Yes, I can see you're nervous." Although Fanny was not a giggler, she let out a strand of tee-hees, relieved the younger woman relaxed her firm posture. Yet, the silence between them became more awkward. Fanny searched her mind for an icebreaker. "Well, we're both wearing white."

Gina eyed her uniform and then Fanny's blouse. "Mine is a ratty uniform, yours a pretty and professional outfit. I doubt we have anything else in common."

Good. The young woman was articulating sentences, let alone conversing with her. A plus, unlike others who brushed her away like dirt under the porch. "I typically wear white or black outfits or a combo of the two colors, whether for work or home."

"Why so limited?" Gina asked.

"I just like those colors on me."

"Is that how you see things? I mean, I'm not saying you're colorblind. If you were, you couldn't help—"

Fanny lifted a hand to pause her. "I understand."

"Is it that you don't see life fitting in the in-between shades?"

Fanny studied the woman, offering her a kind smile. "For the most part, yes. That's how I see things. I view everyday existence as the contrast between right and wrong, needing balancing. Occupational hazard, as they say."

"I'm wasting your time. Let me take your order and give you some privacy. Would you like the day's special—chicken over biscuits with gravy?"

Fanny hugged her middle. "May I have a glass of plain seltzer water? First, though, please tell me your full name."

"Regina Kellerman." The young woman blushed. "Wow. You can tell I'm newly married. I'm now Regina Franks." She tapped her name badge twice with an unpolished fingernail. "You can call me Gina."

"Nice to meet you, Gina. Are you new to town?"

"Kind of. We've lived here since mid-July, with my grandmother. In desperate need of a change, I looked for work and started here last Monday."

"No wonder I didn't see you until today. I usually stop here a couple of days for lunch during the work week. The past few days I've been delayed. Finally, here I am. I've been a Bridgehaven local since my first breath. Where were you born and raised?"

Gina glanced away.

"Pardon me. I should know better than to ask questions that aren't—"

"Grammy and I moved from Rochester after Kenny and I married. We needed a bigger place. My husband..." Gina twirled a strand of hair. "I mean... he's..."

"It's okay. You don't need to tell me." The last topic Fanny wanted to discuss was world news. Similar to the popular topic of weather, the reports out of Germany might serve as a bridge to reconnect with this woman. "So, what's your opinion on this wall in Germany? While preparing for court today, I didn't listen to the news. This development sounds like a spark that will grow into a forest fire. One that will ignite the world with a mixture of conflicting opinions."

Gina's eyes grew wide.

"You know—like bolts of lightning during a wicked thunderstorm."

"Oh, I get the comparison, Miss. No problem."

"Please, call me Fanny."

"Fanny's an old-fashioned name. Are you named after your grandmother?"

Gina was proving to be good at deflection. Fanny would ride with it for a moment. "Do you like classical music?"

"Not really."

"Although my mother hated classical music, she was into names, particularly fascinated by the ones of people who made some sort of difference in the world." Fanny pushed away the irony threatening to flood her mind. "She struggled with a good enough name. Finally, two weeks before my birth, she read about the composer Fanny Mendelssohn. She was one of the first women musical artists who published music under her name, rather than go under a man's name. Previously, only men who released music publicly had their names connected to the beautiful pieces they contributed to the world."

Gina smiled, then jabbed a knuckle at the corners of her mouth as if trying to erase a trace of her pleased expression. "Do you compose music? What instrument do you play? The piano?"

"I play the radio dial." Fanny grinned. "I'm not musically inclined—can barely hum without sending my cat scrambling from the room. Like the great Mendelssohn, I guess you can say I'm a trailblazer."

Gina's left brow quirked up. "Trailblazer?"

"While I can't claim fame by being the first American woman to become an attorney, I practice law. Believe me, despite entering the '60s, with all its advances, it's still not easy for women in a world dominated by men. A woman eager to have a career and to be active outside of her home would find it difficult, to say the least."

"Oh. You're a lawyer," Gina murmured. "That's what you meant by saying occupational hazard." The last trace of pink fled her face. "A lawyer..." she repeated. She grasped the edge of the counter.

On her feet, Fanny motioned to her chair. "Have a seat—you look like you're about to faint."

"I'm fine," Gina said. She reached for Fanny's glass of water and drank it in three gulps.

Return to easy topics, Fanny ordered herself. The eatery emptying would also help ease the tension. "What's your favorite music?"

"I listen to a little rock 'n' roll, or if Kenny's listening to the country station... Well, I should start getting used to talking in the past tense, though it sure isn't easy. When Kenny used to listen to the country station on the radio, I got into the lyrics of the sad ballads as well." Gina squeezed her eyes shut.

"You said Kenny used to listen. Has he passed?"

After a painfully slow minute, Gina said, "Sorry. I still haven't taken your order."

"You apologize an awful lot."

"And way too many people need to apologize more." Gina shook her head. "Sorry. I didn't mean you."

"No offense taken."

"I'm glad. You've been nice to me. I'm not used to kindness."

"That makes two of us." Fanny had taken up valuable time from Gina who had to work. "I'll tell you what. Let me order—"

"My husband's in jail." Gina slapped her mouth; cherry red flamed her cheeks. Taking a sidestep away, she pivoted and fled into the kitchen as if a monster chased her. The door flapped noisily behind her. Fanny was unsure if the sound was an echo of the café's din of seconds ago or a reflection of the commotion surely ricocheting within any woman whose husband was incarcerated.

CHAPTER TWO

Gina, Rochester, February 14, 1961

Valentine's Day was one of the most dreadful days ever invented. Why in the world did Grammy ever suggest that today could be the first day of great things to come? "Sweetheart, it's warm for this time of year. Go take a little walk. I'll clean up the mess," Grammy said after Gina had knocked over a milk bottle from the kitchen counter. The white river spread like a ruptured dam over the green and white checkered linoleum flooring. Holiday or not, the day had gotten off to an awful start. Her favorite brown and yellow plaid skirt, buried on the bottom of the laundry heap in her closet, would never surface at this rate; she had plodded barefoot into a puddle of puppy pee in the hallway; the old Art Deco radio, which sat perched like an ugly statue on the kitchen counter, blared "Only the Lonely" sang by Roy Orbison. Her favorite singer, who had always zinged her heart, now depressed her spirit. Ugh. At eighteen—nineteen on the first of May—she lived the cliché of an old maid.

Since it was a Tuesday and she had off from the dreary five-and-dime Woolworth store where she worked five long and boring days a week, including Saturdays, she could not rightly say no to Grammy. The woman loved her to pieces, evidently more than her mother. Grammy never meant harm. "Okay, though I'm not taking Wags with me."

"Fine. The pup will keep me plenty of company. I'll leave him in the hallway with his blanket when I go to work." Grammy exited the room, returning a few minutes later with Gina's blue sweater draped over her arm. "Here you go. It's so lovely outside, nice and mild. You don't even need your jacket. Take the sweater along to be on the safe side."

Gina snatched the sweater and darted toward the kitchen door, invigorated by the freedom of stepping outside unescorted. Short of leaving the room, she stopped and faced her grandmother. "I stay on the safe side. Sometimes, I wish I was wild and more daring."

A trace of pure sadness crossed Grammy's eyes. Gina recognized the blink-and-you-will-miss-it look in the usually composed woman. She wished her grandmother was more straightforward about her past, especially about Gina's mother, Grammy's only child. When younger, Gina struggled that she would never successfully wring the truth from the obstinate woman. Daily, in school, she observed classmates' mothers walking hand in hand with their kindergarteners and first graders and pecking big kisses on their children's cheeks as goodbyes were shared. Then, despite Grammy's attendance at plays, recitals, and award ceremonies when Gina saw firsthand the moms of her classmates, she struggled to shrug off the emptiness of not having her mother beside her on these special occasions. The lack of knowledge about this mystery woman failed to help her spirits. Once, she even fantasized Grammy was her real mother, having hidden her true identity, for some mysterious reason. Grammy emphatically denied the status. The few times whenever Gina had tried to grill Grammy for more information, she appeared wounded, as if Gina did not trust her. Eventually, Gina let her quest go. She didn't want to continue to make her sad.

"I'm sorry, Grammy. I didn't mean to go against your better judgment."

The older woman gave a slight nod. "It's a changing world, that's all. I want you safe, let alone warm if the temperature should drop."

"Of course. And for you, I'll keep away from danger. Promise." Gina peeked at the red rooster clock hanging above the kitchen sink. "I'll be home by lunchtime to take care of Wags."

With the sweater wrapped over her shoulders, Gina raced out of the first-floor apartment they rented on Gibbs Street. Since the landlord's cranky older brother lived upstairs, she shut the door quietly and wasted no time as she breezed toward the park. It was a joy having a day off during the week. A self-declared loner, she found it beyond thrilling that the schools were in session and kept the rowdy children and the smooching teenagers occupied. And far away from her eyes. Businesses were open as usual, removing most strollers and busybodies out of her way. Upon entering the small city park, she saw two white-haired men sitting on a bench and a middle-aged woman walking with a toddler. Fine with her. The less, the better. She had enough on her mind lately. Namely, what to do with the rest of her life. She had to face the facts sooner or later and move forward. Young, and without a marriage prospect, let alone a boyfriend to snuggle with, or a gaggle of girlfriends to share daydreams or confess fears, she surrendered to the relief of not recognizing one face.

"That's a nice bench to sit on," someone said from behind her. She turned to see a tall, lean man with a thick mop of dark unruly hair. He wore a gaucho shirt, the style popular a few years ago. His brown-and-white-checkered shirt had brown sleeves and a brown collar. Like her, he also was free of a jacket. Standing by the drinking fountain, he pointed to a nearby bench. "I've sat there often. On the bench. It's comfortable."

Words tumbled around in her mouth, not necessarily pleasant ones. "Oh, I understand. No need to go on and on." Just because she did not attend college or slave away at a high-paying job like at Xerox, or like Grammy, teaching dental hygiene at the Eastman Dental Dispensary, she was no fool. The man stood there, facing her and grinning as if she were batty. Or, perhaps that was his way of smiling? She needed to loosen her attitude. He was charming, she had to admit. Dashing, if she wanted to use an old-fashioned word. One to admire individuality, she instantly regretted her defensive knee-jerk reaction, relieved she had not spewed nastier words. "Tucked under the tree, the bench looks like a nice spot to enjoy any time of the year."

He nodded. His silence gave her time to study him. He stood a good seven or so inches taller than her five foot three height, though his stooped posture and hands stuffed in his front trouser pockets made him appear awkward. She wanted to fix that for him.

"Well, then. Hello. My name is Gina. I usually help my grandmother on Tuesdays with errands. When she encouraged me to enjoy the fresh air, I came here instead. What's your name?"

"Kenneth Franks. Everyone calls me Kenny."

She smiled. "May I call you Kenny too?"

"Kenny is good."

"I hope so." She silently chided herself for acting flirtatious. Although she lacked the dating experiences of her former classmates, she knew better than to act all gooney bird silly. She pulled the sweater off and slipping from her hand, it fell to the ground and landed in a pile of melting snow and old wet leaves. She groaned. "Oh, dear."

With the ease of an athlete, Kenny jogged from the fountain and scooped up the sweater. He shook out the woolen garment, then held it snugged against his middle instead of handing it to her or draping it on her shoulders. His expressionless face secreted his thoughts.

"Thank you, Kenny." His name flowed from the tip of her tongue with ease. She took the sweater from him and beamed a large, sincere smile. "Say, Kenny's a cool name."

"It's okay. Your sweater, I mean. Doesn't look broken."

A broken sweater? And why had he stayed on the topic of the stupid sweater when she'd changed the subject? She patted the blue garment she had slipped into. "Not broken, just a little dirty."

"Are you in trouble?"

She squinted. Had he meant the possibility of her receiving punishment over the sweater? Usually a good read on characters, Kenny seemed to be a good-natured guy, in his unique, refreshing way. She wanted to make him comfortable. "Oh, no. I'm not in trouble because of a dirty sweater." She eyed the sleeves of the sweater. "See. It's just the cuffs that got dirty. No big deal."

"Good." He chuckled a warm and cozy sound that cocooned around her like an afghan on a winter day. "You have brown eyes. I do too."

"And you have a nice laugh, Kenny."

"You have a nice smile," he replied.

"Want to sit with me on the bench?"

"Yes, very much."

They walked side by side, keeping a proper distance between each other. When they sat, he positioned himself two feet to her left. She giggled and motioned for him to move closer. He inched toward her, but she shook her head. "Closer." After he moved a few more inches, she again giggled.

Another few inches. This time she lifted both hands. "Stop. Well, unless you like me giggling like a little girl."

He stopped moving. His gaze lingered on her face. Slowly, his cocoa brown eyes swept downward toward her daintily crossed feet. "You're no little girl."

A silly grin hijacked her face. "Looks like you understood my joshing."

"I understand lots." He stared blankly at the tree on the other side of the path. "More than others know."

"I bet you do. Like you, judging by the way people respond to me, they think I'm the one who doesn't understand them. I'm glad you appreciate what I say."

"Appreciate," Kenny echoed. "Uncle Raymond says that word many times to me. He says he appreciates me. That's good."

"Yes, it sure is good." An inkling sizzled in her. "I suspect many people appreciate you."

"Sometimes. At work, people say nice things about me." He tilted his head. "Sometimes, not."

"My Grammy taught me to pay attention and to thank people when they say something nice. And when they don't, she said to pay them no mind. Most of all, she taught me to stop waiting for folks to say nice things to me. Honestly, that's the hardest part. Who doesn't long to hear an encouraging, pleasant word?" She placed her hand over her heart and watched his gaze follow. "It's hard, though. It hurts here."

"People can be mean. Uncle Raymond tells me to walk away from mean people."

"Your uncle is smart. By the way, where do you work?"

"At my uncle's spaghetti factory."

Spaghetti... pasta... Oh, goodness. "Your uncle owns Franks' Pasta Company?"

Kenny nodded. "I love spaghetti. I eat lots of it."

"Wow! What a great place to work. You sure don't look like you eat a lot of spaghetti."

"I do. I don't tell lies." Ready to jump in and clarify that she believed he was telling the truth, his chuckle stopped her from inserting her foot into her mouth even worse. "I just walk a lot. All over the place. Uncle Raymond says I never stay still. No dust will fall on my head, he says."

"You're staying still now."

"Yes," he said. "Because you're next to me."

That was the smoothest, and sweetest line a guy ever said to her. She licked her bottom lip, unsure if nervousness or excitement coursed through her. "What's your job?"

"I'm in charge of delivering messages. Because I like to walk."

"Like a supervisor?"

He nodded. "I take inventory, too. Uncle Raymond says I'm good with math. He trusts me."

"Your job is impressive." She paused, expecting Kenny to ask her questions. He remained silent. The sudden quiet between them became awkward. "Aren't you going to ask me what I do for work?"

He shrugged. "Uncle Raymond says it's not polite to ask nosy questions to strangers."

"Strangers?" She swatted the air, shoving away the frightening notion. "I thought we were becoming friends. I want to be friends with you. Would you like that?"

"Yes."

She smiled. "Good. Then we're not strangers. If you're curious about my work, I'm happy to answer any of your questions, though it's nothing glamorous." When he lifted a brow, she added, "It's not a high-paying, fancy job."

"Do you do your best at work?"

She never thought of it that way. "Yes, of course. I'm nice to the customers and my boss says that's what counts."

"Uncle Raymond says to hold your chin up. You shouldn't be ashamed."

"Aw. You and your uncle are so smart and kind."

"That's the truth." His brow wrinkled and he grinned. "The truth, I mean, when it comes to work."

"Oh? Okay. Well, I still think you and your uncle are wise." She inhaled deeply. "I work at the lunch counter at one of the Woolworth stores. See, nothing exciting or—"

"I like Woolworth. Which one do you work at?"

"The largest one on East Main Street. Since I'm an early riser I find it easy to work the breakfast crowd three times a week. The other two days, I work the lunch shift."

"Which do you like best?"

No one had ever asked her work shift preferences. Grammy never asked her any personal questions. The only thing concerning Grammy was whether she showed up for work and brought home a paycheck. Kenny sounded genuinely interested. "I like the breakfast customers." She snickered. "They're still waking up and keep to themselves, unlike the lunch crowd who dish out their work troubles on me."

"I'll have to go there for lunch. Know why?"

"To see what specials we have?"

"No. To cheer you up."

She thumped her chest with her right index finger and mouthed, "Me?"

"I'd like to see you more."

"I hope lots more." Thinking that Kenny behaved more innocently and tenderly, at least compared to what her wild imagination was conjuring up seconds ago, her instincts told her to dial back the conversation a bit. "So, your uncle is your boss. Is that difficult?"

"Difficult? Like hard to do? No. Uncle Raymond is nice. I live with him too."

"I live with my grandmother. And your parents?"

"My mother went away. She left me with my father. Because I was broken. Uncle Raymond said I was fine. When my father died, my uncle took me in like a son."

Kenny's heartbreak story flooded Gina's eyes with tears. She blinked them away in the hope he wouldn't notice. The last thing she wanted him to think was that she pitied him as an irremediable lost cause.

He stuffed his hand into his trouser pocket and pulled out a handkerchief. Gently, he dabbed the corners of her eyes then thrust the cloth into her palm. "Don't cry, Gina. Uncle Raymond is nice. He's good to me. I'm good to him. We're happy." He flashed his adorable boyish look. "And we eat lots of spaghetti."

Recognizing the need to return to a lighter subject, she sniffled and chuckled. "I imagine. And good tomato sauce too?"

"The best."

Gina playfully slapped her cheek. "Franks' Best Pasta Sauce—of course. Why didn't I connect the dots?"

Kenny stared hard at her. A good stare, though. Not like he was trying to figure her out. Rather, he seemed to appreciate what he saw. "You're like me. Just because we're not perfect all the time doesn't mean we're not good. Doesn't mean we're dumb."

"That's right," she said.

"Lunch break is over." He stood. "I have to return to work. Today's inventory day. I'm good at math. Others don't believe that."

"They're silly. If you say you're smart in math, I believe you." She also stood. "I have to go home and check on my puppy."

"I like dogs. All animals. I want to meet your puppy. We don't have pets. We're too busy. I hope you will come to the park more."

"If you're here, I'd like to visit."

"How many times?"

A smile toyed with his lips and she noted his gentle teasing. A foreign joy now buzzed within her, replacing an emptiness that existed only minutes ago. "A trillion times."

His brows lifted. "That's a lot of times."

"Yes, it certainly is."

"Good. I want to see you all the time."

For once, Gina couldn't care less what others might think of her. Let them snitch to her grandmother. Today, on Valentine's Day, Gina Kellerman was going to make a move on a true gentleman, a good-looking and kind person. She never had a chance. He made the first leap.

Kenny grasped her hand. "I like you, Gina. Is that okay?"

She pressed into his side. "That's wonderful."

•   •   •

"Sorry I'm late," Gina called out when she entered the empty kitchen. The aroma of tangy goulash lured her to the stove. She grabbed the wooden spoon from the spoon rest and tasted her grandmother's best dish. Mm-hmm. Perfection. She covered the pot again. "Grammy? I didn't mean to stay out all morning and afternoon. I hope I didn't worry you."

"Sweetheart," Grammy said as she entered the room. "Worry is my middle name."

"At least you look comfortable out of your work clothes."

Helene twirled around. "Do you think this green housecoat makes a fashion statement?"

Gina winked. "Your pink one is better. More your color."

"I couldn't wear it—it was in the wash."

Gina groaned. "Sorry. I completely forgot the laundry."

"Never mind. It's too late. We'll have to manage until the weekend."

By weekend, Grammy meant Saturday since the laundromat was closed on Sundays, which implied that Grammy would have to lug the rolling laundry cart herself since Gina worked on Saturdays. "Forgive me."

Helene stirred the cooking dinner, then sat at the table. "Have a seat. I had a rough day with surly, lazy students and hope you have good news to explain your absence."

Gina sat opposite her grandmother, though aware the astutely observant woman would readily see her slightest expression. Then again, it would not have made a difference if she sat on the far end of the room or alongside her. Grammy had a reputation among her lady acquaintances as being the *sage woman* for a reason. One could not keep a thing from her, especially Gina. Her soured nerves had her staring at her sweaty hands resting on the tabletop.

"What's wrong, darling?"

"Why do you think something is always wrong with me?"

"No, not every time." Grammy smiled softly. "Believe it or not, I once was eighteen—"

"I'm practically nineteen."

Grammy's smile faded. "Then remember adults don't interrupt. Please."

Although apologizing had become Gina's specialty lately, she kept quiet, bracing for her grandmother to continue.

"I remember what it's like to be young. And lonely." She held up a hand to stop Gina from reacting. "I also know how you operate—you wouldn't stay out longer than expected unless for a good reason. Let me hear what has kept you so busy today."

Words escaped Gina's thoughts. Instead, images of Kenny filled the emptiness of her mind. Smiling Kenny wearing his outdated shirt. Laughing Kenny sharing a silly work incident. Serious Kenny telling how he and his uncle live together because his mom had abandoned—his word choice— him when he was four after the doctor declared he was unfit to attend a normal school when the time came. Magical Kenny making her feel appreciated.

"Regina Frances Kellerman. Talk to me."

Grammy used her full name. Not good. Not at all. Gina peered up.

"What's the boy's name?"

There was no way she could dodge her. "He's no boy, Grammy. He's a thirty-year-old gentleman. His name is Kenneth—Kenny—Franks."

"Thirty? He's twelve years older than you are. What's a man at that age doing spending time with you?"

Like a typical sunny day before a snowstorm, so too was it predictable that her grandmother would get stuck on Kenny's age. Gina battened down her resolve to not roll her eyes like a sulky teenager. She was a woman now and her grandmother must recognize and accept this stage of her life. There was no little girl left in her. "Considering what months our birthdays fall, we're only eleven years apart."

"Oh, yes. I see. One year makes all the world of a difference."

"I'm no longer a child. And Kenny's not senior citizen material, like you." She gasped and slumped partially under the table. For someone claiming she wasn't a kid, she sure just acted like one, and a bratty one at that. She wished she could slip to the floor and down a chute that would transport her far away.

Not true. If she disappeared, then she would never again see Kenny. He was now the one person she wanted to see and be with for the rest of her existence.

"Sorry, Grammy," she said. To test what felt like a widening gulf between them, she added, "I didn't mean to be nasty."

"Apology accepted. First off, where were you all day?"

"At the park—where we met. After a nice discussion, I planned to head straight home. Then, he invited me to his uncle's factory. Grammy, his uncle owns Franks' Pasta Company. Can you believe that? And when he asked me if I wanted to see the factory that makes the spaghetti that we eat, I—"

"I'm well aware we eat the starchy stuff."

Gina telling her grandmother not to interrupt would fire up the irritation between them, not to soothe the palpable escalation of out-of-control emotions. Nor would it help to remind Grammy that one, the pasta tasted good, and two, set at a decent price, the food staple enabled them to maintain their household budget.

"Tell me," Grammy continued, "about this boy, this man of yours. How long have you known him?"

"I just met him today, in the park."

"Today? The way you're carrying on, it's like you've known each other for months." She crossed her arms. "Are you telling me the truth?"

"Yes. I wouldn't lie to you."

Silence seemed to yell at her. Finally, Grammy nodded.

"Did the two of you go elsewhere after the park and factory tour?"

Unable to sit a second longer with her grandmother who acted more like a judge than the next best thing to a mother she never had, Gina jumped to her feet. "Are you implying I'm a loose, wild woman?"

"No. I raised you better. But, I'm familiar with how men operate. And if this Kenneth of yours is thirty, and is honestly unattached, then there must be something wrong with him. Which is it?"

How could she dare say insulting nonsense about gentle and caring Kenny? "We did not sneak off to his place—or a seedy motel room like couples do on your TV soaps. Although you may watch your dramas broadcasted in black and white, there are more colors and shades in real life, Grammy. Like what happened between Kenny and me." Gina realized she had shifted close from simply expressing her views to sprouting off in a tirade. Seldom had she bothered to share her opinions with Grammy. It just did not work. Never until this point had she gone on and on, angrily, with the person who taught her to respect her elders and never raise her voice at a relative. Not that she had other known family members, though that was a different subject. A closed-off, do not even go there, subject. She willed herself to tamp down her attitude and tone and to continue.

"The only things that transpired between us were lots of good conversation and one kiss. A chaste, but the sweetest kiss, ever. The talk was heavenly easy, for a change. No male I've ever met has made me feel so relaxed. He's a swell guy—it's like we've known each other for years. And conversing was—is—a breeze. Until Kenny, no boy or man ever wanted to chat with me. Sure, they'd ask if I had a spare cigarette—though the joke was on them since I don't smoke—or glance at my wristwatch and ask for the time, nothing more. Truly, no pass was thrown my way." She watched Grammy's eyes grow wide. "Kenny is far above my standards of a good man." She cooed a dreamy sound. "This feeling must be true love and it is grand."

"That's not love. Love doesn't happen in one day. It takes time. That's an infatuation."

"Take your words back."

"Call it a brush of passion, then. You need to stay away from him."

"Him? Like I told you, he has a name. Kenneth. Kenny. And Kenny is a respectable, mature man. Maybe to you, it should be Mr. Franks." A thought nudged her and she stood tall. "How would you know about a brush of passion versus true love? From what you've told me, you've never been in love. Are you the right person to dish out advice to me? You're acting like Kenny and I are planning to elope tonight."

Grammy straightened as if a bee had stung her backside.

"Look at us. We're fighting." Gina sniffled. "We stink at bickering."

"Yes, we do," Grammy said, though the dour look on her face remained intact. "Nasty words lead to hurt feelings."

"I shouldn't have squawked. Nothing like sounding like a little kid and thinking others will see me as an adult, huh?"

"That's correct. Especially when you don't know half of it."

I would know more if only you shared, Gina thought. *If only you could trust me and tell me what happened in my past and yours.* "I'm going to my room to freshen up," she said. The excuse was the best she could come up with. At least, she would not further deepen the already icy chasm between them.

"Are you having supper? I made your favorite—goulash."

"I saw. With elbow macaroni... pasta..." Gina watched as her grandmother averted her gaze toward the clock.

Gina needed to calm down more. Otherwise, the subtle coolness snaking between them might escalate into a concrete emotional wall separating them. Nothing hurt her more than the loss of Grammy's smiles and hugs. She was the only family Gina had. "I'll pass on the goulash. Maybe later. I sampled it, though. It's delicious." She walked away from the table and then spun around. "I love you," she said. Like when she was younger and thought Grammy could never do wrong, she blew her a kiss. And like those simpler, golden days of her youth, Grammy plucked the kiss from its air travels, planted it on her cheek, and smiled. "Goodnight, Grammy. Sweet dreams."

She and Kenny had planned to meet after work tomorrow. This was all she needed to think about. It was a relief she had kept this plan from Grammy's censoring, controlling word of *No*. Having heard enough negative words all her life, she never wanted to hear one more. It was time for Gina to become Gina. No longer a girl, she wanted to be a woman. Every part of her heart and mind told her that Kenny wanted that too—to become *his* woman. One she did not have to apologize for.

CHAPTER THREE

Fanny, Bridgehaven, August 14, 1961

The breaking news of this monstrosity of a wall—of all crazy things—being erected in Berlin would have to wait until Fanny could devote her full attention to this developing disaster. Relieved she had no further commitments for the day, and aware Mitch would not ask her to leave, she continued to sit at the counter for Gina to exit the kitchen like the other waitresses quitting for the day. She tried not to stare at the kitchen door's oval window. She should leave. Just walk out. Yet, five minutes turned to ten. Fifteen. Finally, from the kitchen side, a pair of brown eyes riveted on hers. The door cracked open a little more.

"Are you ever going to leave?" Gina asked.

Fanny fixed a smile on her face. "I'm the last person out to hurt you. Let's talk."

Gina shoved open the door just enough to remain wedged between the door and its frame. "I used to think Grammy would never hurt me. She proved me wrong."

"I'm sorry. That must have stung."

"Still does sting, all considering."

Fanny wondered if the two of them shared more in common than not. "If you're done for the day, would you like to take a walk with me?"

"Maybe. Honestly, I'm in no mood for questions."

Fanny pursed her lips. "Okay, then. If I promise not to interrogate you, would you accompany me outdoors?" She batted her hand through the air and sighed. "Am I pushing away the stale cigarette smoke or the echoes of all the lively chatter that filled every inch of this place only minutes ago? The noise is still buzzing in my ears. I can use a hefty amount of fresh air."

"I can as well."

"See? We think alike." Fanny started toward the door without looking to see if Gina followed. With Gina's husband in jail, the young woman needed to trust her.

They stepped into the sunshine. "Isn't this weather grand?" Fanny asked. "I could live like this year-round—not scorching hot, nor below-zero cold. Do you have a preference of where to walk?"

Gina fished out a pair of tortoiseshell sunglasses from her purse. She slipped them on; the dark lenses shielded her expression. "If it's away from others, I'm good."

Fanny led her toward Lake Ontario, the smallest of the interconnected Great Lakes shared by New York and Ontario. The body of water relaxed her and she hoped it did the same for Gina. Most visitors to Bridgehaven, who were from a sizable distance away from the town, asked where to find the bridge. Fanny, in trying to resolve the mystery, would point out that the town's pride was how it sat cozily on the shores of Lake Ontario, and not a bridge. Originally called the unassuming name Laketown, the town's name changed when Thaddeus Bridge, an enterprising resident known to provide swiftly for his large family of eight children, started an ammunition company incorporating his older sons and two brothers. It became a dependable powder magazine when nearby—as the proverbial crow flies—Sackets Harbor was thick in the battle against the British in 1812. The *haven* part occurred when Thaddeus' sons overtook the business operation after the war and Thaddeus put his feet up on the front porch railing of his home, declaring the town his true haven.

"I love it here, don't you?" Fanny took a deep breath of fresh air. "This time of year, with winter about to barrel toward us, it's nice to take in the sights of children swimming, friends picnicking, and sailboats cruising the water. And there's usually a cool breeze to enjoy."

"Bridgehaven has a few extra perks than living in a city." Gina stooped down and plucked a cluster of bouncing Bet. She inhaled the pink flowers. "Mmm. What a sweet scent."

"I agree. My favorite is honeysuckle—a natural high for me." Just when Fanny thought they were bonding and Gina was loosening up, the younger woman turned sheet white. "What's wrong? Does honeysuckle remind you of something bad?"

Gina grinned. "Grammy says honeysuckle is a weed, with its sole goal to take over the world, but I like the flower too. No concerns over me. It's all the tension of the day. On top of working and skipping meals, I admit I'm frazzled."

Fanny imagined having a husband in jail contributed directly to her upside-down state. "Do you and your grandmother often see eye-to-eye on important matters?"

"Not lately. Why?"

"Might Kenny's situation be causing friction between you and your grandmother?"

"I'm impressed you remember his name. Sadly, when people recognize or recall his name it's usually not a pleasant association." Gina's brow furrowed. "Yes, I admit, the friction between the only two people I love is weighing me down."

"I'm sorry about that. That's a tough situation to be in." Fanny pointed toward a bench. "Let's sit."

"It's funny how benches bring people together, like a bridge," Gina said. "Kenny and I met in a Rochester park and seconds later we sat on a bench and talked for a bunch of magical minutes."

"I agree. Benches and bridges are the opposite of walls erected between people, let alone between and within countries. Folks seem to find it easier to put up barriers than to make a bridge of union. Getting back to you, I'm sorry for the trouble between you and your grandmother. With Kenny, was it love at first sight?"

"Practically." Gina set the bouncing Bet cluster between them and stared at the lake. "While I'm no expert in the love department, I guess you can say we fell in love on the fast side. We met on Valentine's Day, after all."

"What a sweet memory, one to treasure."

Gina nodded, smiling softly. "I've asked Grammy if she's ever loved a man so much that she wanted to marry him. She's a hard one to extract the truth from. I mean, she's had a baby—my mother. Sadly, she won't tell me about her, except her name is Liselotte. For goodness' sake, I don't know whether my mother's even alive. Grammy won't tell me why Liselotte didn't raise me, why Grammy did instead. If Liselotte is living, I'm clueless whether she goes by the family name of Kellerman, or uses a different one. She might be married, with a different last name. For all I know, she might have even chosen a new first name. When it comes to my grandfather, I'm assuming he was a great guy who died tragically young or a one-night stand Grammy never married but pined for since. If the latter, perhaps she's ashamed to this day." Gina paused. Anguish flashed across her eyes. "Or, he might be a horrible person who wronged her and she still refuses to speak his name aloud. Not even to me, and I'm the man's granddaughter."

Another person with unknown family members. In Gina's case, an unknown mother and grandfather. In Fanny's situation, her father. A pity. For both of them. "Is this Kenny's first marriage?"

Upon the mention of Kenny's name, Gina relaxed her stiffened posture. "That's what he's told me. I believe him—I believe everything he tells me. He never lies. I'm not sure if he knows how to lie. I'm no one to judge—I didn't date, either. Here's the truth..."

Fanny held up a hand. "You don't have to share anything personal with me."

"I'd like to, though. So, you can understand us better."

"Okay, then."

"Kenny, being a true and respectable man... you know... he didn't want to jump into bed with me unless we were married, though I was ready and wanting to." Gina's face flushed. "He proposed early in our dating days and we married right away. We're happy and committed to each other." Gina grinned. "We sure did shock Grammy."

"I imagine you did." Fanny squeezed Gina's hand. "I'm glad you two met and married."

"Are you married, Fanny?" Gina eyed her left hand, one absent of a wedding band. "Other than knowing you're named after a woman composer, and you're a lawyer, you've kept me in the dark. Tell me a little more."

"I haven't had time to fall in love. After college and law school, I interned at a large firm in Manhattan. I kept so busy that I had no time for a social life." She had left out the parts like adjusting to making adult decisions, securing apartment leases, paying off student loans, and the everyday living issues without the benefit of consulting with her mother. How she wished her life had taken a different turn. Then again, given that she could not have changed her circumstances, she spent her adult life enjoying it to the fullest the best she could, becoming who she wanted to be, without self-pity or worrying over what others thought of her endeavors. With her mother now out of the big picture for over ten years, Fanny lived alone, much to her liking. Ralph, her resident tuxedo cat, kept her plenty of decent company. She had no desire to bring up her past, to Gina, or anyone. "Setting up my practice here in Bridgehaven also kept me busy."

"You remind me of Grammy." Gina snorted. "I didn't mean to say you're old like my grandmother. She's a hard-working woman too. A little too hard. She's a dedicated woman to whatever she sets her mind to. And if she's not devoted to a particular cause or person, the best I can say is to watch out."

"I imagine she had to be strong to care for you," Fanny said tenderly so Gina knew she was more caring than teasing. "Mind if I ask you where she works?"

"At the Eastman Dental Dispensary. She teaches dental hygiene. It's not as lucrative or rewarding as it sounds. Helene Kellerman, though, is a woman with a reputation for being ahead of her contemporaries."

Fanny wondered if she had equal footing with Helene. Perhaps the woman would see her as a respectable counterpart and would work with her for the sake of her granddaughter's husband. "She has some commute to Rochester."

Gina remained so silent and expressionless that Fanny wondered what had prompted their sudden relocation to Bridgehaven. Lesser living expenses? A small-town address usually comes with lesser costs than a city residence. Although Rochester wasn't on the same business and social scale as Manhattan, the smaller city in Western New York had many pluses and she knew several people who loved living and working there. Like any other place, it also had its share of disadvantages. She suspected Gina's relocation hinged on a different reason, such as delaying a reality neither Gina nor her grandmother wanted to accept. She could be wrong, though.

Gina drew in a deep breath and exhaled a sigh. "Although Grammy's not ready to retire, she recently reduced her hours at work and currently teaches three days a week. Then again, it doesn't matter as far as driving goes, since she doesn't find the twenty-five-mile distance troubling. Then again, I'm sure she'd have a whole different opinion in the winter. I'm glad I don't have to drive a long way to work—what a relief Mitch hired me. Grammy's '56 DeSoto, though, is pretty good in the snow. Then again, the car can drive through storms, sail across dirt roads as if they were paved, and with its large windows, keeps us cool on the hottest of days." She chuckled. "Wow! How many times did I say *then again*? Seriously though, you ever notice how many *then-agains* are part of life?"

"For sure. It's good to have a reliable vehicle, though, especially in this Snowbelt area." Refraining from crossing her arms and appearing assertive, Fanny laced her fingers together on her lap. Go gently, she reminded herself. Gina had become chatty and Fanny did not want to ruin the young woman's momentum. "What's your new living arrangements like?"

Gina slipped off her sunglasses, the indentation of the right side of her nose prominent. "Might not falling in love be whittled down to something more basic?"

Fanny blinked at Gina's switch of topics. "Like what?"

"Not meeting the right man?"

Fanny looked at the lake. "You can say that. I'm different from the average woman, though. Can't blame a tall, spirited, and most attractive man turning away from the likes of me." She grinned. When Gina's expression turned serious, considering what she faced with Kenny, Fanny hoped she was not about to say the wrong words. "Perfect men exist only in the fairytales of our girlhood. We're raised to believe such a creature will exist in our future with the single purpose of watching over us."

Gina opened the clasp to her purse and withdrew a photograph. "This is Kenny. I think he's super handsome and perfect, though I'm sure others don't agree. It doesn't matter. I think he's tops and when it comes to me, he thinks the same. And that's all that counts."

Fanny recoiled in self-reproach. Initially, she had typecast Gina as a wee bit less smart than herself because she likely had less education and worked a non-white-collar job. Shame ripped through her. To think she prided herself in not judging others, especially after spending a whole childhood and adolescence in an emotional juvenile purgatory, designated by her peers as the loner, the uppity one, the walking piece of sadness, the unworthy. Pick one. In short, she was the one no one wanted to be bothered with because she supposedly was not worthy of anyone's time. Now, Fanny's perspective of Gina had changed. The young woman was bright and had amazing insights. So what if she waitressed? She worked, rather than sitting around pitying herself. And she certainly thought the world of her husband, despite intimating that others might think of him on a lowly level. Although why was beyond her guess.

Fanny studied the photo. She had seen him before, or at least a photograph of him. Where, though, she could not pin it down. "Kenny is handsome."

"Well," Gina said, laughing the merriest trill yet to reach Fanny's ears. "You can't have him. He's all mine."

With her attention on Kenny's photograph, Fanny had only heard half of what Gina said. Kenny's striking dark features and shock of raven hair demanded her attention. She imagined a few women would long to smooth his hair with their fingers. Photographed wearing a nondescript sweater over an equally plain shirt, Kenny was striking. Pleased for Gina that she saw her husband as movie-star-gorgeous, she added, "Yes, he's all yours, Gina. I don't blame you for wanting him as your husband. I'm happy for you."

A loud sniffle erupted from Gina, startling Fanny and reminding her that Kenny was in jail, not simply tucked away in a workplace office. For Gina's sake, Fanny needed her to stay calm and clear-minded. She gave Gina's arm a reassuring pat. "Okay, then. We've established that your husband is one handsome guy. Tell me more about Kenny other than his looks."

"You're persistent."

"It's the nature of my job to be."

On the water, two seagulls landed on an outcrop of rocks, squawking to each other in a commiseration privy to their ears alone.

"I guess determination is a good trait to have as a lawyer."

"I'll listen to whatever you wish to share with me." When Gina remained silent, Fanny thought of a different angle. "Tell me what you think I should know about Kenny?"

"He's the sincerest and sweetest person I've ever met. For instance, if he says he likes your dress, he means it. Others might say those empty words to persuade you to think they're on your side. With Kenny, he says it as he sees fit."

"And if he doesn't like your dress, he won't hesitate to tell you?"

"No," Gina said with an upbeat tone. "That's where the sweet part comes in. If he's hesitant to say a positive word, he clams up and keeps any unpleasantries to himself."

Fanny noted Gina worrying her bottom lip. What circumstances would it take to push Kenny to disclose his feelings? His anger, or worse? "I applaud his discretion."

"That's the shocker of it all. I doubt whether Kenny understands what the word discretion means. It's not like he's trying to prevent an argument or stop a wrong from happening, but more like he doesn't want to hurt someone."

"He must have a good intuition of what makes others tick, and what aggravates them. Based upon what you've told me about Kenny, he must also have a good sense of how to avoid uncomfortable situations."

A dog barked twice, bringing their attention to a couple walking a beagle alongside the lake's white sandy shoreline.

"Yes, he does," Gina said, still with averted eyes. "It comes naturally to him, I think. From what he's told me about his school years, it's not like he learned tactfulness from his classmates."

Tactfulness? Fanny would have thought savvy was more like it. She sat up straighter. "Pardon?"

"They were mean, pointing the finger at Kenny and saying not one brain cell floated in his head. His sorry lot of his teachers didn't help, either."

"Gina, how old is Kenny?"

"He's thirty. Eleven years older than me—something Grammy has a huge problem with, not me."

He was only five years younger than she. Fanny did the math. "And you're nineteen?"

"My birthday's in May. Kenny's a February baby. He'd just celebrated his thirtieth a week before we met. He didn't even ask me my age until he proposed. Like I've said, he's a true gentleman."

The word gentleman, as in a mature adult, was not exactly the number one adjective that came to Fanny's mind. "Did Kenny graduate from high school?"

"He works—worked—at his uncle's factory." Gina streaked her fingers through her hair. "Franks' Pasta Company. In Rochester. Have you heard of it?"

"Of course. I love all of Franks' pasta." Fanny patted her once flat stomach. "And the pasta sure loves me. I wouldn't be surprised if Franks grows so big shortly that it rivals Mueller." Her thoughts jumped back to how Gina phrased her sentence about her husband in the past tense. "When was Kenny arrested?"

"Early Sunday morning, 1:05 a.m., to be exact."

"Where is Kenny right now?"

"He's at the Monroe County Detention Center in Rochester."

Having met with accused clients there, Fanny was familiar with the prison's location. "Has he appeared before a judge?"

"Not yet. Kenny said he will see the judge tomorrow."

"So, you've visited Kenny?"

Gina remained silent.

"Listen, carefully, Gina. I want to help you. However, without honest communication, I won't have much to offer. Will you please tell me what Kenny is being accused of?"

"Look at the time." Gina waved her white-banded wristwatch in front of Fanny's eyes. "It's after one. Grammy hates it when I'm home late, especially since that's how it all began with Kenny. Late, I mean. I'd arrived home late the day when he and I first met. She says it's an uphill struggle ever since, one thing after another." She stood. "I have to hurry. Maybe I'll see you at Bertines' next week?" She took one step forward and then faced Fanny again. "You did a great job asking me questions I didn't want to hear, let alone address." Her tone was neutral. Not edgy.

Fanny gave a little nod. "And you did a nice job filling me in. Thank you." She had hoped Gina would have invited her home to meet her grandmother. She had envisioned the three of them seated around a table, sipping tea or coffee, becoming more familiar with each other, and then getting down to the nitty-gritty of Kenny's legal troubles. Fanny, however, knew a dismissal at face value. "You just may see me. I'm glad we had our little chat."

"So am I," Gina said and walked away.

Fanny called after her. "Here's my business card if you should want to contact me. Whether business or to chat, I'm available for you."

Gina took the card and looked at its black print on a white background. "Fanny D. Stern. What does the D stand for?"

"Dinah. Although, I like to think of the initial as standing for Difference, as in making a difference in someone's life."

"Fanny Difference Stern." The slightest of smiles came across her lips. "Well, best of luck to you. That's a great goal to have. I wish I could make a difference in someone's life, too."

Gina's long-legged quick step away was nearly a sprint, leaving a funny taste in Fanny's mouth. What did this young woman have to conceal? A piece of evidence? Was she an accomplice to her husband's crime? Or, did Gina fear her grandmother? She had hinted at the tension between the two. Was Gina terrified of crossing her family member, perhaps not for the first time? Or, was she afraid of Kenny and what he might do to her? And why did she and Kenny live with this woman rather than enjoy their own place? There were too many missing pieces for Fanny to take an intelligent stab at answers. Still, no way would Fanny permit Gina's abrupt departure to stop her from gathering the facts surrounding Kenny. First, she needed to meet Gina's grandmother. Fanny searched her mind to recall Gina's maiden name. It seemed like her last name began with a K. Kennings? Kiest? Gina K. Gina Kelly...

Fanny bent over and streaked her palms down her face. Gina was married. No American woman would get hitched only to use her maiden name. If Kenny's uncle was paternal, then likely Kenny was Kenny Franks... The name Kellerman suddenly blazed through her mind. Finally! So, Fanny had two names to search for: Kellerman and Franks. Hopefully, these names would be listed in the phone directory. Once connected to Gina's grandmother, Fanny would convince this relative of the necessity to have a face-to-face chat concerning her granddaughter and grandson-in-law, or whatever she cared to call Kenny. Most of all, she would inquire whether Kenny needed legal help. If so, Fanny would convince *Grammy* that she was the attorney who could provide the right representation.

If she hurried, she would get home early enough to contact the grandmother and meet Kenny during the limited visiting hours. She stood. Something fluttered downward from her lap. Kenny's photograph. She picked it up; the newlywed's gaze jumped off the black and white 5x5 inch glossy paper and met hers so intently it was as if he stood beside her. "Help us," the Kenny phantom said. With those two words, whether magically whispered or imagined, the where and the why of how she saw his image became clear. Earlier that morning when she had stopped at the town's courthouse to search through a stack of CHRSs, criminal history record search reports, she had stumbled across Kenny's mugshot. In needing to appear in court, until now, she had never given the mugshot a second thought. With the likelihood of Kenny's arrest last night, and with a Bridgehaven residential address, it made sense that his photo and booking records were also in this neighboring town to Rochester. The clock was ticking. Gina had said she believed Kenny would appear before the judge tomorrow. There was still time to help. Precious minutes, perhaps. No worries. She had a reputation for walking, talking, and convincing fast for a reason.

·   ·   ·

With only one Kellerman—a Helene Kellerman—listed in the directory, Fanny phoned and introduced herself as an attorney interested in helping her granddaughter's husband's legal situation. When Fanny was invited to meet Helene the next day, she pressed the urgency of the matter, not only for Kenny's sake but Gina's too. Helene agreed to change her plans to accommodate Fanny's visit that afternoon. So far, so good.

Fanny had imagined the grandmotherly woman as a white-haired, plump woman in her seventies, despite Gina saying Helene worked, though reduced hours. She would find out momentarily. Fanny pressed the doorbell. A jarring buzz sounded. The creak of stairs made her straighten. She smoothed down the black slacks and white blouse she had changed into after meeting with Gina earlier. The door opened a crack, just wide enough for a pair of dark brown eyes to examine Fanny, reminding her of when Gina peered out the kitchen door at Bertine's. Chills climbed Fanny's arms at how the grandmother and granddaughter seemed on guard against others.

"Mrs. Stern?" The woman's English was articulate and laced with a distinct German accent.

"It's Miss Fanny Stern. Please call me Fanny." Fanny extended a hand to shake. The older woman remained tucked behind the nearly shut door, neglecting the greeting. "Are you Mrs. Kellerman?"

Without an expression to show pleasure or regret the woman replied, "Miss Kellerman. There's no mister. Not in the past, nor ever in the future."

"Oh. I understand." Fanny did not understand a thing. For once in her life, she came up short of words. Instead, she offered a cordial smile. After an awkward pause, she added, "Well, then. Hello, Miss Kellerman. May I come in?"

Miss Kellerman pushed the door further open. Her dark hair, with a few strands of silver peeking out, was tucked in a conservative-styled bun secured to the back of her head giving her the appearance of the stern librarians that graced Fanny's junior and senior high schools. A pair of black framed cat-eye glasses crowning her head added more to her austere appearance. The navy blue blouse and gray skirt she wore tingled Fanny's arms with a chill as if it were a winter day and not summer. Without makeup to add a warm hue to her face, she greeted Fanny without a smile. "Let's get this over with."

"If it's a bad time we can reschedule, though to be honest, from the little I know, beneficial time to fight on Kenny's behalf is petering out."

"Since I shouldn't be talking about Gina's situation behind her back, let's proceed before I change my mind. I've sent Gina on an errand, which should give us a little time to talk if we jump right to it." Without inviting Fanny to follow her up the stairs, Gina's grandmother led the way to the second-floor residence. Halfway up the stairs, she glanced at Fanny. "The place is a mess with unpacked boxes and crates."

"No concerns," Fanny said as she followed the older woman. She aimed for a pleasant, cheerful tone. "Gina told me you moved to Bridgehaven from Rochester in July."

Miss Kellerman stopped short, her back toward Fanny. "I see. You've chatted a good deal with my granddaughter."

Fanny ignored the knots twisting in her belly. "I can assure you, Miss Kellerman, that other than a slight dip into Kenny's troubles, Gina and I conversed about standard social subjects."

Two grayish brows lifted. "Oh? When it comes to Gina, nothing is standard." After a pause, she motioned for Fanny to continue to follow her into the apartment. A shrill yapping erupted from behind the shut door of a room. "Don't mind Wags. The pup will stay in Gina's bedroom so we won't have to contend with him. He will eventually simmer down. We'll talk in the kitchen—it has the least boxes and clutter."

Fanny was about to say that she adored puppies and it was fine with her if Wags joined them while they conversed. Then she thought twice. Perhaps it would be best to follow the serious woman's lead and stick with the topic that had brought her to Miss Kellerman's doorstep. However, formalities would not serve either of them any good. "May I call you Helene?" When no reply came, she tried again. "I want to help you and Gina. It would be nice to be comfortable with each other."

"I suppose so. Yes, Helene is fine." She showed Fanny to the kitchen with a pinkish Kenmore refrigerator, white Formica countertops, teal-painted cabinets, and a checkered teal and white linoleum floor. "The apartment hasn't been updated since the early '50s, but we weren't in a position to fuss." After a pause, she mumbled, "Desperate times bring desperate actions."

Fanny thought it would be best not to ask for clarification. "A home's a home," she said instead.

Without a gesture to the table for Fanny to sit, Helene settled in the chair closest to the door, her posture so perfectly straight that Fanny was unsure if she admired the older woman or whether jealousy had stuck out its tongue.

Fanny glanced around the crowded room. No teakettle sat boiling on the stovetop, with cups and saucers ready. Just as well. She sat opposite Helene and fished out a writing pad from her briefcase. "Do you mind if I take notes?" When Helene shook her head, Fanny continued. "I met Gina for the first time today. Had she mentioned me?"

"No. My granddaughter has had a lot on her mind the past few days. Actually, for weeks, now."

"The two of us met when I ventured into Bertine's for an early lunch today, on this fine day when America woke up to learn about the wall being built in Berlin. Strange timing, don't you think?" Fanny thought Helene had winced at the reference to the German city. When Fanny gave her space to speak, the woman remained silent. While she typically never rushed to fill a gap in conversation, again awkwardness threatened to trip her and she combated the discomfort with the first words that came to mind. "Lots of commotion—as if the whole town had frequented the malt shop in need to voice their opposing opinions while gobbling lunch."

"I'm glad I stayed home." Helene's lips curled upward. "From what I've observed, Americans make talking and eating a joint sport." She paused for a handful of seconds. "Where I come from, children learned at a rather young age to keep their thoughts to themselves, even if invited to share. We knew better than to offer an antagonistic view. Here, folks are more free-spirited, saying whatever they like. Sometimes, not for the best."

"Why were the children expected to be reticent?"

"The fear of repercussions was real."

Had Helene meant on a personal level by the hand of a parent or on a larger, societal level by the power of a government? Although the Second World War ended sixteen years ago, the years since stripped almost everyone alive today from that time's still unimaginable horrors and helped to form a detachment from the tragedies. People needed to escape calamity; with her background, she saw it daily. What stress had Helene experienced first-hand? Sure, Helene spoke with a German accent but she might have been born and raised in Austria or Switzerland, or even German-born but raised elsewhere. For all Fanny knew, she could be a German Jew, and barely escaped the attempted obliteration of Jews by the Nazi hand. With another glance at Helene, Fanny had a hunch that the fear Helene had alluded to meant that whatever had occurred during her younger years taught her the hard way to be vigilant of others.

"I tried," Helene continued, "to raise my granddaughter to be, let's say, conservative in her behavior and how she shares her thoughts." She shook her head. "Sadly, my attempts haven't worked."

"I understand you raised Gina. What had become of her mother?"

"Forward, are you?"

Fanny grinned. "Why, yes. I'm a free-spirited American, born and raised under the red, white, and blue, and shamelessly not afraid to speak my mind."

"Believing you're more interested in Gina than me, tell me what has brought you to my home today?"

"Your granddaughter has told me her husband was arrested and is currently jailed. She won't tell me the details, at least, not yet. However, a Kenneth Franks was apprehended for murder. I think it's safe to assume this man is the same Kenny Gina is married to."

"Yes, it is. And your concern? We're perfect strangers to you."

"Other than Gina is young, has a lot going for her, and is sad and frightened about what will happen to Kenny, herself, and their marriage of only a few months?"

"It's that apparent?"

"I'm afraid it is. And that's why I'm concerned, as I'm sure you are too. She deserves a future. Kenny does as well." It was time to lure the woman in once and for all. "And most importantly, and I'm sure a major, if not the primary concern of yours, is what might happen to your granddaughter if she was involved in the murder."

Helene reached for the nearby cloth napkin and wiped her palms. "Did Gina out-and-out say Kenny killed someone?"

"No. I believe she came close to telling me more. When I pressed her, as I've said, she left out details."

"I see." Helene's forehead furrowed. "Have you met Kenneth?"

"No." Fanny stood and locked her fingers together across the top of the chair. "Your concern, Helene, legally speaking, is not about me. Your focus should be only on your grandson-in-law, granddaughter, and yourself. If Kenny is indeed wanted for murder and is found guilty, he's facing death by electrocution. If there is the slimmest of chances that Gina and you have helped Kenny in the murder, I need to know."

"To answer for myself, no. Regarding my granddaughter, I cannot imagine Gina killing anyone. For the record, I've criticized her marrying Kenneth. With her stubborn head held high, for better or worse, they eloped. Since both were of legal age, it's not like I could stop their marriage. She wouldn't listen to commonsense advice, especially from me. In all honesty, as much as I don't know this boy-man well, I can't picture him violent enough to hurt, let alone kill another person."

Boy-man? Why had Helene used those words to describe Kenny? Now was not the time to ask. "I want to help, all of you. Even accused wrongdoers, whether petty thieves or ruthless murderers, by constitutional rights in the USA, deserve legal representation, though I'm not saying Kenny is at fault. I'm an attorney. A defense attorney. I want to offer my services."

"Which is a concern. Although my granddaughter and I work, our frugal budget won't accommodate legal fees. If you look hard enough, I'm sure you will find worthy clients who can afford your fees. Ones without complications."

Fanny slipped onto her chair. "I have an established law firm, right here in town. Just me, and David Lorrie, my assistant. I'm offering my time pro bono."

Helene lifted a brow.

"No charge," Fanny said in emphasis.

"I'm familiar with the term." Helene paused, studying Fanny as if she'd just slid her under the lenses of a microscope. "You're a woman."

"Yes, indeed I am." Fanny tamped down the sudden spike of disgust and anger festering within her. She had heard this blunt accusation from countless others, both dismissive men and follow-the-crowd, skeptical women. Best to tighten the reins on her reactions and maintain her dignity. "And you are too, Helene, which means you've also put up with plenty of discriminative nonsense."

Helene gave the slightest of nods. "And?"

"Especially as a woman defense attorney, I'm qualified to handle Kenny's case because I can feel Gina's love for her husband. It is so powerful that it will help them overcome their legal struggle and set a new direction for other women." She smiled confidently. "Plus, because I am a woman and have been discriminated against in my profession, I aim to win each case I represent."

Helene squeezed her eyes shut for a moment. "From the start, this whole matter was disastrous and should have never occurred."

"I do not yet know the details regarding Kenny's alleged crime. I also haven't heard in detail about Gina and Kenny's past histories, or why it should be of concern. In my profession, I hear discouragement all the time. Particularly, when the odds don't favor the defendant, the negatives are more prevalent. However, just because someone says a predicament shouldn't have happened has never stopped me from taking on a case."

"No." Helene averted her eyes. "I meant their marriage. It should have never happened. None of this horror would have occurred if Gina had only listened to me."

"I have a good listening ear," she offered the upset woman. "Although, right now, I think it's best to stick to the topic of Kenny's arrest."

"Hello?" Gina's voice sailed up the stairwell. The pup yapped. "Who's there?"

"Come to the kitchen," Helene called out. "Fanny Stern wants to talk with you."

Gina's approaching footsteps halted. The puppy fell silent.

"Come join us, Gina," Helene said.

"Why? Am I in trouble?"

"For goodness' sake. You're a married woman. Stop acting like a child expecting a punishment and come in here."

A door squeaked open. Helene looked upward and murmured, "She let Wags out. Brace yourself."

Seconds later, a soft-brown wavy-haired Cocker Spaniel puppy zoomed into the room, followed by a more slow-moving Gina. Wags danced in circles on the teal and white flooring, barking like he followed a performance cue. He wagged his tail to do justice to his name. Gina remained deathly quiet.

"Enough! Shut the dog up." When Wags quieted, Helene pulled the neighboring chair away from the table. "Have a seat, Gina. Did you get the milk and chop meat I asked you to pick up? And my prescription?" She looked at Fanny. "The doctor started me on a new medication that's supposed to help blood pressure. It just came out three years ago. With all this ruckus, I have my doubts it will help."

Gina hoisted Wags into her arms and sagged onto the chair. Cuddling the puppy like a teddy bear, she weaved her fingers through the animal's thick fur. Thankfully, Wags remained silent. Gina did not look at her grandmother or Fanny. "No. I didn't run errands."

"Where were you then?"

With the electric Telechron coral clock hanging on the wall behind the table ticking off minutes, Fanny jumped into action. She touched Gina's arm, relieved and surprised the girl did not shy away. "Did you visit Kenny?" When Gina remained silent, Fanny decided it best to be straightforward. "Gina, I know Kenny is being accused of murder. I'm here to offer my legal services—free of charge—to defend him."

"I tried to visit," Gina murmured. "They said I wasn't allowed to see Kenny. Also, they denied us talking on the phone. Why? I'm his wife."

In an equally soft tone, Fanny said, "He's being processed. It's a routine procedure before his initial court hearing, especially if he's not a minor." She lifted her Parker 61 pen. "It's best if you tell me what happened, beginning with Kenny's arrest."

"I wasn't there. I mean, at the crime scene. I'll tell you what Kenny told me. When he phoned earlier this morning from jail, I mean."

"First, back up," Fanny said. "What happened that led to Kenny's arrest?"

"After work on Friday, Kenny chased after Samuel, a co-worker, because Samuel harassed him. Samuel's attacks have happened for a while, which I didn't know until the whole arrest thing took place. Maybe Kenny couldn't take it this time around. I'm not sure, though. He said he chased Samuel into an alley and found him on the ground, dead."

"Did Kenny realize Samuel was dead?"

Gina looked directly at Fanny. "I'm not sure. He told me he rushed over to Samuel and touched him. Maybe he slapped Samuel's face or something to see if he would come around. You'll have to ask Kenny. At that point, though, the cops arrived." She shrugged. "Guess in their eyes, Kenny is guilty. Well, at least suspicious enough to take him in to interrogate him. He phoned afterward and I took him home. Overnight—Saturday into Sunday—the cops came here with a warrant for his arrest and hauled him again to the station and this time booked him."

"Did Kenny say whether he made a statement to the police upon his arrest?"

Gina scratched the dog behind its ears. "Honestly, I'm not sure what he told the cops."

Helene snickered, unsettling Fanny. She stared at the older woman with growing curiosity and agitation and made a note to have David investigate the arrest procedures further.

"Did you witness the arresting officers insult Kenny, treat him funny, or yell at him? Did they do anything to him you would characterize as threatening?"

Gina looked away.

"Gina," Helene said. "Remember when you were a little girl and were frightened, and you needed to tell me something? What did you do?"

"I closed my eyes. I concentrated on my words, not what was happening around me."

"Go ahead and give that a try."

Gina shut her eyes. Fanny mouthed *thank you* to Helene. However, Helene, who kept her poker-faced focus on her granddaughter, ignored Fanny.

"Kenny denied he killed Samuel," Gina said, her voice breaking. Seconds later, a little louder, she added, "He didn't shout or use bad language. He spoke in a normal tone. The one cop asked Kenny why he was talking funny.

Maybe he thought Kenny was doing drugs or something. Beats me. Kenny sounded okay. Then the cop kept telling him to calm down. Kenny said he was calm. The whole ugly mess exploded in a shouting match. Kenny kind of lost it. I don't blame him. The poor guy."

"How was Kenny acting then? Different from his usual self?"

Gina opened her eyes and peered strongly at Fanny. "Excitable. He kept raking his hand through his hair. And he started to pace, even when they told him to stop."

Fanny scribbled *K=anxious. Harassed by cops?* "Under the circumstances, nervousness is normal." She tidied up her notepad and pen and slipped them into her briefcase. "I want to meet with Kenny and see if he will have me as his legal representative. We need to visit Kenny right now. Are you ready to leave?"

"How? Visitors aren't allowed," Gina said.

"Watch. I have my ways of getting what I want." Fanny grinned. "Especially if I'm to be Kenny's attorney."

On her feet, Gina set the puppy on the floor and headed out of the kitchen. "I'm just going to splash some cold water on my face and I'll be set to go."

"Good." Fanny looked at Helene. "And you? I'm presuming you are coming along, right?"

"It probably would be best."

Fanny nodded. "Absolutely. You are family. You need to support your granddaughter and Kenny."

Helene stood. "I'll need a moment." She started away from the table, then faced Fanny. "You remind me of someone in my past."

"Someone you won't reveal, correct?"

Helene crossed her arms. "Absolutely."

CHAPTER FOUR

Helene, Berlin, Germany, 1925

For a late October day with winter chasing everyone's heels, Helene was enjoying a splendid afternoon. Certainly, overdue. It might be due to sitting with her friends at the Terrace Romanische Café at the corner of Auguste-Viktoria-Platz for her twenty-second birthday celebration, or because she was finally out of her parents' watchful eyes. She suspected both.

"A toast to the birthday girl," Erna said, lifting her second glass of white wine.

Martha lifted her recently replenished glass then clinked theirs.

"No, my friends," Helene said. "I salute you. I'd still be stuck home without your rescue invitation to lunch today." She glanced at the vaulted ceilings that helped bring about an airy atmosphere that she adored, though many remarked it simulated a waiting room in a railway station. Even her architect father admired the establishment. "This is my favorite restaurant. I much appreciate you thinking of me today."

"We wouldn't have it any other way," Erna said.

Martha sipped her wine. "This is the absolute best wine I've ever tasted."

"And you've become a connoisseur, since the age of twenty-one last year?" Erna's teasing grin reminded Helene of one of the things she adored about her friends.

Helene placed her wine on the white marble-topped table and grasped her friends' hands. "No bickering on my special day, even if it's playful."

"If it's so special"—Martha interrupted herself by swigging the rest of her drink in three large gulps—"why do you look so glum?"

Helene did not want to spoil the occasion with the truth: loneliness in the romance department magnified yet another year of her life slipping by.

She would do anything to block from her thoughts Martha's recent engagement to her gymnasium sweetheart or Erna's marriage which had already welcomed a baby who had just turned a year old. Helene spent a pitiful amount of time splitting her thoughts. On one hand, she loved them dearly. Yet, contrasted to their exciting lives, she lived a boring existence. If she dared face the truth, it spelled the solitary word: spinsterhood. The thought of her job as an assistant at her father's architectural firm—the title a ruse to skirt around the dull reality of working as his secretary—did not boost her self-esteem. Nor was she cheered by her attempts to scribble silly, meaningless poetry in the evening hours instead of snuggling in a man's embrace. Looking at her two friends who wanted the best for her, she aimed for levity. "My dears, this is my natural expression."

"Perpetually downcast?" Erna asked.

"Yes, that's me." Helene silently counted to ten, then let loose a raucous laugh. Her eyes watered; a stitch from laughing so hard had her grabbing her side. "You sillies. You should see the worried look in your eyes—I thought you'd jump from your seat and ask the maître d' to summon a doctor to cart me away."

Martha wagged a finger in front of Helene's face. "Do you prefer a roommate or a nice private room in the psychiatric wing?"

"Oh, I know," Erna said. "She'd take any room as long as a handsome, unattached doctor tends to her."

Helene swallowed the last of her wine. "Yes, how did you guess?"

Martha and Erna exchanged looks. "We know you," Martha said.

Erna nodded. "We know your empty heart."

Helene's jaw pinched as polite replies tumbled in her mouth, colliding with more caustic comments. Just when she had determined not to say a peep concerning her loneliness, her friends had to drag the nasty truth out of her.

"Dashing man approaching," Martha murmured. Erna giggled.

Despite her gloomy mood, Helene glanced up. A clean-shaven blond man, dressed in black trousers and a gray cardigan over a white shirt walked toward them. He carried himself with ease and an air of confidence. He seemed focused on a nearby table where four other men sat. Likely, he failed to notice that Martha pushed Helene's purse off the tabletop as he approached their table. The mystery gentleman surprised Helene when he swooped down and lifted the small tan bag. He brushed the item off and looked at Helene and her friends.

Martha's eyes darted from Helene to the man. She then flashed a sly grin at Helene.

"*Hallo, Damen.*" He scanned the table and when he reached Helene, he smiled. "Is this your purse? If not, I'll bring it to the proprietor's attention. I know him well."

Helene wondered how a man his age would be acquainted with the owner of this fine city fixture comfortably enough to mention a stranger's purse. A friend of the family? For all she knew, his parents might run the business. She knew better than to inquire, though. Her parents had long ago instilled in her to avoid asking others personal questions. She also knew better than to ask her mother or father questions. *Ask and you may receive an answer you wish not to know about.*

She turned her attention back to the man. "*Danke.*"

He lingered a moment longer, then gave her a little nod and continued to the nearby table of men.

"Thank you?" Martha said. "Is that all you could think of, Helene?"

"What should I have said? Ask his height, weight, and whether he's single?"

Martha grinned. "Yes—an excellent beginning."

Erna looked at Martha and sputtered an unladylike laugh. "That's telling her, Martha." She then whispered an apology to Helene, who brushed her off with a shrug.

As the waiter served their lunch, they teased each other over how they had ordered the same selection. Although all raised in Berlin and were well accustomed to grunkohl, no other restaurant the three of them had dined in served green kale and sausage stew like Romanische did, making it look and taste like a true masterpiece.

"Delicious," Helene said after her first bite. "I cannot imagine celebrating my birthday or enjoying an exquisite feast without you. Thank you, my dears."

Martha sighed contently into her linen napkin. "No wonder why artists, playwrights, and journalists frequent this place and let's not forget filmmakers. Maybe we'll have ourselves a fine encounter to take our minds off of our humdrum lives."

"Who needs any of those when a striking mysterious man fetched Helene's fallen purse from the floor?" Erna winked as if an insect had flown into her eye. "We've already stumbled upon a Prince Charming."

Helene made small talk, diverting the conversation from the topic of men, and ultimately falling in love. The time slipped by as Martha shared her latest wedding plans, despite the confession the wedding was still in the daydream stage. They oohed and aahed over Erna's little daughter's latest milestones. Just yesterday the baby grabbed the leg of a table and stood up for the first time on her own.

"Speaking of," Erna said, "I need to return home—I don't want Otto growing suspicious."

"Of you?" Helene said, then laughed. "He has it good with you as his wife and has not one worry to his name."

"He does." Erma put a finger to each corner of her mouth. "See my lips? I've lived in a state of all smiles since we married, and now that our little girl has come along, we've learned what true bliss is all about. We trust each other like no one else." She smiled. "Well, you two lovelies. I trust you with all my heart."

"You and Otto deserve happiness," Martha said. "It's been seven years since the Great War ended and it's time to make the most of life. Unlike our parents who fretted whether they'd live another day because of the war, we three have much to look forward to. Yes, my friends?"

"For sure," Erma said. "I'm glad we were younger then and our parents shielded us from the tragedies."

The three of them were fortunate enough to have parents in the upper class of German society. In addition to Helene's father's prestigious architectural firm, her mother was a language teacher at a private school. Helene enjoyed her role as an only child, even admitting to being spoiled. However, her parents only lavished exceptional treatment *if* she obeyed every demand they made. The memory from years ago of her mother's approaching birthday underscored that painful lesson well. Previously, she called her mother *Mutti* and her father *Vati,* enjoying the casual atmosphere in her family home that her parents had encouraged. In hindsight, sure, she could admit to acting bratty and rude. However, it was not as if she assaulted her mother with a knife, or for that matter, insulted her appearance or behavior. German custom, though, had long ago determined that one should never wish someone a happy birthday before the actual date of birth. Raised in Berlin, Helene had known this tradition ever since she could recollect celebrating birthdays, whether her own, her parents, or friends. On Saturday, one week before her mother's birthday, while they were eating dinner, Helene giggled and snapped out a *Happy Birthday, Mutti.* For that, she received a narrow-eyed look from both parents. She chalked it off to talking with food in her mouth. The next night she tried again with more birthday wishes. She received a warning to behave. During the third night's meal, her parents lectured her on the polite way Germans behaved and how disrespectful it was for her to mention birthdays in advance. On the fourth night, not only had she made her mother cry and her father swear, but he also threw his linen napkin on the table, stood, and shook his finger at Helene.

"You think it's funny to mock your heritage, and your country, and to show a lack of respect to your parents? From now on, Daughter, we will enjoy stricter formalities between us. Starting right now, you are to call your mother Mutter and I, Vater."

Helene's *Vater* had not exaggerated. Laughs and smiles disappeared overnight. Silence haunted the house. A forever chill took up residence.

This part she kept from her friends. Martha lost her mother years ago. Her father was a surgeon and provided for her and her four younger siblings nicely. She frequently shared with Helene how her father made time for her and her sisters and brothers, taking them to zoos and museums when they were younger and on holiday as they entered their teen years. Erna, like her husband, had parents who also worked in academia in the medical research field. Erna and her mother often frequented dress shops and she and her father enjoyed an occasional evening walk together. Through the years,

Helene had disclosed much to her friends, but the frostiness between her and her parents, and how it originated, would be her secret alone to bear.

Helene looked at her two dear friends. "I'm also thankful. It's our responsibility not to take away opportunities from lesser unfortunate people."

Erna's eyes widened. "Are you referring to Jews? Otto says most of his students and the faculty are Jewish. By the day, it's getting more difficult for non-Jews to enroll in university, let alone find decent jobs." She grasped her water glass. "It's your birthday celebration—must we talk politics?"

"I agree, Erna," Martha said, nearly in a whisper. She glanced at the neighboring tables and leaned closer to them. "Let's not talk about *those* people."

Helene had spoken on a more philosophical level. She did not expect to hear Erna's anti-Semitic verbal jab. Nor for Martha to grow pale as if she were to hurl up her lunch. Helene wanted to rush out of the restaurant, return home, and lock the doors. Forget meeting a potential mate. The faster she got away from people, the calmer she would feel, even if that meant fleeing from her friends.

"It's getting late," Erna said and stood. "Motherhood duties are calling me home."

Helene offered a little smile. "I suspect Otto too would appreciate your company." She walked around the table to hug her friends, pushing aside the questions and doubts now flooding her mind. She swallowed hard. "Danke Schoen, dear ones, for making my birthday memorable."

They lived in the same neighborhood, though Erna and Martha in one direction, and Helene in another. After her two friends left, Helene applied a fresh shade of pink lipstick and then exited through the patio. Despite a little tension, the afternoon spent with her best friends would forever stay in Helene's heart as a lovely memory. And unlike a few minutes ago when she experienced a wave of panic, she decided not to let a few misplaced words from Erna's mouth rattle her. She was too harsh in her thoughts on the two women who stood by her side throughout their childhood and now their early adulthood. If truth be told, she could blame her distorted perspective on the wine they had imbibed.

Sensing that someone was following her, she again linked it to the alcohol and focused her gaze straight ahead. Two blocks later, as she turned right, she stole a look. She was correct and remained still.

"Hello, Mysterious Good-looking Herr from the café." She smiled. "I'm glad I'm not imagining you."

He tipped his gray Bavarian-styled hat. "Hello, Pretty Birthday Fräulein from the café."

A blush fired her cheeks. "Oh, you heard?"

"Only a little. Just enough to know you're a birthday gal today. I'm glad I picked up your purse."

She wondered if his alluring smile was permanently fixed on his face. She hoped so. "My name is Helene."

"I'm Willie."

"I'm glad you're following me, Willie."

"I'd like for something else."

"Oh?" Did she want to hear what he had in mind? She was lonely, not desperate to fall for a man who did not love her. She would take as much time as needed to develop trust between them. Let others stamp her as having old-fashioned intentions—she wanted marriage before intimacy. She could not imagine changing her mind.

He waved a hand. Was that a little blush tinging his cheeks red? "Nein. Pardon me. I meant to ask if you would like my company for a stroll. It would be more pleasant than following you like a spy. A bad one, at that." He took his hat off and scratched the sides of his head, mussing up his hair into a delightful disarray, making him appear more attractive, not less. "I believe I'm making this attempted conversation into one big awkward mess. What I'm trying to say is that I'd enjoy your company. Platonically, of course."

"What a shame, Willie." Was she flirting? She clasped the sides of her face. "Oh, my. I didn't mean to say... to paint a picture of me as... acting untowardly. I shouldn't have had so much wine, let alone a drop. Apparently, I can't handle it. Never again."

"You're too hard on yourself." He flashed a most charming smile. "Birthdays are meant to celebrate." He took three strides and stood beside her, alongside the road. A true gentleman; he knew his manners.

They agreed to walk to the Tiergarten, the largest urban park in Berlin. On one hand, Helene counted her lucky stars for the short distance to cross, allowing plenty of time to enjoy the statues, memorials, and gardens. Then again, a long way would have given them more time to learn about each other without the attractions at the park vying for their attention. She envisioned Willie grasping her hand, his fingers entwining with hers. They would share what made them happy and sad, the foods they enjoyed most, and their favorite pastimes. And when it came time to say goodbye, he would cup her face gently with his long, elegant fingers, and kiss her sweetly. When they departed the park, she going one way, and he another, he would whisper into her ear that this was only a temporary separation. If only that scenario materialized, how splendid it would be. What a sweet birthday present, indeed.

"Do you visit Tiergarten often?" Willie asked, pulling Helene back to the present, away from her dreams.

She held back her answer, reluctant to tell him that despite her being of adult age, her parents preferred she attend a city park only when escorted by a friend or relative. She did not want to scare him away by coloring a shade of parental trouble he might encounter if their casual walk grew into a genuine relationship, so she tiptoed around the truth without crossing the wobbly border and risking the danger of never seeing him again. "Since we only live a few blocks over, my parents and I visit often. We most enjoy the animal and musician statues. My favorite is the memorial honoring Beethoven, Hayden, and Mozart." She clapped her hands twice, like an uninhibited little girl, carefree to do what she pleased, yet having the confidence of an adult woman. "I enjoy music. Do you? My parents and I often take in the concerts here."

"I prefer jazz." He winked. "I'll listen to whatever you would like, as long as it's not to my singing. That's one thing I couldn't inflict upon you."

"Truly? I cannot imagine, especially since you have a rich, smooth-speaking voice." He guided her toward her beloved monument, stopping at the carved figure of Beethoven, her favorite of the three. Perhaps Willie had sensed her preferences and this was not a random coincidence. The thought that this man might be receptive to her likings and wishes so early in their meeting hinted at the dream relationship she had yearned for. A warmth chased away the last of her nervous chills. "I have an idea," she added. "I won't ask you to sing if you don't ask me to dance. How does that sound?"

"Awful." He made a foul face like he had eaten a batch of bad pickles. "I love to dance. I can teach you a few steps and in no time have you dancing the Charleston." He pulled her to his side. "Or we can wow the crowd that would be sure to gather around us when we do the tango."

"Oh, no. I couldn't, especially not in front of others."

"Just for my eyes alone."

"I have two left feet... I can't imagine..."

"Helene?"

She peered into his blue eyes with brown traces, the color of a lake with a sunset simmering upon its surface.

"I want to reimagine a whole different world for us." As if a magician announcing a rabbit appearing out of his hat, he splayed his hands in the air. "I want to make this a spectacular universe for us to enjoy."

"A universe? For us alone?"

"Yes." He extended a hand toward her. "Want to come along with me on the ride?"

"Yes. I do."

"No parents permitted."

She smiled. "That would be lovely."

CHAPTER FIVE

Fanny, Bridgehaven, August 14, 1961
Visitation at the jail ended in two hours. The parking lot had an ample supply of empty spaces. Fanny peered into the rearview mirror of her off-white Pontiac. "Ready?" she asked Gina. When she nodded, Fanny turned toward Helene in the front passenger seat. "And you?"

"I'm ready as can be."

"Remember my pointers on proper, expected behavior," Fanny said, addressing them both. "We will be physically searched—do not object. Leave your purses and any sharp items that can be misconstrued as a weapon in the car." She explained how her briefcase would be permitted, though it too would be searched. "I'll lock the car so you don't have to worry about anyone stealing your possessions. Let's go." The social climate had changed as the '50s had rapidly and clumsily slid into the '60, crashing around between culture-changing music, abrupt clothing-style changes, architectural leaps, political stances, and world hot spots erupting once again. Fanny had no doubt folks would soon lock the doors to their homes and vehicles. Also, security firms would likely become big new businesses, bringing alarm systems to private houses.

They approached the main entrance. Dressed in the required dress code, Gina and Helene wore plain blouses, modest skirt lengths, and low heels, and Fanny the black slacks and simple white blouse she had worn in visiting Helene. Although Fanny had visited clients in this very jail, it was never easy seeing what shape the men—and once, a woman—would be in, whether mentally or physically. She wondered how Gina and Helene would react. They must be holding their breaths in trepidation of what they would find. Fanny wanted to extend comfort. *It will be fine, you'll see.* However, it was a minimum-security facility and the prisoners were still held behind bars. Guards maintained the tension. Both the inmates and their visitors experienced plentiful intimidation. The atmosphere would jar anyone unfamiliar with the setting.

Fanny resorted to her professional side. "While we visit, we will remain united as a strong front and advocate for Kenny. Although we won't tolerate lies, let alone abuse in any form, we cannot contest what we may find. If we break any visitor rules of conduct, we will be escorted out, no matter our motive. So, no emotional or anger-fueled outbursts. Understand?"

Gina and her grandmother replied affirmatively. They proceeded to the Visitor Processing Area. After they were each patted down to check for a potential weaponized object, they showed their identification. They then signed their names to several documents as if allowing an irrevocable contract on their lives as collateral, and took seats until the next conference room became available. This was the easy part. It was all uphill from this moment on.

Fanny gave Gina credit by offering a nod of approval. Calm and composed, especially considering the frazzled state the young woman had dissolved into in the presence of her grandmother back at their apartment, she had cleaned up well. Perfect. Her husband would need all of her support. Fanny, well aware of how one's composure strongly influences for the better, was satisfied with their first step in helping Kenny.

Ten minutes later, a detention officer approached them. His uniform of a navy blue shirt, gray pants, and black shoes would have been indistinguishable from civilian clothes if it were not for the six-point silver badge he wore on the left side of his shirt over his heart, the most vulnerable part of a human being. After a mention of his name, he escorted them to a small conference room and asked them to have a seat. "Keep the door locked at all times, even when the inmate is in your company." He eyed Gina and her grandmother. "No touching is permitted, not even a brief hug. I will watch you at all times. Any questions?"

Fanny sat at the gray metal table in the center of the room and searched her briefcase for a writing pad. Gina cleared her throat; Helene fingered her hair, again drawn back in a tight bun. Fanny sucked in a deep breath. Despite understanding how the law worked, she felt powerless to change the present circumstances to have Kenny immediately released.

"How is he, officer?" Gina asked, in a mousy squeak. "My husband, Kenny Franks?"

The detention officer tilted his head, his thoughts transparent: No need for the reminder—I won't bring in someone else's husband, don't worry. "Calmer."

"Oh," Gina said. Her furrowed brow registered confusion.

"This ain't no deluxe hotel—he had to behave. I'll get him now." The officer stepped out of the room and clicked the door lock secure.

Fanny's jangled nerves threatened to tighten its grip. Nope. Her frazzled state would not help Kenny, Gina, or Helene, let alone maintain her focus. She offered a soft smile to the two women. "How are you holding up?"

"Just like old times," Helene mumbled, without explaining.

"Dandy," Gina said, rubbing her tummy.

Although Fanny's professional role was not to offer words of pat comfort, she wished she could shuck off her *lawyer skin* just for enough seconds to lend a listening ear and caring heart. The professional side of her prevailed. An intimate chitchat would not benefit either Gina or her grandmother. She needed to be objective, not acting on a subjective, personal level. Her jaw pinched at the sound of the door rattling open. She blinked at the sight of Kenny walking into the small room, followed by the same officer assigned to them earlier.

"I'll be right outside," the officer stated, as if they could forget his presence, forget they were in the jail, forget the circumstances of what brought Kenny to a place of bars separating him from the rest of the world. He pointed at the door's narrow glass pane. "I'll also be watching you. Give a rap when you're done." He stepped out of the room and secured the lock.

Kenny Franks was five years younger than Fanny, but compared to Gina's photograph of him he appeared more how a man in his early sixties would look: worn and haggard. Captivity could do that to a person, even in a short period. His need for a shave, his jail clothes of a white T-shirt, forest green pants, and white-rubbery slip-on shoes did not improve his first-impression appearance. Fortunately, Gina held back the visible negative facial reaction Fanny had expected her to show.

Kenny rushed to Gina's side, knelt before her, and pulled her into a hug. "Are you okay, Gina?" He placed his hands gently over her stomach. "Is the baby okay?"

Baby? On her writing pad, Fanny scrawled: BABY. PATERNITY. DUE DATE.

The door clicked open and the officer poked his face into the room. "No touching."

CHAPTER SIX

Gina, Rochester, February 1961

Gina saw Kenny next on February 19th. Despite a half foot of snow fresh on the ground, unlike a few days ago when they first met, they again rendezvoused at the park. She had a little surprise for him. Standing, and facing the same oak tree behind the same bench where they first sat, she nearly giggled out loud in anticipation.

"Hi, Gina," Kenny called. He had arrived on time. She counted on his punctuality. "What's wrong? Why won't you turn around?"

Slowly, she did. Wags, whom she held tight against her chest, let out a loud, happy yap. "I brought my puppy for you to see. This friendly guy is Wags."

Kenny reached out to scratch the dog behind his ears. "You're cute, Wags. I'm glad to meet you."

Wags became more excited and squirmed in her grip. She set the puppy on the ground and extended the leash to Kenny. "You hold him. I can tell Wags and you will become the best of friends."

Kenny shook his head, neglecting to take the leash.

"No? You don't like my puppy?"

"Oh, I like Wags." He pointed to Gina and himself, and then the dog. "I want us to be best of friends."

"Me too. Are you afraid of dogs?"

"No. Dogs are good."

She smiled to soothe Kenny. "Cool. We can all be friends. You and I will be the best of friends." Maybe more. "How does that sound?"

"Like a rainbow."

She pointed up at the gray sky, heavy with dark clouds. "Like that rainbow only the two of us can see?"

"Yes. Since we've met, I've seen a lot of rainbows."

"You sure are making my day lovely." Relief washed through her when he relaxed his stiff posture and stooped to pet Wags. The pup wagged his tail and licked Kenny's hand. "See that? Wags likes you."

"Okay." Kenny took the leash. "I like Wags."

"Want to take a walk?" Gina asked.

"I've never walked a dog."

"It's easy, and he's a good dog."

Despite a cold wind blowing, they strolled at a leisurely pace. They grinned as a man's hat flew off his head, oohed at two children engaged in a snowball fight, and grasped hands as an older couple, arm in arm, made their way slowly toward the park's gate.

"Grammy and I have had different dogs through the years. She claims to tolerate animals because I like them. Yet, when she doesn't think I'm around to see or hear her, I've caught Grammy making lovey-dovey talk to them. It's the cutest, funniest thing ever."

"Uncle Raymond says we're too busy for pets."

"Two bachelors living it up, huh?"

He raised a brow in question. She was happy to help him understand. "You and your uncle are used to living by yourselves, that's all. You're set in your comfortable ways. Right?"

"Yes. And no." They exited the park. Unlike the busy workweek with its bustle of people, congested traffic screeching, and assorted sirens and noises filling the air with a constant thrumming, quiet now hummed through the street. "We like each other. Lots. That's all."

"That's good. Has your uncle ever been married?"

"No. He wanted to raise me because my parents didn't. He had to do it the right way."

She raised a brow. "Do you mean, his dedication to you? He wanted to make sure nothing went wrong for you?"

"Yes. Dedication. I like that word."

"What about you Kenny? Ever married?"

"No. Never. No girlfriend." He pointed to the right. "Want to go that way? Are we having a date?"

A little smile teased her lips. "I hope so. I'm considering our time together as a bona fide date. I mean—"

"I know what you mean. I know a lot of words."

"You're a smart man, for sure, Kenny Franks."

"I like how you make my name sound."

"I like everything about you." She squeezed his hand. "Where are we going?"

"It's Sunday. All the stores are shut today. And it's cold." He looked at their united hands and smiled. "Your hand is warm."

"That's 'cause you're holding mine."

"Let's go to my house. Wags can come too."

"Is your uncle home? I want to meet him." At the intersection, they waited for a couple of vehicles to pass.

"Yes, Uncle Raymond is home today. He'd enjoy meeting you." A U-Haul truck turned the corner. "I want you to visit with us. Today and many other days."

"Is it far?" she asked. "I'm not dressed for a long walk."

"No. Five blocks. I've counted them." He tugged her close to his side. "Together, we'll keep warm."

.   .   .

Two days later, on Tuesday, Gina's next day off, she and Kenny met for lunch on Kenny's break from work. The popular eatery around the corner from the store where she worked provided them a perfect place to chat and get to know each other more. She told Kenny the truth—she would be content to sit beside him, take in his smiles, and listen to his kind words and encouragements. Unlike so many others, not once did he utter a firm admonishment. She had it with reprimands from others for how badly she messed things up. In this past week alone, her life had changed for the better.

During the short and too-long span of precious minutes, without a doubt, she finally found the right person for her. Hopefully, he felt the same way about her.

"Gina, are you having bad thoughts?"

Had she grimaced and worried him? "Do you mean like regrets?"

"Yes," he said, his brow quirking upward.

"Regrets about us? No way. You're the best thing that has happened to me." She reached across the table for his hand. "Sorry. My words came out funny sounding."

"I understand," he said. "Uncle Raymond says not everyone is meant for each other."

"No more uncle-talk. It's just us, alone together." She glanced around the crowded café. "Well, aside from everyone else chowing down their lunches."

He smiled. "We're meant for each other."

"You bet we are. Kenny, though we've only known each other for a short time, I love you." She blinked. "Forgive my forwardness."

"Then nothing to forgive. I love you, too," he said, his words clear but his tone soft. He cast his gaze downward at his empty bread dish. "Are you embarrassed, Gina? Lots of people have called me slow... and..."

Oh. That was what troubled him. "You're not slow. Perfect—most definitely."

He touched the sides of his head. "I am slow. Slower than many. People call me dumb, retarded, Mr. No Brains. Are you okay?"

It took her a second to realize he meant if she was okay with dating—falling in love—with a man society claimed failed to measure up with other supposed intelligent men. She placed her hand over her chest. "Here, in my heart, is the only thing that counts. I love you, Kenny. You're a beautiful person."

"I'm slow. Slow, slow, slow." Each repeat of the word thumped from his mouth like a child's inflatable punching bag springing back after a blow knocked it down.

"Honey," she said, tenderly, yet with a trace of spirit. "You are perfect for me. If I'm perfect for you, nothing else matters, don't you think?"

"You're right. And I want to marry you."

Had she heard correctly? "Marry me? Is that a question or statement?"

"A fact."

She cupped his face. "I absolutely want to become your wife."

CHAPTER SEVEN

Fanny, Rochester, August 14, 1961

BABY. PATERNITY. DUE DATE. With her thoughts swirling and competing for her sole attention, Fanny stared at the words she had written on her pad. She then looked at the others in the small conference room. Thankfully, upon Gina's urging, Kenny quickly stood from the floor where he had knelt and then sat beside her fast enough to encourage the detention officer to leave. Fanny fixed her attention on Helene. The woman showed no shock over Gina's pregnancy, nor a trace of emotion, good or bad. Fanny tabled Helene's lack of reactions for a later time and returned her attention fully to Gina and Kenny. Gina was expecting, supposedly, Kenny's baby. No wonder why the younger woman had appeared gripped by digestive issues. Her pregnancy was also a perfect explanation for her irregular, unbalanced reactions in the conversations Fanny had earlier with her. Although Fanny had no difficulty assessing Gina and Kenny's genuine concern for each other, she planned to talk with Gina later to verify that she and Kenny would state Kenny's paternity of the child for the court record.

"Kenny, I'm fine," Gina said, gently. "The baby is fine."

"How do I know you and the baby are okay?"

Gina placed her hand on her belly. "I feel good, which means our baby is feeling good too. You don't have to worry."

"You and the baby are important. Very important." He looked at the door where the officer stood on the other side, staring at them through the glass. Kenny then faced Gina. "Did you cry when the police took me away?"

"No, sweetie. I know you'll be out soon, and everything will be fine."

"I don't want bad people hurting you."

"Don't worry, Kenny. No one has hurt me. I want you out of here as quickly as possible. Has anyone hurt you?"

Kenny remained expressionless.

"You know, push you or hit you?"

Fanny's breath caught. Why was it necessary for Gina to explain the concept of harm?

"You can say whatever you want to in front of Grammy and Fanny," Gina added.

Kenny eyed Fanny briefly then returned his focus on Gina. "No. I behaved."

Gina lifted her fingers to Kenny's chin, then pulled away. "I'm sorry. We're not supposed to touch."

"That's okay. I don't like the cops." He jabbed at his temples.

"Does your head hurt?"

"No. Just too busy. Lots of thoughts." A grin overtook Kenny's expressionless face. "I'm still slow Kenny."

"Oh, Kenny," Gina said. "And I'm still Gina. Your Gina."

"That's good." He turned and eyed Fanny. "Are you Fanny?"

Slow Kenny? The surprise of Gina's pregnancy was one thing. The bigger shock was that no one had mentioned that Kenneth Franks' IQ may be less than standard. Way less. Unless that was what Helene had meant by referring to Kenny as a boy-man when she had visited Helene at her apartment.

Fanny set her gaze on Kenny. "Hello, Mr. Franks. I'm Fanny Stern. I would ordinarily shake your hand, but we're not permitted to do so here. May I call you Kenneth or Kenny?"

"Kenny is good. I like Kenny. What do I call you?"

"Fanny." She smiled, relieved that the conversation unfolded more smoothly than expected. "I'm an attorney and want to help you."

Kenny looked blank and turned to Gina for assistance. No one responded to Helene's abrupt groan. At least, not outwardly.

"Fanny's a lawyer," Gina replied. "She wants to help you get out of here. You'll like Fanny. She's nice."

"I want to leave," Kenny said directly to Fanny. "I'm glad you want to help."

"And I'm glad we finally got through that part," Helene mumbled.

Helene's words were too caustic for Fanny's taste. However, it was best not to waste time on the ambiguous quip. She directed her attention back to Kenny. "The first step is to get you released on bail. To do so, you must appear before the judge. That will happen tomorrow, Tuesday. If the judge grants bail, can anyone post it for you?"

Kenny stared blankly.

"This is a lot for anyone to understand," Fanny said carefully, skirting around any tones Kenny might construe as judgmental. "Is anyone you know financially comfortable and would help?"

"Kenny... your uncle?" Gina jumped in. "Isn't he coming home from his conference tonight?"

"Yes," Kenny said. "Uncle Raymond will help. He always helps me."

Gina cast Fanny an all-knowing look. "And Uncle Raymond is pretty loaded. More importantly, he loves Kenny."

"Good, Kenny." Fanny then asked for Raymond's phone number and noted it on her pad. "I'll contact your uncle tonight. It may help to know the criminal court system is not only designed to protect society but also helps to secure a better life for the criminal by reintroducing the offender back into society to become a productive member."

"I'm not a criminal."

Kenny's four words percolated through Fanny's mind. His tone sounded neutral, not defensive nor smugly confident. Also missing were traces of fear or self-pity. She could work with that. "I like to take many notes during an interview with a client, Kenny. Do you mind?"

"That's fine."

She toyed with her first question to simplify matters. "Let's start with the basics. Gina said you ran after Samuel and into an alleyway. Who is Samuel?"

"Samuel Klein. We work together."

"What happened after the police found you?"

"They asked me questions. Said it would be good if I talked more with them. At the police station."

"Did they say why?"

"Said it looks like I killed Samuel."

Gina kicked a table leg forcibly enough to shift the table. "They weren't there. What do they know?"

The door to the room opened, thudding against the wall. The detention officer stepped in and glared.

Quick to stand, Fanny said, "I promise it won't happen again, officer."

"See that it won't. No more warnings."

"Yes, officer," Fanny said but eyed Gina.

Kenny murmured Gina's name. "Stay calm. It's good for the baby. And for me."

"I didn't—"

"Please." Kenny cupped his ears. "My head is crowded." When Gina remained silent, he lowered his hands from his ears and returned his attention to Fanny. "Samuel works at Uncle Raymond's factory. With me."

Fanny stiffened when Kenny did not elaborate. She should not have to prompt him to explain. That troubled her. Since the early 1950s, the American Law Institute has been drafting a system to codify the penal law on how to punish criminals, expressly targeting the defendant on whether the subject in question fully understood the criminality of his or her conduct, and if the defendant could conduct one's self to conform to the law. Such a codification was way overdue in the United States considering the vast actions regarding criminals. However, future improvements to the law would not help Kenny now. She needed to explore Kenny's comprehension of the legal charges against him and whether he understood the consequences.

"The police found you and Samuel in the back lot of an out-of-business stationery store. How did you get there?"

"I got out of work. I was walking to Miss Kellerman's job. At the college. Because she drives me home to Bridgehaven. Samuel came after me. He said mean things. I ran after him. He went into an alleyway. I followed him."

"What happened after you ran through the alleyway?"

"I saw Samuel. He was on the ground. I went to him. He said to leave him alone. That I need to leave, right away. Then Samuel stopped talking."

"So, when you found Samuel, he was still alive?"

"Yes. Then he got quiet."

"Was anyone else there?"

Kenny shrugged. "I don't know. I don't think so."

"What did you do then?"

"I yelled for help. A lot."

Fanny frantically wrote the words *yelled for help* and circled them. "Good, Kenny. Then what?"

"I looked around. Didn't see anyone. Then... then..." Kenny blinked. "I can't remember."

"When the police found you, you were bending over Samuel. Why is that, Kenny?"

"I wanted to help him."

"Did you know he was dead?"

"I'm not sure. I never saw a dead person. Before the cops came, I slapped Samuel's cheeks. Not hard. Just tried to wake him up."

"Just to be clear, you said you didn't see another person there with you and Samuel?"

Kenny squeezed his eyes shut and then opened them. "I can't remember. My mind is all black. Like I'm sleeping, without dreaming."

A big sigh flew from Helene, which Fanny chose not to address. She was getting pretty good at ignoring *Grammy*, an endeavor within itself, yet one she wished she did not have to accomplish.

"Kenny, do you remember anyone else who might have seen you chasing Samuel?" When he remained silent, Fanny sought to clarify. "If you don't know, it's okay to tell me."

"I don't know."

"All right, then. After you saw Samuel on the ground, how soon did the police show up?"

He again shrugged. "Fast. Seconds? Minutes?"

Were the police already pursuing Kenny for chasing after Samuel, and why? Or, were they tracking someone else that coincidentally led them to

Kenny and the deceased? Fanny noted to look into the timing of the police's arrival. "What did the police do?"

"They checked Samuel. One cop stayed with me. The other looked around. Then said it was best to go to the police station. In Rochester. Just to talk with me because it looked like I killed Samuel."

"Did the police say why it looked like you killed Samuel?"

Kenny scrubbed the side of his head with his palms. "They said that slapping his face wasn't smart."

"Seconds ago, you said the police showed up after you slapped Samuel's face. Now, you're saying the police saw you slap Samuel's face. Which is it?"

"I don't know." Kenny's brow furrowed. "My mind is foggy."

Fanny thought that if she were in his predicament—and held in jail and facing murder charges—her recollection would also be foggy. However, she did not need his uncertainty to trip her up right now when she could later check into the police report. "Did the police officers find a weapon?"

"I don't think so. I don't know."

"Do you have a history of passing out?"

"Like fainting? No."

Fanny jotted down the words *autopsy report* and *circumstantial*. "What happened when you got to the police station?"

"We talked. For a long time. The cops said they'd look into things. Then they let me call Gina. She picked me up and drove me home."

Fanny bobbed her head, unsure if she was coaxing Kenny to continue or reminding herself to breathe. "Did you tell them you killed Samuel?"

"No," Kenny said without delay. "Because I didn't kill him. I wouldn't kill anyone. They kept asking me if I killed Samuel. I kept saying no. I didn't kill him."

"Okay. That was Friday evening. Then the police showed up Saturday night-Sunday morning to arrest you?"

"Yes. Early. We were all sleeping. They banged on the door and rang the door buzzer. Until I answered the door. Because I wanted to protect Gina and Miss Kellerman. I told the cops to come in. Asked them what was wrong."

Fanny added to her notes that Kenny was initially collected and calm when the police first showed up. "Would you say the officers were respectful to you?" Kenny's brows furrowed. "Pleasant?" She huffed silently to herself. *As pleasant as arresting police officers could be.*

"Yes and no. They yelled a lot. Then they shoved me" He grew silent and looked at Gina, who smiled weakly. He sucked in a deep, audible breath. "They put me in a police car. We went to the police station. In Rochester."

"What happened next?"

Kenny held up his still ink-stained fingers. "They fingerprinted me. Took photographs. Called it a mug shot. They searched me." Bright crimson slashed his cheeks. "Then they took me to jail. Another man sat in the jail cell. The cop told me I had to stay here until Tuesday when I see the judge."

"I understand you were moved to a single cell, without a cellmate."

Kenny nodded. "The cops said I was crazy and noisy."

"Did they ask you to be quiet?"

"No. They called me mean things. I yelled I wasn't crazy."

Fanny scribbled *police antagonism* in her notes. "What happened then?"

"They said I was bad. Said I had to be by myself. And because I was bad, I couldn't call Gina. Not even Uncle Raymond."

Fanny scrawled *solitary confinement* and punctuated it with a question mark.

"Is today Saturday or Sunday?" Kenny asked. "The days are all confusing me."

"Monday," Fanny said gently. "I would also be confused if I were in your shoes." When Kenny looked at his shoes, she realized he had taken her comment literally. They needed to move past this point. "Did anyone explain why you hadn't seen a judge today?"

"When I tried to visit earlier," Gina jumped in, "I was told the court's schedule permitted new cases tomorrow." She glanced at Kenny. "Tuesday."

"Okay, then. Let's talk more about Samuel. Was Samuel a friend of yours?"

"When Uncle Raymond was around, Samuel was nice. When Uncle Raymond was away, Samuel was mean. He was... a..." Kenny raked his fingers through his hair, adding further to his disheveled appearance.

"A bully?" Gina offered.

"Yes, Gina," Kenny said. He returned his focus to Fanny. "Samuel is a bully."

"Was Samuel mean only to you or was he nasty to everyone else?"

"I think others, too. I'm not sure."

"Did Samuel have a lot of friends?"

"He had a few. Not many wanted to be his friend."

"Why's that, Kenny?"

"Just the way Samuel is. He's not easy to be around."

"How long did he work with you at your uncle's pasta business?" Fanny asked, gripping her pen tight, ready for action.

"I've worked there since I was eighteen. I'm thirty now."

She tried again. "Did Samuel start at that time too?"

"Yes. But Samuel is older than me. He's forty."

Fanny's thoughts whirled from Kenny talking as if Samuel was still alive, yet she had not the heart to correct Kenny. In talking about someone's death, people often find it difficult toggling between the present and past tense. She too had the same trouble. With Kenny, she had no choice. She needed to stick with the facts in the past tense. The man was dead. Kenny was accused of his death. "So, Samuel was ten years older than you, correct?"

"Yes. We have different jobs. Samuel says my job is better because of Uncle Raymond."

"What would you say to him?"

"Nothing. Uncle Raymond tells me not to answer mean people."

"Your uncle's a wise man," Fanny said. From what she had heard, Raymond Franks was unaware of his nephew's troubles. Would she be the one who broke the news or would the police or detectives working for the prosecutor shatter his quiet arrival home? Or had he already caught the news in the evening paper? "Let's talk more about your work. Tell me what you do at work and what Samuel did."

"I deliver messages. And count inventory. Samuel is in the mailroom. He says my job is better. Always tells me I'm stupid. That I'm working because of Uncle Raymond."

Fanny tapped her pen on the paper; the ensuing dots looked like a constellation of stars, ready to explode. "Would you say Samuel had called you more names recently, compared to, let's say, a few months ago?"

Kenny jumped to his feet and began pacing. Gina stood, but Helene signaled with her index finger to sit, which Gina fortunately obliged. Fanny whispered to Gina that she should let him be, though the room had become too small for Kenny's growing agitation.

"Kenny," Fanny continued, glancing at her notes. "Other than stupid, what other names did he use to insult you?"

At the far corner of the room, Kenny made a sharp pivot. A screech from his white rubbery shoes raked the small room. He jabbed at the bridge of his nose. "Retarded. Moron. Idiot. Worthless." He looked at Gina, then at Helene. "Other ugly names. Good women shouldn't hear them."

"I understand," Fanny said. "Would you call him names? Get angry? Threaten to hurt him?"

Kenny's eyes widened. "I told you. No. Uncle Raymond says to ignore mean people."

"Let me clearly understand you, Kenny. So, you never called him a name or told him you would hit him or worse?"

"Never. For a while."

Fanny's neck pinched. "Is that a yes or no? Did you call him names?

"No. I told him to leave me alone. Told him he couldn't keep saying bad things about me. Told him to stop lying."

The to-do list grew in Fanny's mind by the second. When she had a private moment, she would phone David and have him investigate potential witnesses on behalf of Kenny. She also needed to meet with Lyman G. Hayes, the DA for Monroe County, who preferred his middle initial to be used, though he refused to reveal his middle name. It certainly did not stand for God, though Lyman often acted as the creator of the universe. Despite it being 1961, with more women stepping out into the work environment, Fanny's career as an attorney was still seen as an anomaly in both the public and professional eye. The state of New York had not engaged one female DA, and she doubted one would be elected. At least, not for a long time, perhaps decades. With all the talking between her and Hayes coming up, she would get the information from him, one way or the other. Once again, she looked into Kenny's eyes. "Had Samuel ever grabbed you or pushed you or hit you?"

"Grabbed me. Pushed me. Never hit me."

"You never told me that," Gina said, hugging her middle.

"Sorry, Gina," Kenny said, still in the corner of the room. "I don't want to scare you. Don't want you to think little of me."

Gina ignored her grandmother's prior warning gesture. Within two strides she stood beside Kenny. She reached out for his arm, but then glanced at the officer standing on the other side of the door and placed her arms to her sides. "I'd never, ever think little of you. You're the best, kindest, and smartest man I know."

"Kenny," Fanny said. "If I understand correctly, Samuel was never nice to you." After Kenny nodded, she asked, "And he pushed you around and called you names, many times, yes?"

"Yes," Kenny said, shame riding his tone. He sidestepped away from Gina by a good two feet. He continued pacing, shuffling his feet, as if prison chains were fastened around his ankles.

Fanny continued. "I sense Samuel's verbal attacks on you suddenly became worse. Did it? When did it become more vicious?"

"Yes. It became bad." Kenny stopped moving and crossed his arms. "Gina said we were having a baby. The next day, I told Uncle Raymond the good news."

"I imagine your uncle is happy for you," Fanny said, as tenderly as she could to encourage Kenny to tell more.

"Yes. I went to his office. Told him about the baby. Uncle Raymond keeps the office door open. Says he has no secrets. That's when Samuel dropped the mail off for Uncle Raymond."

"What did Samuel do or say?"

"He smiled, all funny. Then said, 'That's a gas, man.' Uncle Raymond told him to leave. On his way out, he was quiet."

"Was Samuel's silence a surprise?"

Kenny shrugged. "He kept quiet around Uncle Raymond. Later, with Uncle Raymond away, Samuel laughed at me. Got others to laugh at me.

Said the baby would be dumb, like me. Said Gina must be dumb, too. Poor baby, he said. Poor, retarded baby. Said Gina should get rid of it. Said it didn't deserve to live."

With the cuff of her blouse, Gina wiped her eyes. "We won't listen to Samuel's mean words, will we, Kenny?"

"No, we won't. We're Mr. and Mrs. Franks. Forever. And we're going to have a baby." Gone from his tone, though, were traces of joy.

"Yes, we are," Gina echoed. She whispered into Kenny's ear and then sat.

"If I may," Helene said. She studied her granddaughter as if to gauge whether to continue. When Gina remained quiet, Helene said, "After Gina and Kenneth married, they moved in with his uncle. As soon as I learned of Kenneth's troubles with Samuel, I packed our possessions, phoned his uncle, and told him, especially with them expecting a baby, that with or without his blessings, Gina and Kenneth would not remain living in Rochester. I told him I would pick them up and begin apartment searching. Mr. Franks agreed it might be for the best."

"That's when you moved to Bridgehaven?" Fanny asked.

"Yes. We took the first apartment that opened its doors to us. Since I commuted to work in Rochester, I took Kenneth to his job and then home again. Gina searched for a new job in town." Helene dropped her gaze to the table. "And, here we are, one unhappy family."

"Miss Kellerman," Kenny said, "I'm happy Gina and I married. I'm happy we're going to have a baby. I'm not happy about Samuel."

"Me, too," Gina said softly. She folded her hands on the table's surface.

Still puzzled over Kenny's choice of formally calling Helene by her surname, considering he married her granddaughter and lived with Helene up to the time of his arrest, Fanny made a side note in the margin to look into the peculiarity of Helene and Kenny's relationship. If she were to call Helene to the stand as a character witness for Kenny, she would not want the woman to come across as cold, let alone hostile. For now, Fanny needed to move on.

"So, since Samuel learned of your marriage to Gina and the baby, Samuel intensified his actions toward you. Is this correct?" When Kenny lifted a brow in question, Fanny reminded herself to speak plainly. "Since the day when Samuel heard you announcing your baby news in Uncle Raymond's office, did Samuel become rougher? Meaner? Did he grab you so hard that he turned your skin black and blue? Did he use a knife on you, or other weapons?"

"Yes. A few times, he shoved me against the wall. Kicked me. I had green and purple marks. It hurt to walk." Gina gasped. Kenny cleared his throat. "He used a knife. Didn't cut me. Just waved it in front of my face. He said he knew people who hated stupid people like me. Said I should watch for them."

"Did you ever report Samuel to your uncle? Were there witnesses who saw you and Samuel together when he would say mean things to you or when he hurt you?"

Silence brushed the room into a fluorescent white void. Was Kenny so petrified that he couldn't say a word more?

"Some people heard Samuel," Kenny said after a long minute ticked by. "His friends. No one saw Samuel hurt me. I think."

Fanny scribbled the words *S. bragged threats*, then *possible witnesses*. "Did Samuel bully others at work?"

"I don't know."

On her pad, she wrote *David investigate other S targets?* Curious, Fanny opted for a different approach. "Kenny, let's talk more about your uncle. Did you ever tell your uncle that Samuel treated you meanly? Although he's your boss, he's your uncle—your family."

"No. I said nothing."

"Why?" Fanny asked.

"Because." Kenny closed his eyes, mumbling the bright lights and white walls pained his head. He returned to his seat. "Samuel said he'd hurt Gina and the baby if I told Uncle Raymond."

Gina groaned.

Fanny wondered what was up with Helene. Why did *Grammy* not offer words of comfort, telling Gina all would be fine? Even if it were proven a lie. Fanny swallowed twice, hoping the tears brimming in her eyes would not spill out. She reined in her objectiveness. "Did Samuel threaten Gina before or after the two of you married?"

"Before, he said morons like me shouldn't marry. And, Gina must be a moron too. After he found out about our baby, he said more horrible stuff. Like how he'd hurt the baby too. Said we'll have one stupid baby after another."

"Those are awful things he said, all right. Tell me how he threatened Gina."

"Said he knew where she lived and worked. He'd come after her. Get her fired. Hurt her."

"When Samuel said he'd hurt Gina, did he say in what ways?"

"Just said what he'd do would hurt Gina. A lot. I can't allow that. No one will hurt Gina."

Fanny absorbed Kenny's spiraling distress. Now that he was opening up, she did not need his disclosure to become more thwarted by anguish. "Thank you for sharing, Kenny. Just so I can understand better, what did Samuel say to you after he overheard you tell Uncle Raymond that you and Gina were expecting a baby?"

"Said he knew where we lived. Said after I went to work, he'd visit Gina. He'd do bad things to her. And if he hurt the baby, too bad, he said."

Fanny frantically wrote all of Kenny's statements down while keeping her eyes on Kenny rather than the paper. She hoped she could later decipher her scrawl. "How did you know Samuel wasn't joking or exaggerating when he said these things?"

"Samuel never jokes."

"Do you have good things you want to share about Samuel?"

Kenny scraped his stubbled cheeks. "He lives in a nice house. With his parents. His parents are good."

As Fanny made a note to investigate Samuel's parents and upbringing, a curiosity crossed her mind. "Have you met Samuel's parents?"

"No. I've heard good things, though. I also followed Samuel home. To see for myself."

Fanny swallowed hard, wishing she had never heard his last few words that might be used against him in court if he ever made such a statement. "Did other people see you follow Samuel?"

"I followed him lots. People waved at me. Said hello. I said hi back."

"Did you know any of the people by name?"

"I don't think so. Their faces are blurry in my mind." After a pause, he added, "I thought I could walk anywhere. Is it different now? For everyone?"

"Pardon me for a few seconds." To her growing collection of notes, Fanny added more to follow up on: inculpatory, circumstantial evidence; moral certainty, the consciousness of guilt; relevancy test for admissibility, NY court struggles, see People v. Leyra 1956. She set her pen down and peered into Kenny's eyes. "Let's continue. You followed Samuel home plenty of times," she paraphrased. "Did you follow him because he never invited you to his house?"

"Samuel didn't like me. He never asked me to come over. Told me to stay away."

"Do you believe Samuel or the police might have seen you follow him?"

"I don't think so. I'm good at hiding. I didn't want Samuel to see me. Or the police."

"Did others see you?"

"Yes. They didn't follow me, though. Didn't know I followed Samuel."

Consistent he was. "So, people told you his parents were nice. Which ones?"

"People I asked. At the grocery store. The postman. Others."

"Ooh-boy," Helene murmured. Fanny glared a warning at her. Gina as well.

"Are you saying," Fanny continued, "that you walked up to strangers and asked if they knew Samuel, and if they said yes, you then asked them what he was like?"

Kenny nodded. "I like to talk to people. Even strangers. That's how I met Gina."

"Let's talk about what triggered the incident that ended up with Samuel's death. Did Samuel physically hurt you? Did he push, slap, kick, or punch you that hurt you more than other times?" When Kenny shook his head, Fanny took a deep breath and reworded her inquiry. "Tell me what Samuel said. Then tell me what you did."

"I don't understand." Kenny again ran his fingers through his hair.

"The police arrested you because they say you killed Samuel based upon finding you alone in an unused back lot of a closed-down business. You were next to Samuel's dead body. They saw no one else. We've already established that Samuel had insulted and discouraged you. Recently, he made threats regarding Gina and the baby. How did this make you feel?"

"Angry."

"Tell me again what he said."

"Samuel said the baby would be retarded. That was his word. The baby would be like me. Said Gina should leave me, she didn't deserve me or a retarded baby. I didn't want to hear him talk. But he wouldn't shut up."

Gina let loose a sob. Helene pulled a tissue from her purse and handed it to her granddaughter. While not a softhearted, tender moment, it probably was the next best of efforts.

"Tell me, Kenny, what you said."

"I kept quiet."

"Where were the two of you when Samuel commented about the baby?"

Kenny's eyes opened widely. "We were outside. I was going to meet Miss Kellerman. So we could drive home. She works far from where I work. I like to walk, though. Samuel followed me. He kept shouting at me. Bad names. Mean things."

"Where did Samuel live?"

"Far from work, too. He takes the bus."

"Was anyone else around, watching you two?"

Kenny shrugged. "I don't know."

"You left work, Samuel follows you, and he is saying horrible things about you, Gina, and your baby who isn't even born yet. And you're exhausted from hearing him say this stuff. You said you didn't want him to talk anymore, but he wouldn't be quiet. What did you do? Did you try to make him shut up?"

"Uncle Raymond's words came here." He pointed to the side of his head. "Like people. I saw these words. They told me to keep quiet. I did."

"Did Samuel keep quiet?"

"No. He said the baby would come out all funny-looking. And act funny. He said defected."

"Do you mean the nasty word *defective*? It means having an intellectual disability."

Kenny nodded. "Yes. Like a broken record with no music. Because I'm retarded and stupid. Because Gina is stupid for marrying me."

"And?" Fanny said. "Please tell me, Kenny, did he hit you? I need to know what was different this time. What pushed you to chase him to the lot where he died?"

"Uncle Raymond's words went away," he said flatly. "I stopped hearing them. I turned around. I told Samuel to leave me alone."

"Did he?"

"No. He kept saying bad things."

"What did you do?"

"I told him to shut up. He laughed. He shoved me hard. I fell, then stood. I shook my hand at him. Like this." Kenny fisted his hand and shook it like he was punching the air. "He shoved me again. Then he took off. But I move very fast."

"What happened?"

"I followed Samuel. He ran around corners. And into alleyways. Then out again. Between stores. And houses. Then the alleyway without an out."

"What do you mean?"

"There was a fence. To leave is the same way of going into the back."

"And then what?"

"I got there. He talked to me. Then stopped. His eyes were open. He didn't talk anymore. Didn't move."

"Did you see anyone else?"

Kenny smacked the sides of his head. "I can't remember... I can't remember. Then the cops came. Wanted to talk to me. At the police station."

"Did the police show up right after you found Samuel?"

"I can't remember. It's all fuzzy. Like my head."

Maybe if she skirted the issue a bit, Kenny would recall the details. "Tell me, Kenny, what did you think when you didn't see Samuel move?"

"I was afraid. And sad. I didn't want him to hurt. I don't like when people are in pain."

"Did you think he was dead?"

Kenny shrugged. "I tried to wake him up—I shook him. Just a little. I slapped him in the face. Like when people faint. I see that lots on TV. It's not good when someone dies. They'll never marry. Never have babies."

Out of the corner of her eye, Fanny noticed that Gina and her grandmother sat at the edge of their seats and were as pale as the white paper of her notepad. "Did you worry that because you shook him, you might have killed him?"

"No. Because I didn't kill him. Only touched him. I tried to wake him up."

Hoping Kenny would interpret it as encouragement or empathy to his narrative, Fanny nodded. "When Samuel didn't respond to you trying to wake him up, tell me if anything else was on your mind."

"Gina. I was afraid. Afraid Gina didn't want me anymore. Afraid if the baby found out, it wouldn't want me as a daddy. Afraid Uncle Raymond didn't want me."

"I can understand your concerns, Kenny."

"Afraid I did bad. Afraid I deserve bad things." Once again, he jumped to his feet. "I worry more, now. About what will happen. Because Samuel will never talk to his parents, again. Like I want to talk to my baby."

"Do you remember any time you wanted to hurt Samuel?"

"I don't want to hurt anyone. Ever."

"So, you didn't plan on hurting him?"

"I don't understand. I didn't want to hurt him."

Fanny glanced at the door where the officer stood, watching them. She asked Kenny to have a seat. "I can understand why you were angry with Samuel and why you chased after him."

"No. You don't."

Although Kenny's reply rang as the most assertive Fanny had heard from him, she held fast to her approach. If he could not cope with her line of questioning, and the perspective of how others would view the case, his reaction could spell disaster for them. "I think I understand. Samuel said hurtful things. You were able to ignore him until he said mean and scary things about Gina and the baby." She let Kenny absorb her words. "Let's move on. When the police came to the apartment, were you calm?"

"I was scared. Nervous. But I behaved."

"What do you mean by behaved?"

Kenny gave the slightest of grins. "I didn't act like what Samuel said about me. Like I'm stupid."

"What did the cops say to you?"

"They were taking me to the police station. I was under arrest."

"Did they say why?"

"Because Samuel was dead. They said I looked like Samuel's killer. I'm not. They said they saw my hands on him—that Samuel had marks on his throat."

Throat? Was Samuel strangled? Unlike earlier, with her pushing him the hardest yet, she couldn't stop the momentum gained by taking notes. "How did their words make you feel? What did you do?"

"Angry. I told them it wasn't my fault. They stared at me like I was crazy. Asked me why I talk funny. I told them I didn't talk funny. They told me to stop yelling. I said I wasn't yelling. Outside, they pushed me to the ground. My face hit the dirt. They pulled my arms behind my back and snapped handcuffs on them. They made me stand. Said they were bringing me to the police station. Said if I didn't calm down, I'll go to the funny farm where crazy people live."

"Those jerks were making fun of Kenny," Gina said directly at Fanny. "Is that allowed?"

Helene warned Gina to be quiet.

"No, Miss Kellerman," Kenny shouted. He stood and stepped toward Helene, wagging a finger at her. "No! You can't shut Gina up. The cops wanted me to stop yelling. You aren't the police."

Fanny hooked his arm. She needed to diffuse his detonating agitation. "Kenny, please sit down or the officer will come into the room and there will be trouble. Let's continue talking. I'm not shouting at you. Please don't shout at me. Okay?" When Kenny wrapped his arms around his middle and strode to the opposite wall, Fanny raced to ensure he understood her full implication. "Will you help me get you out of this place?"

"Yes. I don't want to stay here. Will I go home with Gina and Miss Kellerman?"

"I want you to go home. First, you must see the judge tomorrow. He will tell you the reasons for your arrest. I must do all the talking for you. What you must do is remain calm and quiet, no matter what. You must not raise your voice, at anyone, no matter what happens or is said. No exceptions. Do you understand me?"

"Yes."

"Good. Let me explain how I see the way the case can go, either by our control or the prosecutor's control." Kenny's brow lifted. "The DA—state attorney—represents Samuel's case, even though Samuel is no longer alive. This is a case of murder. The state of New York has to find out who killed Samuel." Fanny scanned the faces of Gina and Helene then returned her focus to Kenny. "The DA will try to prove you are to blame. We will work hard to prove you were not responsible. How does that sound?"

"Fanny," Kenny said, his tone more collected. "If I'm with Gina and our baby when it's born, I will be happy. That's all that matters to me."

"Excellent." Fanny studied her notes, thankful not a further peep of contention erupted in the claustrophobic room. "I'm thinking that after a long time of emotional abuse from Samuel, you've held back your thoughts and kept your self-control in check. You were able to tolerate Samuel's harassment until Samuel followed you after work and threatened Gina. Suddenly, you couldn't keep silent. I'm now considering an insanity plea."

"I don't understand," Kenny said, his forehead deeply furrowed.

"I'm thinking about different ways to defend you. The trial's outcome might be easier on you if we get the jury to see you as someone unable to control yourself and your actions. Would you—"

Kenny pounded his fist on the table. "I thought you understood, Fanny. I'm slow. Not insane. I didn't kill Samuel."

"It is up to the judge and jury to decide. My job is to convince them you didn't intentionally or accidentally kill Samuel. By stating and proving that you are insane, your case stands a good chance of being tossed out of court, putting an end to a guilty verdict, and its bad consequences." She offered a little smile. "If we go this direction, you might be released in the care of Gina, and you two can live together and see your baby grow up. Wouldn't you like that?"

"I didn't kill Samuel. I'm not guilty."

At the table, Helene cleared her throat. "Kenneth, listen to Fanny. She's a lawyer. She can help you with the law and your rights. She wants to help Gina, too."

"I am not insane," Kenny said, his tone bumping up more. "This is wrong. I'm slow. Not insane."

"As your attorney," Fanny continued, "I must offer you my legal advice, informing you of all possible ways to throw out the murder charge. And, to find one with a more tolerable sentence. We will need to discuss this in detail. First, when you see the judge tomorrow to plead not guilty—"

Kenny cast a scowl at Fanny, his nostrils flaring. "I am not insane."

Fanny breathed in sharply, reminding herself to tread gently, yet firmly. She would speak softly in the hope he would respond calmly as well. If she could get Kenny to see the two choices he faced—life if found not guilty, or the end of his life via capital punishment if declared guilty—it might become clearer for him. "Do you want to see your baby daughter or son born?"

"Yes."

"Well, when the time comes for your trial, we must say things and provide evidence to convince the jury you are not guilty of intentionally killing Samuel and to convince the judge for favorable sentencing for you." When Kenny looked at her blankly, Fanny tried again to simplify. "When you saw Samuel following you, did you suddenly think *Good, I want to hurt him*?"

Kenny shook his head.

Fanny thumped her heart twice. "And when Samuel said mean things about you, Gina, and the baby, it hurt your feelings?"

"Yes." Like Fanny, he thumped his chest. "In here. My heart."

"Tell me more, Kenny."

"I was scared. And angry. I wanted him to shut up." Kenny scratched his head. "I didn't know how to stop him. He kept talking."

"Do you usually feel scared and angry?"

"No. I'm happy." He glanced at Gina. Instead of a smile, he rolled his bottom lip. "Gina says that's why she loves me. 'Cause I'm happy."

Gina gave Kenny's hand a quick squeeze. She then placed her hands on the table and eyed the door where the officer stood on the other side. "I love you for many reasons. Your happiness is a big reason."

"In your situation," Fanny continued, "fear and anger took over your mind and heart. It overwhelmed you. All you could do was try to stop Samuel from upsetting you. It's like when you accidentally burn your finger and it hurts and all you want is to find cold water to stick your finger in, to cool it off, right?" After Kenny nodded, Fanny stood. "However, the law has its definitions. We all must live by them. The law states what you can and cannot do. Samuel created a new feeling in you. The new feeling took over your mind. You were no longer in control. The law calls this condition temporary insanity, or in some states outside of New York, just insanity. I am not saying you're insane. As of now, I'm not even sure if we will use insanity as an option. However, it would be wise to keep all of our defense options open."

"No!" Kenny grabbed Fanny's writing pad and threw it against the door. "You don't understand. You're like everyone else. You think because I'm not smart that I'm crazy. That—"

"Kenny, I think we—"

"Be quiet, Fanny." Kenny stared at her as if she were the one with questionable sanity.

"Fine. I will listen to you, but unless you want trouble, do not yell. Talk in a low voice. And sit down."

Kenny nodded, sat, and remained silent for a tick of seconds. "My mother was insane. She was crazy when she left me and my father. Said she couldn't take care of us. Like we were trash and she took us out for the garbage men to pick up. My father was insane. I was five years old when he went to Walter's Asylum. He said he couldn't take care of me. Because I was broken. I never saw him again. He killed himself. In the hospital that was supposed to make him better. Uncle Raymond took care of me because he said my parents were insane. I'm not insane."

Just when Fanny believed he had finally understood the legal definition of insanity, it was obvious he did not. Due to his unfortunate family history with his parents, she could understand his perspective, yet she clamped down on her objectivity. She needed to focus on the law and how it operated. "Kenny, like it or not, New York State has a death penalty for murderers. If you are found guilty, you will face electrocution." She resisted cringing when she heard Gina's shriek. "You just said you wanted to see your baby grow up."

"Yes, I do." He jumped to his feet. "Are you and the law insane? Saying I'm insane?"

The door's lock snapped open and two officers rushed in. The officer who had stood guard while they talked said, "Time is up. Come peacefully or you won't like what happens."

Kenny paled. Without a word or a struggle, he permitted the detention officers to cuff him and grip his arms to guide him out of the room.

As if she were a tissue paper origami pulled apart, Fanny crumpled onto a chair. Until today, she had never come close to pushing someone into the psychotic state of insanity, a place she was terrified to visit.

CHAPTER EIGHT

Helene, Berlin, Germany, 1913-1942

Back in 1913 when Helene was ten, she walked home from school with Gisela, a classmate. They slipped into an abandoned storage shed to smoke cigarettes for the first time. Their friends smoked. Their teachers smoked. Their parents also smoked; they might have made their homes stink, but, oh, it made them look so sophisticated. Helene had pinched two smokes from her father's bureau. She gave one to Gisela, then held the other cigarette in the V between her second and third fingers. Pretending to take a drag, she said in a fake nightclub singer's voice, "Don't I look simply divine, darling?" They giggled. On the count of three, they each lit their cigarette, drew in too much and too fast, and coughed violently for several minutes.

Regaining her breath, Helene waved away the lingering smoke. "Wow. It was so bad that for a few seconds, I wanted to die." Tossing the cigarettes out the door and into a nice selection of mud, they vowed never to smoke for the rest of their lives. They settled onto a couple of old crates and talked about their parents.

"What's the one big thing your folks won't tolerate?" Helene asked.

"Tardiness."

"Really? Nothing more serious?"

A little pink tinged Gisela's cheeks. "When it comes to social affairs, Vater is always punctual. He hates it when Mutter makes him late for one of their friends' swanky dinner parties, which is a laugh because, at home, he's perpetually tardy for dinner. You should hear the foul names she calls him then."

"It's a good thing we planned our smoking party so you won't arrive home late."

Gisela batted the air like a cloud of cigarette smoke still hung over them. "It's your turn."

"Lies. My folks won't tolerate the tiniest bitty fib, at all. Whether from the butcher when he tries to cheat us on the amount of meat he sells, or the lies the government supposedly tells us—don't ask me details because I have no idea. I don't follow that nonsense. My parents especially won't accept lies from me, like if I say I have no school assignments or claim I'm sick when I don't want to go to school."

"One day when I have children, I'll never make my little ones worry over silly things."

"And I," Helene said, "will always understand if my child tells an occasional lie."

•   •   •

Now, thirteen years later, Helene could easily see her naivety. Throughout history, there were certain ways that parents never budged in their way of thinking, whether sons should leave the cave and go hunting, which Viking bloodline best suited their daughters to marry into, or whether sailing to the New World was worth the risk. In her case, what would happen if Helene Kellerman fell in love with the first man who paid attention to her? Since she and Gisela first puffed on those horrid cigarettes, they were fortunate enough not to experience upheavals in their personal lives. Their beloved country, though, saw much devastation during the Great War followed by severe food shortages and rioting. Hatred continued to flow. Helene and her friend were sheltered by their well-off parents from harm's touch. They had made it through their teenage years and survived school and first jobs. Helene put on her tough girl face when Gisela's family abruptly departed Germany. Fortunately, fate blessed her when she and her childhood friends, Martha and Erna, became closer. A girl had to have her female friends. With encouragement from her new best friends, Helene became her father's architectural assistant. This was a fancy way of saying that she answered the phone, took notes, and greeted potential clients. Now, a few grown-up years later, she had news that would change everything, permanently.

Without a better time or place to inform her parents, she faced them. And the truth. The dinner table would have to do, especially this singular evening when guests were absent from assembling around their table, for a change.

After Marion served the meal of ham, roasted potatoes, cabbage, and carrots, and topped off their wine glasses before departing for the kitchen, Helene separated her meat from the potatoes and vegetables, pushed them together, then apart.

"You're playing with your food like you're five," her mother said. "Is the dinner bad?"

"Are you ill?" her father asked.

Helene knew it was time to tell them the simple but complex truth. "I met a nice man a few months ago."

"And you didn't think to tell us?"

"Hans," her mother said in as daring as a reprimand she could utter without triggering her husband's dark side. She slipped out a cigarette from a ready pack of smokes beside her dish and lit it. "Look at our beautiful daughter. She's obviously in love."

Her father thwacked his fork down on his dish. "What is obvious is that if our daughter's in love, and is too ashamed to tell us about the fellow, then he must be scum." He rested his elbows on the table, disregarding his wife's disapproval. "How come you haven't mentioned this male interest?"

Helene thought if she cooperated, her father would simmer down and drop the subject. "His name is Willie. Willie Fischer."

"And how old is Willie Fischer? What does he do?"

Although the questions were fair to ask, particularly from her father, Helene trembled. "He's just a few years older than I am."

"I said the same thing to my father when I first met your father," Helene's mother said.

"Frieda, please."

Her mother narrowed her gaze at Helene's father but kept silent.

"Willie is five years older than I am. Until two days ago, he worked for his father's printing business on the other side of the city."

"Until two days ago?" her parents parroted.

"Yes. That's what I said." Helene cringed at her audacity. When her father's mouth dropped open and her mother rocked back, she shot to her feet. The room tilted. She groped for the chair. Her mother rushed to her side.

"Darling, what's wrong?" She helped Helene to sit again. "Catch your breath. It will be fine once the dizziness is gone."

"It won't be fine. Not for the next eighteen or twenty years, if at all."

Her mother had begun rubbing Helene's tight shoulders but stopped at her last words. "What do you mean?"

"Willie enlisted in the army."

"Good for him," her father said, guardedly. "He's to be commended for serving our country. Although, he won't be in the army for that many years unless he chooses to be."

"He's going away, from me. Regarding those years, it's the time to raise a child and see him or her off on their own." She could not take another second of her father staring at her as if he could chisel his shame into her without mouthing a single word of disgust. He knew. She decided to tell her parents the truth and get the subsequent yelling from them over with. "Willie took off on me when I told him I'm expecting his baby."

•   •   •

Helene was terrified of the actual birthing process. If only she could count on her mother's or a friend's encouragement that childbirth—pushing a baby out of a part of her body that defied logic—might be far easier than raising the child, she imagined she would have relaxed a bit. Luck be damned. Her mother, after learning of her pregnancy, treated her like a foreigner who rented the corner upstairs bedroom. A stranger who should only be seen at the dinner table, not heard from. In her father's eyes, she was now a shameful daughter who disgraced her family. He had little to do with her, including her services at his firm. She did not deserve her parents' love or respect. Her friends shocked her more. Her friend Martha avoided her, though if the two met while shopping, Martha did a miserable job concealing her wide-eyed stare around Helene's growing middle. And Erna, who had a loving husband and a baby of her own, also had nothing more to do with her. It was as if Helene was the sole woman in all of Germany pregnant out of wedlock. She was more amazed by the cold treatment from her two supposed friends than the reality of soon becoming a mother. The memory of her birthday celebration just last October, surrounded by her two friends, sipping wine, feasting on a special dinner at a popular restaurant, and daring to daydream aloud, and giggle—lots of giggling—had left her exposed, like a wound after a nasty fall. To think the special day was when she met Willie, fell in love with him, and was certain she would become Mrs. Willard Fischer. All she wanted was to become a good wife to a loving husband and have his children, to love her family with all her heart.

One July morning, while seated at the breakfast table with her parents, Helene's baby made a fast and furious entrance into the world two weeks earlier than the good doctor had predicted. Helene groaned and clutched her large belly. Considering how her parents ignored her during the months of her pregnancy whenever possible, it was a shock that they jumped to their feet. After the first contraction dulled, another one held her hostage. Between her third and fourth contraction, she screamed for her mother to fetch the doctor, though it was her father who ran out of the house to find the older man who delivered most of the babies in their Berlin neighborhood. Liselotte came wailing into the world three hours later. Through the years, one way or the other, Helene's little girl never stopped her cry for attention.

What Helene thought would be easier—the after part of labor like the months of rocking Liselotte to sleep with a lullaby, helping her to take her first steps, introducing a new food while keeping on hand a bib for a rebellious spit-up—proved to be far more challenging than she ever imagined. Severe sleep deprivation did not help. Losing her desire for independence, letting go of daydreams of a committed husband, and ignoring her beloved reading trove, failed to improve her outlook of expecting happiness. What blindsided her most was not the drive of the Nazis to take over the world, but instead, the rapid flying of time. Somehow, seemingly overnight, her little, dependent daughter transformed into a free-spirited teenager.

. . .

For the past four years, Helene had not only endured the hardships of losing the few extended family members she had to the war but also the passing of first her mother and then her father to incurable illnesses. Although grateful her parents had bequeathed the house to Helene, she fought back the anxiety of being the sole person responsible for her daughter. Yet, others had it worse. Far worse. Jewish neighbors were rounded up and transported to camps, which no one dared to speak openly in protest out of sheer fear of being crammed into a cattle car themselves and taken away to unimaginable calamity. Near-daily changing Nazi edicts brought unwelcomed lessons on how to define existence. Standing on sturdy feet became a nearly impossible acrobatic movement.

On a cold late January morning of 1942, Helene's life somersaulted again when Liselotte arrived home late from school. Approaching her sixteenth birthday, she stormed through the front door, bent into herself, and with gaze averted.

"Once again, you're late. School was dismissed two hours ago." Helene eyed her daughter. "Close the door. Keep the cold out, the warmth in."

Liselotte slid the hood from her head, her reddish-brown hair tucked under her coat. "Mutter, what's concerning you the most? Is it the frigid winter temperature and the struggle to heat the house? Perhaps you're concerned about how many neighbors have gone missing. Or are you anxious over my lessons on how to love and obey Hitler? Surely, you're not twisted up in worry over me."

Ever since the German army crossed the Polish border in '39, Helene felt more like she was on the brink of turning seventy rather than forty. She could still hear her deceased parents' murmurs of war having a peculiar way of aging a person. Helene knew the truth, though. Standing at the door, the single fact glared at her, holding its grand head high: her child, not wartime, was the culprit in aging her.

"It's shameful how you talk to me." Liselotte shook the snow from her coat. The thick white globs fell onto the worn red doormat. "I'm tired of your constant suspicions of me."

Helene knew better than to fall into the trap of Liselotte's impertinence and searched her mind on how to right the wrong playing out between them. Any attempt to restore peace between them ended when Liselotte slapped a hand over her mouth and gagged.

She hurried to her daughter's side. "Let me help." She placed a hand firmly on her daughter's shoulders, feeling helpless as Liselotte shook with a round of dry heaves. "You must have the influenza going around." She led her toward the armchair beside the sofa, amazed Liselotte did not put up a stink. Once seated, Helene touched the girl's forehead. "You're not hot with fever."

Liselotte again covered her mouth with a hand and rested her eyes shut. After a few seconds ticked by, with her eyes still closed, she said, "Most pregnant women don't have fevers like they have round-the-clock nausea."

Pregnant?

She was staring at a child. Her child, who was intimating that she was going to have a child.

"Aren't you going to say something, Mutter? At least yell at me, tell me I'm an embarrassment?" Liselotte snickered. "Or, that I take after you?"

Never one to fight the proverbial fire with fire, Helene did not want to upset her daughter, her baby girl carrying her own baby. While she had kept the details of her relationship with Willie from Liselotte, her daughter was smart enough to assemble the missing pieces of the puzzle. Helene, having birthed her baby girl out of wedlock and given the nasty rub from not only her parents but from neighbors and friends, knew the horror of shame. This humiliation, and the truth about Liselotte's father she kept from her daughter's ears, were the two regrets that had colored her life gray to this day.

Loving her daughter, fiercely, she sat beside Liselotte. She determined to remain calm and to speak softly. Surely, her child—rapid-firing into womanhood—was petrified of the challenges she faced presently and for the rest of her life. With the birth of a child, there was no going back. For now, Helene had to begin with the facts. "Tell me who the father is."

Liselotte ran her fingers across the chair's threadbare upholstery. "No one you know."

"Tell me who the father is," Helene repeated.

"Gerhard. Don't ask me his last name because I won't tell you."

Although the pregnancy of her teenage daughter warranted several additional questions that would surely produce a heated argument, it was not the right moment to barrage Liselotte with all the thoughts on her mind. Not that a more suitable time would exist as Liselotte's pregnancy continued, or after the baby was born. However, Helene needed to ask one more. "How far along are you?"

"I've seen a doctor." Liselotte pressed down on her lower lip and parted the thick, bulky sweater she had taken to wearing lately. "He says three months."

Helene gulped. Her daughter appeared more like four or five months. How had she not noticed the changes in her little girl who would soon have her own girl or boy? Could she blame this lack of attention on the war? Whether one held the Axis powers or the Allies responsible depended on who one stood next to at a given second, especially if the other person held a gun. One undebatable truth was that all aspects of life had changed for all of them. No exceptions. Helene could not rightly take the blame for failing to see her daughter's changing body. Not when surviving became a basic, daily necessity.

Then again, a justifiable excuse for hiding her pregnancy from her parents had not existed. They were not at war, then. Another mouth to feed would not strain her parents' well-off household. Nor would expecting a baby interfere with her work obligations to her father. Sadly, her sheer loneliness and yearning for a lover to color her world wonderful would not count in her parents' eyes as a valid reason for not telling them the truth upfront as soon as she had known, not when she could no longer conceal her changing body.

Liselotte smirked, then gagged. After she calmed down, she said, "Yes. You're blind to happenings right under your roof, Mutter."

"Evidently," Helene said. "What else did the doctor tell you?"

"I appear healthy. And pregnant. Probably with twins but he's not—"

Sweat broke out under Helene's arms. "Twins?"

"He's not sure, yet. I mean, he poked my belly and felt around. Things point to one baby, though he says it's too early to know. Despite being queasy all day, I'm eating a lot. The doctor suspects two babies, though."

The good doctor's assessment—or her daughter's interpretation—was as clear as the muck in a barn. Helene tried not to panic. War and its sidekick, death, had become everyday life, an ironic reality. It had become difficult enough to provide daily sustenance for herself and Liselotte. Now, twin grandchildren—innocent, blessed babies who must come first—would be added to the struggle for survival. Helene swallowed back her runaway thoughts. "How do you feel? Other than an upset tummy?"

"Like I said, I'm hungry. All the time. I'm also achy." She ran a hand over her chest. "Here. Is that normal?"

Helene nodded. "Very."

"What should I do?"

"You need to stay indoors," Helene replied immediately.

"Why, Mutter? I'm not Jewish." She stroked her belly. "Doesn't the Führer want us Aryan women to have many babies for the greater good of the German Reich?"

Helene willed herself not to resort to panic yelling. "Listen carefully to me. You are not a woman. You are a teenager. Pregnant, unmarried teenagers, are not accepted by the public. For the sake of your baby— babies—you must remember we're living in a dangerous time. Yes, we're not Jewish..." A worry flooded her mind. "Is Gerhard Jewish?"

"No. Of course not. I wouldn't sleep with a Jew man."

Helene cringed. Who was this stranger sitting beside her? Outside of the house, away from her, had her daughter always practiced anti-Semitism or was this a new side of her that came about from the hatred spewing up and down the city streets like puddles of filthy rainwater, hard to avoid?

"Do not trust anyone other than myself with your baby news. We're living in an uncertain, maddening world. I've heard that babies, especially twins, are being kidnapped. Bad things are happening. Even with one baby, you're an unwed mother, Liselotte." Again, she interrupted herself with another thought. "Does Gerhard know? Would he marry you?"

"I haven't told him yet."

"Are you?"

"I'm not sure." Liselotte stood quickly and groped the air like Helene remembered when she broke the news of her pregnancy to her parents.

Helene grabbed her daughter's arm. "Easy. You need to rest. Would you like me to help you to your room?"

"No. I'll be fine." She surprised Helene by casting her a tender, appreciative smile. Would her pregnancy be the catalyst needed to turn their relationship around for the better?

Liselotte blinked several times as if clearing her vision. "I have no other choice, do I, but to be fine?" She walked toward the stairs. Helene called out. Liselotte stopped walking, resting one hand on the newel post. She did not turn around.

"I repeat, if you want your baby—babies—to remain under your loving care, do not step outdoors until the war or your pregnancy is over with, whichever comes first."

"No worries, Mutter. I already love my babies and will love them forever. No matter what." With her eyes on the stairs, Liselotte climbed toward the second floor. Just when Helene believed she and her daughter might grow closer, Liselotte stopped, and without turning around, added, "I vow to my unborn babies that I will be a far more loving mother than you've ever been to me."

There it was.

After nearly sixteen years, her daughter had accused her of failing to love her enough. Liselotte would not have slung those words like a weapon because of physically feeling unwell or from fear of approaching motherhood... or wondering how she might have to one day grab her baby—or babies—and run to a public bomb shelter in time. One designed, ironically, by her own grandfather weeks before his death. Rather, they were the truth, at least from Liselotte's perspective. Helene now had a new, larger regret—the loss of love from her daughter. More so than the affair which brought Liselotte into the world, fostering scorn from her parents, and subsequently kept her from revealing the truth of her daughter's origins.

CHAPTER NINE

Fanny, Rochester, August 15, 1961

Fanny woke at four Tuesday morning and took pleasure in waking her cat, for a change. After feeding Ralph, and putting up coffee in her trustworthy percolator, she showered and dressed in her lucky court suit, consisting of a polyester pleated skirt of alternating black and white panels featuring keys. She fancied the keys were the passport to freedom for her clients. A white blouse appropriately buttoned to her neck, a finely tailored black jacket, and a pair of black fabric pumps with a high tongue extending up the foot and an oval, ruffled medallion accent made a complete, no-nonsense, and a don't-mess-with-me outfit. Although today's court appearance would be an in-and-out first arraignment, her client, Kenny Franks, the DA, and the judge must take her seriously. She would not settle for less.

A creature of habit, Fanny did not think twice about turning on the radio. Within seconds, misgivings pocked her arms with gooseflesh. Those poor people in Germany. Families, friends, and strangers who had no dissatisfaction with each other were now separated by a wall, a barbwire and cinder block monstrosity, assembled to curb citizens as if they were wild animals. She imagined, sooner rather than later, concrete walls and guarded watchtowers would replace the present structure. She sank to her chair in the kitchen and buried her face in her palms as the reporter and interviewee talked, in English, for the world to hear.

"How old are you, Monika? And where do you live?"

"Sixteen. I live in Bretzenheim."

"That's approximately 600 kilometers southwest of Berlin?"

"Ja."

"Tell us how you and your parents learned about the wall being built."

"We have no television—same with our neighbors and friends. So, we found out the old-fashioned way like any bad news spreads, through people crying on the streets."

A tsk-tsk noise sounded over the airwaves. "Why do you think they were upset?"

"Oh, I just don't think. I know. Everyone is afraid for their families and friends trapped in East Berlin. Why shouldn't we be upset?"

"Trapped, you say?"

"Ja. People have trapped other people. No one can contact them by phone. We're afraid, so afraid. Stories are jumping from one person to another. We're unsure what to believe. Maybe because we don't want to believe—that's how horrible it is."

"Can you tell me some of these stories?"

"Those living in East Berlin will be killed. And the lucky ones—if that's what you want to call them—who won't be killed, how are they supposed to buy food? How will they ever see their relatives on the other side of the wall? We're afraid the building of this wall is the beginning of a war the authorities are keeping from us."

"Surely, Monika, no one believes it's another war breaking out."

"When you live in a country that saw the horrors of war only a few handfuls of years ago, you can be convinced you will never see relatives and friends again. Sir, I was born the year the last world war ended. It's like the awful war that killed millions—multiple millions—of people never ended, but continues. Such a huge number of deaths is difficult to understand or accept."

"Isn't that fear just talking?"

"Fear is real... I have to go..."

"Are those your parents approaching?"

"I can't talk," Monika whispered.

"Leave my daughter alone," a deep-voiced man shouted.

"Folks, this is Jimmy—"

Fanny sprang to her feet and turned off the radio. "Good riddance, Jimmy. Go make a ratings spectacle off of someone closer to your age." The fantasy of guzzling a strong pot of coffee in the peace of her kitchen lost its appeal. Instead, she settled on whipping out a thermos from her pantry and filling it to the miserly capacity with the brown liquid of caffeine and its promise to make her brain cells happy and functioning. She looked forward to taking her first sip as she drove to pick up Gina and Helene and then set off to the Monroe County Courthouse on the corner of West Main and Fitzhugh Streets in downtown Rochester. Constructed in 1822 one year after the birth of Monroe County, the courthouse cost $6,700. It outgrew its size and expanded in 1851 costing $76,000. In 1894, the courthouse was again razed for a third replacement. The Italian Renaissance building consisted of a foundation, steps, and a four-pillar portico made of Onondaga limestone. An addition, built in 1924 at the price tag of $1,201,000, had an exterior noted for its New Hampshire granite and the interior with marble, brass, and wrought iron throughout. The eight-foot-tall statue of Justice— originally carved in wood then later bronzed—was removed from the second courthouse's dome and placed in the new courthouse's front alcove. Unlike other statues of Justice, this one did not wear a blindfold. Growing up in the Rochester area, Fanny had wondered if the lady statue, the personification of justice, with her wise, seeing eyes, fell under the sway of bias or prejudice, likening her to the common person, faults and all. However, when choosing to become a defense attorney, Fanny believed this Rochester larger-than-life figure indicated the accused needed to be fairly represented by someone who saw them as individuals, overlooking prejudices, societal expectations, and financial affluence. Thus, Justice had her eyes wide open to see life as it was, both the good and the bad, and was prepared to take action to protect one's civil rights.

For Fanny, the courthouse was home away from home, not that her clients held the same notion. She grabbed her car keys and briefcase. Ralph stopped licking his front right paw and gave her *the stare*. He knew. She was heading out for the day, and he was prepared to accuse her of neglect if she showed up past his dinnertime. Having to leave, she gave him a peck on the top of his head. "See you later, alligator." She was rewarded with a huge yawn, which usually made her attention him with more adoration, like mothers who cooed over their babies babbling adorably in their strollers. Not this morning, though. Far too many concerns competed in her mind.

Exiting the driveway, she completed a mental checklist of all the warnings and tips she had coached Kenny, Gina, and Helene on behaving in the courtroom. Other than Kenny pleading not guilty to his charges, she would do all the talking. That included Kenny's uncle, Raymond Franks, whom she successfully contacted at 8:00 p.m. last night, via phone, breaking the news to him about his nephew, and dropping the bombshell news that the judge might set a significant bail on Kenny. Mr. Franks reassured her the bail amount shouldn't be a concern for him; his nephew meant more to him than his business earnings. Thank goodness Americans loved their pasta and thickened Raymond Franks' wallet. Although no arguments would be heard in court today, she mentally reviewed the charge of murder the state held Kenny accountable for. She had wanted to meet with the DA face-to-face in his office, however, forgoing sleep, and depriving her adversary of sleep, would be beyond foolish. Instead, she spoke with him last evening on the phone. David, her assistant slash investigator slash hand-holder, would meet them at the court. With everything in place. Kenny's appearance would go well. She would accept nothing less.

Gina and Helene left their apartment when Fanny pulled up to the curb. Gina wore a plain navy blue dress and matching blue slingbacks. The only jewelry she wore were silver studs, a simple watch on her left wrist, and, of course, a wedding band. Her neatly brushed shoulder-length hair did not compensate for her understandably missing smile. Overall, she appeared as a concerned, loving wife. Good. As for Helene, she sported a '50s-styled gray dress of blue pinstripes with side pockets. For the first time since the two met, Helene surprised Fanny not only by wearing her hair loose from the severe bun and brushing her shoulders, her glasses on her eyes rather than parked on top of her head, but most of all, she offered a slight smile. Fanny breathed easier. How the two women dressed and presented themselves would be a plus; Kenny needed as many pluses as possible. She rolled down the window. "Hop into the back seat. Sorry that my pile of paperwork and briefcase sitting shotgun leaves no room for company."

Gina opened the rear door. "No sweat. If it helps Kenny, that's all that counts." She slipped into the rear. Helene followed.

"How are you?" Fanny asked Gina as they pulled away from the curb.

"Hope I'm not jinxing myself—I'm okay," Gina said. "Good, considering I'm a wife whose husband is accused of murder. It will be a relief when today's over with."

"I can appreciate your feelings. If it helps any, remember, today is a first arraignment. Not a trial. The charges we hear may be alarming, yet it's not the end-all. Judge Harrison is presiding today. He has a reputation for being fair."

The rest of the car ride to Rochester was quiet and uneventful. She turned left onto West Main Street then drove two blocks and entered the parking lot for the courthouse.

A slim, average-height man in a nicely tailored brown suit stood outside the courtroom door. Fanny had never met Raymond Franks, nor seen a photograph of him. Yet, she recognized him by how he handled himself, exuding confidence few could claim. Despite his dark hair, she estimated his age to fall between sixty and sixty-five. With Gina and Helene ducking into the restroom, Fanny took advantage of the private moment.

"Hello, Mr. Franks." She extended a hand. "I'm Fanny Stern. It's a pleasure to meet you. Thank you for being here."

"Although Kenny calls me Raymond, please call me Ray. And, of course, I'd be here for my nephew."

Fanny liked Ray immediately. No sarcasm, tension, or airs. She sensed he was not the game-playing sort of guy. Excellent. She would not have to adjust to how she interacted as she did with Helene.

"What do you think of the judge?" Ray asked.

A good question, though ultimately, moot. "I've heard good things. Keep in mind, however, other than setting bail, Judge Harrison will not be the presiding judge if the case goes to trial."

"When we spoke last evening, you mentioned this is the first arraignment. Can you please elaborate?"

"Due to the nature of the crime—murder—the prosecution is pursuing felony charges. The criminal charges will be read to Kenny; bail may or may not be set, depending on the judge. Then, the case will likely go to a grand jury, which decides whether an indictment against Kenny is set. If Kenny is indicted, then he will face trial." As Gina and Helene exited the restroom and approached, Fanny noted their furrowed foreheads and reminded herself to use caution in her explanations. None of them would benefit from a scene. "It's not over until all these parts take place. With each stage of the process, we work on improving Kenny's odds of being acquitted." Fanny raised a hand to prevent the small group from entering the courtroom. "Please, no reactions when you see Kenny brought in wearing handcuffs. Understand?" All three nodded.

She offered a calm, reassuring smile. "Okay, then. Let's proceed."

They entered the courtroom, a basic non-thrill large room with a high ceiling, a splash of gray paneling, gray carpeting, and plain sawed mahogany furnishings. As Fanny had instructed, Gina, Helene, and Ray sat together in the right section of the public gallery. Fanny continued through the gate of the wooden bar separating the gallery from the front of the courtroom and sat at the Defendant's table, the furthest from the jury box, which would remain empty for today's session. She nodded politely at Lyman G. Hayes, the district attorney, seated at the left table. The clean-shaven, silver-haired man whose blank face made readability difficult, returned the gesture.

A door opened on the left side of the courtroom. A deputy guided Kenny into the room. Handcuffed, as Fanny had explained to the others, he wore the jail clothes of the white T-shirt, green pants, and the ridiculous rubber shoes she last saw him wearing. She hoped he was at least permitted to shower this morning, one little way to regain dignity despite the odds. He was led to the defense table and uncuffed.

"Good morning, Fanny," Kenny said quietly, his enthusiasm understandably gone.

She sure wanted it to be a good morning. She greeted him with a smile. "We'll make it a good morning, won't we?" When he remained silent, she added, "Remember what I told you about today?"

"Yes. To stay calm. Let you do the talking."

"Exactly."

The bailiff called out for all to rise for the Honorable Samuel Harrison. "Samuel... of all names," Fanny murmured. How had she blocked the judge's first name? She cringed. Perhaps she was the one in need of direction concerning courtroom decorum. Glancing at the people seated near her, and gauging their indifferent facial expressions, her off-the-cuff comment had not registered on the damage scale. More importantly, a glance at Kenny showed he was unruffled as well. The judge, a dark-haired, middle-aged man, whose short build often betrayed his reputation of having a high batting average when challenging those who dared to chop up his character or size, though she had kept this part from Kenny and the others. She needed to keep herself together just as she had instructed Kenny.

The bailiff asked everyone to be seated; Fanny and Kenny remained standing.

The judge adjusted his glasses. "The State of New York versus Kenneth Franks for charges of first-degree murder."

Relieved no one could see under her black suit jacket at the sweat trickling down her back, Fanny gripped the table's side. From her phone conversation with the DA, she had learned the degree of the charges, yet to hear the term *first-degree murder* officially stated within the courtroom was as jolting as if first learning the charges. Although already committed to a fierce fight on Kenny's behalf, she now upped it to the battle of the century. She would do whatever it took to free Kenny.

Kenny leaned toward her and whispered, "Is this bad, Fanny?"

She tapped her index finger twice against her lips to remind him to be quiet.

"Mr. Franks," Judge Harrison began, "you are charged with first-degree murder by the State of New York. Do you understand the charges and your constitutional rights to remain silent, to have a public and speedy trial, and to be represented by an attorney?"

Kenny looked at Fanny then the judge.

The judge looked directly at Kenny. "Mr. Franks?"

Fanny despised the words she was about to say. More distinctly, the necessity to explain, and the subsequent hoping against hope her client would still be due his respect and dignity as a human being like anyone else in the courtroom. He did not deserve the heinous label of an imbecile or freak of nature which society was all too ready to fling at him. "If it pleases the court, Your Honor, I, Fanny Stern, am counsel for the defendant, Mr. Kenneth Franks. I state for the record that Mr. Franks is mentally disabled."

The judge held up a hand. "Are you saying Mr. Franks is mentally incompetent to stand trial?"

"No, Your Honor. Mr. Franks has a good and clear understanding of what happens around him, toward him, and the consequences of his actions. However, he occasionally needs assistance to simplify definitions and understand matters."

"Let the defendant's intellectual state of mental disability be reflected in the record," the judge said. "Let it be noted Mr. Franks is not the first person to receive this recognition and is not due special treatment above legal explanations during court procedures."

"Thank you, Your Honor," Fanny replied.

"Mr. Franks," the judge continued, speaking in the same no-frill tone and at the same rushed rate of speech as if he had to move his court cases along for the day before they impacted both the court docket and his afternoon plans. "Is Miss Stern indeed your attorney?"

Fanny nodded at Kenny, holding her breath in the hope he would remember the tips she'd guided in addressing the judge. She noted the judge's narrowed eyes on Kenny, believing what she had said seconds ago might correlate with a fresher perspective of Kenny, which might work in his favor. Or, not.

"Yes. Your Honor. My attorney is Fanny. Miss Fanny Stern."

"Do you understand the charge of murder against you and your rights?"

Fanny, with her supposed intelligence compared to Kenny, failed to understand why her client was charged with first-degree murder. She reminded herself this was a legal matter. Not philosophical nor social. And legal issues had to follow a distinct protocol. To the best of her ability, she had prepared Kenny to respond in only one way: composed. She stared at Kenny as if he had a psychic ability to read her thoughts. Who was the true one with a mental disorder? *Why, that would be me.* Fanny visualized everyone else seated in the courtroom raising his or her hand along with her because what was civilization but a motley bunch of folks clinging to life in an upside-down world, zealots with uncompromising beliefs and actions, for better or worse? Who among them had an exceptionally perfect, flawless brain, so fine and right one hundred percent of the time that no mistake, no heated passion of the moment, nor misspoken word ever occurred?

Without a blink, Kenny replied, "Yes, Your Honor. I understand."

"How do you plead?"

"Not guilty." After a tick of a handful of seconds, Kenny added to his plea, "Your Honor."

"Miss Stern," Judge Harrison said, "do you have anything else to add?"

"Yes, Your Honor. The defense asks to waive the preliminary hearing until it receives and reviews discovery from the prosecutor."

"Let it be stated for the record that I am entering a Not Guilty plea by the defendant, plus the granted status of the waiver of the preliminary hearing. Thus, the date for the Grand Jury will be set at a time to permit discovery review." The judge looked at the DA; Fanny frantically worked on keeping a neutral expression despite her perception of favoritism for the prosecutor. "Mr. Hayes, would you like to discuss bail today?"

Lyman G. Hayes stood as Fanny and Kenny sat. He flashed his typical grin Fanny had to quash the temptation to wipe from his smug face. "Yes, Your Honor. The victim suffered a violent crime at the hands of the defendant. Our collected information shows the arresting officers, plus the correction officers at the jail, have attested to Mr. Franks as an uncooperative and mentally unbalanced person, one who acted out during his detainment by yelling wildly. He will put the community at risk. The state would like to have the defendant remanded back to jail without bail."

A cry, which sounded like the whimper of an injured animal, sailed across the courtroom. Without looking, Fanny recognized Gina's grievance. Chatter erupted across the room. The judge banged his gravel and demanded order and respect in the court. Not one more disturbance came from the gallery.

Judge Harrison's gaze swept to Fanny. "Counselor?"

Fanny sprang to her feet. "Your Honor, Mr. Franks, born and raised in Rochester, is not a flight risk. Nor does he have a record of prior offenses. His uncle is Raymond Franks—the owner of Rochester's pride, Frank's Pasta Company. Mr. Franks has raised Kenneth Franks like a son in his Rochester home. He has employed his nephew for considerable years at his company. Up to a few weeks ago, Kenneth Franks had lived with his uncle since the age of four. Today, Kenneth Franks is respectfully married, has a baby on the way, and he and his wife live with his mother-in-law, Helene Kellerman, at her Bridgehaven, New York home." Due to Kenny's charges of murder, her next few words would be a long shot. "If it pleases the court, I respectfully request that Kenneth Franks be released on his own recognizance."

Judge Harrison pulled at his chin and stared blankly for a painfully long minute. "Taking into consideration the defendant's charges of murder, his outbursts in jail noted in the police record, yet his standing in the community, his young family, and his intellectual disability, and that the Defense has not received discovery from the prosecutor, I am setting bail at $100,000 and with the stipulation Kenneth Franks will reside with his uncle at Mr. Raymond Franks' Rochester home, effective immediately, under his supervision. I will also accept Kenneth Franks' wife to live with them and to relieve Mr. Raymond Franks while he is at work. That is if Mr. Raymond Franks and Mrs. Kenneth Franks can remain in Rochester and see that the defendant does not leave the residential premises, other than any medical treatment, and then only in the company of his uncle or attorney, until further court hearings. The defendant is not permitted to return to his job at his uncle's factory, nor seek employment elsewhere. Until bail is posted, the defendant is remanded into custody."

"If I may, Your Honor," Ray said, standing. "I'm Raymond Franks, Kenneth Franks' uncle. I'm prepared to post bail today for my nephew."

"Very well," Judge Harrison said. "This case is adjourned for the day. Further court dates will be set. Let's move swiftly so the next case can begin."

Fanny patted Kenny on the back. "You did well."

"What happens now?" Kenny said, eyeing the deputy who had brought him into the courtroom not even fifteen minutes ago. "Am I going to jail again? Will I ever see Gina again?"

Kenny's life would be in jeopardy if down the road he was determined guilty. Yet, he did not understand what had just occurred. More importantly, his number one concern was whether he would ever see the single person who loved him the most. Living in the present, rather than the past or future, had benefits.

"The deputy will put you in a holding cell for a short time while your uncle posts bail for you. The judge has set you temporarily free, but you must live with your uncle and cannot work while waiting to see if a grand jury issues an indictment for a future trial. It also means that you cannot leave your uncle's property unless there are arrangements to take you to court or a doctor. And Gina will live with you and your uncle."

"Okay. Uncle Raymond is a good uncle. And Gina is my wonderful wife."

Fanny smiled. "Didn't Gina live with you at your uncle's home when you first married?"

"Yes. We lived with him. Uncle Raymond likes Gina."

Then, the transition should go smoothly. "Excellent."

Without a struggle, Kenny permitted the deputy to handcuff him once again. With a tug by the officer, Kenny walked alongside him. Suddenly, he stopped. The courtroom, with people coming and going, was a dizzying swirl of changes. But there Gina stood. Pale-faced and expressionless, she watched each second of her husband she could seize as if her world—her life—had played out like a horrible movie. One still shot after another, and she could only observe, unable to be a vital participant whose input could influence the outcome.

"Gina," Kenny called out. "I'll see you soon."

She kissed her fingertips and blew him a kiss, feet rooted to the courtroom floor until Kenny was escorted out the same side door as he had entered minutes ago, irrevocable steps toward a life he did not want to live.

CHAPTER TEN

Gina, Bridgehaven, August 20, 1961

Gina awoke at 4:00 a.m. She sat up in bed and switched off the alarm clock set for two hours later. She never slept well with the nuisance contraption ticking. Fortunately, her morning-afternoon-evening sickness had backed off, a bodily experience that defied the logical need for her body to nurture her developing child. With a hand over her belly, she imagined she might never need an alarm clock to wake her once her little one was born. They learned the exciting baby news a month and a half after she and Kenny married. The approximate due date, February 22, 1962, seemed far away and also as coming around the proverbial corner. When she first shared with Kenny that he would soon be a daddy, he immediately asked her how she felt.

"A little queasy, off and on." Actually, that was putting it mildly. She avoided telling him the details. He would have taken the blame, which was his not to own.

"That's not what I meant," he had said as they sat side by side on the sofa in Uncle Raymond's living room. In the softest tone she had yet to hear him use, rich yet fluffy sweet, like cotton candy on a cold March day, he said, "Are you happy, Gina? I want you to smile about the baby. I want to see your eyes dance. Your steps light, like you're free. Like you're flying. Without worries. Because I love you. Together, we will love our baby." He kissed her adoringly on the lips. When he pulled back, he added, "I want you to be happy. You're wonderful. Our baby will be wonderful to us."

Straightforward words, there was no room for misinterpretation. Yet, the words addressed the topics that had crossed her mind a few times too often, spanning the days between the time the doctor confirmed her pregnancy to the second she and Kenny sat down on the sofa to have *the talk* that would change their lives forever. Countless people had already narrowed their opinionated gaze when she and Kenny passed by, bumping up the volume of their unsolicited viewpoints of them as a couple. "Look at those two. If she had any smarts, she wouldn't dig that brainless idiot who can't even string two thoughts together." "She must be desperate if she married that creep." Their looks were judgmental. Their words packed cruelty. Their actions—scurrying away from them as if she and Kenny carried the plague—were horrifying. Not for the first time and sadly she believed nor the last, had she questioned who was the true chump.

Kenny tolerated the antagonism well. A usually calm man, he handled adversaries better than most. Another reason, among thousands, why she loved him. "Gina, honey. Just ignore them. They don't understand. So, they say stupid stuff. So what?"

He was right. Of course. Then again, she did not understand most things, lately. Like, Kenny's charges of murder. His living, again, with his uncle. The subsequent growing of her grandmother's frostiness to her. And certainly, not the news from the other side of the Atlantic, in her home country of Germany, of the wall being built.

Germany. It would be ten o'clock there compared to her New York time of four a.m. Groping for the pull chain of the light beside the bed, she switched it on and dialed up her radio on the nightstand. She had a little while until Grammy drove her and her once again packed belongings to Uncle Raymond's. Since all she had left was to shower and eat breakfast, she could listen to a little of the news Grammy discouraged her from tuning in.

"From the Marienfelde Reception Center in the southwest section of West Berlin, I'm Robert Von Biel reporting live." The reception center was a foreign place to her and she grew curious why it made the international airwaves. Wags jumped on the bed and tucked himself beside her left hip. She loved the pup but was glad Grammy had agreed to take care of her furry guy and keep him with her. Although Grammy had become more aloof lately, despite her fussing, she'd never mistreat an animal.

"Operated by West Germany and West Berlin," Von Biel continued, "the Marienfelde refugee transit center is no stranger to the great waves of immigrants that have fled eastern Germany—now East Germany—between 1950 to the time construction began on the Berlin Wall. After obtaining food, medical treatment, housing, and identity papers—as their predecessors had to during the Second World War—these settlers stated they needed a permanent place to live. And, they say, they desire to live in a country that offers them equal political and social rights. American Vice President Lyndon B. Johnson has met with West Berlin's Mayor Willy Brandt. The Vice President had received cheers and applause after crediting President John F. Kennedy for directing him to the meeting. Vice President Johnson says he and the American President will uphold their pledge to West Berlin that the Western Allies will protect West Berliners from an Eastern Bloc advancement into West Berlin. Folks, Mayor Brandt, standing beside the American Vice President has taken a handkerchief to his face... he is wiping his eyes and nose..."

Enough. Gina turned off the radio. She too would have sobbed if she had stood in the packed crowd of people not knowing what tomorrow would bring them. Despite life centering around Kenny's arrest and his upcoming trial, and attempting to take care of the physical needs her changing body dictated, she had snatched glimpses of newspaper photographs of Berlin families ripped apart from each other, pictures of refugees caught between two worlds, yet living with no place to call a true home. Apparently, much more had enfolded than she was aware of. Life again stood in limbo for many, eerily similar to the pre-roundup state of Jews and other non-Aryans during the last war. Gina hugged her middle, wondering when she would first feel the baby's movement, and thinking that if her family circumstances were different, she could have been born Jewish, or disabled as seen from the Nazi viewpoint. If so, she might not have survived the recent world war. *Disabled.* The word squatted on her tongue with a bitter tang.

Kenny.

If her husband had lived in Nazi Germany, would the SS have gone after him, taking him away, only to disappear and never be seen again?

Grammy and she.

If they had remained in Germany rather than moved to the US, they might live on the east side of the Berlin Wall, or trapped in a refugee camp like Marienfelde.

Curious, Gina slid open the nightstand's drawer and withdrew the *Webster's Dictionary* she kept available for her nightly reading. She enjoyed exploring the meanings of intriguing words to expand her vocabulary. Now, she raced to the Rs. Refugee. A person forced into leaving one's country to escape war, persecution, or catastrophe. A displaced person. An asylum seeker. She fanned her fingers across her belly. On the day when she first said hello to Kenny, she had never imagined falling in love and marrying the man of her dreams, the perfect life partner for her, let alone soon having his baby. Nor, had she ever thought, at three months into her pregnancy, she and her unborn baby would become refugees.

She pitched forward and squeezed her eyes tightly shut as images whirled through her mind. Memories? Of shouts and a baby crying. At least, it sounded like a baby. More yelling. *Mama... want Mama... Gimme Mama.* Of a door slamming shut. Silence. Like the void filling her heart back during a not-too-faraway time. Perhaps, Gina was already an experienced refugee.

Good memories had to exist. Somewhere. Right? Would she see the smiles from a long time ago if she concentrated? Hear the comforting words once spoken? The smiles and words must have existed to have been ingrained in her memory, at least occasionally. She hoped.

Reassuring images and sounds failed to come, though. Instead, she was again whipped into the past, remembering a trip that had become foggy in her memories. She saw herself peering out of a plane window. There were clouds so large she thought she could touch them if only she knew how to open the window. Yet, something was not right.

"Grammy," she said, her gaze still fixed on the window. "I want to go home."

"Gina, sweetheart," Grammy said, calling her for the first time the newer version of Regina. "We're going to our new home in a new country. You'll like it in New York. This is a safe plane. It's taking us to our new beginning."

"I don't want to die."

"Die?" Grammy had repeated, her brows shooting up. "Do you know what it means to die?"

Gina shook her head. When she glanced at her grandmother, she wondered if dying was like leaving behind someone you loved. Like her mama? She turned away from Grammy. How could she ask why they were leaving someone if she could not think of a name or summon a face? Instead, she only heard the haunting words fading rapidly from her mind: *Regina... I love you, honey.* Had this person from her past ever truly existed? Upon landing in New York, when Grammy woke her, she tried to remember their old house. No image came to mind. Did it have two brick chimneys on either side of the house, crisscross windowpanes in the parlor, or a large kitchen where Grammy baked cookies? Did the house creak in the middle of winter, or did old steps groan when she walked upstairs to her bedroom? And, what of the smells? She remembered the fresh scent of washing clothes, the rich, earthy smell of potting of flowers, and the sugary aroma of freshly baked cookies. As if they could chase away the insecurity of what dangers tomorrow might bring these scents made her happy. Now, sadness filled her about the country once called home and their left behind lives. Gone. Like it had never occurred. Perhaps this way was for the best. She held back her feelings and memories from her grandmother, sensing Grammy also had painful memories she refused to share or could not recall clearly.

A soft rap came at her bedroom door, jolting Gina back to the present. Still at her side, Wags lifted his head from the mattress.

"Gina," Grammy called. "I see your light is on. Are you okay?"

"I'm far-out fine. Don't worry."

Grammy nudged the door open a crack. She poked her head in. "May I come in?"

Her grandmother sounded polite and considerate. That figured. "Since you're practically in, sure, why not?" Gina wanted to pump her sole caretaker for information about her past whose scattered pieces were scrambled in her mind. She was in no mood for a scrap with Grammy and backpedaled. "Sorry, Grammy. Lately, I can't rely on my mood to save my life."

"Understandable. It comes with the territory of expecting a baby."

"What doesn't?" Regretting her comment, she patted the empty spot in an attempted peace offering. "Want to sit next to me? I'll try not to bite your ear off."

Grammy surprised her with a chuckle. "Given your predicament, I won't hold it against you if you do. Yes, sure. I'll sit with you."

When Grammy sat beside her, the next question sailed from Gina's mouth. "Tell me of your experiences of when you were expecting my mother. You've never shared a peep." Grammy narrowed her eyes and peered over the rim of her glasses as if the look alone could state that plenty of good reasons existed why she kept mum when it came to her personal history.

"Oh, come on," Gina said, managing a playful girlish whine. "Tell me. You might cheer me up—my body is going whacky and I feel like this baby is holding me hostage."

A touch-me-not woman, Grammy shocked her again and grasped her hand. "Don't worry. You'll fare better during the second trimester. I did."

Gina held her breath. *Go on. Tell me more.*

"The big thing for me was that I passed out often. When your mother was expecting you, she did too."

"At least I'm not lightheaded," Gina said, hoping to encourage Grammy to share more. "Tell me how your parents treated you when you were pregnant with my mom."

"Would you like to shower or walk Wags?"

"Was my mother married when I came along? Tell me about my father. Was he charming? He swept my mother off her feet and—"

Grammy stood. "I'm going to make us a nice breakfast. Can you tolerate eggs and a homemade blueberry muffin? I didn't care for the berries at Wegmans yesterday, so I pulled up to the farm stand at the town line. Sure enough, they had the loveliest, hugest blueberries I've ever seen. Sweet, like you wouldn't believe."

"Fine. Don't be disappointed in me if I take one bite and pass on the rest."

"Oh, I won't be disappointed when it comes to you and food. I understand."

Gina watched as Grammy hurried out of the bedroom as if she finally had a purpose in life—cooking her a farewell meal. Troubling, though, were the words Grammy kept from her, words Gina could sense clearly: *I'm disappointed with you when it comes to everything else other than your present eating preferences.*

CHAPTER ELEVEN

Gina, Rochester, September 4, 1961

"Gina, Uncle Raymond says I'm crawling out of my skin. What does he mean?" Seated at the kitchen table where they were finishing up their lunch, Kenny lifted his arms. "Look, my arms still have skin on them," he said with a cheeky grin.

Gina recognized Kenny's joking spirit. Although he took figures of speech literally, the one thing she had picked up immediately upon first meeting Kenny was his cool cat sense of humor. She smiled compassionately at him. No one she knew, including herself, dealt with confinement easily.

Today, Labor Day, folks spent their time outdoors, enjoying picnics, parades, or other festive get-togethers. New Yorkers were no exception, fussing over this special holiday before winter blew in and stayed for five or more months. With Franks' Pasta Company closed for the day, Uncle Raymond planned to host a company picnic at one of the city parks. Earlier at breakfast, he had expressed his misgivings over his need to appear at the picnic. Without hesitation, Kenny told him not to worry and he was happy to have Gina home. The last thing Gina wanted to do was to wave a carefree day in Kenny's face. Somehow, despite the court restriction on her husband making him housebound, she wanted him to have a grand day.

"Oh, you," she said, trying to keep a smile in her tone. "When you crawl out of your skin it's because you want to do something else, usually because you're bored from doing the same old, same old."

"Like the baby. Our baby will be new. I'm excited!"

"Exactly. See, you understand. Uncle Raymond probably means you're tired of staying cooped up in the house. Are you?"

"Yes. I love to walk. All over. I love being outside."

Kenny had no qualms if it were a January and twenty-below-zero day or a blazing hot and humid August one. As long as he was outdoors, he was happy. Since Gina had moved in with Kenny and his uncle, adapting to living with restrictions had gone smoothly. With the house to themselves more often than not, privacy was never an issue for Gina and Kenny.

"Hmm. I have an idea." With lunch now over, Gina stood to clear the dishes from the table. Kenny jumped to his feet.

"I'll do it. You sit." He reached for Gina's dish. "You didn't eat the potato salad. Is your belly still floppy?"

"No. I'm fine—the best in a long time. It just tastes odd." Many foods had become off-tasting lately, but she didn't want to discuss this with Kenny, nor tell him about her emotional state. She snatched the lunch dish from him and set it on the counter beside the sink. "I think I'm crawling out of my skin, too. Want to take a walk?"

"We can't go where I want to go. On a long walk. I love to walk. So where can we go?"

She squeezed his hand. "Kenny, because you adore your walks, and walking is healthy, let's go for one, anyway. We can still walk around the house." She loved this kitchen. A large room with fancy brickwork around the oven, gray and tan slate flooring, and a stained glass window behind the table made for a warm and welcoming area to relax in. However, the Cobbs Hill Rochester neighborhood house certainly was not claustrophobic. Situated east of the downtown section, it had five bedrooms, a living room, a library, an office, and a music room, plus a large eat-in kitchen and a formal dining room. Its terraces overlooked groomed gardens. Best of all, the estate sat on a corner chunk of city property that graced three acres and offered a sense of privacy in a city. Yet, Gina related to what her husband was going through while confined. "At least your uncle's house and grounds are a nice slice of paradise."

"Yes, it is," Kenny said. Gone was the familiar sparkle in his eyes she adored.

When Gina first turned eighteen, she believed being an adult centered around independence. Looking back, the newly founded freedom of making her own decisions based upon what would be best for herself proved to be a power trip. Now, adulthood had redefined itself to mean the acceptance of caring for others whom she loved. The ones that matter the most to her. She gave a sideways glance at Kenny. She never wanted to say a final goodbye to him. At least, not until he was in his upper nineties, and she in her young to mid-eighties. If truth be told, by the time she was in her elder years, she would want to bargain for as much time as possible until their final goodbye arrived.

"Let me soak our dishes in the sink," she said. "And while they're sitting there, we'll go outside and walk around the house a few times and enjoy the late summer air."

"I like walking with you. It's not the same, though. Not like taking long walks."

She wanted to take his hand and stroll along a boardwalk overlooking the Atlantic. There, they would trot down the stairs leading to the sand, slip off their shoes, and collect seashells, walk into the cool water when the waves lapped toward the shore, or build the most elaborate sandcastle time and their imagination allowed. She wanted to hop in a car and drive them to the border, cross into Canada, and play tourist for the whole week. They would stroll through the cities of Toronto, Montreal, and Quebec, then swing to Nova Scotia. And if she could not manage those amazing feats for Kenny, her treasure, her baby's father, they could walk out of the estate's gate and take a five-mile walk in whichever direction he wanted. They could hitch a ride, never to return home. They would walk until they found a place that accepted her and Kenny unconditionally. New friends and acquaintances would greet them with a great big *hello, so glad you're here with us!* They would be seen as a couple committed to each other and their soon-to-be child. What they did not need were interference, discouragement, or condemnation.

However, one major obstacle to her daydream was the harsh reality that Kenny would be slammed into a jail cell if he violated his bail restrictions. She would be seen as an accomplice to Kenny's disobedience to the judge's bail conditions and also take up residency in a cell. Bye-bye dreams. Bye-bye baby Franks raised by two loving parents.

No way could she make a run for *freedom* with Kenny who meant everything to her, despite what the rest of the world thought of him, his supposed lack of intelligence, or folks who claimed she had a shrinking brain for even wanting to marry him.

She looked him in the eye. "Well, then, let's make the best of it."

Together, they piled the two dishes, glasses, and silverware into the sink. She ran the water hot, stopped up the basin, and squirted dish detergent into the sink. While the sink filled with water, its contents submerged like her own thoughts threatening to pull her under. Soapsuds landed on the tip of her nose. A chuckle floated from Kenny's sweet lips.

"Hey, what's that for?" she asked as she faced her lifetime partner. While Kenny's eyes twinkled with a spark she had not seen in a while, her thoughts sobered even more. She wanted to yell across America for all those who easily and eagerly discouraged them as a couple: *By choice, I married this man. Do you hear me? Do you understand? Do you even care about us, or are you out to insult us like you're trying to win a game? Maybe you're the simpleminded folks—not us. Why don't you all grow up and leave us alone? My husband's a good person. He wouldn't hurt anyone... wouldn't kill anyone...*

"Gina? I was playing with you. With the suds. Just for fun."

"Yes, I know," she said quietly. She scooped her index finger in the soapy water and planted a dollop on his nose. Unlike him, she could not muster a giggle. Rather, she shook her head to free the sticky substance of lopsided thoughts stalking her mind. "I need some fresh air."

Kenny turned off the water. "Okay. Let's go."

Gina wiped her hands on a nearby red and white-checkered dishcloth and then led the way. Exiting through the glassed arboretum, they passed by the yucca that reminded her of the desert; various palms for the illusion of sunny Florida; jade and rubber plants; and her favorite, a Weeping Fig tree. They stepped outdoors onto the canopied patio. The blue upholstered chaise lounge chairs called out to her, inviting her to cozy up for a while, prop up her feet, and rest her eyes shut, pushing away all thoughts of life about to visit. Instead, she slipped her hand around Kenny's and they continued down the path that led to a copse of trees providing pleasant shade. Then they continued to the garden. Although past its June prime, the lush greenery gave way to the view of a cloudless blue sky.

"Want to play a game?" Gina asked as they entered the garden area.

"What kind of game?" He grinned. "I love games."

She loved her husband who could sound like an excitable boy while simultaneously coming across as a mature man. He was never dull, for sure. If only others knew the true Kenny, they would not fling their condescending tsk-tsks expressions as they passed by them, or the rare couple of people who shot them pitying glances.

"Gina? You've gone away. Again."

Incident… charges of murder. Ugly words. While she did not want to contemplate those words, she could not stop thinking of them. Married, she would soon welcome their baby into the world, bringing on an eternity of loving, caring, and nurturing. Maybe other children would grace their lives. Years of birthday parties, and the holiday celebrations of Thanksgiving and Christmas and July fourth cookouts. A first school dance. Graduation. Driving grownup Billy or Jane off to college. Weddings. Grandchildren. Anything other than visiting each other behind a Plexiglas window and only being able to speak via a phone on their respective sides of the medium that separates them like a wall built between two countries. Then again, it might come down to graveside chats. Both possibilities were heartbreakingly sad.

Kenny spun her around and kissed her sweetly on her lips. His eyes widened. "You must have played hide and seek. But right in front of me. I found you. Can you stay with me? Don't disappear again. Okay?"

"I'll try not to." She slipped her arms around his slender waist and peered into his eyes. "Ready to play the game?"

He shrugged. "What kind of game?"

"A game of pretend. I'll begin. Can you picture me as looking different?"

His gaze immediately riveted to her middle and he grinned. "You already look different. With the baby."

"No, sweetie." At the beginning of her second trimester, a definite roundness of her belly showed. Although exciting, at that very second, she wanted to escape all things baby-wise. She fluffed up her hair. "I mean, can you imagine me looking different? Maybe with blond hair—I can dye it if you'd like. How about if I grow it long, to my tush?"

"Nope."

"Really? You don't want me to be Hollywood glamourous?"

"You're already beautiful. I like you just like you."

"Aww. You're sweet. I appreciate you. It's so important to talk and to learn more about each other. Know why, Mr. Franks?"

"You can call me Kenny," he said. A little lift in his tone showed he understood her and played along. "Tell me."

"Because I want to stay married to you, forever and ever." *And not worry if you will be found guilty, electrocuted, forever taken away from me.* She swallowed dryly. "Your turn."

"I don't walk a lot, since... You know. The judge told me to stay here." He patted his gut. "I still eat a lot. What happens if I grow old and fat?"

She shrugged her lack of concern. "So what? I'll still love you. Everyone changes as they grow older. It's normal." *See, Kenny. You are normal, after all. Will you be allowed to live, to grow flabby, thin-haired, and wrinkly with me?* That was all she wanted, and of course, to raise their child, together.

He scraped his knuckles against the five o'clock shadow starting to show. "Want me to grow a beard? A mustache?"

"For a sophisticated look, like a college professor?"

Kenny nodded.

She feathered her fingers across his scratchy cheeks. "You already look sophisticated to me. But if you want a hairy face, groovy."

He laughed. "I don't want a hairy face. Let's play more."

"Okay. Let's each name one thing the other doesn't know."

His brow wrinkled. "Like a secret?"

"Well, it could be a secret. Like, if you hate oatmeal but never got around to telling me. I was thinking more along the side of something intriguing." After a pause, she added, "You know, fascinating."

"You start."

"I wrote a song about you."

"You did? Will you sing it to me? What are the words? When did you write it?"

"That's a lot of questions."

"Yes," he said. "Okay. I'll ask one question. What's the song's name?"

Gina shrugged. "I haven't come up with a title, yet. I guess it could be *When I'm Blue*. You know, blue means sad."

"Is it a sad song?"

"Not really. Yes, the song begins when I'm sad. Then I think about you, and how we're together. I become all happy again. And alive. Like all of a sudden, I'm surrounded by beautiful, cheerful colors."

He glowed like a rainbow after a storm. Did she brighten his world with vibrant colors like he did for her?

"I like that, Gina. It makes me happy. Very happy."

"I'll sing it for you later." She winked, and added, "When we go to bed tonight."

"Yes," he murmured, his voice husky. "That would be wonderful. I look forward to that." After a few beats, he said in a more playful, non-sensual tone, "I want to hear this song. Maybe I can learn the words. I like to sing."

Kenny liked to sing? She had never heard him, not even a hum.

"When I sing," he continued, "it's like I become smart. Like my brain is a free bird."

"You mean because your thoughts fly loose and you sing without worry and fear?"

"Yes." He smiled proudly. "No fear."

She learned something new about this beautiful man each day and loved it. She hoped the court case against Kenny went well. Convinced a person changed daily and there never seemed to be enough time to learn every nuance, she wanted life to gift them another sixty or more years together.

"Kenny, you're wonderful," she said as if watching a pastoral scene of sheep grazing in a field surrounded by majestic mountains. "I love learning new, amazing things about you."

"I have something else to tell you."

"All right. Tell me something no one else knows."

"I don't want to change."

A pinch twisted between her eyes. "What do you mean?"

"I like me. I don't want to become smarter and be like everyone else."

Gina thought back to Kenny's court appearance. Afterward, Fanny had cornered Gina alone in the courthouse corridor outside the courtroom.

"I'm sorry, Gina," Fanny had said.

She could not imagine why. It had all worked out well. Kenny had not returned to jail. With Fanny on his side, he stood a chance for a future. "There's nothing to apologize for."

"Yes, there is. I had to say that Kenny is mentally disabled. They weren't nice words."

Gina had glanced at the open door to the courtroom where relief and anguish occurred, year after year. "Fanny, my husband is smart enough to understand who he is, what he is, and he understands what has to be said to help him."

The courthouse and Fanny faded from Gina's mind. Presently, she stood beside her husband. She would continue to love Kenny minute by minute. Any good wife would do the same. The horrors of what might happen could take a hike. She pressed against his chest and wrapped her arms around his neck. "I'm glad you don't want to change because I love you the exact way you are."

CHAPTER TWELVE

Fanny, Rochester, September 6, 1961
The day had dragged by so slowly that it practically pinched Fanny left and right. David, her assistant, thorough in his investigations, finally phoned at six p.m. An hour later he dropped off his report, which she spent the next two hours devouring, making notes, and planning her strategy for her visit with Kenny and Gina the next day.

Despite being born and raised in a neighboring town to Rochester, Fanny had limited association with the city's Cobbs Hill neighborhood as a child. As an adult, she spent countless hours establishing a law practice that kept her busy with the city's courts and related venues. While she expected Ray to have a nice house and groomed grounds, she marveled at the white-stone house—one outstanding, handsome property. A brick chimney on both sides of the house, large windows throughout, a front double-door entrance, and a slate-roofed three-bay garage that matched the house's roof, had her jaw-dropping in amazement. The groomed lawn, potted greenery, and what looked like gardens in the distance added *wows* to her thoughts. Had she expected a less stunning place? Owned by a man who could afford the ridiculously high bail the judge had set for his nephew, the place undoubtedly exuded opulence. Yet, the truth of why she was here rebounded in her mind: no amount of money could save Kenny if the jury found him guilty of murder and sentenced him to death. She needed to do her job without error.

Fanny rang the doorbell and was greeted by Ray, not by a butler like she had imagined. Ray's unexpected dressed-down attire of a blue shirt, blue jeans, and loafers removed her guilt over her casual white black-polka-dotted blouse and black capri pants.

"Hello, Fanny. Welcome. I hope you don't mind me playing hooky from work this morning so I can listen in as you talk with Kenny and Gina."

"Of course, that's fine."

"Excellent." Ray motioned her down a hall. "Kenny and Gina are in the kitchen, less stiff than my office and full of the nutty aroma of coffee. Or, if you're a tea enthusiast, we have a nice selection too."

"You got me at coffee. Thank you."

Ray led her into the kitchen. "Look who I found at the front door."

"Good morning, everyone," Fanny said. She looked about the splendid room. "Wow. This kitchen is larger than the whole downstairs of my house. I love it!"

Ray invited her to join them at the table. She sat, setting her briefcase on the floor beside her chair. She happily thanked Ray when he brought her coffee in a floral Wedgwood cup. "Am I in an elegant restaurant or a lovely home of friends?"

"Friends," Ray and Kenny said in unison. Gina agreed.

"Let me know when you'd like more," Ray said and sat opposite her. "Cream and sugar are on the table."

"Thanks, but I take my coffee black. I'll let you know when it's refill time." Fanny took her first sip and breathed out a contented sigh. She looked at Kenny and Gina sitting at the two opposite ends. She wished her visit was social, what fun it would be for Ray to share about the house's history, and if he had plans to make any changes. She also wanted to ask Gina how she felt. Had she considered baby names yet? Had she bought any baby outfits? And, Kenny. How was he sleeping? Eating? Did he have hobbies to occupy his time? Then, she realized the difference. Her curiosity over Ray and Gina centered around the present and future. With Kenny, the future was dodged, her focus had circled only the immediate present. In the name of concentrating one hundred percent on her client's case, she shook from the sorrow that threatened to engulf her.

Fanny glanced at the kitchen's entrance. "Is Helene here?"

"Grammy's at work," Gina said, disappointment and relief both obvious.

"Okay, then. Let's begin," Fanny said, fishing out David's report and her trusty notepad and pen. "David Lorrie, my assistant, is topnotch at discovering key elements to the cases I represent. He dropped off a preliminary report last evening." How could she tell these three hopeful people waiting on a miracle that not one witness was found to help strengthen Kenny's defense? The facts were the facts; unable to be altered. With all eyes upon her, she continued. "David interviewed the business owners whose shops abut the lot where the..." She mentally said an apology to Kenny for any bluntness she may use, but they were dealing with a dead body. "Where the police found the *victim* and Kenny. David also did extensive interviews with the occupants of the nearby apartment buildings."

"Fanny," Kenny said. His white long-sleeved shirt rolled up to his elbows gave him more of a college preppy look than one accused of murder. "It's okay. Samuel is dead. You can say that. You can say his name, too."

"Thanks. This makes the things we need to discuss easier." Although Fanny was relieved Kenny could now distinguish Samuel as deceased, which lessened her worry about him confusing matters in a future testimony—if he were to take the stand—a wave of jitters seized her. Determined not to bring attention to herself, she examined the list of names in the report. She hoped her voice remained strong. "Beginning with the apartment dwellers, all except one person was elsewhere at the time of the alleged crime."

"Alleged?" Gina pushed her coffee cup between her two hands as if two rival gangs were going after each other, then pushed it away from her altogether. A splash of the creamy brown beverage flew from her cup and splattered the cuff of her soft yellow sweater. "Samuel was murdered. The autopsy report showed he didn't just keel over from a heart attack. And, Kenny is charged with this crime, and yet, it's still alleged?"

"Correct," Fanny said, fishing out the medical examiner's report to reference. "The cause of death of the male victim, age forty, is not attributed to myocardial infarction—commonly called a heart attack—or a stroke. His death was due to strangulation." She set the report down. "I am using the term *alleged crime* in a legal sense. To date, there is no proof that Kenny killed Samuel. By the time Kenny reached Samuel, Samuel lay on the ground, and the culprit responsible for killing Samuel was still on the loose."

Fanny paused to let her words sink into their minds. "We will state that Kenny saw no other person in the rear lot, and most certainly did not attack Samuel. No witnesses have stepped forward to say they saw Kenny act against Samuel. So, the crime is *alleged* at the hands of Kenny because there is no proof. Keep in mind this is all prep work. We're still expecting the DA's discovery information. And, to see if our case will appear before a grand jury who will determine if there will be an indictment. If there will be a grand jury, realize that what's known as the *burden of proof* is on the prosecutor. Not on us, the defense. The DA will have first to convince the grand jury, then the trial jury, that all the evidence points the guilty finger at the defense—at Kenny. In other words, the DA will need to remove any traces of reasonable doubt in the collective minds of the jury. He must present solid evidence, not conjecture or suggestion, which he will accomplish by interviewing potential witnesses, expert witnesses, and other key elements that will work on behalf of the People, in other words, the state of New York."

Fanny looked at each one of them. She saw Gina's worry in her downturned mouth and creased brows. Noted Ray's disgust by the slash of red on each of his cheeks. Kenny concerned her the most. With his right brow lifted higher than the left, and his mouth pursed, he wore the look of confusion. "Understand, so far?"

"As best as I can understand nonsense," Gina murmured.

Ray nodded. Kenny's facial features remained unchanged.

"Now I want to tell you how I will build the case," Fanny continued. "Unlike the prosecutor's job of convincing a future jury and judge that Kenny is guilty, and to do so clearly and rationally, without reasonable doubt, it is the defense's job—my job—to present Kenny's side of the story. I do so by gathering evidence and lining up witnesses who show Kenny is not guilty because there are solid reasons to form *doubt* in the jury's thoughts. Therefore, this will influence the odds that the jury will tender a not guilty verdict."

"Tender?" Kenny asked.

"It means offer," Gina said. "In this situation, the jury will say you are not guilty because Fanny did her job correctly."

Accustomed to clients and their family members dishing out pressure on Fanny that the client would be acquitted of charges *only if she did her job correctly*, Gina's straightforward words did not surprise her. Rather, she was touched and awed by her gentleness and patience with her husband. However, she held back a nod.

"The DA's job is to convince the jury that no other explanation can point away from the defendant's guilt. Whereas, it's the defense's job to make the jury believe the prosecutor's case against Kenny is full of holes, showing reasonable doubt about Kenny's guilt. Thus, Kenny could not have killed Samuel and a guilty verdict cannot be given."

"Innocent until proven guilty," Ray murmured.

Although grateful for Ray's understanding, Fanny needed them to see things through the eyes of the law. "More accurately put, Kenny is not guilty until proven otherwise. Each juror must enter the courtroom with this view. It is the prosecutor's responsibility to flip the no-guilt status around. It is his job to convince each jury member that there is absolutely no doubt Kenny murdered Samuel. On the opposite side, it is my job to convince each juror that *insufficient* evidence shows Kenny is the killer because the case is riddled with holes of reasonable doubt and Kenny is not guilty of Samuel's death." After a slight pause, she added, "I realize I'm repeating myself, but it's important to understand what the DA and my responsibilities are, and the importance of reasonable doubt."

"Sounds like a game," Kenny said. "Not a fun game."

"Yes, indeed." Fanny smiled at Kenny, in full realization, once again, that her client understood more than the supposed intellect who wouldn't give him credit when acknowledgment was due.

"Not one witness has popped up?" Gina asked.

"I didn't mean to jump ahead of myself. From what I've seen of the DA's report, which is limited at this point, Mr. Hayes only has circumstantial—inconclusive—evidence. The material he's gathered may paint a picture of Kenny as guilty on the surface. However, if one looks carefully one would see the so-called evidence does *not* prove a thing. Again, I want to emphasize the *so far* part. This case is just beginning. My job is to make the jury disregard any circumstantial evidence. So that we can all have a full understanding of what happened, let's back up." She took a fast sip of coffee and, with a polite smile, passed on Ray's offer for a second cup. "David talked with one man who had just arrived home from work. A Steven Meinz, who drives a cab. However, he stated he'd headed straight into the shower and hadn't heard a shout."

"Isn't that his word, only?" Ray asked. "Maybe he wasn't telling the truth about the shower business and not hearing a shout."

"It's a possibility. If we use him as a witness, he'd be sworn to tell the truth. In this case, his not hearing any shouts is also testimony he did not distinctly hear Kenny yell. Or, for that matter, notably, Samuel. Mr. Meinz heard *no* one shouting, *no* one threatening the other nor did he hear a cry of pain or a call for help."

"I didn't see anyone," Kenny said.

"Exactly," Fanny said, noticing Kenny had not drunk his orange juice. Instead, like Gina, he had pushed his beverage away. "Which correlates with—agrees with—what you've said from the very beginning."

"And the business owners?" Gina asked.

"The area in question is run-down, with three businesses whose property borders the lot. The first is the out-of-business stationery store with accessible yardage to the area where the victim was found. It has a legal easement of the alleyway and the lot. The store is vacant; its owner, Marcus White, is hospitalized in Florida. David interviewed the owner's niece and she stated her uncle now resides in a nursing home, suffering from dementia. David has a call out to Mr. White's doctor." Fanny sifted through David's report. "The second business, Christine's Beauty Parlor, also shares the easement of the alleyway and the lot. Christine's closes early at three p.m. on Fridays, the day of the alleged crime. Owned by Bernadette Singleton—"

"No Christine?" Kenny asked.

"Christine was Bernadette's grandmother—it's an old family business. At the end of the business day, Mrs. Singleton cleaned up in the shop's front area. She states she saw no one running into the alleyway, nor heard disturbances. In fact, during her interview with David, she appeared more concerned with being alone at the time of the supposed incident, saying she wouldn't have known how to defend herself if a thief or other troublemaker looked to give her trouble. When she exited the shop via the front door, she went home. Her departure preceded the police's arrival." Fanny tucked the report into her briefcase.

"Pardon me, Fanny," Ray said. "I believe you mentioned three businesses had openings to the rear lot where Samuel was found. We've heard about two. The other?"

She had saved the most troubling one for last. "David is looking further into The Rusty Nail, a hardware store, whose front entrance is on the opposite block and faces the other side. The back of the business abuts the lot where the alleged incident occurred. The owner, Rusty Coleman, states he heard one gunshot from the direction of the street frontage, not the lot. Although he phoned the police, not having supposedly witnessed Samuel or Kenny, he did not direct the police to the rear lot where they were." Fanny paused for another sip of coffee.

"Then who did?" Gina asked.

"That, folks, on top of who committed Samuel's murder, is the mystery we face." She looked directly at Kenny. "I need to talk with you. I'm afraid it's not pleasant."

"Alone?"

Fanny glanced at the others. They were his true support team. "Gina and your uncle are welcome to join us."

CHAPTER THIRTEEN

Helene, Berlin, Germany, May 15, 1942
Liselotte's due date in late June did not overly concern Helene. The birth of twins typically made mincemeat of a doctor's calculation. With the heartbeat of two babies finally detected, Helene watched her daughter with a careful eye. Well, as much as Liselotte tolerated, which became more of a creative endeavor as each day rolled into the next. Whether under the guise of sharing family history—true accounts and a bit stretched—noting past generations' birth successes, teaching Liselotte the basics of diaper folding, caring for a baby, and tips on child raising while ignoring her complaints of Helene being the wrong person to offer motherly advice.

"Listen, sweetheart—"

"Stop right there, Mutti... Mutter..." Scarlet streaks slashed Liselotte's cheeks. She had not referred to Helene as the more tender Mutti in years, not that Helene had encouraged her to do so. "I find it strange that you're calling me by endearments upon learning I'm carrying your grandbabies."

Helene had thought Liselotte a challenge to deal with since day one of her entry into the world, but an expectant Liselotte proved more like living within a perpetual tornado. Then again, Helene had to admit she had changed the day her daughter announced she was expecting not one, but possibly two babies. "You're right, Liselotte."

"Pardon? Did I hear what I think I did... what I've wanted to hear throughout my whole life?"

Helene tried not to roll her eyes at her daughter's dramatics, reminding herself, sadness and all, that Liselotte was an adolescent. An overgrown child at her worst. On her better days, a teen flirting with adult reasoning and responsibility. Reality won: a pregnant youth, with no husband in sight, and living in a country that had shoved the world into war. Not that she would state the latter to an SS officer.

"Yes, Liselotte. To repeat, you're right. You've needed more loving and affection from a better mother."

"I didn't mean to sound mean."

An apology—or the closest she might receive from her daughter—was what Helene had wanted to hear from Liselotte for several years. Was this a turning point in their fragile relationship? She looked toward the window darkened with blackout shades that stood between them and the night sky full of enemy planes passing overhead in search of another bomb target. "I didn't have encouragement from my parents. They were ashamed of me, their twenty-two-year-old pregnant daughter, one whose once upon-a-time hopeful husband had left her behind."

"Please. Spare me. The big difference between us is that unlike my mystery father, Gerhard, the father of my babies hasn't abandoned me. He's still in the Berlin area. We're just temporarily out of touch with each other."

What did her daughter imagine? Gerhard, coming around to thinking like a mature man with a baby—two babies on the way, not that he even knew—would gallop up to her doorstep like a prince out of a storybook, kneel upon a knee, and propose marriage? Present Liselotte with a key to their new home. Admit his shame for leaving her to begin with? Helene reminded herself to go easy on her frightened, hormonally cranky teenage daughter pushed into adulthood. She needed a mama more than ever because of the little girl she was unprepared to leave behind. Much of her agony was Helene's fault. She should have raised her daughter with a more observant eye, shaping her to become more mature, respectful of others, and to think level-headedly about practicalities rather than fantasies. However, if pressed, she had to admit she spoiled Liselotte from the start, not so much in material items but more harmful, that she seldom had used the word *no* to her demanding daughter. Now they were both suffering the consequences.

Helene breathed in deeply, summoning her patience. "And this is why I'm trying to make it up to you. Folks say *better late than never* for a reason."

"Mutter, what would you like to do suddenly that you have avoided all this time? Would you sit up with me at night when neither of us can sleep and we take turns sharing what a perfect world would look like, or some other nonsense? Confide girlish secrets with each other like we're old chums? I can't imagine you truly want to do any of these things. That's fine. I've grown used to your ways as separate from my ways."

"Please, Liselotte, I'm trying to be pleasant and you're twisting things into a mess."

"You're doing it again—blaming me." With hands poised on the rocker's arms, Liselotte hoisted herself from the chair, winced, and placing her hands on her lower back, paced up and down across the parlor's braided rug.

"Pain? Cramps?"

Liselotte snorted. "Isn't that the same?"

"Not exactly." Helene fought the urge to step up to her daughter's side and remained in her seat. She wanted to be a mother, to comfort her child, offer encouragement, and lend a shoulder to lean on during the times when Liselotte's anxiety got the best of her. Unsettling, most of all was herself. Helene had become wary of hovering over this lost girl of hers who was about to become a mother. Ironically, she was the one who had alienated the two of them. Yet, she had to try again to reach out to her daughter. "Please let me help. War doesn't make the best time to bring a child into this world—"

"It's a little late for that." Liselotte stroked her belly. "I certainly cannot reverse my circumstances."

Helene refused to take the stinging bait. "It's bad enough you're eating little, not that it's your fault. Even if we're not the Führer's target, rations are to blame for everyone's dwindling food supply." Aware of her daughter's sensitivity regarding weight, baby or no baby, she eyed Liselotte, pitying her and her circumstances. "Please don't take this the wrong way, but carrying twins, you should be larger than you are, which is a concern. You were in the beginning—when you first told me of your pregnancy, but you've been on the slim side these last few months. There are exceptions, like I said seconds ago, a country's rationed food supply doesn't help."

A grin—the first Helene had seen on her daughter in months—hung lopsidedly, dangling from her lips like a piece of food she was unsure if she liked enough to swallow whole.

"Too funny," Liselotte said. "All my childhood I wanted to be skinny, and here I am, unlike at the beginning of my pregnancy, needing to be fatter. Besides, I'm not sure why you're talking about food. Do you think a lack of good food pokes one with pain?" She stopped pacing. Her eyes bulged in surprise.

"What is it? Queasiness again? I shouldn't have talked about food."

"Mutter, there's a trickle down my leg."

·   ·   ·

Liselotte's labor crept slowly into the early morning hours. Helene tried to find out whether her daughter had pre-labor symptoms the past day or so, but with each question asked, she only received a groan. Not wanting to leave her daughter's side and alerting others of Liselotte's condition they had fortunately kept hidden from neighbors and acquaintances, Helene was torn between fetching a doctor herself or relying on the mercy of a neighbor to do so. As another hour slipped by and Liselotte's pain and anguish did not subside, Helene concluded she had to take a risk and reach out to the woman next door for help.

She squeezed Liselotte's hand. "I'm going next door to Frau Herman to ask her to summon the doctor. I promise a quick return."

"Don't go. I need you."

Helene heard the huff of her daughters' words, saw the terrified wide-eyed and brows peaked together expression, and absorbed her shudder as another contraction racked her body, all emphasizing how alone she and her daughter were in this big, scary world. The little medical studies she undertook—before she had to halt her studies altogether because of the severity of the war—had done little to prepare for the delivery of twin babies. With memories of her delivery of Liselotte sixteen years ago having faded fast and furiously, she could not summon practicalities to help. Without a phone in the house, she had no choice but to leave to ask for help.

"And that's why I must go for help. I'll hurry."

"No," Liselotte cried. "I'm going to die. Don't leave me."

Helene kissed her daughter's forehead. "Darling, you're about to become a mother to two wonderful babies. You will not die." *You will not leave me. You will not exit from my life, not now. Not ever. And you certainly will not take my grandbabies with you to the afterlife.* Helene raced from the bedroom, trotted down the stairs as if she were the teenager and not the adult, flew from the house, and pounded on her neighbor's door to beg for the good woman she barely knew to fetch the doctor for her daughter.

"It's the middle of the night. I can't go. It's dangerous to be outdoors past curfew." Frau Herman bracketed her hips with middle-aged beefy fingers. "Why, I'd be stopped like a worthless *Jude* and then the authorities will—"

Helene silenced the woman's prejudicial nonsense by shoving her hand into a skirt pocket and pulling a handful of Reichsmark notes. She'd feel the pinch but would do whatever it took to aid her daughter. "This will make it worthwhile."

The neighbor swiped the money from Helene's palm, peered down the street, and rushed into the night without shutting the door. In a charitable mood, Helene closed the door. She then hurried home to comfort Liselotte, praying the doctor would arrive shortly.

•   •   •

"I'm on fire," Liselotte screamed at the doctor. "Do something."

"The first baby's crowning. It's almost over." The bald doctor whose heavy-lidded gaze was a telltale sign he had witnessed his share of tragedy during the past few war years, murmured to Helene that he arrived just in time.

A perfectly healthy-looking baby girl made her appearance in the world. "Congratulations Mama. You have a girl," the doctor said. He showed Liselotte the baby and then gently handed the child to Helene. "You will hold your little daughter soon. Let's concentrate on getting the next baby out."

"Mutter," Liselotte said. "Is she breathing?"

"Of course." Helene beamed. "She has little tufts of blond hair, ten cute fingers and toes. She looks like an adorable, precious doll." On cue, the baby let out a wail. "And a fine pair of lungs."

"Regina," Liselotte called out. "That's her name."

Whether from a silly superstition, or a case of indecisiveness, Liselotte had oddly kept mum about naming her babies throughout her pregnancy. Helene wondered what the other child would be called.

"A lovely name for a beautiful girl," Helene said, squeezing her daughter's hand.

Liselotte thanked her. "I'm trying, Mutter. Trying to be a good daughter to you...but sometimes I fail... sometimes..." She screamed.

"No worries," Helene said. She hoped this talk between them was not out of fear, but rather from a sincere heart. "I'm here for you. I'm here for you and your children."

"The second baby is crowning," the doctor said. "This one is a fast little duckling."

"There's so little pain," Liselotte said.

"A good thing," Helene said, then gasped.

"What's wrong, Mutter?" Liselotte flicked her attention from her mother to the doctor. "Tell me. What's wrong with my baby? Is it alive?"

Helene sidestepped in a way she hoped would obstruct Liselotte's view. "Yes, your second baby girl is alive." She stared at the newborn as the doctor guided it from Liselotte. The little one, thank God, did indeed breathe, despite her body weight appearing to be half of her older sister's, despite her head so tiny, despite her delicate looks.

"All children are different," the doctor said in a hushed tone. His fleeting glance at Helene expressed what he didn't say in words. *This baby, if she survives, will indeed be different. Not in a good way.* "From today and onward, you should not compare them."

"My second daughter is Rosa. My little blossom." Liselotte's heavy eyes were shutting.

"Rest, sweetheart," Helene said. "I'll wake you for your babies' first feeding shortly."

She placed Regina into the same bassinet Liselotte had slept in as a newborn. She gingerly took Rosa from the doctor, nervous to touch her as if she might break in half. After she placed Rosa beside her sister, she smiled at her granddaughters. "May you two help each other grow to be strong, beautiful women and a blessing to each other and your mama."

She jumped when a hand touched her shoulder. She turned to see the doctor.

"Oh, I need to pay you."

"No worries. There's no charge for my services today."

Was his gesture an act of kindness and compassion? Or, guilt and regret?

"Regina should be fine. As for the second one, do what you can," the doctor said. "I'll see my way out." Without another word, he left the room.

"Do what you can?" Helene said, repeating the doctor's orders. She then realized how the good doctor referred to Regina by her name. When it came to Rosa, he had called her by a number. *The second one.* If the doctor did not want to attach a human name to the baby, as if already choosing not to remember her, then what would the rest of society do when it came to Rosa? Discount her? This was 1942. Nazi Germany. As per the Nazi view, when it came to spoiling the Aryan stock, a baby like Rosa could not only endanger Rosa's life but put each Aryan in peril. There was no way Helene would accept and comply with this inhumane policy. Rosa was an innocent child... a newborn. Helene would risk her life before she would step back and watch harm come to her daughter or granddaughters.

CHAPTER FOURTEEN

Fanny, Rochester, September 6, 1961

Still seated beside Ray's French doors that opened up to the patio, Fanny said, "It looks like the rain may be holding off for a while." She reminded herself that, by court order, Kenny was restricted to the premises. "Is anyone up to continuing our discussion outdoors? A good stretch of legs and fresh air helps one to think better, and I would love to walk around the grounds."

On his feet, Kenny headed for the door. "Walking is good," he said. "I'll meet you outside. On the patio."

"After a visit to the bathroom," Gina said as she stood. "I should hang a sign on every bathroom door I see that says Home Sweet Home."

"It's kind of exciting," Fanny called after her as Gina hurried down the hall.

"Not really," Gina said, but giggled. She ducked around the right corner.

"Now that it's just the two of us—do you have bad news?" Ray asked quietly.

Fanny shrugged. "Not really. Whatever we have, it's to be expected. I'm just sorry your nephew is going through this unfortunate situation."

"He didn't do it." Ray's words stopped Fanny short of reaching the patio doors. He closed the doors enough to block his words from reaching Kenny's ears. "I've raised Kenny like my own son. And a father knows his child. Kenny couldn't, wouldn't, intentionally hurt or kill another person. You believe that, don't you?"

Often asked whether she believed *deep down in her heart* whether someone's son or daughter, parent, or grandfather, grandmother, grandchild, or simply the kid next door, committed a crime, Fanny loathed this question most of all. It was not her role to say one way or another. And it was in everyone's best interest if she did not defend a client from some emotionally entrenched viewpoint. Aware she had often come across as a hard-hearted, cold woman, and heard frequent derogatory insults attached to her name as she walked by, she had no other choice but to conduct herself to the degree the law dictates. That meant seeing that emotions did not interfere. Like a doctor needing to keep his eye on scientifically treating the patient without incorporating the pain and anguish of the patient, she needed to focus on objectivity or she could kiss a case goodbye. They would all be losers, then. Not one of them would say hello to a desired future.

"I believe, Ray, if we all work hard on behalf of Kenny, a jury will see, without a doubt, that Kenny did not kill Samuel."

"I'm concerned that what you will discuss might upset Kenny." He winced. "Just call me overprotective."

Fanny noted he had spoken his last few words without a trace of a smile and heard anguish in his voice. She aimed to reply in a soft tone. "Spoken like a true caring uncle... a dad. I see Kenny as intuitive when trying to understand the ins and outs of our tilted world. Maybe instead of Kenny having to learn from us, we need to learn from him."

"Is that your way of saying he'd do just fine?"

Another difficult question. Despite offering distinct evidence for or against an alleged crime, despite offering concrete-solid expert testimony, despite holding one's head up in confidence and ignoring the inner plague of doubt, at times, winning or losing in court—in life—often boils down to a matter of a toss of a coin. Heads or tails.

Gina called out their names. Fanny and Ray looked toward her. Ray excused himself, saying he would join Kenny outside.

"My, look at you," Fanny said, trying to sound bright and cheerful after her little discussion—and dodging the answer—with Ray. "You're looking more and more motherly."

Gina fanned her hand across her belly then lifted her chin toward the outside dining area. "I'm no longer flat like the patio stones outside this kitchen, but look at you."

Fanny gave herself a once-over. "Me?"

"You're still dressed in black and white. You need more color."

"Black and white—"

"Sheesh. You claim the two colors define you." Gina swatted the air. "I'm not digging it."

For an unsettling tick of seconds, Fanny froze. Then, her mind cleared. "Duly noted."

Gina reached for Fanny's arm. "Please, no aloof legalese-speak between us. You know I didn't mean any harm, right?"

Fanny was set to do whatever it took to win for Kenny. When it came to herself and altering her lifestyle, she was not sure. There was a certain comfort in doing the same old same old, and dressing in her preferred black and white had become a sort of mainstay she was not quite ready to depart from. Yet, beside her stood a lovely, strong woman who wanted the best for her. She gave Gina a slight nod. "Let's catch up with the guys."

"Fine." Gina shook her head in contradiction. "When Kenny's ordeal is over—and it will be—you need to surround yourself with color."

•   •   •

They caught up with Kenny and Ray at the small pond adjacent to the neighboring property. Two benches faced the water. Gina sat next to Kenny, reaching for his hand. Fanny sat on the other, and Ray sat cross-legged on the grass, appearing more like an older college student rather than the sixty-year-old president of a well-established and beloved pasta company.

"Kenny," Fanny began, "the district attorney and his team are assembling witnesses and expert testimony against your case." A quick wrinkle across his brow signaled she needed to explain more. "It's Mr. Hayes'—the DA—job to prove that you murdered Samuel."

"But I didn't."

"In court, the DA will say what he needs to convince the jury that you did. He will introduce people with special knowledge to prove otherwise. He does this to sway—to influence—the jury that he is right because you were wrong in your actions that resulted in Samuel dying. Any questions?" When he remained silent, she continued. "The good thing about the DA gathering information is that we have the right to see it. It can help us build a sounder argument for you. This is what I'm trying to do, to be ready with weapons against the prosecution."

"Argument? Weapons?" Kenny echoed. "I don't want to fight."

"It's all right, Kenny," Ray said. "In this situation, it's not like a boxing match. It's more like talking. Sharing information in court."

"Talking can hurt." Kenny pulled at his chin. "Is this what you meant earlier, Fanny? You said it won't be pleasant."

"You have a good memory," Fanny said quietly, aware she couldn't affix a smile to the compliment. Originally, at this point of today's visit, she had imagined that she would invite Kenny to go off separately with her from Ray and Gina and talk privately. Now, she rethought her strategy. Kenny appeared more comfortable with his uncle and Gina around. He trusted them; she did as well. "We need to talk about your parents. At our first meeting, you'd grown upset when we mentioned your mother and father."

"My parents aren't part of my life." Kenny looked toward the water, its surface growing darker with the heavy rain clouds thickening the sky. "What do they have to do with Samuel?"

"Excellent question," Ray said. "By the way, you're doing a good job staying calm today, Kenny."

Kenny continued to stare ahead. He remained silent.

Time to jump in, Fanny thought, though she wondered why Ray had praised Kenny's rein on his calmness. Had he a hidden temper issue she had yet not witnessed? A behavioral issue could indeed color the argument against Kenny. Ray might have spoken simply in general terms, hoping to encourage his nephew. "I've received word from the DA's office that he intends to present expert testimony—"

"Will we do that, too?" Kenny asked.

"Yes. I'm also lining up experts. One of the DA's experts is a psychiatrist. His testimony is to show that when things don't go the way you want them to, you have a genetic tendency to violence, like your father."

"Genetic?"

Fanny racked her brain to explain a highly complex, still inconclusive study, of human tendency based on hereditary factors to its most simplistic terms. "In this situation, a genetic predisposition means that people are likely to behave like their relatives. And the behavior inherited from these relatives—in your case, your parents—is something you cannot control, no matter how hard you try."

"My father wasn't violent. He didn't hit me. He didn't hurt me. He killed himself, not other people."

"I understand, Kenny. However, it is unlikely—let's say impossible— that the DA can convict you of murder based on circumstantial evidence alone. What is meant by this is that the evidence needs to be concretely clear and will leave no doubt in each juror's mind that you either killed Samuel or you did not kill Samuel. Yet, the DA can, and will, act to persuade—to influence—the jury to see things the way he wants them to."

"That makes no sense."

If Fanny were cloaked in Kenny's skin, she would see things exactly his way. She could only explain and subsequently act based on how the legal system plays out. "Genetics is all about how the biology we inherit from our families when we are born shapes us. For example, if both parents are blond, the baby is likely to be blond, too. Or, maybe not. And that's because he or she might have inherited the genetics of his or her grandfather who had red hair. The environment—our surroundings—can also influence us. Take, for example, a baby who is born with weak lungs just like his parents. Although his parents grew up in a heavily polluted city and coughed a lot, they moved to the country with cleaner air. Their baby grew well in the cleaner environment and showed no health problems, despite his weak lungs. Do you understand the differences between genetic tendency and environmental circumstances?"

Kenny gave a slight nod.

From the corner of her eye, Fanny noticed Ray looking at them intently. "Do you have a question, Ray?"

"Is the belief that genetics influence one's behavior new?"

Fanny glanced at her notes. "It dates back to 1933. Han Brunner, a Dutch geneticist, documented a gene connected to human violence. In simple terms, this gene influences mood, emotion, sleep, appetite, and how the body reacts to stress. The study points to how a person with this specific genetic disposition, coupled with negative environmental surroundings like childhood stresses and upheavals, can produce the tendency for a person to be more violent." She glanced at Kenny. "The DA is fishing for the psychiatrist to show that with the upheaval of Kenny's early years from his parents leaving him, coupled with his father's aggression of taking his own life, Kenny has a great chance of being violent and therefore has the capability of acting violently against another person, especially when push comes to shove. In this case, Samuel's bullying and threatening Kenny."

"This sounds very funny," Kenny said.

Fanny nodded at him. "Do you mean iffy? That it might not hold up in court?"

"I think that's what I mean."

"Although I said Brunner's study originated in 1933, and despite others presently researching it, yes, it is all debatable." Fanny held back a sigh. "Remember, though, all a good attorney has to do is to plant a seed of doubt in each of the jurors' minds. In your case, to make each juror believe this indeed shows a correlation—a connection—that a genetic tendency, coupled with the wrong environment, can produce a murderer." Kenny and Ray opened their mouths but Fanny held up a hand to pause them. "Keep in mind, that no matter how convincing the DA is, or despite his expert witness, the judge may not allow any of this to be admissible in the trial. We don't know at this point." She winked. "However, I have my genetic tendency to be aggressive and therefore like to be prepared in court. I'm lining up a psychiatrist to counter any possible assertions the DA's witness might throw at us. While my job is to make the jury believe that you could have never hurt Samuel, the DA's job is to convince the jury that you can easily cause harm to someone and, because of this, you hurt Samuel to the point of causing death. In other words, by using this expert, the DA will show that you act violently because your father chose a violent way— suicide—to end his worries over raising you. I'm sorry to say these things, to risk sounding like I don't care. However, this is the way a trial works. The DA will bring out bad things, sad things. It's all a matter of perception— making others see things you want them to see. Kenny, have you ever watched a movie with good guys and bad guys?"

"Yes. Lots of cowboy movies."

"So have I. What color hats do the good guys wear?"

"White. The bad guys wear black hats."

"Right, you are. Think of the DA as an artist. He's painting a picture of a man wearing dark clothes and a black hat. If he were to show a picture of this man to the jury, what would they first think?"

"That he's a bad guy?"

"Yes, sir." Fanny breathed in deeply. "That's exactly how the DA will portray you and your family. When things became difficult for your father because he was suddenly the only one to care for you and the stress became difficult for him, he didn't reach out to his brother, Uncle Raymond, for help. He didn't ask other relatives, friends, or doctors for help. Your father became overwhelmed because—according to what the DA's expert found in his research of your father's father—he had a genetic tendency to act violently against himself."

"My grandfather?" Kenny faced his uncle. "He died before I was born. Uncle Raymond, you knew my grandfather."

Ray's mouth flattened. "Paul Franks—your grandfather, my father—was a strong man. At times, though, he was also weak. He bottled up his resentments and anger until he couldn't hold back a minute longer and then he would explode in anger. Anyone around him had to be careful to keep out of his way."

"Did he hit you, Uncle Raymond? Did he hit my father?"

"Yes, both of us." Ray paused, rubbing the back of his neck. "Sad to say, he also struck your grandmother. It's something I try not to dwell upon. Perhaps that's why I've worked hard, avoiding thoughts connected to my past, thinking it's best to put my energies into making my business excel. I'm sorry I haven't talked more about your father and grandfather."

"I'm not mad at you. But, Uncle Raymond, you're a nice person."

Ray stood and walked behind Kenny and patted him on the shoulder. Fanny wondered whether the stoic man would shed tears. He remained somber, keeping his facial expression impassive. Often to survive tough times, people dodged their ugly past by keeping busy, sometimes excessively, to channel energy into creative activities, offering goodness to others in need, all of which Ray Franks did. As for the others who could not control a sense of overwhelming sadness or anger? The troubled person often reached out to alcohol and drugs. Other times, he or she lashed out abusively to others, which the DA stated in his report on Kenny's grandfather. Although Paul Franks kept his violence within the family, away from outsiders, violence was violence, and it was never acceptable. Domestic violence was not a lesser level of aggression, but rather a sideways step. Once the jury had the visualization of hostility—in any form and on any level—it would be permanently etched in their mutual thoughts.

"Thanks, Kenny, for the compliment," Ray said. "Based upon the little more you just learned about your grandfather, can you see why the DA will use the evidence to say your father acted up, at either himself or others?"

"My father got broken." Kenny's right eye twitched. "He killed himself, not me. Not anyone else."

Ray turned toward Fanny. "Your thoughts, counselor?"

Fanny kept her gaze on Kenny. "This expert will say that killing one's self is an act of violence. And, this violence is a genetic tendency you inherited, Kenny. You were five years old at the time. At this young age, you were influenced to end your life—anyone's life—when things don't go the way you want them to go. The prosecutor will push that it shows your lack of respect for others and yourself. In other words, your upbringing fits the profile—a description—of a person who grows up and becomes a criminal who can easily murder someone."

"My father didn't kill me. Didn't kill anyone but himself."

"Fanny understands," Ray said to Kenny. "Remember, the attorney on the other side will say things to sway the jury that it may be a natural tendency for you to have the capability of killing Samuel. However, Fanny will work to make the judge and the jury not accept this as evidence. This would be a great thing for us."

Kenny stared at Fanny. "Do you believe I can kill someone, that I can kill Samuel?"

"No," Fanny said. Minutes ago, she had to dodge the same question asked by Ray. Kenny needed more, both in legal understanding and personal comfort. "Not at all, Kenny. As your attorney, I must inform you about what will happen during your trial. It will be very rough. It will not be fun. And it's best if we are prepared. Do you understand how the DA must act on behalf of Samuel and how I must act on your behalf?"

He nodded. "I wish I didn't understand. It's not a nice thing to understand."

"Wise words, Kenny."

"And my mother?" Kenny asked.

Images of Fanny's mother flashed in her mind. With her father out of the picture, Louise Stern had raised Fanny, her only child, as a single mother. Her mom, when Fanny was age five: "Our friends and neighbors are far too generous, spoiling you with toys and candy, especially compared to what I had as a little girl." Her mom, when Fanny was thirteen years old: "Don't complain boys don't like you—I can tell you all about what it's like to be the least appreciated in your class." Her mom, when Fanny faced high school graduation: "You want to become some hotshot lawyer and do good in the world? Good luck with that dream. My parents never expected me to do anything other than marry and have baby after baby. And look where I am today."

Not once had Fanny ever rebutted her mother. How could she, when in the name of competing against her only kid, Louise Stern would shoot down all lines of reasoning out of Fanny's mouth? The only thing she could do when her mother *flung verbal trash*—as Fanny had viewed it—was to ride out Storm Louise. She would eventually run out of steam and pass by.

"And my mother?" Kenny repeated.

Fanny licked her bottom lip. "The DA will have his expert show the jury that your mother's action of leaving you as a toddler in your father's care happened because she didn't want to be *bothered with you*. This is how the expert will describe it. Not at all pretty or kind words. The expert will describe your mother as emotionally and socially detached from you."

"Detached?" Despite a raised quizzical brow, he nodded.

Gina groaned. "How? This so-called expert had never met Kenny. Nor his parents. Will he make one sweeping statement to cover all the bases, a one-size-fits-all?"

"This is what expert witnesses do," Fanny said. "Although the expert may request an interview with Kenny, he doesn't have to know the person directly or even have observed the person remotely. However, based upon years of study and cumulated knowledge, the expert can establish that his or her information is reliable, and a jury can use it in the decision-making process of a guilty or not guilty verdict."

"That's not fair."

Fairness. Fanny looked intently at Gina, this young woman, this mother-to-be, with her own set of mysteries. The big wonder of life Fanny had pondered during her early years in law school, wrapped not around the debate over the existence of fairness but rather, why people thought life was supposed to be fair.

Rather than address Gina's last statement, and wanting to stick to the needed subject of the opposing expert testimony, she responded to Kenny. He was, after all, her client. He was, after all, her sole concern.

"Kenny, a right-minded mother loves her child, no matter what the child does. For example, if little Billy accidentally breaks his mom's favorite vase, she would be disappointed in him, but wouldn't stop talking to Billy or the worse action of giving Billy up for adoption. Rather, she would encourage Billy to think for himself, even if different from how she thinks. His mom would also mentally prepare for when Billy leaves the family home to be on his own as an adult. An emotionally detached mother doesn't prepare Billy for independence when it's time for Billy to face life as an adult. An emotionally detached mother tends not to react to her child. When a child has problems, needs talking to, or wants emotional support, the mother cannot offer understanding and comfort. Sometimes, she can be defensive, as if she only cares about her needs. Although I'm referring to mothers, an emotionally detached parent can also be a father."

Kenny smiled at Gina. "Like when I walk five miles away from Gina. I mean, like I used to. Before the trouble happened. Now I have to stay here."

"I know what you mean," Fanny said. "Go on."

"My body is away from Gina." Kenny covered his heart and then touched the side of his head. "Here, in my mind, I'm not away from her. So, I'm attached, not detached."

"Aww," Gina squealed. "Me too. You're always in my thoughts and heart, Kenny."

"Right, again," Fanny said. "You're not at all detached emotionally from Gina just because you are not physically near her. Let's return to this expert against you. He or she will say that your mother acted detached from you. And because of her behavior, she was irresponsible to you and others and had an irrelevance to you and whoever she met."

Ray shot to his feet. "Fanny, may I speak with you alone for a moment?"

She questioned him silently about his timing. His slight nod told her it would be best to step aside with him.

"Let's be quick," she warned. She excused herself to Kenny and Gina, then walked halfway around the pond with Ray, outside of earshot. "I think Kenny's beginning to understand and I'd like to return to him sooner than later."

"I agree, but there are a few things you need to know. First, and nothing against you, tell me where you're coming from." His cheeks flushed rosy.

"Having a family history like Kenny's does not help matters. I want to be ready to shoot down whatever Lyman G. Hayes pitches against us."

"This is outrageous." Ray brushed the sides of his head, then withdrew his hands and studied them. "Am I too to blame? Do I have a natural tendency toward violence because of my father? Have I influenced my nephew the wrong way?"

"Please, Ray, don't think that way. It's too dangerous, too unhealthy. The law is perpetually updating. Based upon what doctors are discovering about the human mind, the role of genetics, and how society is changing regarding the perception of others, I hope to see an argument against the assertion of one's past influencing a commitment to crime. However, today, no such law exists. We need to be prepared against what the DA may introduce to the court against Kenny. And so far, based on what the DA has forwarded to me, he's lining up an expert witness in genetics and behavior. With this in mind, what did you want to tell me?"

"I'm sure you've heard Kenny say—because no one who knows him gets away without hearing his favorite assertion—that he is slow, not dumb. When Kenny was four, he said he wanted to be like everyone else. At first, I didn't understand and told him he was a nice boy. I tried to encourage him by saying he was creative, handsome, in short, a bright child. My words didn't take. It only got worse as he progressed through kindergarten and first grade. Or, more aptly put, when he failed to progress through his early school years. He became frustrated because he couldn't learn like the other children around him. I explained that for some children it took extra time. Know what? Despite failing tests, and being shamed by his teachers and classmates, Kenny flourished because he understood he wasn't like the other children in his age group and moved forward the best he could."

"Was he frustrated?"

"Some. At other times, sad. He did the best he could and accepted who he was. I believe he's made the most of what God gifted him with, probably more than so-called smarter people who don't tap into half of their talents and potentials."

"I see Kenny as a very positive person. He's especially committed to Gina and their soon-to-be growing family. He's especially upbeat and encouraging to others. Downright hopeful. Yet, I'm hearing angst in your tone."

Ray folded his arms against his chest. "I should have never employed Samuel."

"Samuel's murder is not your fault, Ray. You won't help your nephew by jumping aboard this erroneous ship." Her gaze traveled across the pond. Kenny and Gina sat close to each other, apparently conversing quietly. "Look there, Ray. I see two sound people talking calmly with each other. The word *maturely* also comes to mind. To me, that's a distinction of intelligence. What do you see?"

After seconds of silence, Ray nodded. "I see the same."

"Well, then. The defense will present to the jury a man who is not capable of murdering another person, one who can cope with opposition. And, though Kenny—like all human beings, even of greater, tested higher IQs—can grow frustrated, and give chase after a tormentor, he would not kill him because he can control his anger and can differentiate right from wrong."

"Okay, then." Ray gave a little smile. "I'm encouraged. Shall we return to the two lovebirds?"

"Let's hurry," Fanny said. She approached Kenny and Gina, confident there was no need to check on Ray to see whether he followed. He never deserted his nephew during the years he raised Kenny under his roof, and was not about to change his plans to leave Kenny behind in this crucial hour of need.

"You talked a lot," Kenny said when Fanny and his uncle returned.

"That's for sure," Gina added, her tone unclear if she was teasing or complaining.

"Let's pick up right where we left off." Fanny looked at Kenny. "Your mother. Remember, it's a tough subject to discuss, though we need to."

"I understand, Fanny," Kenny said.

"I have a hunch," Fanny continued, "the DA will bring up that your mother believed you and others were not important enough to her to take care of, and that's why she left. In court, the DA's expert will say that because you have inherited social and emotional detachment from your mother, you treat others as insignificant and not worth your time. Meaning, that you would have an easy time murdering someone if the person upset you. Therefore, you would not think twice about killing Samuel who had said very mean things to you, and then mean things about Gina and your baby. The expert will say that you do not understand right from wrong, or good from bad. In other words, he will say you believed it was fine to kill Samuel— anyone—if troubled by them. Almost like stepping on an ant when you walk on the grass, you do so without hesitation or guilt."

"I'm not like that," Kenny said. "I'm not angry."

His matter-of-fact, calm reply said everything of importance to Fanny. "Yes, I can see that."

Gina twisted a strand of hair around a finger. "You're saying the other side's attorney will lie about Kenny? That's not right."

Fanny wished Gina had kept her agitation to herself. One glance at Kenny showed his holding-tight look a second ago had morphed into wide-eyed alarm. Fanny reconsidered. She could not blame either of them. This was a stressful case. Not only was Samuel killed, but if determined guilty,

Kenny's life would be sacrificed to appease anyone who hungered for *an eye for an eye*. The only guarantee was that emotions—from all—would be as volatile as a moody teenager.

Kenny faced Fanny. "This is not good. This is mean. How can you allow this? How can the judge—"

Fanny lifted a hand to signal that everyone needed to pause and listen. "The DA will do whatever he deems necessary to win in court. It's his job. He has a dead man to account for. Mr. Hayes' bottom line is Kenny's confession to chasing Samuel and cornering him in the lot, coupled with Kenny admitting he saw no one else, is proof alone that Kenny is guilty of murdering Samuel. The DA will go on and on about Kenny's family, and his supposed inherited nature of anger and detachment showing how he has a genetic tendency to commit a violent crime. We, the defense, will argue against this conjecture. This is how a case is brought to court. Accept it, and roll up your sleeves. We have a lot of work to do."

"Who is the crazy one here?" Gina mumbled.

"Try to think of it this way." Fanny reminded herself to breathe. "If things were on the opposite end, and the DA defended you, you would want him to do the very best job he could, right?"

"Will you do the same, Fanny?" Kenny asked. "In court? Your best?"

Fanny struggled with achieving the right type of tone to use. Should she go easy, like a concerned friend? Playful and light, like a big sister? Guiding, like a good mother? She chose her attorney's voice. That was who she was, who she needed to be. "You bet. That's one of the reasons I'm with you today. To talk and to plan."

"Good," Kenny said. "That's what I want."

"Okay, then. Let's work out our plan of action by starting with your mother. May I have her full name?"

"Betty. Betty Hanson." Kenny stared at his feet. "She never married my father. That's why they had different names."

"I never knew that," Gina said.

Fanny kept her gaze on Kenny. "When did she pass?"

"She didn't," Kenny and Ray said simultaneously.

Fanny's mouth was shaped around the missing two-letter word *oh* wedged halfway up her throat. She jotted a reminder note to ask the judge whether she could take Kenny to meet with his mother. Working around her surprise, she asked, "Where does Betty live?"

CHAPTER FIFTEEN

Fanny, Bridgehaven, September 6, 1961

Relieved to be alone, Fanny placed a freshly poured mug of peppermint tea on the side table and then sat in her favorite easy chair, the one she usually reclined in with a novel. Tonight, was an exception. She needed to think.

Her cat jumped on her lap and purred in her face. "My goodness. I didn't mean to ignore you, Ralphie-baby."

Well, you could have fooled me. Good thing I'm a forgiving guy.

"You're so right, you big ball of purr."

Ooh. That scratch behind the left ear feels so good... just a little down and I'll remain your best friend forever... there are better things to do in life than worry all the time.

"Thanks for your visit, Ralph. You're right. At times, I take myself too seriously."

For sure. Just focus on your next scrumptious meal. Then imagine sleeping it off on a five-hour nap bender, discounting life to the fullest. It's heaven, I'm telling you. Heaven.

Fanny tugged Ralph to her chest. A little TV entertainment would hit the spot nicely, especially a comedy or variety show. A knock at her front door quashed the idea. She eyed Ralph.

Don't look at me like that, pal. I prefer you stay here and give me one hundred percent of your human attention.

"And believe me, I wish I could cuddle with you rather than investigate who's at my door at nine at night." She stood and set Ralph on the chair. Without a fuss, he settled into the warm spot on her chair.

"Yes? Who is it?"

"Helene. Helene Kellerman."

Fanny opened the door and invited into her home the one person she never imagined would grace her doorstep. "I just made myself a cup of tea. The kettle water must still be hot—care for any?"

"No thank you." Helene remained by the door, clasping the V of her navy blue cardigan with a look of irritation. Rather than the polyester material causing such discomfort, Fanny suspected a much greater distress. She offered to hang up the sweater but Helene declined, saying she was fine wearing the garment.

Sidestepping around Gina's grandmother, Fanny shut the door. "Come on into the living room. I'm a casual, no-thrills person. So please don't mind the mess." Helene followed her into the next room.

"Oh, you have a cat."

Grateful for the needed icebreaker, Fanny picked up Ralph and stroked his head. His purr relaxed her. "This cute guy is my version of your Wags."

Helene smiled. "We all need a little source of sunshine in our lives. Please don't tell Gina I'm saying kind things about that pooch, even if indirectly."

Fanny set the cat on the floor and gestured outward with her hands. "Have a seat wherever you'd like."

Helene nodded and sat on the recliner and remained silent.

Fanny thought Gina and the baby might be a halfway decent segue from the subjects of pets. She sat on the rocking chair opposite Helene. "Speaking of adorableness, I imagine you're looking forward to welcoming your great-grandchild. I saw Gina today. She's looking good… finally looking like she's in the family way."

"That she is," Helene said, smiling. "She didn't tell me you met with her today. Since living at Mr. Franks' house, Gina rarely phones, nor stops by for a visit."

"Visiting might be difficult. The judge appointed both Gina and Ray to watch Kenny."

"Like he's a five-year-old in need of watching," Helene said, not quite a question, nor for that matter, a statement, though with a distinct note of disgust in her tone. "Well, he certainly knew what to do in bed with…" Her breath hitched; her cheeks flamed red. She averted her gaze to her knees.

Fanny was not about to touch that subject. Whatever Gina and Kenny did in their bedroom was not her concern. "With the judge ordering her to keep her husband under surveillance—sorry to be blunt—being cooped up in a house that isn't hers—"

"Living in a mansion is not exactly tough doings."

"Still, it's not the cozy home she ever envisioned to make as a newlywed. On top of Kenny's keeper, which I'd think puts an extra burden on her and might strain the young relationship she has with Kenny, there's the stress and fear of wondering if her husband will be found guilty and sentenced to death. Between the possibility of becoming a single parent and presently dealing with a changing body, she must be in great turmoil. Poor Gina. She has plenty to contend with, don't you think?" Fanny had surprised herself with her rant. She had every intention of acting civilly. This woman brought out the worst in her, which frustrated her more.

Helene sat straighter and laced her fingers. "She's not the first woman, especially in our family, to deal with problems."

As in maternal *problems*? Was this a clue why Helene had kept so tight-lipped, refusing to talk about the past with Gina? Or, was it more of a general or mundane declaration, like Gina's great-grandmother having to decide to choose lamb or fish for dinner? Perhaps something more heartbreaking, like whether to lug a drunkard husband to bed or to leave him on the cellar floor where he had collapsed? "Sadly, we each have our own particular set of difficulties. Despite the circumstances, it appears your granddaughter is handling things well. Better than I would if I were in her shoes."

"Me too," Helene said, softly.

Fanny never expected to hear this admission from her guest. "What was Gina like when she was little?"

Instead of reclining more comfortably, Helene straightened further in her chair and crossed her ankles. "She was the cutest, nicest darling, ever."

"I can't imagine Gina, otherwise. Was she a good student? What were her favorite subjects?"

"Did she tell you we came to New York when she was four?"

"Yes, I believe she said four."

Although the living room curtain was drawn, Helene peered hard at the window as if she could see the outside world, the good and the ugly. "With the war over, and traveling opening up and becoming easier, I thought it would be a good time to begin a new chapter in a new place."

Images came to Fanny of the morning's newspaper, with the lead article of how the diplomats, military, and the Allied forces, were harassed as they moved across the East and West Berlin borders. With each day rushing by without a peace accord, the concept of a united Germany may have become a pipe dream. "Strife is never good. I can't imagine what living through the Second World War was like. What I cannot understand is why, after the world battled two wars the number one goal of every world leader isn't peace between countries."

"You probably were too busy as a young woman in 1950 to remember when the first issue of *Sing Out!* hit newsstands with the cover featuring the song "If I Had a Hammer" by Pete Seeger and Lee Hays. It was a song about spreading love between everyone."

"I don't remember the magazine. I'm familiar with the song, though. The idea of everyone loving each other certainly has a great appeal. At least, it should."

Helene turned away, but not fast enough to hide from Fanny her eyes brimming with tears.

"It was a different world then, fresh from the atrocities of war." Fanny had spoken more reflectively, but when she didn't observe Helene turning around, she slipped into the role of hostess again. "Are you sure you wouldn't like a hot drink?"

"Oh, no thanks. I'm fine."

"I have a nice Scotch whisky I can bring out. A satisfied client gave me a bottle as a thank-you gift."

Helene sank her chin, convincing Fanny she would break out in sobs. Instead, she lifted her face to reveal a furrowed brow. "Honestly, I don't want to indulge in alcohol out of fear I wouldn't stop."

"I hear you," Fanny said.

"Really?"

Fanny gave a little nod. "I don't drink except on a special occasion, and then it's just a few sips."

"All righty. You've expressed curiosity about Gina as a little girl." Helene finally leaned back into the chair. "She was a bright child. And, oh, did she sparkle in the charming-department. Regina could wrap anyone around her small fingers. She knew it, too. Knew how to use it to her advantage."

"You came from Germany, correct?"

"Yes. Berlin."

Again, the current separation of the city of Berlin into two entities by a wall, peppered with the eastern military ready to kill any man, woman, or child with escape on their mind, haunted Fanny. "I imagine Berlin must have been a fine place to live."

A reflective nod came from Helene. "Between the two wars, ja. I had a good time growing up in Berlin. Fortunate enough not to be in want, my family delighted in the joys of theatre and the opera. We enjoyed seasonal tickets to the Berliner Philharmoniker, the zoo, parks, and the finest of restaurants, it was a lovely place to live."

Fanny wondered whether Helene had realized her accent had thickened as she spoke while riding a wave of sudden nostalgia. "Until it wasn't?"

"Ja."

"I'm sure the war changed everything."

"Oh, it did. Both for the Jew and the German."

Fanny gritted her teeth over Helene's need to differentiate. "Native Germans, who happened to be of the Jewish faith, were plentiful."

"Relax—I'm not a Nazi." Helene held up a hand. "Please. Hear me out. I'm not looking to start another war, especially between us. One can't blame everything on what happened in 1933 on the newly appointed chancellor, though he sure changed the world, horrifically."

It would be best if Fanny kept the peace, or as the kids said these days, kept things groovy. "Sounds like a personal matter developed for you, which slanted life toward the unpleasant side."

"Irreversibly so." Helene reached over to pet Ralph who had settled on the nearby chair. "Gina began kindergarten in Rochester."

For a moment, Fanny was mentally dizzy from the return to their initial conversation. "How did you end up coming to upstate New York? Certainly, not for its warm and sunny winters?"

Helene chuckled dryly. "When it comes to winter, there's no drastic difference between Berlin and Rochester. I wanted to pursue a career in dentistry." She paused. "Originally, I wanted to become a nurse. After attending school, my interests changed to dentistry." She narrowed her eyes. "Do you realize much of our health is shaped by having good teeth? Anyway, a major change in life occurred for me and I had to put all my interests aside for a while. When a little time passed, my parents rerouted their daily activities so I had the time to attend school."

"Was this change for you a baby?"

"Do you have children of your own?" Helene glanced at the bookcase and then on a side table beside the sofa as if searching for framed photographs of a smiling boy or girl. Not one existed.

"No. I've never married, nor had a child."

"Do you want children?"

"Must I answer?"

Helene shook her head. "You never have to reply to a nosy question. Remember that. Please pardon my lack of manners. Perhaps I'm talking like a drunkard without the benefit of a drink."

An element of truth to Helene's last statement rang clearly. She was indeed rambling on whatever came to mind. Perhaps with Gina living at Ray's, Helene longed for company. Fanny, though, suspected something more had to be the compelling impetus to bring her here for a visit. A sense of guilt? Like loneliness, guilt also leads people to do the unexpected.

They stared at each other for several awkward moments. "Helene, in building a strong defense for Kenny, I will gather as much personal and relevant information as possible. That said, I have a question for you."

Helene's eyes widened. "Yes?"

"How come you call Kenny by his full first name of Kenneth, especially when he prefers Kenny? And why does he call you Miss Kellerman?"

"That's two questions."

Aware the odd formality between Helene and Kenny occurred before Kenny was charged with Samuel's murder, Fanny would chance a wager that the answer connected to Helene's past. She was hiding something, not only from Fanny but more distressfully, from Gina. Sooner than later, Fanny would find out. She hoped for anything other than a haunting pain that could not be overcome.

Helene abruptly stood and headed toward the door. Halfway there, she pivoted and faced Fanny. "I'm sorry to have taken up your time, Miss Stern—"

"No."

"Pardon?"

"Please." Fanny crossed her arms. "Let's not restart the game-playing between us. We had agreed you were to call me Fanny. I will continue to call you by your first name, Helene. I may be Kenny's attorney—and one doing so on gratis terms—but let's agree we should not mess around with each other's minds. Two young people are at the beginning of their marital lives together. A baby is on the way. Other than this incredible murder hanging over their heads, threatening to turn their lives permanently upside down, and leaving an innocent baby without a father—"

"Runs in the family."

Fanny glared at Helene. "Pardon? What do you mean?"

Helene remained quiet.

"Listen, Helene. A baby's whole life is on the precarious edge of ruination. The baby of two people madly in love with each other, despite what society labels them. Two people who will love this baby like no other family member or friend can. I will give this case my all. My legal expertise, my heart, my every breathing minute to make a win for Kenny. I—all of us— need your cooperation and support. May we count on you, Helene?"

Fanny's guest remained quiet long enough for her to wonder if her silence substituted for the word *no*. Finally, Helene gave a little nod. Then, she added, "Yes, Fanny. You can count on my cooperation and support." She proceeded to the door.

"Good. Have a pleasant night, Helene."

"And you as well." Helene let herself out of the house.

It took Fanny two minutes to realize two things. First, Helene reminded Fanny of her mother. Secondly, this meant that Helene was also like Kenny's mother. Emotionally detached.

Emotionally detached people acted to protect themselves. In Helene's situation, what troubles was she trying to avoid? Or, were they memories? Undoubtedly, her actions were to ultimately safeguard her granddaughter, though Gina might have appreciated and benefitted from a hefty dosage of tenderness.

"Ralph," Fanny called and headed to her little furry boy. She scooped him up from the chair and nuzzled his face with her nose and cheek. "Let's call it a night."

Just short of walking into her bedroom, Fanny paused and leaned against the doorjamb as a nagging thought revisited. Without a doubt, Helene harbored a secret—possibly more than one—which was getting the best of her. By their very nature, secrets had a way of imploding upon the poor person keeping them. Possibly, Helene's hidden truth had driven her to visit. However, the last thing Helene, Gina, and Kenny needed was this truth to backfire and ruin Kenny's chances of success in the trial.

CHAPTER SIXTEEN

Helene, Berlin, Germany, May 18, 1943

A light rain fell after their breakfast, though precipitation of any nature did not disturb Helene. Dealing with people was a different matter. With two one-year-olds to care for and their mopey mama, the luxury of letting the weather botch up the household atmosphere was the least of her concerns.

A whir of pink and yellow crawled past her. "Mu... Mu...Roo."

Regina's babbling planted a smile on Helene's face. The little *Prinzessin* was calling out for her mama and her sister. Why was Regina scurrying through the house without her mama watching to ensure the energetic toddler avoided trouble? Helene's stomach pinched. She lifted from her parlor chair, took three steps, then stopped. "Liselotte! Liselotte! Look at Regina!"

"What now?" Liselotte said, from within the kitchen.

"Your daughter is walking. By herself."

"So what? Regina has walked for a week, already."

"Only with a helping hand. Now, she stood, and without supporting herself, she..." *It wouldn't kill you to be enthralled over your daughter.* Just as fast as her thoughts had formed, a more disturbing contrast blazed its truth. *Your healthy daughter, that is.* It would not be fair for Helene to continue singing more about Regina taking her first independent steps. Not with Rosa strewn across Liselotte's lap, swatting away her bottle, and squinting with vision problems. The poor little honey. Like Regina, Rosa should sit upright, unaided, and point at objects. And, babbling. *Gimme. Gimme.* In addition to the girl's vision, Helene worried about other delays in behavior. Maybe it was unfair to Rosa to compare her to Regina. However, developmentally, Rosa suffered. No disguise could mask the fact. And with a war going on it was a given not to seek medical treatment, at least not in this situation.

They did not need the Third Reich to interfere with their lives under their roof; it was bad enough that they were monitored as soon as they left their doorstep. Their suffering would have been far worse if they were Jewish. Or Roma. Rumors abounded of these folks, commonly called Gypsies despite their objection to the derogatory term. They were *disappearing*. Were they also rounded up and carted away to camps like the Jews? Jew or Roma, no one needed a government, let alone one sole person, to decide if they had a right to live as they choose and to worship their God.

Little Rosa? The doctor who delivered Rosa and her sister had given Helene a sharp perspective of how Aryan eyes would view Rosa as a blemish, one who would bring disgrace to the country. No amount of reasoning or pleading would change the hardened hearts that determined the destined paths for all the Rosas in the world. Back then, Helene had vowed to herself that no one would harm her granddaughter, however, she also knew it was all a matter of timing.

Helene entered the kitchen and proceeded to Liselotte sitting at the table with Rosa on her lap. Helene bent over, putting her face right in front of her granddaughter's, smiling, saying her name several times. She knew not to expect a reaction from the child. None came. Regardless, she enfolded Rosa's hands within hers.

"Be careful," Liselotte scolded. "This one will poke your eye out. She doesn't care."

Helene willed herself to talk gently with Liselotte. "I'm holding your little one's adorable hands. She can't poke me." Helene pecked a kiss on Rosa's forehead. No cooing ensued. In lifting the baby from Liselotte's lap, Helene expected another admonishment from her daughter to handle her in a specific way or suffer the consequences. None came. Liselotte remained silent, unnerving Helene. Wasn't some interaction among family members better than none? That Rosa was severely mentally and physically impaired—further disheartened Helene. "Let me relieve you of Rosa for a spell." Holding the baby tightly against her chest, Helene crossed the room, taking large steps. The faster the better. She would not upset her daughter more, not with her own fat, hot tears rolling down her cheeks. "See to Regina," she said. "Then get dressed and start your day."

"Stop telling me what to do."

"Liselotte, you're a mother," Helene said, tenderly. "Please, act like one. Tend to both of your babies."

"Don't want to."

Helene willed her silly tears away and faced her daughter. Half of her knew this confrontation would end on a sour note while the other half clutched the last bit of hope she had to rebuild a loving relationship between them. She wished she had been a better role model of love all these years she had raised her daughter, doing the best she could but knowing her efforts were not enough. "Then what is it you want? I question whether it is your two daughters."

Liselotte groped the table's edge and struggled to her feet. Helene took a step toward her to help, then thought twice.

"You know what I want," Liselotte said, staring directly into Helene's eyes. "But you never consider my needs, my desires, my dreams. What's the sense of talking about it?"

Liselotte was adult enough to stop pitying herself and to end mourning her non-Prince Charming. Gerhard was not coming for her. If Liselotte's one letter addressed and sent to him two months after the twins' arrival, informing him of his fatherhood to two baby girls, failed to send him running to her and the twins' sides, she should forget him, once and for all. That is if she was in her right mind. Helene resisted groaning. Liselotte was a lovesick teenager, the mother of one healthy girl and one unwell girl. Helene now had three babies to take care of.

A crash came from the other room. Helene and Liselotte exchanged looks; baby Rosa even stopped her fussing.

"Regina!" Liselotte called and rushed from the room.

Helene feathered a finger across Rosa's cheeks. Did Rosa just smile? Could Rosa react to a stimulus, or had her expression stemmed from a natural bodily function, like a burp? Helene clung to the notion of a smile. "If your sister causing trouble gets your mama acting like a mama, and gets you to smile, I hope she misbehaves more often."

CHAPTER SEVENTEEN

Gina, Rochester, September 10, 1961

The bread basket nudging Gina in the arm snapped her out of her swirling thoughts. She eyed the plain white basket with its contents tucked under a yellow cloth as if it were a venomous snake showing its fangs. "Get it out of my sight."

Kenny set his slice of bread on his dish. "What's wrong, Gina?"

A pang of guilt squeezed her heart. Of all people, she did not want to upset Kenny. "Sorry, honey. One minute I can't eat enough food, the next, I can't stand the sight of food."

"My secretary went through the same difficulty with food throughout her last pregnancy," Uncle Raymond said. "Constant heartburn."

"Terrific." Gina wished she had another woman to talk to concerning the changes happening to her body. At first, the daily adjustments were exciting. Now, her body, and life, changed by the second and it seemed all out of her control, ruled by the baby growing within her. Her little girl or boy commandeered her like a general in an army, determining what she ate, the amount of sleep she got, and of course, her appearance. The tag of *routine* no longer existed. The more she thought about it, the more the baby would subject her to the unusual and spontaneous for the rest of her years. Yet, she wanted everything connected to her baby, nothing less. Why Grammy could not be a more giving, supportive nurturer was beyond her guess. And, her mom? Why had she exited her life? She needed her mom more than ever. Fanny was now in her life, which Gina could not link to random coincidence. Yet, Fanny had never married. Could they relate to each other on the level Gina needed? For all Gina knew, the woman may not have ever dated. Whatever the situation with Fanny, Gina felt uncomfortable seeking her out to discuss private female matters. Let her do her attorney thing. Let her make all of their lives better.

She squeezed her eyes shut, pushing away the other, more major factor robbing her of control over her life, hanging over her like a noose, taunting her with fear and panic: the loss, due to the death sentence of her husband for a crime he did not commit. She would rather face the challenges and discomforts of pregnancy than say a final goodbye to Kenny.

"Gina?"

She looked up at Uncle Raymond and smiled at the man who deserved an A+ for all he did for her and Kenny. "Her last pregnancy? How many children does your secretary have?"

"Three. Maybe I can—"

"I'm surprised she works." Gina was sure Uncle Raymond would suggest that he could arrange for her to speak with his secretary. Seconds ago, she thought talking with another woman who had borne a child would be sensible. Now, talking with another woman who struggled with pregnancy was the last thing she wanted to do unless she too had a husband accused of murder. Then, sadly, they could relate to each other.

She pushed her dish toward the center of the table and stood. "I'll try to grab a bite later after I relax." She excused herself and exited the room, aware her center of gravity had shifted again to accommodate herself and her baby. Once again, she had to find a new balance. That seemed to be the way in life—finding the center of gravity and continuing onward. Somehow.

"Is Gina okay?" she heard Kenny ask his uncle.

"Just womanly things," Uncle Raymond responded.

"Like pregnant woman stuff?"

She wanted to growl. And laugh. Instead, she padded up the stairs to the large bedroom she shared with her husband. *Her husband.* Just a few months ago she never envisioned having a man of her own to call a husband. She brushed her fingertips across her belly. She also never imagined she would be expecting a baby.

A baby whose father may be found guilty of a crime he could not have possibly done. And if he were determined guilty, then he would fry in an electric chair. Buried, society would remember Kenneth Franks as the murderer of Samuel Klein, the lippy *degenerate* who might have opened his mouth once too often. Kenny's family, though, would forever grieve over him. Gina would take little Deborah or Wayne to visit their daddy's grave. She would begin by reminding her little one of her or his handsome and charming father. *He was the kindest, gentlest, most thoughtful man I had ever known. He made me happy and proud to be his wife. And, as far as looks go, he was truly handsome—and you take after him. Never, ever, forget who your daddy was.* Then, any news would follow. *Deborah's first baby tooth fell out yesterday as she bit into an apple—she's so excited about the Tooth Fairy coming. Grammy bought a dress for Deborah, and she loves it so much that it's a struggle to change her outfit. Wayne is looking more like you by the day. His joking reminds me of you—the two of you can always get me to laugh... well, how, you, sweetie, used to make me laugh.*

Used to. Past tense.

Gina slapped a hand across her mouth and rushed to the bathroom. Thinking her morning sickness had passed as she had begun her second trimester, this nausea must have resulted from all the chaos buzzing in her mind. She gagged and slapped up the toilet seat, wishing for once Kenny would stop listening to her request to shut the seat and lid when he was done.

She had tossed up several dry heaves when Kenny called her name.

"I love you, Gina. You'll be okay."

Her wonderful husband loved her even when all she wanted to do was puke up her guts.

He squatted beside her and slipped his hand to her back, thankfully not rubbing it in the tiny circles she usually appreciated. "Want to talk? I'll listen."

She looked into his marvelous dark brown eyes and surprised herself by nodding.

"Let me help you up." Kenny stood and with one hand on her back and the other taking her by the arm, he helped her to stand. "Where would you like to go? Want to go outside?"

"No," she said, testing the sturdiness of her voice. She thought of Uncle Raymond and her need for privacy. "Would you be disappointed in me if we stayed in our bedroom?"

"Gina, I can never be disappointed with you."

She kissed his cheek, sighed easily, and they walked to their room, the silence between them comfortable. The twilight's brilliant streaks of copper and pink shining through the window welcomed them, offering a sense of peace. They sat, hip to hip, on the bed's side, their backs to the wall. Kenny grasped her hand but remained quiet. He would stay that way as long as necessary. She could have all the breathing room she needed. If she wanted to talk, that would be fine. If not, that would also be fine. That was just his lovely way. However, she did not want to keep bottled up.

"I have a question," she began.

He nodded. "Ask."

"When you were a boy, did you want to change anything about yourself?"

"I dreamed silly things. Like becoming a scientist or doctor. I even dreamed about becoming president of the United States. Gina, you know I have no smarts."

She shook her head. "No... no...no. You are smart."

He kissed her sweetly on her lips. "Gina, I knew I wasn't smart enough. Even as a little boy. Not like my father. He was broken. I just wasn't smart."

"Honey, I asked you to name what you once wanted to change about yourself. Not what you wanted to be. For instance, when I was little, I wanted to be a trash collector and drive those big trucks. Boy, am I ever happy I didn't become one. However, that's a job. Here's an example of changing something about me." She took a deep breath. This was the first time she had shared this with anyone, a bittersweet comfortableness. No, she thought. She needed to stay in the present. He was alive. He was with her. The present counted, not the awful *what-ifs*. "In sixth grade, my face broke out in pimples. All my classmates made fun of me. I was embarrassed. So, if I could change one thing about myself in the past, I'd say I wanted to be pretty... at least, for others to see me as pretty."

"I'm glad you didn't become a trash collector, too." He pecked her cheek with a tender kiss. "I'm sorry you were made fun of. That wasn't nice. Gina, you are pretty. You're gorgeous."

"Thank you," she murmured. "When you were a kid, did you want to change yourself? I mean, if you could."

"Like what?" He pointed to the side of his head. "Have a new brain put in?"

"Yeah. Something like that." She offered a gentle smile.

"No," he said without hesitation. "I wondered, a lot. What it would be like. To be smarter. Now, I'm glad I couldn't change who I was. Who I am now. I like me."

She could see how he might not have always been *glad* how he measured up, intelligence-wise, to the other boys his age. Thankfully, he had made peace with whom he had become, a remarkable trait considering the most intelligent people she knew often lacked self-respect.

"Know what, Gina?"

"No," she murmured.

"If I were smart, things would be different. We probably wouldn't have met. I would be very sad if I didn't know you."

"I would be very sad, too."

"That's smart, then? I mean, that we love each other."

"Oh, it is," she said, her three words renewing her strength. "I'm glad we said hello that day in the Rochester park."

"So am I."

CHAPTER EIGHTEEN

Fanny, Rochester, September 12, 1961

Betty Hanson did not resemble the woman Fanny had visualized as Kenny's mother. Compared to Kenny's six-foot frame, she was short, skinny, oozed tension, and could not be over fifty years old—if that.

"Hello. Miss Hanson?" Fanny inquired. Kenny and Ray buttressed her sides.

"Yes." Betty slipped the cigarette from her mouth and dropped it to the concrete step. She stubbed out the abandoned smoke with the toe of her weathered sandal. "Miss Stern?"

A miracle surely had occurred when the judge permitted Fanny to take Kenny from Ray's house for a visit with his mother. The very least Betty could do was to be more cordial, let alone look at her son. Judging by Ray's large huff, he too absorbed the awkward friction.

"Let's stop the formal absurdity," Ray said. He stepped toward Kenny and hooked his elbow. "Remember your son, Kenny? Well, this is Fanny Stern, your son's attorney."

"Nice to see you too, Raymond." She eyed Kenny. "Can you speak?"

Ray groaned. Fanny placed a protective hand on Kenny's arm.

"I can speak," Kenny said, blazing a scowl at his mother. "I talk when I have important or nice things to say."

Fanny rocked back, scanning the small group to see who else beside her stood slack-jawed. Go, Kenny, go!

"I'll tell you what, then," Betty said without an emotional clue of how she felt seeing the son she'd abandoned twenty-six years ago. "Why don't the three of you walk to the back patio? I'll meet you there in a moment or two." She pointed to her left where an alleyway separated her house from the one next door. She had not invited them indoors... no looking through old photo albums of baby Kenny's pictures. No peeking at bookshelves or coffee table knickknacks revealing her interests. No sighting of a couch potato squatting lover indicating her taste for companions. "I'll grab another pack of cigs and be right with you." She shut the door, practically in their faces.

"A shame," Ray said. "She never asked if I preferred lemon with my iced tea."

Kenny faced Fanny and Ray with furrowed brows and a pale complexion. He pressed a hand on his stomach.

Fanny wondered if Kenny struggled with a case of indigestion. The poor guy. Seeing his mom suddenly after an absence of so many years, reflecting on why she left him and his father, and consequently if his father's tragic death would have occurred if she had remained home, must be incredibly difficult. "Are you okay, Kenny?"

"Yes. Just thinking. That's all."

"Want to talk as we walk around back?" Ray asked and led the way.

"Yes. And no."

"I see," Ray said. "It's a tough memory?"

Kenny nodded. "I remember her. She's my mother. Remember her smoking."

"Did she smoke around you?" Fanny prompted, awed that he could remember the details of his early childhood days. She vaguely recalled celebrating her seventh birthday.

"She smoked in the same room. She sat away from me. I think. Far away."

"Do you remember her saying anything?" Ray asked.

"Yes. She said she was sad. She wanted to leave. Leave me. Leave my father. And then she laughed."

When Ray exchanged looks with Fanny, she sensed they shared similar thoughts. Kenny's sudden fear of a mom threatening to say a forever bye-bye. Of being swept up in his mother's swinging emotions of sadness and out-of-place amusement. Of Kenny wondering if he was the source of her unhappiness. Although at his tender young age, it was too difficult to comprehend. Fanny thought of her mother. One could be older, and according to society's standards, more *with it*, yet she could not understand why a parent, who supposedly loved you, would flaunt the possibility of severing all family ties.

"That was a long time ago," Fanny said. "You have a different life now."

"Yes. I have Gina. Soon, we'll have a baby. We'll raise him or her, together."

Fanny tried to shake off the bittersweet realization of the big *if* Kenny had avoided saying: if he didn't lose his life if found guilty of murder. Or, was he being optimistic? She needed to keep her thoughts upbeat for her client's sake. "Kenny, you certainly have a lot to look forward to."

Ray swung open the gate and they stepped into the small, private yard.

"There you are," Betty said from her seat at a glass-topped patio table. "Guess I moved faster than you. Sit." She motioned to the mismatched cushioned wrought iron chairs around the table. "Despite needing paint, they're still comfy. Help yourself to a drink and some cheese and crackers."

"What's that?" Kenny asked, pointing to the green and white soda cans with labels reading *here's Sprite. Taste its Long Lasting Tartness.* The h of the first word was in lowercase and each word, except for Sprite, was in script.

"It's a new pop." Betty studied Kenny for a handful of seconds. "It's a lemon and lime mix."

"Like 7 Up?" Kenny asked.

Betty blinked. "Well, yeah. They say it's supposed to taste better, though."

"Who says?"

"Um... I don't... who knows? Who cares?"

Kenny reached for a can and snapped open the lid. "I care."

Ray passed the platter of cheese and crackers. "Want some, Kenny?"

"No thanks." Kenny passed the platter to Fanny, who placed it back on the table's center. Not one of them sampled the food.

"Since this visit can't be easy for any of us, let's begin from the beginning." Betty sipped from her open can of Sprite. She looked squarely into Fanny's eyes. "I've minded my own business for years. Staying out of trouble. Working hard at the laundromat I own and—"

"Gina worked at one, too," Kenny said. "A long time ago. Then she worked at Woolworth. Then waitressed at Bertine's. Now she's pregnant. And she has to watch me when Uncle Raymond is at work. The judge says so."

Betty's eyes widened. "Who in the world is Gina?"

With a pat on Kenny's hand, Ray paused his nephew. "We have a lot to catch up on, Betty. Maybe another time?"

"You bring my son to me for the first time in over twenty-five years—"

"What are you talking about?" Ray said. "I've tried to arrange visits for you with Kenny. You refused, coughing up excuse after excuse. And you certainly didn't invite him over to your place."

This was the first time Fanny had seen Ray angry, though more toward the Papa-bear role than belligerent. *Yay, Ray.*

Betty slammed her pop can down on the table. Foam gushed out like a warning signal from an active volcano. "Do you really have the gall to come here after years of having nothing to do with me and to frame me as the bad one because I needed to support myself by working seven days a week?"

"Your husband and child never told you to leave."

Betty shook a finger at Ray. "How do you know what happened? You certainly didn't live with us."

"My wife," Kenny blurted. "Her name is Gina. She's my wonderful wife. That's who she is. And I love her. And I will love my baby, even if you never loved me. You'll be a grandma. Maybe you'll see our baby, and not me. Because the prison guy might electrocute me." His words threw a blanket on the flame spreading around the table and smothered the tension into stunned silence.

That did it. While Fanny noted not one stinking tear trickling down Betty's cheeks, she needed to swipe her own eyes dry. She snatched a fist full of the paper napkins in the center of the table, sniffled, reset her attention on Kenny's mother, and chose to stick with the facts. "We'd like to speak with you about Kenny's pressing legal matters."

Betty lit up another cigarette and inhaled a long drag. "Get to the point, will ya."

"Kenny is accused of murdering a co-worker," Fanny added. "He needs your help." She stopped for a moment to let the cold reality sink in.

On her feet, with her cigarette in tow, Betty crossed from one side of the fenced-in patio to the other. "I don't know you people." She looked at Fanny. "And, of course, we didn't meet until you forced your way here. Never even heard your name until Ray phoned out of nowhere." She leaned against the fence, stuffed the cigarette in the corner of her mouth, and crossed her arms. "Tell me, Kenny. Did you do it? Did you kill the miserable SOB?"

"Samuel?"

"Whatever his name was." Betty rolled her eyes. "Yeah, your coworker."

"No."

"That's it? No elaboration?"

Kenny raised a brow and looked at his uncle.

"She means details," Ray said.

Betty tsk-tsked. "Of course. What would my sonny boy ever do without his Uncle Raymond?"

Ray opened his mouth to reply. Fanny immediately pressed her hand on his clenched fists resting on the table. She murmured in his ear, "Save it for later."

"I would never kill or hurt anyone," Kenny said, slapping the table twice with a palm. "I did not kill Samuel. I've said this lots of times. Already."

Betty returned to her seat. "What do you want from me?"

Fanny inched forward. "Your son's case is in the very beginning stage. Kenny's charged with first-degree murder—"

Betty gasped. "So, he's right? He's going to fry?"

Fanny sprang from her seat. Ray stopped her from raging by grabbing her elbow and tugging her back to her chair.

"Not now," he hissed, nearly repeating her earlier warning.

Fanny gave a begrudging nod and returned her focus to Betty. "We're readying Kenny's defense for a possible grand jury indictment."

"Power to you," Betty said, her tone edged with sincerity. "Again, I ask, what do you want from me? I'm still not ideal mother material." She waved her hands inwardly. "I mean, look at me—I've failed to keep in touch with him. No holiday cards, let alone birthday cards. No phone calls. I never even married his worthless father—"

"Betty," Ray said with a snap.

"I've made one step toward so-called progress." Betty took another drag of cigarette and blew the smoke out slowly. "I work six days a week, not seven. Today the place is closed. After paying rent and groceries, I barely have a dime to my name. I'm not a churchgoer, don't get involved with social clubs. No jury in their right mind will look at me and see a good mom, let alone believe what I say. I abandoned my child." She wrapped her arms around her middle. "Of all people, how can I help?"

"Betty, the DA is planning to present expert witness testimony showing that because you took off on your son, Kenny has the inclination to disrespect the sanctity of human life, and therefore can easily kill another person."

Betty groaned. "What's this hotshot lawyer doing? Judging others—Kenny—like he has it over everyone?"

Would Betty ever be able to say the words *my son*? Fanny pictured a Calm Button and mentally smacked it. She heard a loud ding echo in her mind, inhaled deeply, and offered a weak smile at Betty. "The DA is doing his job on behalf of the state of New York. While it is true you did—sorry for my baldness—leave your son's father and your then four-year-old son in the man's care to pursue a separate life, I wonder whether you can shed how you interacted with your son from his birth to the time you left your family."

Betty stabbed out her cigarette in a glass ashtray and lit another one, holding it without taking a drag. Her knotted forehead unfurled. She looked at Kenny. "I wasn't a horrible mom back then. I loved you the best I could. Why your father didn't want to marry me is still a mystery." She glanced at Ray. "Did Jerry ever say a word to you?" Ray shook his head.

Kenny pointed an index finger to his left temple. "My father had problems."

"Guess so," Betty mumbled. "Listen, I took care of you. I fed you, changed your diapers, and saw to your naps. All the typical mom stuff." She sighed. "I even sat on the floor and played with you, read your storybooks, told you stories. Baked cookies—can you believe it? Well, at least in the beginning. Until things got too nasty between your old man and me." Her lips turned downward. "I admit it—he went his way and I went mine. I guess you can say I crawled into myself. Didn't spend time with either of you. It wasn't right, but that was what happened."

Relief flooded Fanny with warmth that Kenny had a little good before the bad times took up residence. Sadly though, he did not seem to remember the happy times. Why did bum memories seem to crowd out the good ones?

"Maybe it wasn't wrong, either," Kenny said.

"I did what I could," Betty said, a smile tugging at her lips. "Despite the doctors' warnings."

"What did they say?" Fanny asked.

"He was slow to do normal baby things. And he appeared abnormal in looks. The docs all said he was... retarded. They all used that R word. Said he had a low IQ. That he'd never be normal. We were advised to put him in an institution, and never visit him... in other words, forget him. Said to try for another baby to replace him. Like getting a different car when the old one wears out." She looked into Kenny's eyes. "I didn't want to do that. Neither did your father."

Kenny rolled his lips. "Then why did you leave us?"

"Not because of you, Kenny. As a young mother, I did the best I could for you. According to your father, I wasn't good enough."

"Ray," Fanny said. "Did your brother talk to you about his concerns for his family?"

"No. He kept it all to himself, just like our father did. But it was obvious there was a lot of tension and unhappiness." He glanced at his nephew. "The small advances Kenny had gained nosedived once Betty left the home scene."

"Don't go blaming me for any of his failures," Betty shouted.

"Betty," Ray said, "what I meant, is that after you moved out, Kenny didn't flourish without your touch." Ray jabbed two fingers between his eyes. "My brother wasn't a good parent."

"Let's calm down." Fanny faced Betty. "What was the turning point? What was the one thing that pushed you to leave without taking your little boy with you?"

"I had no choice." Instead of looking into either of their eyes, Betty took a puff of her cigarette and stared at the glass table surface. "It was the middle of the night. Kenny was asleep. Jerry and I were going at it as if we were two boxers in a ring going for the grand prize, at least verbally. One thing led to another—you know how that goes. He hauled me to the front door, opened it, and told me to leave, or else. He said he'd drop off my things once I phoned him and told him my whereabouts. I went to my sister's and called him the next day."

"Did you ever try challenging Jerry for custody over Kenny?"

Betty shook her head. "I didn't have the means to hire an attorney. More importantly, I didn't have the funds to raise him as a single parent, unlike his father, who owned a jewelry store and did a reasonable business."

"Until he lost it altogether," Ray murmured.

"Well, no one contacted me." Betty glared at Ray. "I learned of Jerry's death by reading the obituaries."

"You didn't call or visit," Ray said. "What did you expect?"

Fanny took a deep breath. "Betty, would you be willing to testify on behalf of Kenny? He would greatly benefit from your help."

Betty set her gaze directly on Kenny. "Would you like my help, son?"

"Yes," Kenny said without delay, his eyes growing wide. "Very much. I am your son. You are my mother. I like that."

CHAPTER NINETEEN

Fanny, Rochester, September 14, 1961

With the last sip of her chocolate milkshake, Fanny pushed the empty glass aside and looked at Gina seated beside her at the Woolworth's luncheon counter. "Enjoying your roast turkey and creamed potatoes?"

"And these heavenly corn sticks." Gina moaned contentedly, taking another bite. "You bet. And without a smidgeon of guilt. It's so nice not worrying about eating what I want, and when I want. Maybe I should be pregnant more often."

If Fanny still had been guzzling her drink, she would have spewed the chocolate beverage all over the countertop. "Although I can't offer motherly advice based upon my own experiences, you may first want to try this baby out for size."

"You're probably right." Gina stabbed her last piece of turkey. She glanced around. "It's strange we're eating in this particular Woolworth because I used to work here. With my belly beginning to show, I'm catching former workmates who had ignored me now giving me either the stink eye, a look of disbelief, or envy."

"In a way, the attention must be kind of nice."

"It's more like the right thing at the wrong time. Where were they before I got married and wanted their friendship?"

"Envy can materialize in various ways."

"Ha. They never admired me when I worked with them and hardly spoke to me like I was a lowlife they didn't want to be seen with. Certainly, it's not a case of the envies when it comes to my marriage with Kenny, or having his baby."

Fanny smiled a supportive smile. "What's wrong with being Mrs. Kenneth Franks and expecting his baby?"

"Not one thing. I love Kenny." Gina fidgeted with a straw wrapper. "Love being his wife. Love we're going to have a child. I have no shame. You know how folks are, though. I can hear their whispers; see their pitying, looks. *Oh, you're the one expecting the murderer's child—and to think he's a simpleton, too.* Believe it or not, despite ranting to you right now, I'm beginning not to care. Shocking, isn't it?"

"Do you realize you're talking with someone who has had to hold her chin up for years, no matter what family and supposed friends had thought of her?"

Gina nodded. "Did you ever want to marry and have kids?"

Fanny dropped open her mouth and pressed her hands to the side of her face. When Gina snorted, Fanny played the silly face up more. "Me? Give up my prestigious career and goal of becoming one of America's top ten attorneys?"

"Stop." Gina wrapped her arms around her middle. "All this laughter... it's not good for me or the baby."

"Yep. Laughter's never a good thing. I'm sorry. I should have known better."

Gina laughed again. When she simmered down, she said, "Thank you. I needed a taste of glee."

"That's what friends are for."

Gina reached down and rattled the large brown shopping bag with the store's name in red lettering in its center. "You're so sweet for taking me out for lunch and to shop for clothes."

"You're welcome. David came into the office this morning and freed my day up. I've wanted to get to know you better, so today was perfect."

"I needed a breather away from Uncle Raymond's house. Don't get me wrong—it's a magnificent place. And he has become a mix of a big brother and uncle to me. And surely, I love my husband. Thank goodness Uncle Raymond's off from work today and can stay with Kenny. A change of scenery helps the spirit."

"Perfectly understandable." Fanny winked. "Soon, you'll be needing more clothes, not only for you but for the baby. Do you have a preference for a boy or girl?"

"As long as he or she's healthy, it doesn't matter. I'm glad technology to determine a baby's gender doesn't exist. I like fun, joyous surprises." Gina sighed. "Correction—my preference is for Kenny to be alive, happily married to me, and raising our child—or maybe a bunch of children." Quiet settled between them, and then Gina looked at Fanny and smiled gently. "You didn't answer my question. Did you ever want to marry, have a family, and forget having a career?"

"A long time has passed since I breathed in my law school studies, interned, and set out my shingle. I doubt if there's anything else I'm meant to explore. To conquer, so to say. I barely have enough time to cuddle with my cat and give him the chin scratches he demands."

Fanny drifted back to her little girl days of playing house with her dolls. There was the boy doll, the girl doll, and the baby doll. They had a nice home. Boy doll was a good husband and daddy. He worked hard and came home for his dinner. Girl doll cared for the baby doll, did laundry, and cooked big and delicious dinners for her boy doll. That way of living was a simple, more sensible lifestyle, according to Fanny's mother, her two aunts, and her grandma. Careers were for men, not that her father lived under the family roof as a sterling example of a loving husband and father, and a good provider. Women could not have a career and be expected to care for children. If a woman dared dream of a profession she was seen as a laughable wannabe, a foolish and selfish dreamer. Or, as some folks referred to, *different*. The old ways of the man out of the house and the woman indoors once made the world rotate. Not any other version. Well, that was once upon a time. Now, things were changing by the day.

Fanny returned the smile. "I suppose if I pushed myself into memory-land, yes, of course, I wanted to marry and have a brood of babies. If I think about it further, what I wanted the most was to silence my mother each time she asked the *when-will-you* question." Heat slashed her cheeks and she looked away.

"Fanny," Gina said. "I shouldn't have asked such a nosy question. It's none of my business."

"And I should have been more respectful of my mother." She paused to form clearer words to an unclear part of her life. "Mom was just being a mom. A woman of her time. She meant well."

"It might be a slice of normal life for mothers to become excited about their daughters' lives and eventually become grandmothers," Gina said. She had made air quote marks when she said the word *normal.* "Still, it's pressure for us women. A lot of pressure." She balanced her chin on the tip of her thumb and pressed her mouth against her index finger. "I wish my mother was active in my life. I wish I knew if she is even alive." Gina shrugged. "Who knows? If she is alive, I'd do just about anything for her to help with the ins and outs of marriage and the sometimes overwhelming fears of childbirth and raising a child. I'm not sure I would even complain if she pressured me to have heaps of more children."

Fanny heard Gina's unspoken words: Maybe my mom could comfort me of the possibility of losing my husband to a crime he didn't commit and subsequently, becoming a single mother. About to offer supportive words, Fanny eyed a different waitress approaching them.

"Good afternoon, ladies. I'm Cathy. I'm taking over for Trixie whose shift has ended, the lucky gal." She gawked. "Gina?"

"Oh," Gina said. She glanced sharply at Fanny then returned her attention to Cathy. "Wow. I haven't seen you since graduation. How are you?"

"Fine. I just transferred from another store two days ago. Where're you living?"

"Bridgehaven."

"Bridgehaven, huh? Funny, when I heard you used to work here, I thought the other gals were confusing you with someone else."

"What have you been up to, Cathy?"

Cathy extended her left hand to show a sizable diamond ring. A beaming smile took over her face. "Happily engaged."

"Congratulations. I got married back in April."

"He's one lucky guy."

Gina dropped her gaze momentarily. "By the way, what did you mean by the others confusing me with someone else?"

"Don't worry. They clacked like old biddies gossiping over a girl who used to work here a while ago—the one who married the dummy accused of murder. And my goodness, she's even expecting his baby. Can you imagine?"

Gina stood and interlaced her fingers under her slight but distinctly growing belly. "Yes, that's me all right. I'm proudly married to Kenneth Franks. We're expecting a baby in February and planning to have more children. And, yep, he's the one being accused, wrongfully so, of murder. Although you have neglected to ask, my friend—our attorney—and I would not care for dessert. Have a nice day." She motioned to Fanny to collect her purchases. "It's time to check on Kenny. I sure wouldn't want him getting into further trouble."

Fanny tossed four dollars onto the counter to cover their lunches and a tip. Gina might not appreciate Fanny leaving a gratuity, but after the brilliant way Gina handled her former schoolmate, Fanny took pleasure in doing so.

Standing at the main exit facing East Main Street, Gina giggled. "That was fun."

"Your encounter with a former schoolmate wasn't what I expected. You dealt with that well... better than I would have." Fanny reached for the door handle. "Where to?" When Gina failed to reply, Fanny followed Gina's transfixed gaze through the glass door as people of various ages carried picket signs and marched past the Woolworth store. While fashion chiefly still resembled the more modest styles from the '50s, lately more women wore bold patterns and shorter hem lengths and were abandoning their gloves. Most guys kept their hair buzzed-cut and in a mixed crowd wore ties and hats, though here and there, a shaggy waist-length-haired one appeared, defying the norm. The protestors out on the street were clean-cut in appearance, though a few had donned jeans with wide bottoms and dared to wear T-shirts, some with cartoon characters, others with political messages. Fanny could only imagine what the rest of the decade might look like. Annoyed with cultural rules that she knew would backfire, she could only hope for more independence in attire.

"What in the world is happening out there?" Gina asked. "Is it safe to venture out?"

"I don't have a clue," Fanny said, sincerely. Her mind traveled to a year ago when the *Greensboro Four*, four black college students, staged the first non-violent sit-in at a Greensboro, North Carolina Woolworth lunch counter to protest the company's policy of refusing service to blacks at its lunch counter. The four young men had remained seated until the store closed. The next morning, they returned with twenty-five more college students. When the police arrived, because no violence occurred, no arrests were made. Fanny returned her attention to Gina. "Let's go out and see what we can learn. If there's any sign of danger, I'm taking you back indoors, immediately. Agreed?" Gina nodded and they exited the building.

Gina hooked the shopping bag over her arm and covered her ears. "The protest is much louder than I realized."

"I'm not surprised," Fanny said, her eyes on the protesters.

"Hey, hey! Ho, ho! The Berlin Wall has gotta go!"

More chants blared from bullhorns, matching the messages painted on signs held by many in the crowd.

"Support two million Berliners in their rights to peace and a progressive lifestyle."

"Keep the peace!"

"Give peace a chance in Berlin."

"Destroy the wall, build peace instead."

"The demonstration... the Berlin Wall," Gina said, her words swallowed by the surrounding noise. Barely able to hear her, Fanny nodded. They pressed against the storefront as two teenage boys raced by on bicycles. Between them, they carried a sign which read: Down with the wall, up with freedom for all!

A silver-haired man dressed in brown slacks, a striped tan and white shirt, and chukka boots, appearing more like someone who worked in an office rather than attended demonstrations, ducked into the hidden, safer place against the store and stood alongside Fanny and Gina. Fanny hoped he had information to share about what spurred the protest. Did the marchers have permits to rally? Surely, the police would arrive on the scene any second. She had to get Gina out of there, and fast. Appearing at a rally would not be the right image for her client's wife. Neither would it help Fanny gain bonus points in her professional reputation.

"What's happening out there?" Fanny asked the stranger.

The man slid his hat off. "Yesterday, more than eighty British people of prominence sent a letter of solidarity to Willy Brandt, the governing mayor of West Berlin. It stated freedom in Berlin must be upheld, and all people have the right to live without fear and foreign intrusion and control."

"Results?"

The man shrugged. "Just happened yesterday. Same day as two women in East Berlin—right on the border of the west side—tried escaping from an apartment."

"Are they okay?" Gina asked, then covered her mouth as if her words alone could provoke the unimaginable.

"Sad times. The police stopped them by using tear gas and water cannons. From what I heard on the news last night, a West Berlin fire brigade had stood on guard with a safety net for the women to jump out the apartment window and land on the west side of the wall. Those Easterners stopped them cold. I imagine they were arrested and thrown in jail."

For all of Fanny's education, wide scope of reading, and monitoring the news, she had trouble comprehending how Gina's former classmate saw her as a fool for marrying Kenny and wanting to have his baby, contrasted to a short sixteen years ago when a devastating world war ended, followed by the Korean War five years later. And now, once again, authorities in control desired to rob citizens of their human rights to enjoy freedom. Where was the humanity in all the madness? Who was the true fool?

"Let's go, Fanny," Gina said. "We either return home or make the evening news by grabbing a protest sign and participating in the march. I don't think it would help Kenny's situation if I made the headlines."

"You're right—not even for a good cause of advocating human rights for all." The sad irony of it all. She glanced around for the older man. He was gone. "Where did our friend go?"

"He snatched an extra sign and joined the march."

Fanny looked at the last batch of protestors storming past them, chanting, with signs held high above their heads. "Yeah, we need to leave."

Gina sighed heavily. "If circumstances were different—no murder charges for Kenny, nor a baby's welfare—the two of us would have joined the demonstration. Right?"

"Absolutely," Fanny said without delay, pushing aside any concerns about her participation possibly impacting her career. For once, it was nice not to only think about life and how it seemed to revolve around work. She was more than a woman who wore a suit five days a week to win cases for her clients because she believed it was the right thing to do, not to prove her worth to society. To see an agreeable smile on Gina's face was priceless. "Are you up to a talk once we return to Ray's? That is, just the two of us. I had an interesting visit the other day from your grandmother and now I'm more perplexed than ever. Our fifteen-minute car ride home won't cut it."

"Sounds serious, but sure. You have me curious about Grammy's visit." They headed in the direction of Fanny's car three blocks over. "I hope more groups of citizens will unite to protest the Berlin Wall and the lack of freedom it symbolizes. How any one person or governing power can have the audacity to divide people by a wall saddens me. The awful part is that this calls for those in authority to segregate people into groups, like the supposed better versus the worthless. Talk about prejudice!"

Fanny nodded. "Sadly, this is nothing new."

"After what the world's gone through, horrific trouble can start all over again because of this forced division."

Fanny reached out for a thread of hope. "However, I believe goodness prevails."

"So true," Gina said. They reached the car and slid into the front seat. "Once we arrive home, I'll listen to whatever you want to share. I'm sure I can handle it."

With Gina's last words, Fanny realized the positive changes in her. Sure, Gina would pounce defensively if provoked, sometimes on the straightforward side, daring to come close to crossing the line of more polite social conversation. The mom-to-be, however, was becoming a stronger woman, one she had grown to respect. Yet, what she had to say to Gina would undoubtedly be a challenge.

CHAPTER TWENTY

Gina, Rochester, September 14, 1961

"That was a lot of excitement for our girls-only outing," Gina said. Scenes from the past few hours paraded in her thoughts. Shopping for maternity clothes and enjoying lunch. Running into her mouthy former classmate. Witnessing a protest march against the developments between West and East Germany. She was exhausted. No wonder she struggled to stay awake as they headed back to Uncle Raymond's.

When Fanny didn't reply, Gina shifted and relaxed her head against the passenger window. In her foggy state, she wondered why Grammy had paid an uninvited visit to Fanny's house. Gina could not imagine the nature of the visit was positive. Suddenly, a memory stepped out from the darkness. She and Grammy still lived in Germany. Grammy was about to change things. Again. They were seated on the sofa in their Berlin home. She remembered eyeing Grammy's lap and wanting to snuggle with her. Since Grammy was not the type to pat her lap and invite her to cuddle, Gina knew better than to ask. Instead, she sat stiffly a little distance away.

"Listen, carefully, sweetheart."

She had to be in trouble. Grammy never used cute words like sweetheart or honey unless bad news followed.

"We're moving to America, Regina" Grammy stated.

"Why, Grammy? I don't want to leave."

"Sometimes, we must do what's best. Even if we don't see it that way at first."

"I like it here."

"Do you like carrots?" Regina shook her head. "Because you want to grow up healthy and strong, you should eat carrots and other healthy foods, no matter if you don't them."

"Germany has carrots. We can stay here. We don't have to go away."

Grammy's eyes watered. Her smile disappeared like a bunny in a magic trick. "Sad memories are here." She pointed to Regina's ankle. "The war may be over, but there are scars and it's time to heal. Like the boo-boo you got yesterday when you fell. In a few days, you'll be all better. Well, I want to start a new life in a new place and feel better too. It will be good for both of us."

What did Grammy mean by sad memories? "Will my mama be in America?"

"No. Remember, I told you she is gone. You can't see her again."

"Grammy, if I try hard, I can see Mama. Here. In our house. We can stay."

"She's gone, sweetheart. It's time for a change. Moving to America will make me happy. Don't you want me to be happy?"

"Yes," she said, without hesitation.

Grammy's smile returned. "Wonderful! We leave tomorrow."

Why was Grammy shaking her?

"Wake up, sleepyhead. We're home."

Grammy? Fanny? Gina wanted her mother.

Gina batted her eyes open and found Fanny sitting beside her in the car. "Home? Oh, we are?" She shook her head. "Sorry. I was dreaming of when Grammy and I lived in Germany. Wow. I'm glad I'm not there, especially considering the forced division between west and east."

"Are you okay? You were twitching around for a while."

"Sheesh. How embarrassing." Gina glanced at Fanny, relieved she was in America, not Germany, let alone four years old again. At that age, she had not wanted to come to New York. Her whole life would have turned out differently, radically so, if she had remained in her native country. Especially, not meeting Kenny. And these days she might have ended up living on the East side of the wall, restricted by the government on how to live. Then again, here in New York, people around her glared accusatory, judgmental daggers at her for sticking to her husband's side. They lived in a huge world, yet, apparently, it was too small for folks to stop vying for control of others. "Yes, I'm fine. Just plain exhausted."

"I imagine you are. We had ourselves enough excitement for some time to come."

About to say she preferred the excitement of protest rallies than the anxiety of a court battle involving her husband, Gina stopped short when an off-white Ford Fairlane pulled up behind them in the driveway. "Who's that?"

"It's David, my associate. I suspect his sudden appearance may not be exactly interesting."

"One way to find out.

Fanny opened the driver's door and stood as David exited his vehicle. "What's up?"

Gina's attention strayed to Uncle Raymond's front door. She blinked at Grammy, the one person she never expected to see here. Tired or not, Gina hefted herself out of the car. She tried her best to push away the sinking sensation chiseling her stomach.

David handed a file folder to Fanny. "We received a phone call from an unexpected potential witness. A Floyd Osman. I invited him to the office and we had a good conversation, though it may or may not make a difference. I thought you might want to review my initial report."

"Thank you..." Fanny broke off and stared at the front door where Grammy stood. She looked at them as if *they* were the unexpected visitors of concern. Then, Uncle Raymond opened the door further and stepped out.

"Would everyone like to come in?" he asked. "I have coffee to offer. The magic brew has a reputation to spark energy and world peace."

Although Uncle Raymond had attempted in his charming way to make everyone relax, no one smiled, nor had they entered the house. With arms wrapped around herself, Gina stepped toward the newly formed cluster. "Where's Kenny?"

"He's setting up the cups and saucers." Uncle Raymond pointed toward the house. "He mentioned you all afternoon."

"Oh?"

"Like, how wonderful you are," Kenny said. He stepped beside Helene, and by cupping his hands around his mouth, he called out megaphone-style, "I missed you."

Grammy's mouth dropped open, yet she remained quiet. Gina knew her grandmother well enough that she could hear, at least in her mind, Grammy sighing her exasperated two cents.

Gina had no patience for confusion a second more. "Coffee sounds marvelous right now." She scanned the small crowd. She placed her hands around her belly for emphasis since she did not think politeness would do the trick. "Since the baby and I are tired, let's get going."

"I second the motion," Kenny said. Everyone turned to face him. Brows lifted. Foreheads crinkled. Kenny shrugged. "I hear that a lot when I go to movies. I mean, when I used to go to the movies. Now, I'm home. At Uncle Raymond's."

"I'm glad you're here," Raymond said, patting Kenny on the back. "Let's all go indoors before the coffee cools off."

"One moment, Gina," Fanny said as she hooked her elbow and drew her back as everyone else piled into the house. "Kenny's a trouper," she said in a low voice, keeping the exchange between them. "And you are too— exceptionally so. While I still want to share with you about your grandmother's visit the other evening, I want to tell you that after we visited Kenny's mother, I think it's safe to say that Betty realized we weren't visiting to condemn her for leaving Kenny. He was delighted when she warmed up to him and called him *son*. While she can't go back and change their personal history, there might be a chance for mother and son to rekindle family ties." Fanny looked off into the distance.

"Fanny? Is it ever too late for lost family members to heal the brokenness of separation?"

Slowly, Fanny faced her. "Let's hope not."

"A fair enough answer," Gina said as she watched Fanny again turn away. Was this daring woman who chose the profession of law despite many women remaining home on the wife-mother front, now wondering how her life might have developed if her relationship with her mother had turned out differently? Might she have been content as a housewife and mother, raising a handful of children if she had married someone like the surgeon who lived across the street from Uncle Raymond? Perhaps she would have worked fewer hours, just enough to insert independence. Or, if she had more encouragement and emotional support at a younger age, she might have gone the other extreme to have a more prestigious law practice and become the sole owner of the magnificent house next door. Or, having both a family and a career.

Gina did not do badly despite her mom's absence as she was growing up. Although she often did not see eye to eye with Grammy, Gina was grateful to have her grandmother as a guardian. When it came to Kenny—aside from their legal battle—she was beyond extreme happiness for meeting and falling in love with him, and soon having his baby. She could not fairly point the finger of blame—whether at Grammy or her *lost* mother—on not enrolling in college or failing to date men society shaped as go-getters and social climbers. Kenny would be declared *not guilty*; in her mind, innocent. Presently, though, this legal mess was like a diagnosis of advanced cancer, without hope of a cure. Only a miracle and the possibility of a breakthrough development would restore one's health. In the case of Kenny's criminal charges, a miraculous breakthrough would provide the success he needed to be a free man again. Thank God they had Fanny on their side, working hard and diligently on Kenny's behalf.

"I believe in happily ever after endings," Gina said. "And miracles."

Fanny pivoted. "Pardon?"

"Just thinking aloud. Sorry." Gina conjured Kenny's often typical calm look. "I'm determined to remain positive."

"There's no reason to apologize for staying positive."

"Good." Gina held the door open for Fanny. "Let's charge into the fray, bravely."

•   •   •

The kitchen, where Gina had assumed the others would be seated around the table with coffee mugs cradled in between their palms, stood empty. She shrugged at Fanny. "I can't guess where they are."

"Me, either."

Gina heard a distant chuckle. She pointed at the open French doors and blew on her fingernails then brushed her chest as if she had just scored higher than others in a grueling task. "I would make a great detective—they're outside on the patio. If only that were the most difficult problem to resolve, right?" Fanny nodded. They proceeded out.

"We saved you some coffee," Uncle Raymond said.

Fanny took the seat beside David. The only other chair for Gina remained between Kenny and Grammy. Wonderful, when it came to Kenny. Nail-biting anxiety when it came to her grandmother. She sat, wondering what the woman was thinking, or judging. Not wanting to involve herself with Riptide Grammy, getting dragged out to sea, and robbing her of energy to swim back, she faced Kenny. "Are you okay?"

"Yes, Gina. I missed you. Did you have fun today?"

"Definitely. I'll tell you more, later."

"I'm glad to see you again, Gina," Grammy said.

Gina's mind emptied.

"Gina," Kenny whispered, "say hello to your grandmother."

Of course! "Hi, Grammy. Thanks for visiting us today."

"How are you?"

Additional words refused to form in her mind. Kenny grasped her hand. She immediately relaxed. "I'm good. Tired, all the time."

"That's normal."

Gina mouthed the words *thank you*. After a tick of seconds, she added, sincerely, "It's so nice to hear you say that there's something normal about me."

"You need to stop by for a visit. Wags misses you. He's not the same without you."

Was this Grammy's way of saying she felt her absence?

Fanny cleared her throat. "Let's begin. Although we're gathered in this amazing, fine house—thank you, Ray, for hosting an impromptu meeting—it's not my place to extend the meeting time. Also, I'd like to begin so we don't keep David during his off-time." She thanked David for coming to Cobbs Hill to meet with them, took a large swig of coffee, and then gathered what appeared to be a report from the tabletop. "David, though I've given the report a quick perusal, why don't you fill us in on this development."

"Sure," David said. His business-like tone clashed with his casual clothes of blue jeans and a black and white striped shirt with a red collar. With Fanny wearing black slacks and a plain pullover white blouse, Gina could see how Fanny and David made an interesting team.

"A potentially good witness for us," David continued, "Floyd Osman, phoned us today. Mr. Osman lives in the apartment building to the left of the lot where the victim was found. His balcony faces the lot. If I'm not mistaken, Mr. Osman is age forty." He paused for verification and Fanny checked the report and nodded. "He lived at home with his bedridden father and was often there to see to his father's needs. Since June, Mr. Osman had only ventured from the apartment to the grocery store, and attended to banking, and other necessary tasks." David eyed Kenny. "On the day when the police found the defendant alongside the victim, Mr. Osman states he heard someone shouting for help. He believes the voice matches Kenny's from the recording sample I played for him."

"When I shouted for help for Samuel?" Kenny asked.

"Yes," David said as he took the report Fanny handed him. After scanning it, he looked up at Kenny. "Mr. Osman distinctly heard a call for help. He remembered a deep male voice, shouting *Samuel's hurt... help... help Samuel*. He said the person called out several times."

"That's good he heard me, right?" Kenny added.

David titled his head. "Yes and no. First, Mr. Osman testified it was a consensus among—"

"David," Fanny interrupted, "if I may, I'd like to explain the rest to Kenny." David nodded and handed her the report. "Kenny, what David learned today by talking with Mr. Osman is that the back lot you and Samuel ran into is a hangout for street gangs."

"Like teenagers who fight with other teenagers?"

"Yes. It's usually a pack of teenage boys and young men. They go after each other viciously. Sometimes for drugs, other times for money... or both. At times, they're after making a name for themselves."

"Saying they're the best?" Kenny asked.

"Correct," Fanny said. "During the past year, two rival gangs made a hangout of the lot. Several times, the cops had reported there to investigate.

That might, or might not, explain why the police had arrived as quickly as they did."

Gina, hopeful again, inched forward in her seat. "Did someone hear Kenny crying for help?"

"The potential witness, Floyd Osman, says he heard someone shouting for help. His father then experienced a seizure and Mr. Osman needed to attend to his care. Understandably, he couldn't pursue identifying the person calling for help."

"How unfortunate," Uncle Ray said.

"This was in August," Fanny clarified. "A few days after Kenny's arraignment, Mr. Osman's father passed away. Again, understandably, Floyd Osman went through a period of mourning. As he climbed out of his grief, he wanted to follow up on the crime committed, especially after reading in the newspaper what had occurred. When David had dropped by his apartment building to interview the residents, Osman relayed his surprise over Samuel's death and Kenny's initial arrest. He said if he could be of help, to contact him."

"Can Mr. Osman be a witness on behalf of Kenneth?" Grammy asked, surprising Gina with the sudden question after minutes of silence. Gina had assumed she was there to listen, not to contribute. She heard a different twinge in her voice, one of hope.

Fanny looked away from the document and directly into Grammy's eyes. "Kenny," she said. "He prefers the name Kenny, not Kenneth."

A jolt sizzled through Gina. Accustomed to Grammy calling Kenny by his full first name of Kenneth, it had taken a few extra seconds for Gina to realize Fanny had instructed Grammy to view her grandson-in-law on a more familiar basis.

"Yes," Grammy said. "Kenny, it is."

Kenny smiled at Grammy, though he remained silent. Was he anticipating an invitation to call her Grammy? When none came, he pushed aside his untouched coffee and glanced at Fanny. "Is this good news? Will Mr. Osman help us?"

"I sure hope so," Fanny said. "However, I believe the court will see him as a weak witness because he tended to his father. He is unsure if he distinctly heard you call for help. He didn't see you, didn't see what happened. This may not be the strong evidence we need, but with the knowledge of active gang activity in the area, it's a good direction for us to pursue." She turned to David. "Are you up for additional investigation?"

"Of course," David said. He stood. "If you don't mind, I'll split and see what I can further dig up."

"Aren't you off-duty?" Fanny asked with a smile in her tone.

"Never for you."

"I'm so glad I can count on you. Oh, David? Can you arrange a meeting for me to meet Osman directly?"

"Sure." David excused himself and left.

"I still don't understand," Kenny said.

"I appreciate your honest communication," Fanny said. "Let's think of what we just learned as a positive development. We'll figure out how to make it work for us, not against us. Okay?" After Kenny gave a little nod, Fanny stood. "What a day we had." She smiled at Gina. "Girl fun, a protest rally—"

"A rally?" Uncle Raymond said, his eyes wide.

Fanny waved a hand. "It was extraordinary—exhilarating—seeing people gather in the name of peace. Nothing of concern—we weren't in danger. I'd never purposely put Gina—or anyone—in harm's way." She smiled at Gina. "If you aren't too exhausted, I'd still like to chat with you."

"Sure," Gina said and headed toward the bathroom. "The baby's controlling me. Again. Just give me a moment and you'll have my complete attention."

CHAPTER TWENTY-ONE

Helene, Berlin, Germany, December 20, 1943
At the front door, Helene stomped off the snow from her shoes. Unlike her childhood holidays in a house decorated with a Christmas tree, evergreen branches strewn on the mantel, and paper stars in the windows, today, her home looked pitiful. While Hitler had tried his best to obliterate the Christian position of celebrating Christmas, replacing it with a nod toward the winter solstice with its rebirth of the sun, and at one point, attempted to do away with Jesus and instead push for the *Savior Führer*, German citizens still celebrated Christmas with traditional customs. Whispers whooshed through the air that an unexpected fringe benefit of the war was that Hitler kept too busy taking over countries to pursue the abolishment of the holiday. Now, Helene glanced about the house. The lack of holiday décor made the place appear downright grim.

"Liselotte?" She took one step forward toward the parlor. "Where are you? Are the babies okay?"

Silence greeted her like the death stare of a wolf. With a hand gripping her coat collar, she raced into the kitchen, praying Liselotte and the girls were there. The room was empty. While Liselotte could remain quiet, the twins—at least, Regina—would not unless asleep. At four in the afternoon, Helene doubted the twins were napping.

She walked back into the hallway. "Liselotte," she called again, aware it sounded more like a shriek. At the base of the staircase, prepared to call her daughter's name again, a rattling noise came from upstairs. No one would scare her short from preventing harm to her daughter or grandbabies. She flew upstairs to confront the intruder.

After a complete search of the two bedrooms and the makeshift nursery in a small sewing room, an additional clatter did not sound. It had to be the miserable visitor. "You worthless mouse," she yelled. "Show your scrawny rodent-ugly face once more and it will be the end of you. No cat's necessary in this house—not with my big, fast feet." Painfully aware that yelling exorcised her pent-up frustration, she gulped a large breath of air to let loose once more and nearly choked when, from below, she heard the front door open and shut.

"Go to the kitchen, Regina. I'll be right there."

Liselotte. Helene had warned her several times not to step foot outdoors. And she had taken the twins?

"No sad faces for Mama. I have to change your sister's stinky diaper. I'll be in the bathroom."

"No, Mama. No."

A big sigh. "Fine. Come along, then. Maybe I'll check yours too—I have nothing else to do except to check dirty diapers."

"Liselotte," Helene said, halfway down the stairs.

Liselotte stood by the door with Rosa in her arms. Regina clung to her skirt. "Hello, Mutter."

"Save your salutations for others, Liselotte. You have no business—"

"Oh, I have already given my greeting to someone else—cheerier than the one I just gave you."

Helene rested a hand on the oak newel post. "I don't care for your smirk."

"And I don't care for you bossing me around like I'm a naughty toddler." With a gentle hand to Regina's bottom, Liselotte instructed her to sit on the sofa while she changed Rosa's diaper. After Regina cooperated, she faced her mother. "It's too late, Mutter. You couldn't have stopped us."

"Us? Who are you referring to?" Helene crossed her arms. "Exactly how many times have you left the house despite me forbidding you to? Just last month Berlin saw a major bombing—we barely escaped. Now is not the time to take chances."

"Repeating your own words, if I'm old enough to bear children, I'm old enough to make adult decisions. It's time for you to be happy for me,

Mutter. Please, I so want your encouragement since I've taken your advice to heart."

Her daughter had listened to her? "My advice? I told you to stay home, that was my advice."

"What I did involves a certain someone."

Wobbly-kneed, Helene slumped onto the bottom stair. The dry old wood squeaked, contradicting her slim figure—courtesy of the rationed foods they were subjected to. Nervous to hear her daughter's replies to what she was about to say, for all of their sakes, she had to pursue the subject. "I rarely step outside. When I do, it's for the long food lines to obtain a measly portion. Other times it's to search for an item for the girls, often on the sly. And why? Because I only have you and my granddaughters on my mind. I risk my life for you three, and will continue to do whatever it takes to keep you well."

Liselotte glared. "Stop the drama. I can't take it any longer."

Helene would have laughed at her daughter's scowl, if it were not for the awful circumstances plaguing them, and the real danger to their lives. She wished with all her heart for a better time, frivolous and fluffy.

"Mutter," Liselotte said, jolting Helene from her wishes for more joyous days. "Clearly—like you've bragged through the years—out of the two of us, you're the better woman. Why don't you scout around for a medal the next time you're out? I'm sure the Nazis can spare you one."

On her feet, Helene took Rosa from Liselotte's arms. "Now that you have two empty hands, shrug out of your coat and change your daughter's diaper. Or, is this too a ruse, like so many things you've declared? The air is missing a nasty stench."

Liselotte groaned, yet kept her coat on. "One second you have me convinced you're acting nice to me. The next, you're the same old biting mother I can't stand being around, though I've certainly tried."

Helene refused to fall for that bait. "How often have you left the house behind my back?"

"To meet with boys? No boys for me." Liselotte smiled and batted her lashes as if flirting. "A man, yes."

"Step away from the door and tell me who."

Liselotte half chuckled; half groaned. She remained rooted by the door. "Two months ago, while you were out of the house, Gerhard visited."

"What did he wear?"

Liselotte's eyes widened. "You're asking that question first? Not, what he wanted? Or, if I introduced him to his daughters?"

"You heard correctly." After Liselotte mumbled, Helene demanded her to speak up.

"A uniform. He's proudly serving the Nazi Party."

With the rate of Rosa's fussing matching Helene's growing fear, and the two approaching a sparking point of fire, Helene gritted her teeth. "What color was the uniform?"

Liselotte looked away. "Gray-greenish."

"Waffen SS."

"Well, he has to serve Germany, somehow. He's not a Jew."

Helene covered her mouth with a hand. Fear? Nervousness about what could slip off her tongue? Outrage and disappointment about her daughter's prejudice. All three?

"Mutter? You're whiter than a new bedsheet."

Helene, careful to hold Rosa firmly in her grip, said, "Did he see the girls?"

"Of course. I had to tell him—he's their papa. I asked him to come in."

"What did he say about Rosa?"

"At first, not a word. He looked concerned, a good, caring concern, not condemning or judgmental. I could tell by Gerhard's expression he knew something was wrong with our daughter, but if he had negative thoughts, he kept them to himself."

Our. The word had not escaped Helene. The louse of a man. He should have known better than to involve himself with her young daughter. Now, Liselotte, once again entranced under his spell, saw him as suitable husband material and the ideal father to the girls.

"He picked up Rosa," Liselotte continued. "He kissed her and said *I love you, my little one.* Just like a proud father would say. He then did the same with Regina."

"He made no comments concerning Rosa's health?"

Liselotte shrugged. "He asked more about me. I told him having two babies wasn't easy, though Rosa's condition didn't complicate their birth. We played with Regina while Rosa slept."

"So, he suddenly wants you in his life again? Has he proposed to you? Is this what you think I was advising you—to marry someone who marches to Hitler's command?"

"Propose, as in marriage? Mutter, Gerhard's reappearance was unexpected, though I'd hoped like anything to see him again. Don't rush us into marriage."

"Why are you giving him the time he wants? Don't you see, he's not taking the time to take you or the girls seriously." When Liselotte opened her mouth, Helene charged on. "For once, open your eyes. The father of your children is a Nazi. It doesn't matter whether he'd volunteered or was conscripted. To serve the German ruler, he had to sign papers recognizing the Nazi party. He's serving a leader who mandates a perfect Aryan race, one who will stop at nothing to obtain his goals. Everyone who serves under Hitler must obey all of his demands or face the consequences of removal, which translates to death. Don't you..." Helene swallowed dryly when her daughter held up a hand to stop her.

"Once again, Mutter, you're wrong. Yes, Gerhard is a Waffen SS member. In title only."

"Why is that?"

"Because he's on the run from them."

Until that given second, Helene considered people's description of dizziness as seeing little white stars circling one's head an exaggeration. She was wrong. White stars circled her. Certain they had sucked her into a vortex and pulled her into permanent darkness, she staggered to the wooden bench seat of the hat stand beside the door. "What do you mean he's on the run?"

"Three months ago, not even aware of his children, he got thinking about the two of us and took off from the SS and returned to his family's Berlin home."

"Yes, of course," Helene muttered. "Berlin is the epitome of a haven for SS deserters."

"These days, he's hiding under his parents' toolshed."

"And now he wants you and your daughters to hide with him? My, what a cozy and safe place, living under a shack. Perfect for bringing up your children."

"*Our* daughters. They're just not mine. It's okay—don't worry. His parents give him food. Besides, no one comes knocking on their door. Not when his father was the chief chemist in developing Fanta for Coca-Cola. Who would suspect a man working for the company that produces one of the Führer's favorite drinks? Besides, this is all temporary... we plan to relocate as soon as we can secure a place that his father is helping us to find. We're trying to be practical in an impractical situation—war. We want the best for each other and our daughters. Don't you want that for us as well?"

"Of course, I want that for you and my granddaughters. That's why I want you here, away from Gerhard and his family."

Liselotte wiped her eyes with the back of her hand and sniffled.

Helene crossed her arms quickly before she too needed to wipe tears from her eyes. Silence filled the entranceway. She struggled for words to address her incredibly naïve love-stricken daughter who followed her hormones more than a common-sense approach. Like mother like daughter? Once, a man she thought could do no wrong had blindsided her like this lover had done to Liselotte. She looked into her daughter's eyes. "Gerhard is a deserter of the SS," she said, determined to keep a civil, calm tone. "What is to stop the Nazis from raiding his family home and searching the place from cellar to attic to toolshed?"

"As I said, Gerhard's father is well-respected—at work and in the community. His neighbors can vouch for him. Besides, there are ways to escape the Nazi eye."

Helene gulped. When it came to how the Nazis would judge Liselotte's cover-up of hiding her Prince Charming-less, her daughter would also be seen as blameworthy as Gerhard's parents.

Liselotte snickered. "Mutter, you should see your face now. You look as if I just told you his father was Hitler's long-lost brother."

"Liselotte, this is Nazi Germany. It's being culled of undesirables; of which Rosa is one. The country's being shaped into an ultra-Fatherland like we've never imagined possible. Gerhard is putting you and the girls at risk each time he visits here and when you visit him. You can't count on Gerhard's neighbors coming to the rescue by putting in a good word for his family, not when neighbors are turning against neighbors by the minute. It's everyone out for himself."

"Calm down. He only came here once. I visit with him on Mondays at his place." She dropped her gaze to the floor. "I'm usually... usually manage... to get back before you return. Except for today. Do you know why?" She made eye contact again. "Because we got carried away with fun—telling the girls stories, daydreaming aloud about our future, little, big things that real adults do when they're not terrified to live."

That explained her absence. However, this raging war could not be dismissed. They were all vulnerable, all sitting targets. Mondays were the one long day when Helene was gone from the house from early morning to late afternoon, standing in line after line for the necessities her little family needed. She hated leaving their sides, but knowing her daughter remained home caring for the twins and would not venture outdoors, Helene had settled for that slight comfort and continued with the tasks. She was wrong. She should have never trusted her daughter, especially not with the lives of Regina and Rosa dependent upon her actions.

"Don't worry, Mutter. I don't drop the girls off at random neighbors for them to watch. I bring them along. Gerhard and I keep a good eye on them to make sure they remain safe. No one sees us, Mutter." Liselotte smiled widely. "You should see how Gerhard's mother oohs and aahs over the twins."

"I'm frightened for you and my granddaughters. It's only a matter of time until this boy of yours is discovered. If you and the girls are there when this happens, you will need all the mercy possible to avoid trouble."

"We have it under control." Liselotte's sudden grin was too cocky for Helene's nerves.

"How?" Dry-throated, Helene had trouble asking the one-word sentence. Worse, she feared her daughter's answer.

Liselotte stood. "I have to see what Regina is up to—she's too quiet. Please, have confidence in me." She headed for the parlor, calling Regina's name.

The thing was, when it came to Liselotte, Helene's doubt ruled. Two years ago, her daughter had hidden her involvement with Gerhard until she could not conceal her pregnancy a day longer. Then, in his absence, Liselotte had wilted like a droopy willow deprived of water, retreating into herself, sullen to the point of perpetual unpleasantness. Helene blamed it on the pregnancy and all the physical changes Liselotte was experiencing. Yet, after the babies were born, her daughter continued to pine for Gerhard and left most of the baby care to her. With Gerhard back again in her life, Liselotte suddenly glowed, a carefree girl oblivious to the war around her and the rest of the world. If it was any other man, Helene might view Gerhard's turnaround thinking as maturity, and he might have come to realize he truly loved Liselotte and that he should no longer avoid or neglect her. However, he owed his allegiance to Germany. The price tag for his desertion spelled imminent danger to himself, Liselotte, and their children.

"Mama's here now, Sleepyhead Regina," Liselotte said from the other room.

Was her daughter cooing to her child?

"Want bed," Regina said.

"I'm sure you do sweetheart. We've had ourselves a long day."

With Rosa in tow, Helene stepped into the room. She stared at her daughter conversing tenderly with her daughter. What was going on? "What are you and Gerhard planning?"

Liselotte didn't respond. Helene repeated her question.

"I'm not deaf," Liselotte said.

"Answer me, then."

"All I can say is that soon, you will no longer have to worry."

"Take off your coat and spread it on the floor."

Liselotte narrowed her eyes. "Pardon?"

Helene repeated herself. When Liselotte slipped her coat off and placed it on the rug, Helene gently eased Rosa onto the warm garment and watched the little girl yawn, blink her eyes, and promptly fall asleep. Regina had tucked her face into the sofa's pillow. A lone snore escaped her mouth.

"Come with me, Liselotte."

Liselotte's forehead furrowed. "Why? Are you going to spank me like a child and make me stand in the corner? I'm a grown woman."

"Grown women who have children act like adults and put their young ones first... unless the mother is mentally unfit." At Liselotte's huff, Helene narrowed the distance between them, grasped her daughter's blouse collar as if she were indeed a child, and steered her to the kitchen. "Let's talk, away from the sleeping girls. We can keep a good ear out from within here, so there's no need to worry about the girls. Have a seat." Anticipating Liselotte's objections, Helene sighed in relief when she obliged.

"Are you going to tell me I can no longer see Gerhard?"

"Are you going to admit that you two are planning to leave Berlin?"

For the longest of seconds, Liselotte kept quiet. To battle her nerves, Helene needed to stay busy. She stood to make a pot of tea.

Liselotte reached out for her arm. "I can't answer you because I honestly don't know. Gerhard is still planning things. The best he could, considering his situation with the army." She averted her gaze. "Listen, I realize you don't have confidence in me or respect for Gerhard. Truthfully, I can't blame you."

Shocked by her daughter's confession, Helene could only stare at Liselotte.

"Falling in love with a wonderful man," Liselotte continued, "then having two babies, one of them who will never be well, isn't easy. I'm not asking for your pity." She streaked her hands down her face. "I'm not sure what I want from you except for your love and respect."

Of course, Helene wanted to give her daughter love and respect. However, the element of danger that threatened their lives took priority. She needed to make her daughter understand the gravity they faced.

Helene shook loose from Liselotte's grip. She anchored her gaze to the unchanging fixtures of her kitchen: the wall of oak cabinets behind the table, the cast iron white enamel sink, and the old, reliable icebox on the opposite side of the room. Not the first time, nor the last, she suspected, she wished that the planet could slow its rotation and that life could calm down. She blinked her foolish desire away and focused on Liselotte, the child she bore and loved with all her heart, aware that it wasn't enough for her daughter. Regardless, trusting Liselotte was a nonissue now, not with the care of two babies. Not with Nazis patrolling the streets, ready to cart away each person who threatens the purity of the Aryan gene pool.

"For the sake of your daughters' well-being, and of course, yourself, you must remain put. You must, must, must never see Gerhard again. He's a danger to you, to Regina and Rosa. If you love your daughters, listen to me and stay here. This is your home."

"If I love my daughters?" Liselotte's voice, bumping up in tone, came close to a bird-like squawk. "Of all people dishing out motherly guidance on how to love a child? You, who had raised me like a military general shouting out command after command on how to think, behave, and breathe?"

"Don't condemn me for the only way I've known to love you." Helene pointed toward the parlor and the two sleeping girls. Sadly, one would remain childlike. "The last thing your daughters need is for you to jeopardize their lives."

"And me, Mutter?" Liselotte said, barely audible. "Does it not matter what I need?"

Helene recognized the anguish and fear in her daughter's eyes; the heartache making her breath choppy, her voice weak. She shoved away the temptation to again remind Liselotte of a mother's priorities. "What I'm about to say is out of love and compassion for you, not out of anger." She paused to see if Liselotte would dismiss her words, saying she had no idea what she was talking about. Instead, her child—this young mother—blinked once as tears streamed down her cheeks. Helene inhaled deeply to steady her tone, bathing it in as much tenderness as she could summon. "Boys like Gerhard are only interested in their happiness—this I speak from experience. He doesn't care about you. Nor the twins."

Helene expected her daughter to scream her head off at her. Or, the other extreme, of throwing herself at her, asking for forgiveness and help in caring for her daughters until the war ends. Instead, Liselotte walked out of the kitchen without uttering one word.

Helene rushed after her so quickly that she battled fleeting dizziness. "Promise me you'll stay put."

Liselotte turned and faced her. "Will you promise me to respect my decision to one day marry Gerhard?"

Marry? Helene swallowed dryly. A slew of negative words lodged in her throat. They hurt as if pebbles by the bucketful threatened the precious airway she needed to breathe.

"Your silence says everything, Mutter. I didn't think you would be happy about me marrying a good man."

Helene watched as her daughter walked past the twins and then proceeded upstairs. Helene cleared her throat and called out. "Under no certain terms will I permit Gerhard into this house. And if you must take chances and continue to visit him, will you at least agree to leave the girls with me?"

On the landing, Liselotte spun around and stooped enough to meet Helene's gaze. "If that's what it takes, yes. I'll return to Gerhard tomorrow. He and I have important matters to discuss. Regina and Rosa will stay with you."

Helene tried to smile but faltered. "With five days until Christmas, please watch each step you take. I'd love a nice holiday for us... for all of us."

CHAPTER TWENTY-TWO

Fanny, Rochester, September 14, 1961

Fanny held the patio door open for Gina as they stepped outdoors. "It's a lovely evening. Are you sure you're up for a walk?"

"I'm completely sure. It will be good to catch a breath of air. Besides, I'm curious about what you want to tell me about Grammy."

"Want to walk around the gardens?"

"I may cry or go berserk if I see the same old, same old again, even if Uncle Raymond's gardens are lovely," Gina said, chuckling. "With Kenny under good watch, let's walk around the neighborhood. Believe it or not, I have yet to explore the area."

Fanny slipped her sunglasses out of her blouse pocket and put them on. With Gina having to remain at Kenny's side while Ray was at work, Gina typically had little time for an outing. At least today had been different with Ray staying home and providing a little more freedom for her to get away from the house, even if it was a grand estate. Earlier they had enjoyed shopping—and protest-watching—and now they could extend the pleasantry with a walk. "Sounds like fun."

They left Ray's property and turned left. Three houses over sat a yellow-sided structure with a mansard roof. Fanny was unsure if the estate made the grounds or if the expansive, groomed lawn and gardens showcased the house. "That's my type of place."

"Yeah. I could easily chill with a novel sitting on a porch while Kenny plays badminton with the kids and keeps them out of my hair."

"I think the fancy porch arches are known as Italianate in style." Fanny pointed to the side of the house. "And look at the two bay windows—just wow. Not only can I envision myself and a herd of cats cuddled on a cushioned window seat, but if I were outside, admiring the spirea and rows of sunflowers, I'd look proudly at the fresh paint job I just gave on the friezes above the windows." She chuckled. "I take that back. If I lived in this house, I would have the means to admire the paint job of the contractors I'd hired to do the job for me."

"First, the way your career is going, I bet you'll soon be able to afford any of these fine houses without thinking twice. You've made no mention of a husband, or the desire to have one. Oh, come on, Fanny. This is all pretend, but still, no life partner?" Gina shook her head as red fanned her cheeks. "Goodness. Sorry. That's your business. Not mine. I guess it's difficult for me not to play matchmaker."

"Gina, I haven't met the right person yet. If one exists. So, I'm daydreaming in the context of my present reality—me and a cat or cats. Like you're dreaming in terms of Kenny and children. No worries about overstepping anything, so no need to apologize."

"Then, you are open to meeting a Mr. Wonderful?"

"Is he a Mr. Wonderful and Handsome?"

"Sure, why not?" Gina said. "Kenny certainly is."

"If it's meant to be, yes, I'm up to meeting a man who thinks of me as Miss Wonderful and Beautiful. And smart. Very smart." They approached a white-brick house with a pristine slate roof and stopped to admire the large fountain in front of the house surrounded by purple, blue, and white asters. "Okay, then." She inhaled deeply. "I'll begin by saying there's no smooth way to lurch into a conversation about your grandmother."

Gina nodded. "Grammy is Grammy. Although I can't use the words *smooth* and *Grammy* in one sentence, I love her dearly despite a few challenges. Her closed-mindedness is one. Understand, though, I'm not making excuses for her standoffish ways."

"To be fair," Fanny said as they crossed the street, "she grew up between two world wars and then raised you alone in Nazi Germany before coming to New York. If you ask me, that's a lot of gumption and love."

"Yes, it is. I've tried to learn why she was a single mom. As I've told you, she won't speak about it."

"When she visited me the other night at my home, I sensed she needed to talk to someone... to another woman. She might have come close to opening up to me, to admitting whatever has weighed her down but when I told her I wasn't a priest and that she didn't need to confess to me, she clammed up again. All this came after a big revelation. One you're probably aware of already."

Gina motioned toward the neighborhood park a block up and they headed in that direction. "What did she say?"

"Children without the benefit of fathers were typical in your family."

After a brief silence, Gina again nodded. "My mother, Liselotte, didn't know her father—Grammy's lover if indeed he was a boyfriend as opposed to someone who... you know..." She dropped her gaze.

"Yes," Fanny said. Her instincts told her that Helene was not raped. She hoped she was not mistaken.

"And, I'm clueless about my father, Liselotte's lover," Gina continued. "Oddly, it's my mystery mother I long for the most. But this thing regarding children, plural? Grammy's parents were together until they passed. I can't guess what Grammy meant. Was she implying there were other relatives besides me and my mother without active fathers? Who knows whether I'll ever discover the truth about my past?"

Fanny touched Gina's arm lightly. "Having babies out of wedlock usually brought shame and disgrace to families back then. Even now, society's judgment hasn't changed... though, pregnancy without a wedding ring isn't talked about as much as it used to."

"Yeah, it has become more like dirty laundry than the sin of the century. The true shame happens when family members get disappointed with each other. There's nothing pretty about that, for any of the parties involved. I don't want to imagine the difficulties if we were expecting our baby and not married, especially in addition to Kenny's criminal charges." She cupped her belly and looked at Fanny. "Legal scenarios aside, it doesn't matter to Kenny or me what people think—we will love our child."

"That's how it should be," Fanny said with a tender smile, holding back the tears threatening to flood her eyes.

A collie yapped playfully as a tennis ball rolled toward them. Fanny scooped up the ball and tossed it to the dog as a man holding a leash jogged up.

"Ranger. Come, boy," the man called. When he leashed the dog, he tipped his brown fedora toward them.

Fanny could have sworn the stranger eyed her directly while disregarding Gina. She ignored the spike in her heartbeat.

"Hello, ladies. I'm sorry if old Ranger disturbed you."

"Not a problem," Fanny said, smiling. She and Gina waved after him as he and the dog continued down the path.

"That's it?" Gina said. "A handsome guy—and an animal lover, like you—says hello and all you can do is reply that his adorable dog isn't a concern?"

Fanny sank her chin downward and mumbled, "Guilty as charged." She then grinned to lighten up the moment. "He's just a stranger in passing. What should I have done? Ditch you and beg him for his name, and telephone number, and ask if one of the beautiful homes we just passed might belong to him and if so, could he give me a personalized tour?"

"Absolutely, yes."

"Here's a better idea." Fanny pointed to a nearby bench. "Let's sit for a spell."

They sat side by side. Gina slouched back and fussed with her hands, apparently unsure of where to place them. Finally, she put her hands below her belly, linked her fingers, and shrieked.

"Are you okay?"

"Look at that—I can't see my hands 'cause of the baby. What is it going to be like when I hit six months?"

"How about nine months?"

"What are you trying to do—scare me to death?" Gina sat up straighter and exaggeratedly wiped her brow. "Whew. Much better. I must have reclined too much—I can see my hands again. With my appetite in full gear, I'm probably eating like I'm trying to make up for lost time. I didn't think I'd put on that much weight, yet."

"You're funny, Gina."

"I try to be. That's one of the things Kenny says he loves about me."

"What's something you love about Kenny?"

"He accepts me for who I am," Gina said without a pause. "All my life, folks have wanted to change me. When I graduated high school, everyone around me tried to mold me into what they thought I should do for work. In my new role as a wife, and soon a mom, it seems society wants to dictate what I should look like, and how I should act, and that's aside from their views of me being Mrs. Kenneth Franks."

"Sweetie," Fanny said. "I get that too. All women do. It's always been like that and I'm afraid it will continue to be, no matter the advancements in the future. It's the nature of the beast... I mean, people."

"Well, at least Kenny has never expressed disappointment in me. Nor I over him. We accept each other for who we are, pluses and minuses, and whatever falls in between. Honestly, I don't see one minus in my husband. And, I don't think I'm speaking from a newlywed-bliss state of mind."

With all that Gina and Kenny faced since the start of their marriage— an early pregnancy followed by Kenny's murder charges and various living arrangements—the one ticket Fanny could not tag onto Gina is a *blissful* start to her marriage. Yet, the one amazing distinction that separated Gina from other young women, whether married or single, was the look of unwavering love and confidence in her eyes when it came to Kenny. Aside from his legal mess, Gina was a woman with no regrets. She saw Kenny as intelligent; the opposite of what society had labeled him. The strength of their relationship lined the road they walked together with golden glitter.

"You two set a true standard about what makes a marriage blissful and sustainable. Let's put aside the topic of your grandmother and her association with Kenny. Addressing what you've just told me about your family without active fathers, I want to add that I'm sorry your grandmother and mother had to go through their troubles. And, of course, the eventual outbreak of the last world war, and the troubles endured. Helene must have had difficulties raising a daughter by herself only to lose her." After a pause, she added, "So, to confirm, your grandmother has never clearly told you what happened to Liselotte?"

"She avoids the subject of my mother. I'm assuming she died. Then again, I'm not sure. It's all a cruddy mystery." Gina stroked her belly and sniffled.

"What is it?"

"Just me feeling sorry for myself, wondering what it might be like if Kenny's case goes to trial and he's found—"

"Stop. Don't even think it, or say it. We'll get Kenny free." Fanny hoped to the heavens she would win the case on behalf of Kenny. "Maybe it's the wrong time to bring up your grandmother."

"It's fine. What's up?"

"I'm glad that Helene finally calls Kenny by his preference of Kenny rather than Kenneth. Although, I'm curious why your grandmother insists that Kenny still has to call her Miss Kellerman?"

"When I originally told Kenny about Grammy's stern ways, he thought I was exaggerating. Then I introduced them and he called her by her first name. Without first taking the time to learn more about Kenny, she ordered him to call her Miss Kellerman. Kenny, though, used the title of Mrs. instead of Miss. I'm telling you, the Third World War almost erupted. For several weeks he was terrified of facing her again."

"What happened when the two of you married? Did he call her Grammy as you do, or another family name?"

"You know we had eloped and were married by a justice of the peace, right? No Grammy in attendance."

Fanny nodded.

"Grammy made the first move. Practically the second she learned we were married, and saw Kenny, she told him, again, to refer to her as Miss Kellerman. That was the first thing out of Grammy's mouth. No congratulations. No welcome to the family. It's like she has to take control of the situation, even if it's not directly involving her."

"I can see her seizing control. Do you remember her calling you Regina? What was the turning point?"

Gina shrugged. "I was young when the name change happened, so it's foggy in my memory. I think the change occurred when we emigrated from Germany. Grammy wanted to leave our native land behind... perhaps leave the memories of her parents, grandparents, and my mother behind. When we got to Rochester, I was suddenly Gina, not Regina." She smiled. "I kind of like it."

"Me too. It fits you better." Fanny suggested they return to Ray's. "Maybe if we work on your grandmother the iceberg between her and Kenny can fully melt. At least, the chink in the ice has started—a good thing. It would be more helpful to Kenny, strengthening him psychologically as his trial approaches. That is if the grand jury decides that's the route they will take. Either way, it would be good, don't you think?"

"It would be nicer, yes."

"Also, I can't help but compare Helene to Betty, Kenny's mom." Fanny ignored the grimace Gina made. "Both are adamant in detaching themselves from Kenny, though Betty deserves credit. She not only called Kenny *son* but surprised us all when she agreed to be a character witness if we needed her, so maybe she's changing after all these long, lost years. I suspect detached people act this way with anyone they love. It's probably out of self-preservation since they've experienced hurt countless times themselves."

"While I can't speak for Betty, I've long suspected in Grammy's case her attitude might be linked to a secret she wishes could go away and never come back to haunt her again."

"I think we've made a little progress with Helene. I noticed earlier when we sat around the kitchen table to talk with David about the witness, in addition to her finally saying the shorter version of Kenneth—*Kenny*—that she'd taken your hand and smiled. I was pleased."

"Oh, me too," Gina said. "I hope it will happen again and again."

At the corner, they stopped at the traffic light. Fanny continued. "There's one more thing I want to mention about the visit with Kenny's mom, Betty. When she did call Kenny by the familial term *son*, he acted more neutral than anything, but after we left, I could tell he was touched. I'm saying this because there's hope for your grandmother and Kenny to grow closer to each other."

Gina nodded. "And how did you react back at Betty's place when she called Kenny her son?"

"I held my act together until I got home." Fanny smiled. "Alone, I bawled like a newborn over the long overdue tender moment."

"I don't think us clients think of you attorneys as having feelings. You must see plenty of tough cases. I hope it doesn't take a nasty toll on you."

A twinge of nervousness surged through Fanny. Fiddling with her black-framed sunglasses, she tried to downplay it. "We often play doctor, taking the objective, clinically detached approach."

"And the other times?"

She thought about how she admitted to crying over Kenny when it came to his mother. Had she let loose with her emotions out of self-pity for herself? She couldn't rightly reply to Gina.

"Fanny, may I ask you a different question?"

"Sure. I hope I have an answer."

"Oh, I think you do. After visiting Kenny's mother, he asked me again to explain what detachment from others meant. I hate to say it, but the only example I thought of then was how Grammy keeps her distance from others. For her own sanity's sake, it's safer and hurts less to distance one's self from certain—if not all—people. Or, perhaps it's *the truth* they're distancing themselves from. And certain people—for lack of a better way to say it—are custodians of this truth that no one wants to hear."

"I think you're spot on correct. And the question you mentioned seconds ago?"

"Actually, questions, plural." Gina sucked in a deep breath. "Was your mother detached from you? Is this why you don't talk about her—because you're also emotionally removed from her? I wouldn't blame you. In the name of survival, people have to do many things—sometimes the unthinkable."

For a split second, Fanny wondered whether Gina had read her mind. She wanted to tell Gina the truth. That yes, it was often safer to place one's past behind a thick veil, not to be seen, ever. By blocking the memories from visiting again, one can move forward past the hurts and griefs. It was best to live in the present, not the past, nor a future that did not exist yet. At least, this was what worked best for her.

"Gina, regarding my situation, sincerely, I haven't figured it out, yet. I just have a hunch of what would be best for Kenny in his legal situation." She jutted her chin in the direction of Ray's house. "We're almost back. Are you ready to return?"

"Yes," Gina said without delay. "It was wonderful to enjoy a little change of scenery today, with you. Both earlier, and just now, on this walk. I needed a woman's company—a friend's company." She yawned. "Now, all I want to do is to cuddle with my husband."

Fanny glanced sideways at this remarkable young woman. "I'm sure Kenny will have no objections."

CHAPTER TWENTY-THREE

Gina, Rochester, October 2, 1961

Seated at the kitchen table, Gina watched Kenny open the refrigerator. He withdrew a package of American cheese and opened the oak bread box, but did not take out the bag of white bread. "What are you looking for, honey? Want me to make your lunch?"

"Grilled cheese. I can make them for us. I like cooking."

"Thanks. You're a great cook." While Kenny's cooking creativity ranged from sandwich making to scrambled eggs and toast to producing a flawless Betty Crocker ginger cake, she could not complain one drop. Her food tastes favored simple comfort foods. Despite her recent cravings for egg rolls and buttered egg noodles, grilled cheese would have sounded scrumptious— especially cooked by someone other than herself—if she was hungry. "I think I'll pass on lunch right now."

"Okay." He stepped toward the table and sat next to her. "We're Mr. and Mrs. for six months now."

"I'm well aware of that." She cringed at her edgy tone.

"Don't worry, Gina." He slipped his hand around hers and gave it a little squeeze. "I still love you. It's okay if you're grumpy."

She sighed. "Sorry. I'm lacking sleep, lately."

He eyed her mid-section. "You have a lot to handle."

Uh, in more ways than just the baby. The thing was, she wanted to shield her life partner from slipping into the dumps of depression. His life was at stake—he was the one who had way too much to handle. He was a beautiful man who did not deserve the cruel nonsense occurring now. Or ever. She needed to remain positive for him.

"Thanks for understanding, Kenny. For not taking me personally."

He kissed her sweetly on the cheek. "Let's go in the living room. You and the baby need to be comfy."

"Don't you want to eat lunch?"

"Later is good."

"Okay. Comfy sounds wonderful." She appreciated him hooking her elbow and leading her out of the kitchen. The large, elegant yet unpretentious living room proved relaxing with its pale yellow walls, oil paintings of calm, scenic old California landscapes, and an antique rosewood square piano angled in a corner. Two large sofas faced each other with a round glassed-top coffee table between the two.

They sat together in silence. After a few seconds ticked by, Kenny sprang to his feet. With four strides he stood by the record player. "Want to listen to records? Music cheers you up. I have Patsy Cline's "Walkin' After Midnight" handy."

The song about a person walking for miles after midnight in search of love used to be a favorite. Unable to trust her emotions over endlessly trying to track down love and consequently finding loneliness instead, especially not with her thoughts swirling around Kenny's trial, Gina could only shake her head.

"Okay. Want to sing your song for me?"

She scrunched her brows.

Kenny chuckled. "The one you wrote for me."

Goodness. She still had not sung her song for him. What kind of wife was she to tease him with a song title but not share the lyrics that thinking about him made her happy?

"I know your song is better than Patsy Cline's," he added.

She wiped her cheeks furiously from the sudden tears cascading down her cheeks. In a snap of seconds, he was beside her again. He wrapped his arms around her and rocked her gently until she simmered down.

"Sorry," she said, sighing. "I feel too droopy to sing. I promise to sing the song later for you."

"That's fine. You don't have to apologize. About anything."

"Are you sure?"

"Think happy thoughts, Gina. About us. I think about us all the time."

Gina nodded against his chest, touched and amazed that in this time of crisis, her husband focused on them, and their love of each other, not on the horror that may be around the corner. This, she was learning, is what love between two people truly is about: love has the power to heal, to bring peace, and to soothe. Love makes one stay in the now, not the past. Love is the dearest blessing a human can receive from another and can offer another. And thankfully, love is never conditional. A swirl of pink ruffled dresses flashed in her mind. Red hair ribbons. Brown, puffy teddy bears. Dolls with golden hair ringlets. White toy ovens and black pots and pans. Their precious love has blessed them with a baby on the way.

"You're right," she said, blinking her eyes open. "Here's a happy thought—I think we're going to have a girl."

"Oh? Last week you said a boy."

"Do you want a boy?"

He squeezed her hand. "Doesn't matter. Just that the baby is good."

"What do you mean?"

He pointed to his head and dropped his gaze. "You know. Nothing broken."

A cold tingle settled between them. She inched away. Fear. Panic. It was happening again. She detected it in his voice, in his looking away from her.

"There's nothing wrong with you. There will be nothing wrong with the baby."

Silence. The one thing Gina did not handle well.

"Come on, sweetheart," she tried again. "We've gone through this plenty of times. Everything is okay. Everything will continue to be good, if not, magnificent."

He kept his gaze fixed downward. "I'm slow. The baby might be slow, too. Then what? Then you have two slowpokes to take care of. Then you won't be happy, Gina. Ever again. Taking care of two babies. Two of us who can't do anything."

Gently, she lifted his chin and peered into his beautiful brown eyes. "What's wrong?"

"I am dumb. We'll have a dumb kid."

It was her turn to lift his spirits. She combed her fingers through his thick dark hair. "You, Kenny Franks, are the smartest man I know. In many, many ways, I'm proud that you're my husband. I'm proud you'll be our baby's father—"

"Gina, that's if..."

If. The longest two-letter word, ever created.

She heard a distinct snort. Saw him brush his hand across his face as if to erase the evidence that only tears could make.

"I love you, Kenny, and everything will be fine," she said. Her throat clogged with fear and doubt, preventing more words of hope from reaching his ears.

"I love you, Gina. That's my problem." He placed his large hand on her belly. "And I love our baby. That's also my problem."

"Why?" she asked. Terror filled her heart at hearing him articulate the words of the conversation she wanted to avoid. Still, sensing he needed help, she prodded him. "Do you think our child won't be proud of you? That our little darling will be ashamed of you? No way. He or she will see you for who you are—a kind father who loves his children."

One lone sob puffed from his mouth. A sound, like dandelion fluff she wanted to trap in her hands, make a wish his concerns would never materialize, and release the fluff into the air. Then with a strong breath, she would send the wish toward the heavens, demanding that tragedy would never again disturb them. Was living in a fantasy of sunny days without one challenge or sadness wrong? Since expecting a magic spell to make life full of perfection and flawless joy was ridiculous, she did what she knew how to do: she whispered a prayer, wrapped her arms around him, and held him until he stopped crying. Until his breathing evened. Until he leaned back onto the sofa and fell asleep. She pressed her head against his chest and shut her eyes.

• • •

When Gina awoke, she had no clue of the day, month, or year, or for a still second, where she was. Then, the mantle clock striking four stirred her fully awake and roused Kenny beside her.

"We were tired," Kenny said, leaning forward and scrubbing his face with his palms.

"I can't remember the last time I took a nap."

"You have a good excuse," he said. "A baby. I have no excuses."

"Oh, you have a lot on your mind." She watched his telltale lift of a brow. "Meaning, there's plenty any man in your shoes, with a baby on the way, would chew over."

"You mean, with a trial happening. A murder trial."

"Maybe, maybe not. I doubt it will happen. You'll see, Kenny. You will be a free man. You can watch your baby grow, become a cute kid and a sulky teenager, go off to college and get a great job, and then get married and give us grandchildren. In other words, you'll see me grow old with wrinkles, flab around my middle, and stooped over because of stiff bones."

"Sounds wonderful."

She grinned. That was all she wanted—to grow old and happy with her beloved husband. "It does."

"And me too. I'll also grow old. I want to grow old."

"Yeah, us growing old together has an appealing charm." She streaked a fingertip down his cheek where his tears ran not long ago. "You sound better. Maybe you were just tired."

"No. I'm still tired. A lot."

"Really?" Had she been too tunneled into herself and her changing body to notice how exhausted he must feel? The prospect of possibly having a jury declare him guilty, strapped into *Old Sparky*, and never living one of the everyday parental moments she just paraded around him would send anyone off a cliff of despair. What were a few tears? She would have ridden the emotional roller coaster, up and down repeatedly, if in his shoes. This battle of keeping his spirits in check while facing the possibility of awful consequences highlighted his strength and resilience.

"Yes. I didn't want to tell you."

"Were you ashamed? You don't have to be. I love you. I love everything about you."

"I didn't do it."

She blinked at the possibilities. "You mean, kill Samuel?"

"I didn't kill him. I never killed anyone. I never want to kill anyone. It's wrong. It's—"

She pressed her index finger against his mouth. "Hush, my love. I believe you."

"What if no one else believes me?"

She understood exactly the crux of his agony. Letting go of fate. No one, including herself, proved good in surrendering ultimate control of one's future.

Gina squeezed Kenny's hand. "Fanny will make sure the jury will see you as not guilty. She's really good—I have all my trust in her."

"She is," he said. He took two strides away.

"Please, don't leave me," Gina said, painfully aware the word *leave* had a scary double meaning, about the present and the future. She told herself to stay positive despite feeling close to again spiraling into a murky lagoon of despair. If her husband were declared guilty, she would become a single mom, just like her own mother and her grandmother. She would be doomed to repeat family history. What would she say when her little girl or boy asked about Daddy? Tell her that others condemned him as a murderer? Tell him his daddy was a hostile man who took someone's life? How could she ever marry again when other men would think negatively that her soul was worthless—she who had once loved a man that not only did society see as a simpleton but also as a ruthless killer? And she could not forever sponge off of Kenny's uncle, never mind that he was kind, rich, and generous. Then again, how could she get a job when she had to raise a child by herself? She could not dare ask or expect Grammy to help. The baby would be Grammy's great-grandchild. Gina needed to respect her grandmother and let her live the rest of her elderly years without the responsibilities Gina created herself... responsibilities that had occurred from falling in love with Kenny, a wonderful, charming, and yes, brilliant man.

She willed a smile on her face. "Come on, sweetheart. Look at me."

He peered into her eyes. "Gina, are you okay?"

"Of course, I am. And that's because you're in my life." She leaned toward his sweet mouth and kissed him.

CHAPTER TWENTY-FOUR

Fanny, Rochester, October 2, 1961

With a peek into the rearview mirror, Fanny was pleased to see a relatively relaxed-looking Kenny and Gina. At least, externally. Absent from their foreheads were furrowed lines across their foreheads, pale complexions, and silence between them. She hoped internally, that they were relatively at ease, as well.

"Is that a new store?" Kenny asked.

"No, it's the same shoe store that's been there for years," Gina replied. "The red awning is new, that's all."

"I like it."

"They have a nice selection of shoes."

"Do you like their shoes too, Fanny?" Kenny asked.

"I've never shopped there." Due to a mixture of lack of spare time and wanting to avoid the standard crowds of more *typical* women out shopping with a gaggle of girlfriends, Fanny shopped for her shoes and outfits from the *Montgomery Ward Wish Book* and the *Sears Big Book*. "Maybe one day I will, as a treat."

"A treat? You never know how long you will live, Fanny." Kenny glanced at Gina. "Enjoy life now."

"Very true, Kenny," Fanny said, wishing he was wrong. Wishing she wasn't taking him to a doctor who would be an expert witness in a trial that would ultimately decide whether Kenny would live or not.

"It will be okay, sweetheart," Gina murmured.

"Yes," Kenny said, without a trace of emotion. "It will be."

"Just another block and we'll arrive," Fanny said.

Kenny combed his hair with his fingers. "I remember from last time. Was the test good?"

Kenny had referred to the intelligence tests conducted on him by Dr. Theodore Grant. Although Fanny was originally hesitant to pigeonhole Kenny into the same negative category that most of society did, she wanted to be prepared if the case went to trial. Last week, Dr. Grant shared the test results with Fanny, pointing out what she suspected: Kenny had the IQ of an approximate pre-adolescent boy, yet had acquired a good chunk of commonsense, everyday knowledge of a more typical man his age. She had not yet shared the findings with either Kenny or Gina. Interestingly, Kenny had not asked, until just now. She assumed their lack of inquiry was because they supported each other and had pre-determined the test results would not impact their relationship. Scientific proof of Kenny's intellect did not matter. A number, whether a high or low rating, would not change their lives as Mr. and Mrs. Franks.

Kenny's words replayed in Fanny's thoughts: *If I was smarter, would that mean I wouldn't be married to Gina?* Although he had posed the question hypothetically, Kenny had spoken the ruling truth between him and Gina. The only thing that mattered to them was remaining happily married, together through time. With the divorce rate spiking, and the growing popularity of living with another without the benefit of a marriage certificate, Kenny and Gina were hundreds of years ahead of others with more supposed intelligence.

Fanny, unsure how to reply to Kenny's question about last week's test, again reflected upon what mattered most to Kenny. If he heard a unique number that judged him as intelligent or not, would that change his life? "Dr. Grant's test showed us exactly who you are." Fanny smiled. "No surprises, Kenny. You have fine intelligence for a man your age that will help you make important decisions as a good man, a loyal and loving husband, and a devoted father."

"Too bad," Kenny said.

"Why's that, honey?" Gina asked.

"I want to be a great man. Not a good man."

"In my eyes, you are a great man. However, if Dr. Grant says in court that you're a good man, that's excellent."

"Okay. I'm glad."

Gina giggled. Fanny resumed breathing.

"Then why am I having this test today?" Kenny asked.

Fanny had already explained the reason. She searched her mind for a simpler way of telling him. "Last week's test results presented conclusions about you on a physical level to one day share in court—if the occasion rises. Today's test is to examine you emotionally."

"How, Fanny? A doctor can't look into my head or heart and see emotions. Only blood and veins, right?"

"Dr. Grant will ask questions and your answers will give him insights into your emotions. From these new understandings, he'll get ideas on how you cope with stress and how you might react if bad things happen."

"Like the times Samuel annoyed me?"

"Yes. Exactly."

"What about when I make mistakes? Like when I chased Samuel into the alleyway? I wish I never ran after him. I was bad."

"Here's the thing," Fanny said. She pulled into a diagonal parking spot in front of the Rochester building housing the doctor's office. "Dr. Grant is confident that today's exam will provide a clear understanding of what makes you a good person. Ready to go?"

Kenny glanced out the passenger window. "Will you and Gina be with me?"

"Yes," Gina answered. "Fanny and I will be in the doctor's waiting room."

Fanny nodded, though she and Gina knew it was a stretch of truth.

·   ·   ·

On one side of the one-way mirror, Kenny and the doctor sat at a table in a pleasant-looking examination room with four prints of colorful floral arrangements hanging on off-white walls. On the other side of the mirror, where they could observe and not be seen from within the examination room, Fanny and Gina sat alongside the doctor's assistant who would record the session and take notes. Fanny's thoughts drifted to last week when she had explained to Gina that in 1955 the Mental Health Study called for a nationwide examination of the problems of mental illness on the human and economic levels. The findings resulted in a joint commission and the report was titled *Action for Mental Health*. In 1956, based upon the *Action for Mental Health* report, Congress passed the Health Amendments Act, expanding community-based help in mental health and drawing the interest of President Kennedy.

"Gina," Fanny has said, "I have confidence that President Kennedy will pursue legislation that will benefit the mentally ill in the United States."

"Kenny states he's not mentally ill," Gina had replied. "You've heard him. While he admits he's not as smart as others, he says he is of sound mind, that he is not mentally ill."

"Yes, I recall. And I'm not doubting Kenny, nor you. However, Dr. Grant, who I think will be an excellent witness in defense of Kenny—and remember, we're talking legal procedure and defense preparation—will inevitably conclude one can be of a sound mind—not mentally ill—and still kill. And the reverse. One can be mentally ill, though not oriented to committing a crime, let alone a murder, and not kill another person."

"Fanny, it sounds like it's all over for Kenny. Whether he's mentally ill or of sound mind, the DA can say he can easily be Samuel's killer."

Fanny had eyed Gina, good and hard. "Not after I get done defending him."

Now, behind the observation window, they watched as Dr. Grant told Kenny to get comfortable. Fanny glanced at Gina. "Ready?"

"Definitely," Gina whispered, not that her husband could hear, or see her. She settled into her chair and stared ahead. Fanny did the same. Since she would later receive the transcript, she could absorb what would transpire between Kenny and the doctor and not concern herself with scribbling notes.

Dr. Grant: Thank you, Kenny, for agreeing to take this special examination.

Kenny: I want to be here.

Dr. Grant: Why's that, Kenny?

Kenny: I want to help. I didn't kill Samuel. I want everyone to know.

Dr. Grant: Okay, then let's begin.

Kenny: Do you want me to tell you what happened? Like what I told the police?

Dr. Grant: No, thanks. I have all that information. Instead, I want to learn more about you. Tell me, are you comfortable around other folks?

Kenny: What do you mean? I like people.

Dr. Grant: Well, that's good. (chuckles) Do some people make you nervous?

Kenny: No. Sometimes, I think I make them nervous. Sometimes, people get funny around me.

Dr. Grant: What do you mean by funny? Do they tell jokes? Laugh a lot?

Kenny: (shakes head)

Dr. Grant: Please speak out loud your answers.

Kenny: Okay. I want to help. I mean, when people meet me. Like they don't understand me. People are afraid of me. (shrugs) I think they are.

Dr. Grant: What do they say?

Kenny: Not much. They don't like to talk to me. They walk away from me. Sometimes, like Samuel, they call me dumb. Other bad names, too. Gina never does. She only says nice things to me.

Dr. Grant: You're beginning to pull at your shirt collar. Do these people upset you?

Kenny: They're not nice people. They would make anyone upset.

Dr. Grant: Tell me what you think when you hear the names they call you.

Kenny: Like if I get angry?

Dr. Grant: Yes.

Kenny: Not really. When I was a little boy, I would get sad. Like I wanted to be with them more. But they didn't want me. Like when all the kids in my class got invited to a party. Not me. That was sad.

Dr. Grant: I can see how that would make you sad. How did you cope, then? Would you hit them? Call them names?

Kenny: No. I tried to be nice. Uncle Raymond taught me to be nice. Even when no one else is nice.

Dr. Grant: Now, as an adult, are you still nice when people call you names or do you have bad thoughts about them?

Kenny: (Stops pulling at collar) I count to ten. Sometimes, I count to twenty or more. To myself, I mean. After I finish counting, if they still say bad things, I walk away.

Dr. Grant: Would you say you fear people and how they might act to you?

Kenny: No. I like people. I give them a chance. To be nice. To show me how they are.

Dr. Grant: And if they're not, do you get depressed?

Kenny: You asked if I get sad. Is that the same as depressed?

Dr. Grant: Think of depression as a sadness that doesn't go away for a long time. Have you ever felt that way?

Kenny: No. I look for other ways to be happy. Not everyone will make me happy. And I can't make everyone happy, either.

Dr. Grant: Would you describe yourself as outgoing or as quiet?

Kenny: Depends. Some people make me laugh a lot. Think a lot. Talk a lot. Gina does that for me. Other people make me quiet. When they talk more than me. I can tell if they care about me. If they don't, I become quiet. It takes time to be the person they want, but I can't be. So, I don't try.

Dr. Grant: Do you make friends easily?

Kenny: Yes and no. I make friends with people who like me. And want to be friends. Like Gina. Like Uncle Raymond. Like Fanny. They're nice people. I like nice people. I don't worry about mean people.

Dr. Grant: If you were a magician and could make anger into a real thing, like a gun, or the other extreme of a calm ocean, which would you choose? Would you then carry this anger with you, in your pocket?

Kenny: A calm ocean. Anger is nasty. It hurts to be angry. (Points to his stomach then the side of his head) Makes me get twisted, like a knot. Makes me get headaches. I don't want to feel that way. I don't like it.

Dr. Grant: It's normal to be angry, occasionally. Do you try to get rid of your anger or carry it around inside of you?

Kenny: I get rid of it. I count a lot. I like to take long walks. After Samuel died, I was told to stay in Uncle Raymond's house, unless when I went with Fanny, like to see my mother or a doctor. Or here, with you. Now I walk around Uncle Raymond's gardens. I talk with Gina. And other things in the house, like listening to music.

Dr. Grant: Those are all healthy ways to cope. Do you remember when you would become so angry that none of these things—like talking with Gina or taking walks— helped you? Did you ever have to yell? Throw something. Bang a door?

Kenny: I'm not perfect. But I never hit anyone. I don't want to hurt them. Even if they don't do nice things to me or others. (Looks away) Once, though, I got angry at Fanny. At jail. She said she could say in court that I was insane. I'm not insane. Just slow. I yelled at Fanny. I think I threw something, too. It's blurry in here. (Points to head.) I didn't throw it at Fanny. I like Fanny. I didn't want to hurt her. Not even when I felt angry.

Dr. Grant: So, would you say that you can control your anger?

Kenny: Yes.

Dr. Grant: What makes you angry at the thought of being insane?

Kenny: Because it's scary. Like you can't control it. I control my feelings, though. My mother couldn't. And she left me and my father. My father was insane. He killed himself. I'm not insane. Just slow. Some people are insane and smart. Some people are insane and slow. Some are slow, but not insane. Everyone's different.

Dr. Grant: So, you aren't confused about the difference between insanity and slowness?

Kenny: No. I'm not confused. Insanity is like a cube of ice that will never melt. It can't. It refuses to melt. Slow is what I am. I'm like an ice cube that can melt. I need more time, that's all.

Dr. Grant: Would you say anger or other feelings make you impulsive?

Kenny: I don't understand.

Dr. Grant: Do you do things without thinking about the results?

Kenny: Depends. If I want to take a long walk or have a chocolate ice cream cone, I don't think much and just do it.

Dr. Grant: What happens when someone calls you hurtful names?

Kenny: Depends. Like when Samuel called me names. I would walk away from him and not worry.

Dr. Grant: What things did you think when it came to doing something about Samuel?

Kenny: Just tried to stay away from him. He wouldn't change. I think he was crazy. Like the ice cube that refuses to melt. I never tried to change him. I tried to keep out of his way.

Dr. Grant: Did you ever fantasize—dream—about what it would be like if you could make Samuel change, make him a nicer person?

Kenny: Like making him my best friend? No. I knew that would never happen. I couldn't change him. I didn't want to. Like I didn't want him to change me.

Dr. Grant: Do you like being who you are, Kenny?

Kenny: Yes. It's all I know. I don't dream about being anyone else. I mean, I dream when I become a father. When Gina has our baby. But I'll still be me.

Dr. Grant: Let's talk more about Samuel. From talking with you and reading the police reports, and what you told the police, and your attorney, Fanny, you and Samuel had a long history of working with each other at your uncle's pasta company.

Kenny: Yes. We worked in different departments. He was jealous. Said Uncle Raymond was nicer to me. Called me names. He got others to call me names.

Dr. Grant: How did that make you feel?

Kenny: Different ways. Annoyed. Disgusted. Hurt. (Points to head) I got a lot of headaches.

Dr. Grant: From what I've read, before you met Gina, you never chased after Samuel or threatened him, correct?

Kenny: Yes. I tried to ignore him. When he wouldn't let me alone, I just put up with it.

Dr. Grant: What changed when you met Gina?

Kenny: You mean the change with Samuel?

Dr. Grant: Yes.

Kenny: He called me a lot more names. He pushed me more. When he learned we got married, and Gina was going to have a baby, Samuel got crazier. He called me more names. Called Gina names. Said horrible things about the baby. He threatened to hurt Gina.

Dr. Grant: What did you do?

Kenny: That's when I chased him to the alleyway. It led to a back lot. I didn't think about it. Just did it. Just chased him. Because he said bad, horrible things. I didn't want to hurt him. I just wanted to scare him.

Dr. Grant: What were you planning to do when you caught up with Samuel?

Kenny: No plans. It just happened. Like my feet thought for themselves. I pictured in my mind that we would talk. I would tell him to act like an adult. To leave Gina and me alone. That we can be married like other men and women.

Dr. Grant: Did you tell Samuel what you just told me?

Kenny: I couldn't. He died. I didn't see who killed him. I yelled for help. I didn't like Samuel. But I didn't want him dead. He can never marry. Have a wife to love, like Gina. Never have children to love.

Dr. Grant: (Hands Kenny a box of tissues) Can I get you a glass of water?

Kenny: (Wipes eyes) No, thanks. May I see Gina? Are we done?

Dr. Grant: One last question. Do you want to tell me anything else?

Kenny: (Nods) You asked me a lot about thinking. And talking. I don't understand why other people can say what they want. Or do what they want. But they won't listen to me. I'm not sure who is smart and who is dumb.

Dr. Grant: That's a big mystery in this world, all right. Okay. We're done. You did an excellent job in helping me see who you are. Thank you, Kenny. I want you to remain here for a few minutes while I talk with Fanny and Gina. Then I'll get you and bring you out to the others.

Kenny: Good. I want to see them.

Dr. Grant: I'm sure you do.

• • •

To Fanny's liking, the car ride back to Ray's was fast and calm. She said little, half thinking about the insights the doctor brought out from Kenny, and half listening to the conversation between Kenny and Gina. All she wanted to do was to go home, enjoy a rare glass of white wine, curl up with Ralph, and pet him to the point of shedding as they watched TV. Work had kept her busy for the past few weeks, and made it impossible to watch her favorite escape, *Wagon Train*. Tonight, she would catch up with Charlie Wooster and Bill Hawks, her favorites of the series, and see what hot water had befallen them and the rest of those bold and gruff characters.

"Fanny, did you hear me?"

Poof. The movie stars were gone. Fanny peered into the rearview mirror. "What is it, Kenny?"

"I talked to you."

"I'm sorry. I was lost in my daydreams."

"That's okay," Kenny said, sounding cordial and relaxed. "Gina told me what she thought. What do you think? What does the doctor think?"

"From what Dr. Grant told me about his interview with you, yes, it went well. I'm eager to see the transcript—the printed recording of what you two talked about. It should help your defense plenty if the case moves to trial."

"Good," Kenny said, bobbing his head in emphasis.

Gina leaned toward Fanny. "Do you still have doubts about the trial?"

"I wouldn't use the word *doubts*," Fanny said, honestly. "I've practiced law long enough to avoid second-guessing jury verdicts, whether grand juries or trial juries. And this is set aside from what the prosecution might throw at us. The DA still has five months to seat the grand jury. The unexpected can surprise us with an awful shock or a wonderful one. I like to be prepared as thoroughly as I can be." She turned left onto Ray's street.

"That's why we like you, Fanny," Gina said.

"Aww, thank..." Fanny couldn't continue when she saw the familiar red and white DeSoto parked in Ray's driveway.

"Is that your grandmother's car?" Kenny asked.

"It certainly is," Fanny and Gina said in unison.

Ray greeted them at the door. "She just stopped by seconds ago—she didn't mention why."

Fanny doubted Helene brought over homemade banana bread to cheer their spirits.

"Where is she?" Gina crossed her arms, tugging away from Kenny when he went to hook her by the elbow. "I'll go straighten her out. We've had enough of a long day."

"That's unnecessary," Helene said. Dressed in gray pants and a black blouse, she matched the somber mood she'd already created. Yet, for the first time since Fanny met Helene, she wore her hair loose from the tight bun, a softer, more approachable look. "I'm here to straighten *you* out, Gina," she said, yet with a gentle tone.

"I'm fine, Grammy. I might not meet your standards of a perfect granddaughter, but there's not one thing about me needing to be *straightened* out. I'm a good person."

"Gina," Kenny said, narrowing again the distance between them. "Stay calm. For the baby."

Helene's gaze swept to Gina like a tender caress, lingered on Kenny for a handful of seconds, then returned to Gina. "With a baby on the way, and who knows what will happen with Kenny's legal matter—"

Kenny gave a little jump. "Miss Kellerman! That's the second time you called me Kenny. Not Kenneth."

"Right, you are, Kenny." Helene slipped her hands into the pockets of her gray slacks. She again faced Gina. "I'm ready to tell you the truth about your past. Prepare yourself. You won't like it." A handful of seconds ticked by. "It's something I don't like, as well."

CHAPTER TWENTY-FIVE

Helene, Berlin, Germany, December 20-21, 1943
"I need to run one last errand tonight," Helene announced to her daughter at half past five. "Watch Regina and Rosa."

"At this time of evening? It's nearly curfew."

Helene did a double take. "Are you truly concerned that I'm leaving the house? Or, do you want to ensure I'm alive and available to watch your children tomorrow while you visit what's his name?" Helene realized how vile she sounded. Since she needed her daughter out of the house the following day, she counted on her tone to work for the better.

"Go ahead. Flirt with death." Liselotte groaned. "On second thought, don't die on me—you're right. I'm counting on you to watch the girls tomorrow."

At the door, Helene stopped but didn't turn around. She smiled to herself. "I have dinner made for the three of you. Please don't neglect the girls. I'll come home as soon as I can."

A shrill chuckle zipped across the room. "Mutter, do you have a lover you're keeping secret?"

Helene refused to dignify the question with a reply. She also despised how they permitted their negative emotions to bounce off each other. They sounded like children. They were adults, at least, age-wise, she was. She knew better. Inhaling a deep breath, she left the house before she chickened out. Before Liselotte could see her eyes brimming with tears.

The whole matter took an hour and fifteen minutes. Thankfully, the wind wasn't as blustery as last week's trip to the same place and she made good timing, which gave her more precious minutes to talk and to sign the final paperwork. With each mention of Gerhard from her daughter's mouth, reminding her of how he exposed Liselotte and her daughters to certain danger, and with hints of marriage, Helene was now whole-heartedly certain she had made the right decision.

When Helene arrived home, the place sat dark and silent. For a second, she feared Liselotte had taken the girls to Gerhard's hideaway quarters under his family's toolshed despite agreeing to leave them in her care tomorrow while Liselotte met again with him... she could not bear to think his name again. What a numbskull he was to put his newly discovered family at severe risk. These war-torn days of living in Berlin proper were like wearing a target pinned to one's shirt and begging the enemy to drop a bomb or two on one's head. This was why she'd devised this last part of her plan. She just needed to be patient. If luck favored them, they would all survive the next few days. Liselotte, too.

A light switched on from within the parlor. "Everything okay, Mutter?"

"Yes," Helene replied as she walked past her daughter toward the kitchen. "Earlier, I'd arranged with a neighbor to fetch an item from the market she needed in exchange for doing the same for me." She lifted the brown sack for emphasis "I just picked it up. I'd be home quicker, but we got talking. Let me set it in the pantry and I'll return to check on the girls."

"Don't trouble yourself over them."

The five words tripped Helene's feet and she stopped moving.

"For goodness' sake," Liselotte cried out. "Don't act like I sold them into slavery."

"Where are they?"

"Exhausted and cranky, I put them to bed early."

"All right. I'll be just a moment." Without a word more, Helene entered the kitchen and opened the pantry closet, pretending to store the nonexistent food item from the sack she had brought. Where to stash the signed document, the one thing she had forgotten to plan for? She grew frantic as she combed the kitchen for a hiding spot. The flowerpot on the windowsill. Ah. That would work. She lifted the small pothos plant and placed the folded envelope underneath. Despite neglect, the plant survived, and as long as another pair of eyes never discovered it, the signed papers would also survive well. At least until tomorrow while Liselotte was away and she could secret it away.

"Did the girls eat?" she asked as she rushed out of the kitchen.

"Regina, yes. Rosa..." Liselotte waggled her fingers. "How she lives is a guess."

"A miracle," Helene said under her breath.

"What did you pick up tonight? Anything good?"

"Rice."

"Rice, again? All we eat lately is rice and beans. Gerhard's mutter is a good cook. She canned—and hid—most of the vegetables she'd grown before the Nazis fine-picked the area. Scavengers, that's what they are."

Guilt and shame twisted Helene. How had her family gotten to this point of falling apart? She could not ignore the bigger question: what kind of mother was she that her daughter wanted to leave her for a worthless man? If not tomorrow, then the next day. Liselotte's departure was inevitable. With her daughter choosing to follow her heart instead of family commitment, she had endangered her daughters. Rosa, being so needy, was greatly impacted. It was all her fault—Helene had failed her only child. She was a disgrace of a mother.

The situation, especially with a war raging, cried for someone to take charge. Helene pulled herself from the pity of self-reproach and looked Liselotte directly in the eye. "You're in love with one of these *scavengers*." She had not meant for the nasty words to drip from her mouth like a snake's venom oozing from fangs. Too late.

"Gerhard is a good man. He's the father of my little girls. I love him. He loves me. Don't you want me to be married, to straighten out my so-called tarnished reputation that you and the neighbors have labeled me with? I'm trying to do the right thing. Of all people, you should be the happiest for me." Liselotte's voice hitched. Her eyes brimmed with tears. "Look what you've done, Mutter. Not the first time. You've made me cry more days than not of my miserable life with you. Why should today be different?"

And there it was. The truth. Liselotte hated her. Perhaps, it was time for Helene to turn off whatever feelings she had left for her daughter. Love? Fondness? Her parents had dished out love at their convenience. When she met their approval, she was their beloved daughter. And when she disappointed her parents? They had stopped talking to her as if she did not exist. She thought she had finally found love in Willie. What a joke he turned out to be, and at her expense. He took off on her upon news of their baby. Now, as if love was a piece of paper, Liselotte had torn the last of what existed between them into shreds. Anguish blazed throughout Helene's inner core. She could not hate her daughter, though she had to remain strong for her grandchildren's sake while keeping herself from falling to pieces.

She headed for the stairs.

"Where are you going?"

Helene wanted to ask why Liselotte cared but held her tongue.

"Answer me," Liselotte shouted.

With feet on the first stair, Helene paused. "I'm going to check the girls, then go to bed. I'll watch Regina and Rosa tomorrow, as we agreed if you pay another visit."

"Oh, I'm seeing Gerhard. At least he's civil to me. Beyond civil. And his parents too. With them, I'm adored and respected. I'll arrive home after dinnertime. Best to travel in the dark."

The timing for Helene could not have been better.

•   •   •

Little Regina knew. Helene had no doubts about it. From the moment Regina had awoken from her late morning nap, it was obvious she knew that a great chunk of life for her had changed. She spent the day looking for Rosa in closets, under furniture, exploring each room, and chiseling at Helene's heart.

"Gram-Gram."

"Yes, sweetheart?"

"Rosa. Rosa bye-bye?"

"It's lunchtime. Would you like cornbread? You can have apple slices, too." A measly lunch. At least it was food, more than others had these days. Would Rosa have eaten her lunch by now? Had she fussed and refused to eat? Maybe she was tucked in a new crib, sound asleep. Or, was she too looking for her sister?

"Rosa?" Regina called out. "Mama?"

At first, Helene had tried to occupy her by playing games, reading a story, holding her up to the frosted parlor window, and asking her to name the things she saw outside. A neighbor's cat. A postman. A boy. These things only went so far as to divert her attention away from her new reality for a handful of seconds.

"Regina, it's time for dinner."

"No. Rosa."

"Be a good girl and eat for Gram-Gram."

"No. Rosa. Mama."

Helene would not stop sobbing if she attempted to explain, on the simplest of levels, the truth to her granddaughter, the only granddaughter who now mattered. The soon-to-erupt maelstrom was overwhelming enough to deal with. Having given up on cheering Regina, she'd spread a blanket on the rug and let the child play quietly with her dolls. Now and then the little tyke whimpered and asked for Rosa. At least, she had stopped asking for her mother, though Helene suspected that too would change over the next few days, perhaps over the next few months.

At seven in the evening, the front door banged open. Liselotte stomped off the snow from her boots and swept additional white flakes from her head. Helene placed the book she held on the side table beside the sofa. With her mind crowded with countless thoughts, she had no clue which book she had clutched for the past hour or so like a teddy bear from her childhood days.

"Mama," Regina cried as she barreled against Liselotte's legs.

Unaccustomed to showing affection, Liselotte stood still as a statue.

"Pick her up and hug her," Helene said. "She's missed you."

Instead, Liselotte pushed Regina away. "Where's Rosa? Is she asleep?"

"Rosa bye-bye," Regina said. She started to cry. Again. "No Rosa."

Liselotte charged toward the sofa; Helene jumped to her feet.

"What did you do with my daughter?"

"Oh? Did you remember you had a daughter named Rosa, one who needs a lot of attention?"

"Mutter, tell me right now what you did with her. I'll call the police if you don't."

Helene pointed toward the front door where Regina had balled herself up tight on the floor, wailing her heart out. "You better care for your daughter so I can get a word out."

"Listen to me. If I head to the door it won't be to care for my daughter. I'll fetch an officer and have you arrested."

Helene walked around Liselotte and scooped up the sobbing Regina. She hugged her tight and carried her to the sofa where she gently settled her down and tucked a pillow under her head. She then pulled a yellow and red afghan off the furniture's back and covered her emotionally exhausted granddaughter.

Helene hushed Liselotte the moment her daughter opened her mouth. "She's been through enough today. Let her simmer down, perhaps she'll fall asleep and we can talk."

Liselotte glared at Helene as if she had grown three heads, each sprouting devilish horns. "I come home to find my one daughter hysterical and the other daughter unaccounted for. What horrible thing did you do to my Rosa?"

"Your Rosa? She's mine too—my granddaughter." Helene backed away. She paused at the end of the sofa. She had two choices: dodge her daughter or stand her ground. Her decision about Rosa was not done to torment Liselotte, but rather to save precious, fragile Rosa's life.

"Why are you playing games?" Liselotte stepped forward, hands fisted and lifted in the air. "Or the bigger question, why do you hate me?"

"Quiet," Helene shouted. "I do not hate you. They came for Rosa. I had no choice in the matter and had to comply with their commands."

"What?" Liselotte wrapped her arms around her middle. "Who came after Rosa? Why?"

"Someone must have alerted the Gestapo to Rosa... a neighbor, perhaps. Did someone see you walking with the girls?

"The Gestapo…" The color drained from Liselotte's face. She sank onto the sofa, nearly on top of Regina who, awake, stared wide-eyed at her mama.

Helene wished they were having any other discussion but this one in front of Regina. Fortunately, her granddaughter was young and would not process this spoken exchange.

"The authorities showed up while Regina napped." Upon the mention of her name, Helene hoped her grandchild would remain quiet. So far, so good. "They didn't say how or when—as if the Gestapo owes anyone an explanation—they'd learned about Rosa's… her…" Helene couldn't bear to typecast her granddaughter into the forbidden Aryan category of the mentally and physically unfit.

Liselotte grunted. "I bore her. I nursed her. Of course, I'm well aware she's damaged."

Damaged? Is that how she thought of her child? Bile rose in Helene's throat. She swallowed several times until feeling calm enough to continue. "Damaged is how the Nazis see people like Rosa. I tried to tell you—never take her outdoors while this war is going on or it will be all over for her. You wouldn't listen to one word of caution because you had to see your lover."

"Are you blaming me for what the Gestapo did? They took away my daughter. What did you do to stop them, Mutter? Nothing, right?"

Helene crossed her arms. "And you're blaming me for not fighting with the Gestapo?"

Liselotte groaned. "You just handed her over—and I imagine without a little kiss goodbye? You're probably the one who alerted the authorities. I can picture you flinging open the door and shouting 'Come and get her, she's all yours.' You'd do whatever it takes to revenge me for not listening to you about Gerhard. Rosa will be tossed into a camp where who knows what will happen to her. And you just let her go—"

"Be quiet, Liselotte. You're hysterical."

"I'm hysterical? When you're the one out of her mind to surrender a grandchild to the Nazis?"

"I had no other choice but to obey their command. They weren't interested in me. It was a good thing they didn't ask about…" Not wanting to say Regina's name aloud and get her further involved, Helene gestured with her chin toward her remaining grandchild. "...about her, who was asleep upstairs. They don't think kindly of twins."

"And if you refused? You could have done that. Could have told them to leave the house, to stay away from Rosa."

"The Gestapo isn't a pack of polite youths. They're ruthless officers working on behalf of Germany's vindictive leader whose passion is making up new edicts each new day to accommodate his needs of taking over the world and killing everyone in sight who fails to obey or to make the *Aryan race* appear perfect."

"I'll never see her again," Liselotte murmured.

"What happened to Rosa is not my fault."

"It's certainly not mine." Liselotte tottered to her feet. Without a glance at Regina or Helene, she rushed toward the front of the house, slid into her boots and coat, and yanked open the door.

Helene had not imagined their conversation would turn so heartbreakingly venomous, way beyond Liselotte's childish behavior, and her own bitter, sarcastic responses. While she knew it would not have a happy ending, a cold terror sliced through her over what she sensed her daughter was about to do. "Where are you going?"

Liselotte brushed the tears running down her flushed cheeks. "I'm going to the only person who accepts me for who I am, flaws and all."

"So, these objections center around you? Not the children? Will Regina and I ever see you again, or am I also losing you like I've lost my one granddaughter today?"

Without a word, Liselotte stepped over the worn threshold and shut the door behind her.

CHAPTER TWENTY-SIX

Gina, October 2, 1961

Gina did not know whether to be more puzzled or alarmed by the look on Grammy's face. Her lips were spread wide, not so much in a smile but with a hint of compassion. Gone was the constant companion of disappointment edged with what Gina suspected was profound sadness. Grammy certainly had news to share. Gina braced for the worst, yet hoped for the best.

Gina crossed her arms. "What's up, Grammy?"

"I see you're already nervous." Helene flinched. "Sorry. I sound like I'm judging you. I don't mean to."

Gina could not recall the last time Grammy had apologized.

Kenny wrapped an arm around her. "Are you okay, Gina? You look wobbly."

Suddenly everyone gathered around her. While she appreciated their concern, just because she faced the woman ready to reveal *big* news, let alone that Gina was pregnant, did not equate her as being a fragile mess. She spread out her arms sideways. "Please. I'm fine. Give me air."

"Helene," Fanny interjected. "Would you like some privacy with Gina?"

"No, my granddaughter trusts all of you and I'd like to make her comfortable, so please, keep us company."

"Let's go into the living room, shall we?" Uncle Raymond suggested and motioned to his left. "It's a comfortable room that might help us keep calm."

"Excellent suggestion," Fanny said and led the way.

"Gina," Grammy said, as they entered the room. They all stood awkwardly like party guests not knowing what to do with themselves. "Why don't the two of us sit beside each other." She eyed Kenny. "Kenny, you can sit next to Gina."

"I like you calling me Kenny." Kenny hooked Gina's arm and they sat with Grammy, opposite of his uncle and Fanny.

Although no smile crossed Grammy's mouth, coldness didn't radiate from her either. For a painful tick of seconds, she remained silent. Finally, she tapped her bottom lip. "This is harder than I thought it would be..."

"We had good news today," Kenny said, jumping into the sudden silence. "The doctor said I did good. Do you have good news, too, Helene?"

"Doctor?" Grammy stared blankly at Kenny.

Gina grasped her husband's hand, grateful to have support. She willed away the fears of what it would be like if Kenny was found guilty and she had to say a forever goodbye. She looked at her grandmother. "Fanny thought it would be wise to have a psychologist's professional take on Kenny." She reminded herself that Kenny still had no idea she and Fanny had observed him with the doctor through an observation window. "The doctor is confident that Kenny's replies will help him if his case proceeds to a trial."

Grammy gave a nod to Fanny. "I'm glad my granddaughter and her husband have you on their side and can comfortably tell you everything necessary to help them."

Gina blinked. Was this woman really her grandmother? For someone who had insisted on keeping matters between the two of them, limited to outsiders, stating to Fanny that privacy could take a hike, was exalting the term *turning over a new leaf*. Grammy also had referenced Kenny as her husband, a tender term Gina could not remember Grammy using in association with Kenny. Plus, she had praised Fanny with a note of sincerity in her voice. Grammy seemed ready and wanting to reveal any truths. People could change, including Helene Kellerman. Sure, the truth could hurt, but Gina had wanted to hear the truth she had suspected Grammy kept from her as far back as she could recall. Perhaps she too had to change and become more receptive to what Grammy had to share.

"Gina?" Kenny said. "You're shaking. Are you okay?"

"I'm fine." She returned her attention to Grammy. "Please, continue."

"Very well, then," Grammy said. "I've wanted to tell you as much as I didn't want to tell you." When she paused, Gina rushed in.

"I can't deal with more secrets. Just spill them out. I'm a big girl."

"Yes, you are," Grammy said, smiling kindly. "And you're expecting your own little girl or boy. I should have recognized your maturity years ago."

"You know what they say—it's never too late to change or to learn the truth."

"Yes, Gina. I do. And what I have to share is something that still shames me. When I heard on the morning's news that an East Berliner man escaped despite getting caught in barbed wire and getting shot twice by the guards patrolling the wall, I got thinking..." Grammy grasped Gina's arms. "With my great-grandchild on the way I decided it was time for me to be brave and to share the truth with you."

Gina thought about Grammy's visit to Fanny's home. She must have been ready to divulge the truth with her then, only to back out, too mortified over the facts that had haunted her all these years. Perhaps she sought acknowledgment she was doing the right thing. No matter what Grammy was now ready to reveal, Gina vowed to keep her heart and mind open and her tongue civil. "Well, then. I'm relieved you're here."

"I was a good daughter." Grammy's eyes turned glassy-eyed in reflection. "My parents never had to think twice about me getting into trouble. My girlfriends ribbed me. Because I never flirted with boys like they did, they said I should have become a nun. Raised by two strict parents, I was not one to make the first advance when a boy seemed attracted to me. Looking back, I think it was because I never met the right man." Her brow furrowed. "Things became suddenly different for me on my twenty-second birthday. Although surrounded by friends, I still ached to have romance, like a normal young woman." Helene inhaled deeply. "That day, I met Willie Fischer and my life changed. While a few of my friends were already married, and others engaged to beaus, no boy had ever kissed me, let alone a man. When Willie paid attention to me, I knew he was meant to be my husband."

Gina saw a sparkle in Grammy's eyes. One she knew well because she also was consumed by a lifted spirit whenever she and Kenny were together or in her thoughts if separated. This special force would sweep over her, and wrap her with an intensity to the point that she could not stop thinking about him. She reached for Kenny's hand. Pity the person who tried to separate her from the special person in her life who mattered the most.

"I'm pretty sure I can read your thoughts, Gina," Grammy said. "And I can't blame you. My parents had a fit when they learned about Willie. In hindsight, looking back as a protective adult over a child—even if she, you, are an adult now—I can no longer hold a grudge against my mother and father. And I say this after listening to them for years categorizing the man I loved as scum, and for treating me as a shameful embarrassment to them. But look what I did to you and Kenny—I'm sorry if I was cold to both of you, especially at the beginning of your relationship when encouragement would have benefitted you instead of my negativity."

"Why did they call Willie such awful names?" Gina asked. "Why did they treat you so poorly?"

Grammy stared at the floor. "Because I told them I was pregnant... with your mother. And without the benefit of marriage, a big *No* in their eyes, one they never let me forget."

Gina swallowed hard. "What happened? You didn't marry Willie, right?"

"No." Grammy lifted her gaze to Gina's face. "I couldn't, though I wanted to. He took off when he learned the news of my pregnancy. He joined the army. I never heard from him again, never saw him. Honestly, I don't know if he is alive. I don't care to find out—those days are behind me. It's taken me a while, but I'm ready to move on, beginning right now."

"Tell me more about how your parents treated you when you broke the news that you were pregnant?"

A light pink tinged Grammy's cheeks. "They did their best to ignore me."

"That must have hurt."

"It did. And I was wrong to continue that foolish, austere way to you and Kenny."

"At least we were married before we learned of our baby on the way," Gina said, quietly.

"A pregnancy should not matter. There's no shame in having a baby. What I am ashamed of is how I mistreated you both." She swept an apologetic gaze at Kenny and then back at Gina. "I'm so sorry."

Grammy's apologetic confession encircled Gina like a tug of a thread to pull them closer. However, she wanted to know all. "Tell me more."

A soft smile crossed Grammy's lips. "Liselotte was born in July 1926 and it was the happiest day I've ever known... until you were born."

The clang of a phone ringing in the distance filtered into the living room. On the fifth ring, Uncle Raymond said to ignore it.

"Uncle Raymond, someone might have a pasta problem," Kenny said and winked.

"Pasta crises!" Uncle Raymond grinned. "What's the world coming to?"

A badly needed round of laughter spread across the room.

"My parents passed," Grammy continued, "before Liselotte turned fourteen. A good thing, because with the news of her pregnancy, they would have turned against her. You see, at the tender young age of barely sixteen, Gina, Liselotte informed me she was pregnant. If her grandparents were alive, their frosty treatment would have continued."

"Wow," Gina mouthed. She stroked her belly. "That's sad."

Grammy glanced away. "More sadly, I had picked up a few of my parents' negative ways. Again, I'm sorry about that." She returned her attention to Gina, pointedly at her middle. "I hope to make it up to you and your child—my great-grandchild."

"I think—"

Grammy held a hand up. "There's more. A lot more."

Gina could not imagine. A tingle crept down her spine.

"Liselotte had twin baby girls."

Despite her vow to remain calm, Gina shot to her feet. "What? I have a sister? And you didn't tell me? What happened to her?" As if a colder truth smacked her across the face she sank back on the sofa. "My mother didn't die like you made me believe, did she?"

"One thing at a time."

The phone rang again.

"Disregard it," Uncle Raymond urged. He leaned forward, rested his elbows on his knees, and continued to eye Grammy.

Grammy fixed her gaze on the opposite wall. Her eyes widened as if the past showed like a movie on a screen. "You were born first, Regina."

"Regina?" Kenny said. "I like Gina better."

"Me too," Gina said, softly.

"You were a beautiful, healthy little girl—the cutest honey-bunny, ever. Your mother called you the sweet name of Regina as soon as you were born without one moment's worth of hesitation. Then, your sister was born. Her name was Rosa."

"Was?" Gina's stomach pitched with queasiness. "My twin? Was she stillborn?"

"Oh, no. Others would believe Rosa probably would have been better off. Not me. She deserved to live. And though Liselotte had her thoughts tied up with Gerhard—your father—I truly can't imagine she wanted the worst for this little babe of hers."

With her mind swirling, Gina pressed a finger tight against her bottom lip.

"Gina, stay with me," Grammy commanded. "Please. I know what you're wondering, but don't. Especially in your condition."

She was not battling a *condition*. She was pregnant, not as delicate as a wish. She told herself to stay calm. To listen. To learn about this mystery, this void she had sensed existed throughout her. "I'm fine. Continue."

"When Rosa entered the world, she appeared differently," Grammy continued. "Grant you, twins are often born on the early side, plus, with a war going on—"

"Right," Gina said. "The Second World War. That only added to the problems at hand, I imagine."

Helene nodded. "With food scarce, Liselotte didn't eat properly, especially for twins. This lack of nourishment might have impacted Rosa. Or, sadly, good health for your sister wasn't meant to be. Who knows for sure? She was underweight, smaller than you were. Plus, her small head size was another telltale indication of an abnormality. Compared to you, other little characteristics made her not... let's say... not right, health-wise. She grew, some. She tried to thrive. At least, I sensed she tried to blossom the best she could. I'd think that's a natural tendency of all living creatures. With Rosa, though, one couldn't be certain. You were milestones ahead of her. She never talked or walked or sat up by herself. And that was the trouble."

"I don't understand," Gina said, regretting she could not remain silent; regretting the next words shoving their way to her lips. "It sounds like she... my sister... didn't live long."

"We lived in Nazi Germany."

"Yes, I know. In Berlin." They lived there until moving to New York in 1946, one year after the war ended. In her mind, Gina slipped into the past and glimpsed a slice of life hidden in the dark recesses of her mind for years. She could now see them, could now hear them. The streets were flooded with folks she had not seen in some time. Neighbors? People in hiding? Men cursed. Women wept. They grieved over children and other family members lost during the war. Their words echoed through the stench of the Berlin streets, past destroyed houses and businesses burned by torching and bombs. *We'll never see them again. My whole family's gone.*

Jews. Roma. The mentally ill. Homosexuals. The physically unfit. Whoever the Nazi Party believed disgraced the beautiful Aryan race. Whoever weakened the Third Reich was deplorable. And had to be disposed of.

Rosa. Her sister.

Germany slipped away.

Gina was again in New York State.

Grammy's face soured. "I disapproved of Gerhard—your father. I didn't want to be like my uncaring, unsympathetic parents, but Gerhard was in the Waffen SS and he left me no choice when it came to protecting your sister. Whether he truly supported the Nazis didn't matter. He had to listen to Nazi orders to turn over all children who could compromise—from their atrocious viewpoint—the pure, perfect, golden blood of Aryans. Nazi Germany wanted to rule the world. All these so-called imperfections, *blights*, had to be obliterated."

"Grammy," Gina said, unable to recognize her own shattered voice. "What did you do?"

"Gerhard deserted the Waffen SS, which put his life in jeopardy and anyone who associated with him, especially his parents, who hid him under a toolshed at their residence. At first, your mother took you and your sister to visit Gerhard. When I learned what she was doing I pointed out the reckless danger she put herself and her daughters in. I then instructed her to leave you two home, with me. I told her to be careful because a multitude of Nazis were on patrol ready to protect the Reich. I also ordered her to stay home. She refused to listen to that part. I had to act. Had to..."

Tears streaked down Grammy's eyes. This was the first time Gina saw her cry. Had Grammy—whom she had thought of as stubbornly strong—hidden sadness and misgivings from her all these years? Gina inched closer, but Grammy wiped her face dry with her fingertips, sniffled, and continued.

"Liselotte came home one snowy evening, days before Christmas. You and I were home. Not your sister. You'd searched the house and kept asking for Rosa. I couldn't bear to tell you she was gone."

"What did you tell my mother?"

"I said the Gestapo came pounding on the door, evidently having learned about Rosa. And that they took her away. Your mother then walked out on me, and you. We never saw her again."

Gina again sprang from her seat. "Did you..." Her stomach churned, but she had to push the question out. "Did you surrender my sister to the Nazis?"

"No. I could have never done such a miserable thing to my grandchild." Grammy gestured to Kenny to help, and he hooked arms with her and they resumed sitting on the sofa. "I would have surrendered myself or fabricated a lie to chase those brutes out of the house and away from my family. However, the Gestapo never came. I was not prepared for your mother to storm out of the house thinking I handed your sister over to the Gestapo. But for the sake of your sister, I let her..." Grammy sniffled and swiped away more tears.

Gina feathered her fingers across her belly. Her little girl or boy was growing, hopefully, full of health. No matter the condition or shape of her baby, she would love her child with all her heart. Fiercely. She stared her grandmother in the eyes.

"How could you let Liselotte... my Mutti..." Constricted from the rush of years of grieving for a mother she had never known, Gina's breath momentarily stopped. From the corner of her eyes, she saw Kenny reaching for her. She put up a hand to stop him. She forced out the accusatory words she wished she did not have to say to this woman who raised her. "Leave? How could you let my mother leave me? She was my mother. Your daughter. What right did you have? I have no memory of her. No memory of my sister."

"What I did was all in the hope Rosa would survive. If Liselotte knew where Rosa was, she'd have searched for her despite putting herself, Rosa, and you and me at great risk. Why? For not turning Rosa over to the authorities immediately when she was born. And you, being Rosa's twin, would have also been taken away. Liselotte wouldn't have stopped until she found her missing daughter, not flinching at the heartless souls in command who would have killed her for her reckless behavior, questioning their actions, and making demands."

Gina again stood and stepped away from Grammy, then stopped as if she had walked into hardening cement. Fanny moved to her left side; Kenny on her right. They both held her upright.

"Grammy?" Gina murmured. "Tell me what you did with Rosa."

"I arranged with the Benedictine nuns to take your sister. I'd heard they were placing orphan children into homes, no matter the child's physical or mental condition. The Sisters didn't ask who I was, nor did I volunteer information because I didn't want word getting out to your mother and risk the Gestapo tracking down Rosa like the worthless bloodhounds they were. Or you. You being Rosa's twin—even a healthier one—would have shaded their opinion about you. Gina—"

"So, Rosa is alive?"

Grammy struggled to her feet. "I bear the responsibility of breaking up our family. I'll take this blame to my grave."

"I repeat," Gina said. "Is my sister alive?"

Grammy's whole body sagged. She too looked like she needed support.

Kenny stepped to her and put his arm around her. "Let me hold you, Helene."

Grammy stared Kenny in the eye. "Thank you, Kenny," she murmured.

"Grammy, tell me if Rosa and my mother are alive. Unless you've hired a private detective and kept it from me, also explain why you have never searched for them all these years. And most of all, why did you let me believe my mother was dead?"

"If Rosa survived the war," Grammy began, her voice stronger, "it might be difficult to track her down, or for that matter, any information on her. It was customary for the Sisters to give children new names before placing them with a host family. If Rosa's health worsened, she might have transferred to a hospital." Grammy's throat caught. "Hospitals weren't the best of places, then. Not with the Nazis combing through them, selecting who should live or who would make the next best test victim. They loved experimenting... on twins... doing awful, inhumane tests that under no certain terms were anything but torture. Realistically, I have my doubts Rosa is alive." Tears ran down her cheeks; she did not wipe them away. Kenny did. He blotted her face with his fingertips and gave her a tender smile.

"And?" Gina prompted. "Why did you mislead me into thinking my mother—your daughter—was dead? Why didn't you search for her?"

"I had to stop thinking of her as alive."

Gina streaked her fingers through her hair. "But... how..."

"Right or wrong, I did what I did. To this given minute, I've been racked with guilt. And no, I'm not asking for your pity. I acted to save my grandchild... both my granddaughters—"

"Stop right there, Grammy." Gina silently counted to ten. "There's something you're not telling me. I suspect it's a big something."

"Yes, you're right." Grammy wrapped her arms around herself. "Fear is a horrible companion. I was terrified that if I found Liselotte, she would tell me she wanted nothing to do with me. And, for a second—and final time— she would leave me."

A *final time*. Gina glanced at Kenny. She understood. The anguish of losing someone forever made one do whatever was possible to continue, to escape. For her, Gina tried her best to fill Kenny's days with the bright colors of joy. She focused on their unborn child. She blotted out a future verdict from the jury of whether her husband would live. And Grammy? She moved them to the United States, began a profession, and loved and raised Gina the best she knew how to, even if it was on the stern side. For Grammy, being serious and strict meant being in control... and not taking a chance on losing Gina.

"I put my energy into us," Grammy continued, verifying Gina's thoughts. "I fed us, sheltered us, and loved you the best I could. Eventually, when the war ended, I found a way to leave Germany and the past behind. You seemingly forgot about your place of birth." Grammy squeezed her eyes closed and then opened them. "I had to, as well. And that meant not daring to search for your mother or sister because any thought of doing so—at least back then—cracked open the door further to mentally falling apart." She drew in a deep breath. "You're the love of my life, Gina. I did what I had to do to ensure you would have the chance of a good life... just like what I tried to do for your sister. Speaking these words to you—finally telling the truth—I realize I've been outright cold to you. I'm sorry. Again, right or wrong, that was my way of hanging onto a protective hand to you... and to my sanity."

Grammy remained quiet for so long that Gina thought perhaps she had nothing more to say about Liselotte or Rosa. "I—"

Grammy held up a hand to pause her.

"For all I know, Gina, your mother is alive. She and Gerhard might be married. Maybe she started a new family. She might be living on the wrong side of the Berlin Wall. I can only guess." Grammy shuddered.

"Are you okay, Grammy?" Gina asked.

Her grandmother, who seemed to have aged twenty years within minutes, shrugged. "How can I be okay? My only daughter never contacted me from the time she walked out of my sight, believing I would have surrendered her child to the murdering hands of the cold-blooded Nazis... believing I was a heartless mother and grandmother."

The phone rang. No one moved to answer it.

"How did we ever escape Berlin, Grammy? Back in high school, I learned of the devastation Berlin suffered because of the Allied bombings."

"Yes. A lot of lives and property were lost," Grammy said so softly that Gina had to strain to understand. Out of the corner of her eye, she noticed Fanny had stepped closer toward them. "First, our family... my daughter and your sister..."

"Then?" Gina prompted.

"My gut told me to grab your hand and flee. On Christmas Day, abandoning the only home we'd ever lived in, I took you away from the horrors, the ones caused by war, and by my own hands. First, to my cousin who lived in Bamberg, southwest of Berlin. Unlike Berlin which was heavily bombed right after we left, Bamberg, with no industry, nor weapon production, escaped the bombing by the Allies. When traveling became permitted—and financial arrangements made—we came to Rochester where a job offer awaited me."

"Gina, are you okay?" Kenny asked, echoing the question she had asked Grammy moments ago.

No, of course not. Yet, with his own worries stampeding his mind, the last thing Gina wanted to do was to drag him further down a dark hole about herself.

"What are you thinking?" Kenny pushed.

Kenny rarely nudged her in a direction she did not want to go, though she noticed that in addition to Kenny's concern, Fanny and Uncle Raymond, with attentive eyes and a press to their bottom lips, wore the expression of caring. She owed them all a response, including Grammy.

"Honestly, I'm torn," she began. "Is this too much or too little? The crazy irony of discovering the overdue truth is that I now have more questions than answers. I'm no longer Gina, who has no mom. I'm no longer Gina, who has no siblings." She eyed her grandmother. "Do I—can I— forgive you for your deceit in making me believe my mother had died? For not telling me about my sister—that I was a twin? Do I attempt to find a mother who didn't want me in her life? Is Rosa alive? What condition would she be in? The troubling part of this whole mess is that I don't know what to think because I no longer know who I am."

Kenny grasped her hand. "You're my lovely, wonderful wife."

Fanny reached for her. Uncle Raymond stepped toward her. In need of privacy, Gina squirmed away from the caring group. She knew they meant well, and loved her, but she needed personal space and time.

Again, the phone rang.

Gina eyed Uncle Raymond. "Maybe you should find out who keeps phoning." She scanned the faces of the others. Her friends, her husband, and Grammy. "Pardon me. I need to be by myself. I'm going upstairs to rest. Please, just leave me alone for a while." She continued to the staircase that would take her to the bedroom she and Kenny shared in a house not their own. One day, perhaps like her mother, she and Kenny would carve out a life of their own and they could live the way they wanted to without the worry it would one day be taken away from them. At the top landing, she paused when she heard Uncle Raymond's voice.

"Fanny, it's for you."

"Me? The only person who has your phone number is David."

"Maybe he has good news," Kenny said.

"One way to find out," Fanny replied.

Gina loved her optimistic husband. However, she needed to stretch across her bed and hold still, despite the thoughts about the mother she never knew, and the twin sister she never knew existed, racing at full speed through her mind. Without a word more, she continued to the bedroom, her oasis.

·   ·   ·

When two raps sounded at the door, followed by a pause and then one more rap, Gina opened her eyes. Kenny's distinct knock.

"Gina, I want to come into the room. With you."

She hoisted herself upright against her pillows, not ready to surrender the dream she was having of her baby. Although the dream was unclear as to the baby's gender, she saw herself excited about telling her little one that having a grandma and an aunt was now a possibility. "Wouldn't that be sweet?" she had said to her baby-to-be in the dream. "And that's in addition to Grammy being your Great Grammy!" The baby cooed then delighted Gina with a big smile.

"Gina? Can you hear me?"

"Yes. I'm just thinking about a dream I had."

"I hope it was a nice dream. I'm opening the door now." Kenny entered the room but remained by the door. "You took a long nap."

"What time is it?"

"Past dinnertime. We let you sleep. You and the baby need rest. Do you feel better?"

"I'm confused. You know—about my family."

"Like me when I visited my mother—Betty—after not seeing her since I was four. All of a sudden, she's there. Breathing, like me."

"Yeah, kind of." She puffed in vexation. "I still don't know if my mother is alive and where she is. I didn't know her... can't even remember her. If she is alive, maybe she never wants to see me again. And then there's the shocking discovery that I have—or had—a sister. I don't know what to think."

Kenny strode to the bed, knelt, and kissed her lips. "You are my Gina. I love you. Soon, you will be our baby's mother. That's all that counts. Anything else in life is extra."

"Like a gift?"

He nodded.

Her husband, the wise one. While others easily hurled insults and caustic barbs at him and gave her the stink eye for marrying him—now an accused killer—and wanting his baby, her eyes, ears, and heart only knew Kenny Franks to see the world as it should be: un-tilted, unadulterated goodwill between all. She had her own sanctuary with Kenny, and soon, their child.

"Where's Grammy?" she asked.

"Helene went home. She said to phone her if you want. She can visit again tomorrow. She said she likes me calling her by her name."

Good. Grammy had not again slammed shut emotional doors between the two of them. She should take Grammy up on the invitation to visit. They needed to talk more.

"Gina, are you worrying what other things Helene might say?"

"Maybe." Was her father really a Nazi? Could Gina's baby be born like Rosa, physically and perhaps mentally forever challenged and in need of constant help? Frighteningly, she selfishly wondered if Liselotte re-entered their lives, if Grammy would suddenly dote on her daughter, disregarding Gina who had become the daughter Grammy never really had. These fears pointed out the concrete realization that she needed Grammy to continue to be a part of her life. Simply and complexly, she loved her grandmother. Grammy was there for her. What about the fears and concerns Grammy had expressed? Gina needed to reassure this special woman that she loved her unconditionally, that she did not think any less of her because of the decisions she had made about Rosa and what and why she had told Liselotte about Rosa being taken away by the Gestapo.

She sniffled, banishing the scary *what-ifs* to the furthest corners of her mind. "You're right. What counts is that we have each other, and soon, our child. And, Grammy. And, of course, your uncle. We have a family. A family that loves us." Perhaps Kenny's mom would now be an active member, too, especially if they welcomed her into their lives.

With a pat on the mattress, she invited Kenny to sit beside her. She wanted to ask him for advice on what to do, how to think about her lost relatives, and whether it was too late for a reconciliation. And if her mother and sister were deceased, should she at least look forward to reuniting with them, she hoped, in heaven? The thought of her passing to be reunited with them made her eyes well with tears. Not wanting to make Kenny upset, she turned away.

He gently touched his fingertips under her chin and shifted her head until they were eye to eye. A place she did not want to tug away from. "Uncle Raymond says David will help."

"Help? How?"

Kenny's eyes sparkled. "David's good at finding people. Like now. He's busy finding the gang."

With each word from Kenny's sweet, loving mouth, Gina became more confused. "What do you mean?"

"On the phone. David told Uncle Raymond that he'll see if your mother and Rosa are alive."

Although excellent, hopeful news, it was not what she meant. "What's this about finding a gang? What gang?"

"Before. The phone calls were from David. The police arrested a gang member. In the lot."

"Where Samuel was found?"

Kenny nodded. "No evidence, though. Connected to Samuel. David says he's still a suspect."

"What? He was released from jail?" She leaped to her feet. "I thought you said this gang member was arrested?"

"He's still in jail. Where David called from. David's hoping this gang member will confess—"

"And Fanny?"

"She's happy."

Gina's mind whirled at a dizzying pace. The promising, breaking news might prove, once and for all, Kenny's innocence of his accused crime. However, if it was not the gang or one particular gang member who was responsible for Samuel's murder, then it meant the person or persons involved were still out there. Had this person heard about the other perp's arrest? And what better way to return to the scene of a successful crime and try for additional victims than when the police were tucked away at their precinct, rejoicing over the bust of a gang?

She tried again. "Did Fanny leave? Did she say where she was going?"

"Yes. She wanted to see the lot again. She—"

"We have to find her... have to make sure she's safe."

"I want you to stay here."

On her feet, she raced downstairs, whether Kenny called after her she had no clue. She had to find Fanny before the worst imaginable could strike.

CHAPTER TWENTY-SEVEN

Fanny, Rochester, October 2, 1961

Fanny had honed a solid backbone for a reason: she liked to fight a good fight and win. With the news from David that a suspect in the murder of Samuel was apprehended, could she dare believe Kenny's case might be resolved without having to go to trial? While she liked the challenge of the courtroom scene, it would be more than perfectly fine if Kenny never had to appear before a jury and judge set to determine his fate.

When she had spoken to David on the phone at Ray's, she learned that Floyd Osman had contacted David because he had just witnessed a handful of *punk youths*, heard a scream, and then saw the thugs fleeing from what appeared to be a lifeless body. He called the police, then went outdoors where he encountered a man—the suspect now being held at the jail— bending over the body of a battered, definitely dead, young man. Fed up with street gangs destroying his neighborhood and taking lives, Osman bulldozed the suspect, knocked him unconscious, and pinned him down until the police arrived. The suspect now faced the next step of the justice he deserved. The only chink in this latest chapter in Kenny's case was the missing murder weapon.

Sure, in the case of Samuel's murder, there were telltale signs of strangulation, like purple marks on his face, burst blood vessels in the eyes, and swollen neck muscles. These marks were not from a weapon but by hand. Yet, who was to say the perp didn't like variation, using his bare hands for Samuel and weapons on others? If only Fanny could find a bloody bat or a knife, left behind evidence, with fingerprints, that matched the suspect in custody. That, along with the professional experts she had lined up, and the testimony from Kenny's mother, and with Helene coming around, Fanny could make all these pieces work on Kenny's behalf. She still did not know everything the DA planned to throw at Kenny. Although Lyman G. Hayes never struck her as careless in his investigation, preparation, and subsequent delivery in the courtroom, he would also have to contend with her. Yet, as prepared as she was, she would not blink an eye if Hayes called off his case against Kenny if an admission of guilt from this newest suspect proved without a reasonable doubt, that he was Samuel Klein's killer, not Kenny who was at the wrong place at the wrong time.

Until her fantasy became reality, Fanny would look around more before calling it quits for the night. In addition, she needed time to think about Helene's revelations made earlier at Ray's. The possibility that Gina's mother and sister might be alive was excellent and hopeful news for Gina, Kenny, and Helene. Fanny felt genuine happiness for them, yet it emphasized a familiar dilemma in choosing the direction of her career and personal life. Ever since she began to practice law, she thought it best not to mix business with pleasure. Here she was, though, barely two months after first meeting Gina, she felt she had a true friend. And, she felt like a welcomed part of this growing family. Although Fanny and Gina's mom, Liselotte, were roughly the same age, Fanny saw herself more like an older sister/friend than a mother figure to Gina. She admired Gina's solid love for Kenny. She had spunk, a killer sense of humor, and hope, the latter the key necessity to living in this spinning world. Since they first met, Fanny had witnessed a growing, commendable maturity in Gina. Considering her background, and that she'd soon be a mother, Gina had a rich future to look forward to... *if* her husband's life was not taken away because of Samuel's murder. Could Fanny objectively continue to fight on Kenny's behalf? Then again, was befriending Gina unconscionable conduct? Should she even be concerned? The independent creature she was, she had never worried about social mores. Then again, she had, hopefully, years of a career to look forward to and...

To the right of her, a rock landed on the ground. She was shoved, landing face-up on the broken asphalt. A hard force gripped her throat. The stench of rotten food mixed with tobacco reached her nostrils and prompted her to open her eyes, despite the huge energy it demanded. Holding her down—with gloved hands—was a filthy, twenty-something-old punk. His blond hair swept over his forehead. No facial hair. The darkness made it impossible to detect eye color, whether he had all his teeth, or a tattoo to identify him by. Not good. Well, he had met his match. She would fight and win. She began to kick and shove his hands away. He shifted his fingers tighter around her throat.

Like Samuel?

No way.

She tried to scream.

He laughed, loosening his grip on her throat as if a tease. "No one will hear your pathetic squeak."

She closed her ears to him and attempted another scream.

Again, he clamped his fingers around her throat and inched his face closer to hers. Then, continuing his brutal game, he let up on the pressure against her throat.

Aware she had mere seconds until she took her last breath, she swallowed her nausea and squirmed more to make enough room to shove him and run.

"Hold still," he ordered. "Or don't. Doesn't matter. I'll get you like the others."

Others? She had to keep him talking. The more seconds that tick by, the better chance help could arrive. "What others?"

"The others I caught." She kicked more. He pressed tighter against her throat. She fought for breath. "The others I killed. Now, stop moving and you'll suffer less." He loosened his hold.

"Why kill?" she pushed out.

"Because it's what I do best."

One thought flashed through Fanny's mind. She had to live... to tell Kenny he was absolutely correct that he was sane. He had one of the finest minds she ever encountered. He was one of the kindest, if not *the* kindest, person she had ever known. She owed him that respect. And an apology for even thinking twice about using an insanity plea for his defense.

She could not breathe.

Could hardly think.

Life was rushing away.

The killer was suddenly gone. Fanny gasped. Air filled her lungs. She heard voices. Kenny? Ray? She could not talk. She could not see. She slipped into blackness.

•   •   •

"Look at you go!"

Fanny set aside the packing of her belongings from her two-day observational stay and pivoted around. "Well, Gina," she began, a playful note crawling out from her still scratchy throat, "if you hadn't brought my whole closet, I'd be ready to leave. Believe me, I can't wait to leave."

"At least the degenerate didn't rob you of your sense of humor." Gina's eyes welled with tears. "He almost... killed you."

"He didn't." Fanny stepped fast to her side. "What he did was to confess he was Samuel's murderer."

"This monster would have killed you—he took pride in confessing to killing Samuel like he wanted a gold trophy. He also confessed he was a mass murderer. At least ten others that he's so far confessed to. That doesn't freak you out?"

"I wouldn't opt to be in his path again, or another murderer's, that's for sure. He's facing his debt to society behind bars, waiting for the electric chair." She inhaled deeply, to collect herself. Her aspiring killer was wrong, if not mentally insane, to kill. Still, she could not wish him to receive the death penalty. Perhaps a nice sentence of life in jail without parole. "As for

Kenny, the DA has dismissed the case. Your husband's a free man. Ray says Kenny is returning to work next week. You and he can now breathe easy and enjoy your life. And soon, your child."

Gina sniffled. "You're right, of course. Kenny has suffered enough. We—and our two babies—need to enjoy life the way we want to."

Babies? Plural? Fanny squealed and tugged Gina into an embrace. "When did you find out?"

"Yesterday. Looks like twins run in the family. Kenny's ecstatic."

"I'm sure he is. What did he say when you told him the news?"

"You should have seen Kenny," Gina said with a smile of pride on her lips. "I told him when we were alone, after singing him a song that I wrote just for him—"

"You wrote a song? Wow. I didn't know you composed songs. Will you write more?"

Gina nodded. "Kenny's love—and triumph over his criminal charges—has inspired me. I want to write many more songs... when the babies give me a minute to myself, not that I'm rushing it. Anyway, the song is about why I'm not blue around him. After I sang the song, I told him our big news about the babies... you should have seen him. To say that Kenny jumped for joy is the understatement of the century. I think he's the happiest man on Earth. And, regarding Grammy's fuss over fatherless kids running in the family, well, no more. Not with my husband loving and adoring our children."

"You two have so many blessings to count. How are the others reacting to your news about having twins?"

"Grammy's planning on making a dozen quilts and purchasing every stuffed toy animal and baby outfit she sees. And Uncle Raymond's getting a forever gold star in my heart with his invitation to live in his house as long as we want, which is fine for now. Eventually, Kenny and I want our own home."

Fanny was sure Ray would help finance a mortgage—probably buy them a house paid in full knowing him. They'd have it good, deservedly so. "I'm happy for you."

"I'll be happier if two things happened."

"Okay. I know this because of David's visit yesterday—he's investigating whether Rosa and Liselotte are alive."

"Yeah," Gina said, bittersweetness edged in her tone. "I suspect Rosa is no longer with us, though I hope I'm pleasantly wrong. My mother... I have a hunch she's alive. It would be interesting to find out if she's living on the east or the west side of the Berlin Wall. Or for that matter, for all I know, she lives in Alaska with her darling husband and six children. I could have a bunch of step-siblings. That would be kinda nice."

"I read in the morning's newspaper that the west and east authorities are discovering tunnels people are digging to escape into West Germany. With more people upset over a nonsense wall forcing a separation that should have never occurred, I'd think that the wall might be knocked down not too long from now. Maybe in just a couple of months. Wouldn't it be wonderful if East Germany would say a big, fat hello to West Germany and they'd unify as one country?"

"For sure," Gina said.

"Times are changing. Rock 'n' roll didn't fade as some had hoped; people worldwide are speaking up for their human rights; and slowly but surely women are gaining more opportunities and respect." She grinned. "And *hey*, for better or worse, mothers are dropping their line that *hay is for horses* and not for people to say to each other." Fanny thought for sure her last words would have made Gina chuckle. Instead, she groaned.

"What's wrong?"

"What happens if Liselotte is living in East Germany and the crazy separation between the two halves of Germany continues for eternity? And I can't see her or communicate with her? Talk about torment."

"Let's stay positive. The wall *will* come down during our lifetimes. When Liselotte is located, the two of you will easily be reunited. Will you remain hopeful with me?"

"You're right—I will remain hopeful and positive. It's all cool. The most important thing for me has finally happened—the secrets Grammy kept from me have risen to the surface. Sure, on the one hand, learning about my twin and my mother is a lot to digest. On the other, it's like darkness has lifted from my soul." She palmed her belly. "Ha. I'd say that I could stand straighter and hold my head up firmer, but my little sweethearts are messing with my posture these days."

"Not for much longer."

Gina stepped to the bed and snapped Fanny's valise shut. "If you're set, I'll notify the nurse and we'll wheel you out the front entrance where Uncle Raymond has the car for us. Then, we'll drive you home, only if you promise to come visit on Saturday for a wee surprise."

"If it's a good surprise, sure." She suspected the occasion to be a celebration party for Kenny's victory, and perhaps a thank you to herself. Fanny touched her throat. "I've had it with awful surprises."

"No sweat, my friend. You will be pleased."

Fanny smiled at Gina. She had a hunch that she would not stop smiling until way later into the night when she rested her head on her pillow and Ralph curled beside her and purred her to sleep. She again thanked Gina for taking care of her cat.

"So, what's up with you for the rest of the day?" Gina asked. "Are you going to take it easy?"

"Me? All I've done the past two days is rest. Other than a choppy voice, the doctor says I'm fine. No restrictions." Actually, the good doctor said she was lucky to be alive, and that it was a matter of seconds until she died. She kept from Gina this little tidbit, though, especially since she had chosen not to focus on her brush with death. Rather, she would continue to march forward. "The first thing I'm going to do when I go home is give Ralph a hug and a treat, then drive over to that park by Ray's house to see whether the man who walked his collie is taking another stroll."

"Fanny, do you mean that handsome man we met, the one with the tennis-ball-loving dog named Ranger?"

"You remembered the dog's name?" Fanny winked. "I just remember his owner's looks."

"That's because I'm already married. Now it's your turn."

"Okay, then. Let's get out of here. I've seen enough white walls for a long while."

Fanny had a lot of catching up to do. Like Helene, she too had a secret she kept far too long, perhaps because she had not wanted to face the truth of a situation that should have never occurred. Silences can be broken. If all went well, she would share the good news with her friends on Saturday. Friends were friends for a reason. If the uncovering of her secret backfired, she would lean on Gina and Helene's support. She was sure that Kenny and Ray would offer their encouragement as well.

However, a walk in the park would happen tomorrow, not today. Man, or no man, she would keep her head lifted high, taking one step in front of the other, and enjoy the rest of her days. First, though, she had a definite visit to make as soon as she freshened up in her own home, and that involved digging through her downstairs closet for clothes she had boxed up intending to donate to a Goodwill store, yet never got around to doing so. The last time she wore them, the outfits had fit fine. They just had not matched the black and white attire she had imagined would be the only colors defining her wardrobe. She was alive. She did not live in a black-and-white world, but one full of color and vibrancy. Today, she would splash color back into her life, wearing reds, greens, and yellows like she used to. Tomorrow, pink and blue. Perhaps a shock of purple.

At three that afternoon, she stepped out of her car and smoothed her orange dress with large gold sunflowers, studded with green leaves, and with a small red Peter Pan collar. Breathing in deeply, she proceeded to the front door of the modest brick one-floor house, only twenty miles from her own. She rang the doorbell.

At first, Fanny thought no one was home. Then, slowly, the door creaked open. A woman stared; her blue eyes wide. Her familiarity, a delight.

"Hello, Mom."

"Fanny—I was just thinking of you." Tears welled in her mother's eyes. She opened the door wide. "Come in. Hurry, I don't want you to change your mind."

"Oh, don't think twice." Fanny stepped over the doorsill. "I'm not going anywhere." Not with the time to forgive, to heal and most of all, to love, staring her right in the face.

WHEN I'M BLUE, A SONG FOR KENNY
BY GINA FRANKS

When I'm blue
And see you
Rubie red and lemony gold
Span the sky and grip me in its hold

You got that smile
You have me for more than a while
You got that finesse
You have me spellbound with one caress

When I'm down and out
You chase away the last of doubt
Rainbow violet and lucky green
We're real together, no in-between

When I'm blue
And see you
Rubie red and lemony gold
Span the sky and grip me in its hold

You got that smile
You have me for more than a while
You got that finesse
You have me spellbound with one caress

For you, I'll cut a slice of paradise
Waltz the wedding aisle for the toss of rice
I'll be your missus forever and ever
Giving love to you, my one endeavor

When I'm blue
And see you
Rubie red and lemony gold
Span the sky and grip me in its hold

You got that smile
You have me for more than a while
You got that finesse
You have me spellbound with one caress.

ACKNOWLEDGMENTS

With deep gratitude, I thank Reagan Rothe, the creator of Black Rose Writing, and the extraordinary BRW team, for making The Last Secret Kept a reality. I also thank my fellow BRW authors for their camaraderie and for sharing writing and publication insights.

Many hours of research have gone into what I think of as Fanny, Gina, and Helene's story... what is an author without her characters, especially the ones who keep her constant company and dictate to her what matters most? I would, however, be remiss not to acknowledge the legal advice of Susan Antos, Assistant District Attorney Ariel Fallon, and the spark of excitement from Walter Spiro on the initial shaping of Kenny's legal troubles. Any legal errors are mine and not intentional.

My patient husband needs his own cheering squad after the whirlwind of my writing wedged between working the day job, cooking dinner in the mornings, my semi-meltdowns, and playing house. Remember—it's WHEW forever.

Last but certainly not least, I want to thank all my friends and readers who have encouraged me in this novel and my writing in general. A special shout-out is extended to authors Lelita Baldock Lisa Montanaro, and Jacquie Herz, and reader extraordinaire Susan Roberts, the latter whose words "I'm not ready to say goodbye to this family!" jump-started my mind on a big hmm-I-wonder-how...

READER'S GROUP GUIDE FOR
THE LAST SECRET KEPT

1. How do you define justice? Do the characters in The Last Secret Kept define it differently?

2. Are there similarities between the social and political movements of the 1960s and today? Do you think "dilemmas" can always be resolved diplomatically?

3. The original title of this novel was When We Said Hello. Thinking the story might be mistaken as a pure romance, the title was changed to its present one. Do you initiate saying hello to strangers or reconnecting with someone from your past?

4. How would the story's tone and urgency change if Kenny faced life in prison if found guilty of murder as opposed to death by electrocution? Do you support capital punishment?

5. How does loneliness influence Fanny, Gina, and Helene? Do you see loneliness as a catalyst for decisions you have made?

6. Throughout history, governments erected walls rather than attempted peace negotiations. On a personal level, have barriers of communication been built between your family members or yourself and friends?

7. What does the term "civil rights" mean to you?

8. Kenny's top concern is not the verdict for his criminal charges, but whether he would be with his wife and together, would raise their child. What is your #1 concern?

9. In less than a month, Gina had to leap from her teenage years and embrace a version of adulthood that took her by surprise. Through the years, had the meaning of adulthood redefined itself for you?

10. Have you mistaken a person's hardened ways as irreversible and unredeemable? Which character in the story has surprised you? Discuss the circumstances that had made this person "tough."

11. Is there ever a good time to keep a secret?

12. Who do you think Fanny reminded Helene of when they first met?

13. Have you ever participated in a protest march?

Bonus Question: What are the *colors* in your life, and why?

ABOUT THE AUTHOR

When Elaine Stock penned the novel, *We Shall Not Shatter*, inspired by her paternal heritage from Brzeziny, Poland, she discovered her passion for writing what she loved to read: historical fiction. It became the first of her bestselling Resilient Women of World War II Trilogy. What pleases her the most is that readers have reached out to say her books have encouraged them to face their tomorrows.

Elaine is a member of the Women's Fiction Writers Association and The Historical Novel Society. Born in Brooklyn, New York, she lives in upstate New York with her husband and enjoys long walks down country roads, visiting New England towns, and of course, a good book.

NOTE FROM ELAINE STOCK

Word-of-mouth is crucial for any author to succeed. If you enjoyed *The Last Secret Kept*, please leave a review online—anywhere you are able. Even if it's just a sentence or two. It would make all the difference and would be very much appreciated.

Thanks!
Elaine Stock

We hope you enjoyed reading this title from:

BLACK ROSE
writing™

www.blackrosewriting.com

Subscribe to our mailing list – *The Rosevine* – and receive **FREE** books, daily deals, and stay current with news about upcoming releases and our hottest authors.
Scan the QR code below to sign up.

Already a subscriber? Please accept a sincere thank you for being a fan of Black Rose Writing authors.

View other Black Rose Writing titles at
www.blackrosewriting.com/books and use promo code
PRINT to receive a **20% discount** when purchasing.